HURRICANE AFTER DARK

GANSETT ISLAND SERIES, BOOK 26

MARIE FORCE

Hurricane After Dark
Gansett Island Series, Book 26

By: Marie Force
Published by HTJB, Inc.
Copyright 2023. HTJB, Inc.
Cover Design: Diane Luger
Cover image: *istock.adobe.com/478343810*
Print Layout by E-book Formatting Fairies
ISBN: 978-1958035382

The Gansett Island Series

Book 1: Maid for Love (*Mac & Maddie*)
Book 2: Fool for Love (*Joe & Janey*)
Book 3: Ready for Love (*Luke & Sydney*)
Book 4: Falling for Love (*Grant & Stephanie*)
Book 5: Hoping for Love (*Evan & Grace*)
Book 6: Season for Love (*Owen & Laura*)
Book 7: Longing for Love (*Blaine & Tiffany*)
Book 8: Waiting for Love (*Adam & Abby*)
Book 9: Time for Love (*David & Daisy*)
Book 10: Meant for Love (*Jenny & Alex*)
Book 10.5: Chance for Love, *A Gansett Island Novella* (*Jared & Lizzie*)
Book 11: Gansett After Dark (*Owen & Laura*)
Book 12: Kisses After Dark (*Shane & Katie*)
Book 13: Love After Dark (*Paul & Hope*)
Book 14: Celebration After Dark (*Big Mac & Linda*)
Book 15: Desire After Dark (*Slim & Erin*)
Book 16: Light After Dark (*Mallory & Quinn*)
Book 17: Victoria & Shannon (Episode 1)
Book 18: Kevin & Chelsea (Episode 2)
A Gansett Island Christmas Novella
Book 19: Mine After Dark (*Riley & Nikki*)
Book 20: Yours After Dark (*Finn McCarthy*)
Book 21: Trouble After Dark (*Deacon & Julia*)
Book 22: Rescue After Dark (*Mason & Jordan*)
Book 23: Blackout After Dark (*Full Cast*)
Book 24: Temptation After Dark (*Gigi & Cooper*)
Book 25: Resilience After Dark (*Jace & Cindy*)
Book 26: Hurricane After Dark (*Full Cast*)

Gansett Island Extras

More new books are always in the works. For the most up-to-date list of what's available from the Gansett Island Series as well as series extras, go to *marieforce.com/gansett*

View the McCarthy Family Tree *marieforce.com/gansett/familytree/*

View the list of Who's Who on Gansett Island here *marieforce.com/whoswhogansett/*

View a map of Gansett Island *marieforce.com/mapofgansett/*

CHAPTER 1

Only for Laura Lawry would Piper Bennett be on this ferry ride from hell. The crew had warned the passengers that the ride would be rough, and that it would be the last boat from the mainland to Gansett Island before they shut down service in anticipation of Hurricane Ethel.

Piper had received a text from Laura the night before, asking if there was any way she could come back to work a few days early because all three of Laura's little ones were down with the flu, and her top helpers—her mother-in-law and grandmother-in-law—had gone to Italy, right when most of the summer help had returned to college. *Clearly, we didn't think this all the way through,* Laura had said, including a grimace emoji. *And now there's a storm headed our way!*

As she tried very hard not to puke up her breakfast, Piper was starting to think she should've listened to the crew and sat this one out. She'd never been on a boat in seas like these and would be happy to never do anything like this again. While she tried to psych herself out of getting sick, she thought of Laura, who'd been such a good friend to her from the first day she landed at the Sand & Surf Hotel on Gansett Island earlier in the summer.

That'd been one heck of a week. After her fiancé, Ben, decided to end their engagement, Piper had come to Gansett Island to take a break from the madness of canceling her wedding and looking at her mother's crestfallen face. Since the wedding meltdown, Piper had decided her mom had loved Ben way more than she did. That's something she'd realized with hindsight, when it occurred to her that she didn't miss him the way she should have and maybe it was for the best that he'd put a stop to the whole thing.

Suddenly single for the first time in years, she'd gone a little wild during that first week on Gansett and gotten herself into a mess by going to a hotel room with a man she met at a bar. That turned out to be a huge mistake when he got aggressive with her, forcing her to flee from him and run back to the hotel, where Laura had been such a source of support as Piper reported the attempted sexual assault to the police.

That and the job Laura had subsequently given her at the hotel, along with the warm friendship they'd developed, were the main reasons why Piper was on this ferry ride from hell.

There was also the matter of a sexy state police officer who'd been "in the picture" on and off since the day they met, ironically when he and Gansett Island Police Chief Blaine Taylor had come to take her report.

Months later, her attacker had taken a plea deal and was serving a jail sentence, Piper was the assistant manager at the Sand & Surf, and she was still trying to figure out what, if anything, was happening with Jack Downing, the sexy state trooper. Other than some major flirting, not much had come of the attraction she felt zinging between them any time she saw him on the island. He'd been off-island more often than not lately, dealing with a big trial on the mainland, but supposedly, he was due back any time now. She was looking forward to seeing if anything would come of the flirting.

It was funny how she barely missed Ben, but she thought about Jack all the time. Other than an occasional text to say hello and what's up, she wasn't sure if Jack ever thought about her. She was giving it a month after she returned to the island from an end-of-summer visit to her family, and then would move on if nothing happened with Jack. Life was too short to sit around waiting for things that were going nowhere fast.

Piper was ready to date again, and Jack was the only guy she was interested in, but she was tired of wondering if he was into her or if he was just playing some sort of game by flirting with her any time they saw each other. If that was the case, she was out. Since Ben called off their wedding, she'd spent a lot of time focused inward, asking herself what she wanted—and what she didn't want.

She kept coming back to the same thing—she wanted to spend more time on Gansett Island and have the chance to get to know Jack better. She felt ready to put the hard work she'd done on herself into a new relationship. If not with him, then with someone else.

As the ferry rocked and rolled, people were getting sick all around her. She prayed the smell wouldn't reach her as she kept her head down and tried to focus on anything other than where she was and the sounds of retching.

A check of the time on her phone showed they still had forty minutes to go. She was never going to make it.

"Piper?"

His voice sent shivers down her spine as she looked up to find her favorite state trooper standing in front of her, looking as happy to see her as she was to see him. That he was also in full uniform only made things worse. Or better. Depending on how she looked at it.

"I thought that was you," he said. "Are you all right?"

How was he able to stand there like the boat wasn't heaving and rolling under him? The state police uniform was gray with red trim. A brown strap crossed his chest and connected to a thick brown belt that held a variety of items. Knee-length pants were tucked into tall brown boots, and he held a tan hat under his arm. He had the number twenty-four in red on his chest and silver bars on his shoulders. She'd never been one to go goofy over a man in uniform, but this man in that uniform packed a wallop.

"I, uh, I'm trying not to puke."

"It's a rough one, for sure." He gestured to the seat next to hers. "May I?"

"Sure."

As he took a seat, she hoped she could talk to him while trying not to vomit. That'd be a challenge.

"How've you been?" he asked.

"Pretty good until I made the mistake of getting on this boat."

"They said it was going to be bad."

"I know, but Laura needs me back at the hotel, so I decided to brave it. I'm wishing now that I hadn't."

"It'll be over soon enough."

"Not for thirty-eight more minutes."

"You're doing great. If you haven't gotten sick yet, you're probably good to go."

"I hope so." Puking in front of her sexy crush would be mortifying. "How's the trial going?"

"Thankfully, it's done. After weeks of testimony, the defendant took a plea deal that locks him up for the next twenty-five years. I would've liked for the sentence to have included no chance of parole, but at least now he's in jail where he belongs."

"You must be relieved to have it done."

"I am. Living between the island and the mainland for the last nine months has been a pain. It's funny," he added with a chuckle. "When I first got assigned to Gansett, I was furious. I wanted nothing to do with a tiny, remote island in the middle of the ocean. But after a few months there, I was hooked, and now it feels like home. I've missed it."

That was the most he'd ever said to her at one time. "I know what you mean. I came for a long weekend, and now I live there."

"I'm not sure what it is about that island, but I love it, and I can't wait to get back, although I could do without the looming storm."

"What's the latest on that?"

"It's grown to a Cat 2, and it's making a direct line for our favorite island." Reading from his phone, he continued. "The National Weather Service has issued a hurricane warning for Gansett Island, the southern coast of Rhode Island, the Cape and Islands and are advising residents to prepare for a slow-moving storm bringing high winds, torrential rain and life-threatening storm surge. They've also recommended that Gansett Island residents evacuate, but I heard that most are staying put. That doesn't surprise me."

"Wow." Piper was overwhelmed to hear the storm had gotten that bad. "I was probably crazy to come back with that coming for us, but I couldn't leave Laura to deal with it all, especially since her kids are sick."

"It's good of you to do it."

"I admit I didn't take as close a look at the forecast as I probably should have. All I knew was there's a hurricane coming. I didn't know it was aiming right for Gansett."

"It'll be fine. We'll batten down the hatches and then ride it out. Have you ever been to a hurricane party?"

"Nope."

"Well, now you have something to look forward to."

. . .

RHODE ISLAND STATE Police Lieutenant Jack Downing wished he had a dollar for every time he'd thought of Piper Bennett over the last few endless months spent mostly on the mainland, helping to convict a man who'd murdered his wife during an argument, leaving three young children without parents. Jack had been heavily involved in that investigation two years before he was assigned to Gansett, thus the back-and-forth in recent months.

With yet another scumbag successfully convicted and off to prison for decades, Jack could finally exhale and get back to the island he'd come to love. That still came as a surprise to him. He'd expected to go mad with boredom, but to his surprise, he'd been anything but bored.

The main reason he liked Gansett so much lately was the young woman sitting next to him on the ferry, who'd come into his life when she reported an assault at one of the island's hotels. She'd stayed on his mind ever since. What he remembered most from the day he met her had been her strength and courage in reporting the attack. Her calm recitation of the facts to Gansett Island Police Chief Blaine Taylor had allowed them to quickly apprehend the man and charge him. The guy had since pleaded to a felony assault charge and was serving eighteen months at the state prison in Cranston.

It was a relief to have that taken care of so Piper could get on with her life without having to testify about the assault in court. He was glad she wouldn't have to revisit that painful episode in such a public forum.

And maybe now that he was back on the island to stay, they could get on with pursuing the friendship-slash-flirtation dance they'd been engaged in for months now. Not that he was looking for anything serious, because he wasn't. But he didn't think she was either. She'd mentioned a bad breakup with a fiancé before she came to Gansett, but he didn't know the details.

What did it matter? They'd enjoyed hanging out a few times, they had interesting conversations, and he was attracted to her, which was a big deal in and of itself. But who wouldn't be attracted to her? She had shoulder-length brown hair with red highlights that looked like it might be curly if left to its own devices, light brown eyes and a dusting of freckles across her nose that were the cutest thing ever. But it was her smile that was the showstopper, at least for him. Whenever she directed that dazzling smile his way, he went a little stupid in the head.

Jack's phone chimed with a text from Blaine. *You coming back any time soon? We're all hands on deck here right now. People are panicking about a direct hit.*

He wrote back right away. *On the boat now. I'll report to the station when I arrive.*

Great, thank you.

You got it.

The state police didn't keep an office on the island. Rather, they used space provided by the town police department. Not only did Jack enjoy working with Blaine, but he considered him a close friend, too. He was looking forward to seeing him, as well as Blaine's brother, Deacon, who was the harbor master, and the fire chief, Mason Johns, who'd also become friends. Jack was sure they were all exhausted from preparing for the storm, and he was ready to help.

But once the work was done, he'd be interested to know where Piper planned to hunker down for the storm.

"How much longer?" Piper asked as the ferry crested a particularly large wave.

Jack looked behind him to see where they were. "There's the island now. About fifteen more minutes." From a distance, the island reminded him of the mud pie dessert, with layers of water-darkened rocks at the bottom and a wall of sand that looked like coffee ice cream. He kept the reference to himself since he didn't think Piper would appreciate him talking about ice cream when she was trying not to be sick.

"I don't think I'm going to make it."

"Hang on. I've got an idea."

He stood, waited a second to get his legs under him and went to the concession stand to purchase a ginger ale. He also grabbed a packet of the oyster crackers that went with the clam chowder they sold. No one seemed interested in that today. "Try this," he said to Piper when he returned with his offerings. "It might settle your stomach."

"Thank you." She took the drink and crackers from him. "That's very nice of you."

"No problem."

She opened the crackers and ate a couple, chasing them with the ginger ale. "Now let's see if it'll stay down."

"I'll await the verdict with bated breath."

"Don't make me laugh. It might make me lose control of the vomit."

"We don't want that. Take another sip of ginger ale. My mother swears by it as the cure for everything."

"Are you close to your family?"

"Very. I'm the third of six kids. We were born within ten years, so we grew up tight."

"Wow, six kids in ten years."

"My dad jokes that they had six of us before they figured out where we were coming from."

Piper's laughter was infectious and made him smile. "You're not making me laugh, remember?"

"Oh, sorry."

"That was funny, though. Do you have nieces and nephews?"

"Two of each, with another on the way."

"That sounds fun," she said wistfully.

"Do you have siblings?"

"Two younger sisters. They're still in college."

"Are you close to them?"

"I'm five years older than one and seven years older than the other, so I was like a third parent to them when they were younger. That's changing as they get older and more grown-up."

"The years between you will disappear over time."

"That's what my mom says."

"Did you grow up in Rhode Island?" he asked.

"Connecticut. Almost to the New York line. How about you?"

"Boston area."

"Oh no. You're a Red Sox fan, then. I knew there had to be something about you that I didn't like."

"Haha, yes, I am. Don't ruin everything by telling me you're a Yankees fan."

"Sorry."

"Ew."

"Did you just say ew?"

"I did. The Yankees are gross."

"I can imagine it must seem that way looking up from the cellar the Sox have been sitting in the last few years."

"That was rude."

"Truth hurts, huh?"

"It really does. They've gone from best to worst in a few years."

"So sorry for your troubles."

"You're not one bit sorry."

She giggled, causing the strangest feeling of lightness in his chest.

That'd happened before when she was around, which was one of the many reasons he'd thought of her so often while he was away.

"Is this going to be a deal breaker?" he asked.

"Did we have a deal?"

"I sort of hoped so."

She gave him a side-eyed look and took another sip of the ginger ale. "Are you sticking around this time?"

"That's the plan, but I have another question for you before we close the deal."

"I'm listening."

"Giants or Jets?"

"Bills."

"*Really?*"

"Uh-huh."

"Hmm, didn't see that coming."

"I like to keep you guessing."

"Clearly."

"Any other questions?"

"Just one," he said.

"Shoot."

"Will you hide from the mean old hurricane with me?"

CHAPTER 2

*M*ac McCarthy Jr. had been working since dawn to board up the family's marina in North Harbor. On the ladder next to him, his business partner, Luke Harris, held one end of the large sheet of plywood they were nailing over the windows in the gift shop. Mac's cousins, Shane, Riley and Finn, were at the Wayfarer in town, boarding up the massive plate-glass windows that overlooked the beach.

"Are we gonna undo all this for two more weeks of the season after the storm?" Luke asked.

"I don't think it's worth it. Do you?"

"Probably not."

"We can offer dockage through the long weekend in October, provided we still have docks after this storm," Mac said as he hammered a nail into a wood frame. The large window looked out over the island's famous Great Salt Pond.

"You think it's going to be that bad?" Luke asked.

"I don't like what I'm hearing."

"Yeah, me either. What's after this?"

"We need to button up the hotel and tie everything down at the alpaca farm." The farm was currently under construction to become a wedding venue by the following summer. Mac hoped the storm wouldn't knock them so far off schedule with the renovations that they'd have to cancel weddings already booked for next year.

"Have you done your house yet?" Luke asked.

"That's on the list for later today. You?"

"Not yet."

"We can do them together, if you want."

"I won't say no to that."

"I'm glad I bought all this plywood a couple of years ago in case of something like this," Mac said as he drove in the last nail.

"Remember how all the old guys said you were nuts for spending the money?" Luke asked, grinning.

"Two of them have called me today to ask if I had any extra," Mac replied.

"Did you?"

"Of course I did."

"What would this island do without you?" Luke asked.

"That's what I'm always saying. How'd you people survive before Mac McCarthy came home to save your asses?"

"And now you're talking about yourself in the third person."

"It's what I do."

"Trust me, I know. How are Maddie and the babies?"

"She's doing great and so are they, but we're both tired. It's very hard to get twin babies to sleep at the same time. One of them falls asleep, and then the other starts crying, and before we know it, they're both crying. Sometimes all five of them are crying at the same time."

"Yikes. Five crying kids."

"Thomas is only crying because he can't hear the TV over all the racket."

Luke laughed. "It's tough to be the oldest."

"It's a difficult burden for him, especially with two new baby sisters adding to the chaos, when he was all set with the one sister he already had."

"Poor guy."

"I feel his pain. Everything was fine in my world until Janey showed up." His sister was the youngest of the five McCarthys. They'd learned in recent years that their father had had a daughter he hadn't known about before he married their mother, which was how Mallory had knocked Mac out of the position as the eldest in the family—a role he still played to the hilt with his four younger siblings.

"You're so full of it. You love her to pieces."

"I do now. Then? Not so much. That reminds me. She called me an hour ago. I need to call her back. Let's take five."

"I'm ready for some coffee."

"Make it a double."

"You got it."

Mac took his phone to one of the picnic tables. Before they left, they would carry the tables inside the large building that housed the restaurant and office. He placed the call to Janey, who answered on the first ring.

"Mac."

"What's up, brat?"

"Joe has lost his ever-loving mind."

That she didn't tell him not to call her brat put Mac immediately on alert. "Why do you say that?"

"He's taking one of the boats out to sea to ride out the storm—alone—and Seamus is taking another." Joe's family owned the Gansett Island Ferry Company, which was the lifeline the island community relied upon to get them back and forth to the mainland.

"What's he doing that for?" Mac asked.

"Joe says that's what you do when there's a big storm coming, and you don't want to lose your most valuable assets or some such nonsense. Even though they're insured, apparently the time it would take to replace them would put us and the island out of business. You need to talk him out of it. They could take them up the Connecticut River just as easily. That's what Carolina's father did in the past."

"I'll talk to him."

"I'm thinking about coming there. He's leaving the kids and Carolina with Mom and Dad, since Carolina is still laid up with her broken leg, while he and Seamus take the boats out to sea."

"You can't get here, brat. They just sent the last boat over, and planes are already grounded."

Janey let out a sound that was a cross between a moan and a scream. "I'm losing it sitting here in Ohio while my whole family is under threat from this massive storm—and my husband thinks it's a good idea to drive a ferry out to sea."

"I'll see if I can talk him out of that."

"Thank you," she said, sounding relieved. "I tried to tell him the most precious assets are him and Seamus, not the boats, but they aren't listening to reason." Seamus, the ferry captain Joe had hired to run the business while he went with Janey to Ohio so she could attend vet school, was now married to Joe's mother, Carolina.

"I'll do what I can," Mac said with a weary sigh as he added another thing to his lengthy pre-storm to-do list.

"How's it going there?"

"Chaotic. Everyone is scrambling to batten down the hatches, so to speak. Luke and I are just finishing up at the marina."

"I'm so scared, Mac. Everyone I love is on that island. My kids…"

"We'll be fine, Janey. I know it's hard not to worry, but we'll get through this."

"How am I supposed to focus on school and studying when there's a huge storm heading for Gansett?"

"Keep your head down. You know Mom and Dad will take good care of the kids, and everything will be fine. I promise. I'm the big brother, so you know you can count on me."

"Always, Mac, but I'm worried about you, too. I'm worried about everyone."

Mac hated to hear Janey so upset that she was on the verge of tears. "I get it, brat. I'll find a way to get word to you after the storm, even if I have to do it by Morse code."

"For all the good that'll do me," she said with a laugh.

"We'll get word to you one way or the other. Try not to worry. We're all together, and we'll take good care of each other."

"I know you will. I think I'll go have a gigantic glass of wine and try to chill out."

"Good plan."

"You'll talk to Joe?"

"I will. I promise."

"You're the best big brother ever, except when you call me that stupid name."

Mac laughed. "It's tradition. Too late to change it now."

"It is *not* too late. I'm going to be a doctor of veterinary medicine very soon, and my brothers still call me that ridiculous name."

"I'll tell you what—the day you get that DVM, we'll stop calling you that."

"I'll believe it when I see it."

"Although, Dr. Brat has a nice ring to it."

"Mac!"

He laughed harder than he had in days. The threat posed by the looming storm had taken the humor out of his life and that of everyone else on the island. "I gotta run and get back to work, but I'll check in later after I talk to Joe."

"Thanks again, Mac."

"Anything for you, kid. Love you."

"Love you, too. So, so much."

As Mac ended the call, Luke walked over to him and handed him a coffee and a hot sugar doughnut.

"Every time I swear I'm giving up the doughnuts," Mac said, "I crumble like a sandcastle the first time someone hands me one."

"Why would you do something so dumb as to give up the doughnuts?"

"Because they're full of fat and other crap that's not good for me."

"So?" Luke took a sip of coffee and a bite of doughnut. "How's Janey?"

"Freaked out about everyone she loves being on the island with a storm barreling down on it. Joe and the kids came after Carolina broke her leg, and they're still here. Seems Joe and Seamus have decided to take the two biggest boats to sea rather than running them up the Connecticut River."

"And Janey isn't liking that plan, I take it."

"Not one bit."

"That's what the Navy does when a storm is headed for one of their ports. They take all the ships to sea."

"Still, it's risky, and they'd both be alone on the boats."

"Why wouldn't they take someone with them?"

"Probably because they don't want to risk anyone else."

"That's insane."

"Which is exactly what I plan to tell him when I talk to him. Should we move up the hill and knock out the hotel before we head into town?"

"Sounds like a plan."

"We've got miles to go before we sleep," Mac said as he finished the doughnut and downed the coffee. He only hoped they could get it all done in time.

CHAPTER 3

"This is absolute insanity," Carolina Cantrell O'Grady said to her husband and son as she sat with her healing leg propped on the ottoman. The two of them ran around packing for themselves, her and the two boys she and Seamus had taken in after their mother died. The plan was for Carolina, Jackson, Kyle and Joe's kids, PJ and Viv, to ride out the storm with Big Mac and Linda McCarthy while the two fools took the ferries out to sea.

"We've already had this argument, Mom." Joe tossed toys into a bag. "It's the best way to protect the boats."

"Who will protect my son and husband while they ride out a hurricane *at sea?*" The thought of it gave her nightmares.

"We won't be anywhere near the storm, love," Seamus said as he came into the room. "That's why we're going tonight, so we'll be clear of it by the time it arrives."

They were like two little boys anticipating a big adventure while playing down the risks for her sake—and Janey's. Carolina had heard her daughter-in-law screaming at her son on the phone earlier. Suffice to say, Janey didn't approve of this plan any more than Carolina did.

"We'll be fine." Seamus dropped a kiss on Carolina's forehead and headed for the bedroom before she could respond.

They were packing food and clothes for three days, but they didn't expect to be gone that long.

14

"What am I supposed to do while you guys are out in the middle of the ocean?" Carolina asked.

"Take care of yourself and the kids," Seamus said from the bedroom. "That's your only job."

"How am I supposed to function while you two are at sea in a monster storm?"

"Nothing to worry about," her charming husband said. "I swear."

Right, Carolina thought, *nothing to worry about with my husband and son at sea during a hurricane and four young children to care for with a broken leg.* Thank goodness for friends like Mac and Linda, who'd offered to take them in when they heard about Joe and Seamus's plan to take the two largest ferries to sea.

Since it seemed there was no way to talk them out of the harebrained scheme, Carolina decided to make herself useful—or as useful as she could be on the dreaded crutches that had made her hands and armpits as sore as her healing leg. She got up slowly and carefully and moved to the bedroom to pack for a few days at the White House, as the locals called the McCarthys' home.

"What're you doing, love?" Seamus asked when he returned to the bedroom they shared. "I can do that for you."

"I've got it." Sure, it would take about ten trips from the dresser to the bed, but she was determined to pitch in.

Seamus stopped her with his hands on her shoulders and an imploring look on his handsome face. "Caro, please. Let me do it so you aren't exhausted later."

To her great dismay, she broke down.

"Aw, love." He gathered her into his warm embrace. "Don't do that."

"Can't help it. I hate this plan."

"I know, but we'll be fine. Do you honestly think I'd ever do something that would take me away from you and our boys or that would endanger your precious Joe?"

"No, but—"

He kissed her before she could finish the thought. "I would never, ever, *ever* do anything to mess with the sweetest thing in my life. You and our family are all that matter to me, and protecting the business your parents founded is also very important. Those two boats are our bread and butter. We're taking them far away from the storm. We'll be nowhere near it. I swear on my life, the life that began the day I met you, that your son and I will be safe."

Carolina leaned into him, letting her crutches fall to the floor as she breathed in the familiar scent of him. She'd spent decades alone after Joe's father died and had never imagined she'd ever love a man again, let alone a smooth-talking Irishman sixteen years her junior. "This is all your fault."

"How so?" he asked with a tinge of amusement in his voice.

"You made me fall madly in love with you, so the thought of you being in any kind of danger is simply unbearable to me."

"Aw, I knew it. You *do* love me."

She swatted him on the ass. "Don't get sassy with me."

"You like me sassy."

"I like you *here* and whole and driving me crazy."

"I'll be back before you miss me."

"No, you won't. Will you be able to call me?"

"I'm not sure we'll have cell service out there, but I packed the handheld ship-to-shore radio for you to take to Linda's. We'll monitor Channel 72, so you can reach us that way."

"What do I do if you don't answer?"

"We'll answer."

"But if you don't?"

"If it's been twenty-four hours, notify the Coast Guard."

"Seamus…"

"You're thinking worst-case scenario, and there won't be any need for that. Joe and I are both seasoned professionals, and this is no big deal."

It was a very big deal to her, but she'd said enough. He and Joe wouldn't change their minds about this, so she would have no choice but to go along with the plan and hope for the best. Jackson and Kyle would help with PJ and Viv, and so would Big Mac and Linda.

In the next room, Carolina could hear Joe on the phone with Janey's brother Mac, telling him there was nothing to worry about, and no, they couldn't be talked out of the plan. Janey had probably asked her brother to try to talk some sense into his best friend.

Carolina recognized defeat when it was staring her in the face. "Let's get going," she said, resigned now to days of worry.

"Will you be all right?" Seamus asked.

"Not until you and Joe are back, so you'd better keep your word that everything will be fine."

He hugged her tightly and kissed the top of her head. "My only goal will be getting home to you and the boys as fast as possible."

Since she couldn't ask for anything more than that, she clung to him and his assurances, knowing she'd be a nervous wreck until they had safely returned.

JARED JAMES HELD one end of a sheet of plywood while his brother Quinn operated a nail gun that would secure it over the windows of the Chesterfield, the wedding venue Jared and his wife, Lizzie, owned. "I'm glad I listened to Mac when he told me to have supplies ready for a hurricane," Jared said.

"I'm sure a lot of people are glad they listened to him. He'll be even more smug than usual after this." As Quinn was married to Mac's older sister, Mallory, he was allowed to say stuff like that about his brother-in-law.

Jared laughed. "Probably so, but he's allowed to be smug as far as I'm concerned. He saved our asses with that advice and by telling us to install whole-home generators."

"Indeed."

With the Chesterfield thoroughly buttoned down, the brothers got into Quinn's pickup truck to head over to the senior care facility.

"I'm also thankful for the generators we invested in at the senior home," Quinn said. "I wouldn't want to deal with a storm like this without auxiliary power for the people on oxygen and other monitors."

"No kidding," Jared said. "That was money well spent."

"Since you've got a generator at home, too," Quinn said, "Mallory and I are coming to your place if the power is out after the storm."

"My home is your home. You know that."

"Thank you. Any word from Coop lately?" Quinn asked of their younger brother, who'd recently moved to Los Angeles with his new love, Gigi Gibson, a reality TV star.

"Just that he and Gigi are living it up in LA, and they're looking forward to coming back next summer to get his business launched."

"A party boat for bachelor and bachelorette parties," Quinn said with a chuckle. "Because nothing can go wrong there."

"He's got a great business plan and has covered all the bases with insurance. They're limiting guests to two drinks each. I think it'll be a big success."

"If you think that, I'm sure it will be."

For so long, his older brother had been somewhat of an enigma to

Jared. Quinn left home when Jared was in seventh grade and had never come back. After college and med school, he'd done a tour as a trauma surgeon in the Army. He'd lost a leg in Afghanistan, which he'd kept private from the family for a long time. He was so mobile that Jared had to remind himself at times that his brother relied on a prosthetic leg.

Now Quinn lived a couple of miles from Jared on Gansett Island, was married to Mallory and was the medical director for the senior facility Jared and Lizzie had founded on the island. Jared loved having Quinn close enough to see regularly and was delighted with the friendship that had grown between them over the last few years.

"How's the baby?" Quinn asked.

Jared couldn't help but smile when he thought of his baby daughter. "She's amazing. It seems like she does something new every day." Violet had come into their lives when Lizzie helped her mother, Jessie, after the child's birth. Later, Jessie had abandoned the baby with Lizzie and Jared, who were now adopting her.

"What do you hear from the birth mother?"

"Nothing."

"I guess that's for the best."

"It is for now. Lizzie promised to keep her updated with photos."

"When will it be final?"

"Not for a few more months."

As Quinn tightened his grip on the steering wheel, a muscle in his cheek pulsed with tension.

"What?" Jared asked.

"I'll be glad when that's legally settled for you guys once and for all."

"Me, too, but we're not worried about something going wrong. Jessie has no interest in being a mother."

"Still… The people who love you and Lizzie will sleep better at night when it's final."

"Thanks for caring, Quinn. I appreciate it."

"I do care. I'm sorry if I ever gave you the impression that I didn't. I was so caught up in my own shit for so long… And, well, I'm sorry."

"You don't owe me any apologies. It's all good."

"It is now, but for a lot of years, I didn't have much to do with you or the rest of the family, and I regret that. I mean, Coop went and became a *man* on me. What's up with that?"

Jared laughed. "That was a tough one for me, too. Seemed to happen suddenly."

"For real. What do you hear from Kendall?" Quinn asked of their sister.

"She's filing for divorce and moving out with the kids."

Quinn's deep sigh said it all. "I'm so sorry to hear it's come to that."

"It's been coming to that for a while," Jared said. "Phil refuses to get help. What's she supposed to do?" Their brother-in-law's issues with drugs and alcohol were no secret to any of them, but only recently had Kendall started talking about leaving.

"Nothing she can do, I guess. Thank God for the Jared James trust fund that makes it so we can all do whatever we want. I'm sure you're making it possible for her to leave a difficult situation."

"Anything for you guys. You know that."

"Not everyone would've been as generous as you were, Jared."

"I couldn't imagine having what I do and not sharing it with the people I love the most. Kendall was thinking about coming out here for a bit, until the storm started threatening. She might come after it passes."

"I hope she does. It's been too long since we've seen her and the kids."

Jared's phone rang, and he took the call from Lizzie. "Hey, hon. What's up?"

"Violet and I were wondering how it's going."

"We've got the Chesterfield boarded up. On to the senior center now. I'll be back soon to board up the house."

"We'll be here."

"You'd better be." He loved her laughter. "See you shortly." After he ended the call, he glanced at his brother. "Lizzie is so happy since we settled things with Jessie. She was born to be a mother."

"Yes, she was."

They arrived at the Marion Martinez Senior Care Facility a few minutes later and were surprised to find Mallory, the director of nursing, engaged in a verbal altercation with an older man.

Quinn brought the truck to a stop at the curb and jumped out. "What's going on?"

Jared followed him in case he needed backup.

"Mr. McDade is insisting on taking his wife to their home for the storm," Mallory said, sounding exasperated. "I recommended against that since we'll have medical staff on hand during the storm should the need arise."

"She's my wife, and I can take her out of here any damned time I want!"

"Mr. McDade, it's our job to care for your wife," Quinn said. "In our professional opinions, it would be a mistake to remove her from the center with the storm coming. If you have an emergency during the storm, EMS may not be able to get to you."

The older man's expression was full of outrage, his eyes flooded with tears. "I can take care of her. Who do you think did it for five years before she came here?"

"And I'm sure you did a wonderful job," Mallory said gently. "But the fact is, her condition has deteriorated considerably, and it wouldn't be safe to take her home. Not anymore."

Mallory's kind tone seemed to get through to the older man.

"I want her with me," he said in a softer tone. "She belongs with me."

"Yes, she does," Mallory said. "You're welcome to ride out the storm here with her, if you'd like to, that is."

His well-lined face brightened when he heard that. "You'd let me do that?"

"Of course we will," Jared said. "I'm Jared James, the owner. You're more than welcome to stay here for the storm."

"I, well… I appreciate that. I, um, didn't mean to get so hot under the collar. I apologize."

"No problem," Mallory said. "Why don't you go pack what you need for a day or two, and we'll get you settled with Mrs. McDade."

"I'll do that. Thank you again."

After Mr. McDade walked away with a new spring in his step, Quinn glanced at Mallory. "Are you okay, hon?"

"All good. I feel sorry for him. He was probably afraid to be alone during the storm."

"No doubt."

"You two are quite a team around here," Jared said, impressed by their handling of the situation.

"Thanks," Quinn said. "We love what we do. That helps."

"And we love who we do it with," Mallory said with a saucy grin for her husband. "That helps, too."

Jared covered his ears.

Laughing, Quinn said, "Not in front of the boss, babe."

"Oh yeah," she said. "I forget he's the boss."

"I've clearly lost control around here," Jared said, smiling.

"Did you ever have it?" Quinn asked.

"Good point. Let's get this place ready for the storm so I can get home to my girls."

"Right this way," Quinn said.

CHAPTER 4

*P*aul and Alex Martinez had spent the morning in a frantic state of activity, securing the equipment they relied upon to run their landscaping business and assisting numerous customers who'd called asking for help at their homes. After stops at the homes of six different island clients, they were on their way back to the compound where they lived and worked.

"Put the news on," Paul said as he drove a company truck toward home. "Let's see if there's an update on the storm."

Alex tuned the radio to a Providence-based news station and caught the latest weather forecast of a direct hit on tiny Gansett Island around two o'clock the next morning. A plane flown into the storm had clocked sustained winds at ninety-five miles per hour, with rainfall estimates topping two inches per hour. Most concerning of all, however, was the expected storm surge, which could exceed ten feet.

"Damn," Paul said, "it keeps getting worse."

"I'm worried about what's going to be left after it's finished with us."

"I know. I guess we hope for the best and prepare for the worst."

"Funny how this island used to feel like a prison when we were kids," Alex said, "and now…"

"Now it's our favorite place on earth, and there's nothing we can do to protect it from a massive threat."

"Yeah, that," Alex said with a sigh.

"We've done everything we can to prepare."

"Doesn't feel like enough, though."

"It's not a fair fight."

"No, it isn't."

"On the upside, the cleanup will keep us busy long after our season usually ends," Paul said in a cheerful tone.

"I suppose so." Every year, after the frantic pace of spring and summer gave way to autumn, Alex looked forward to the off-season and more time with his wife, Jenny, and their son, George. After Halloween, they sold Christmas trees and seasonal items, but otherwise, they were off until the spring.

"You checked on Mom again this morning, right?" Paul asked.

"I did. Mallory said she's comfortable and oblivious to the threat posed by the storm."

"I guess that's for the best."

The senior care facility that now bore her name had been founded in response to Alex and Paul's efforts to care for a mother with dementia with limited island services.

"Yeah," Alex said. "For sure. I'm going to have lunch with Jenny and George and then meet you back in the office to see what else there is to do."

"That sounds good. I could use some time with the family, too."

They'd been going straight out for the last few days, working sixteen to eighteen hours a day, and were exhausted.

Paul parked outside their retail facility, which was closed until pumpkin season began later in the month. "Meet you back here in two hours?"

"Yep."

While Paul headed to the home where the brothers had grown up and he now lived with his wife, Hope, her son, Ethan, and their baby daughter, Scarlet, Alex hung a left toward the two-story house he and Jenny had built a couple of years ago. Everywhere he looked on the vast property, he saw memories of his late father and their mother. Marion's battle with dementia had been brutal and relentless. After enduring that nightmare, a Category 2 hurricane was a minor inconvenience.

At least he hoped that's all it would be.

He went up the stairs to the porch, as tired as he could recall being since the first week George was born, when they'd hardly slept for days. Before he went inside, he removed his muddy work boots and left them on the welcome mat. The second he stepped inside, his son let out a shriek of excitement and came running to him on still-wobbly legs.

If there was anything better in this life than a joyful greeting from a toddler, Alex had yet to experience it. Well, everything with the toddler's mom was rather awesome, too. He knew she felt the same way about George as he did. He'd become the center of their world. Alex swung him into the air, making the little guy squeal with delight.

"How's my buddy today?" Alex asked as he kissed George's plump toddler cheeks. He'd snuck out early while Jenny and George were still sleeping.

"Dada."

That was Alex's new favorite word. His son was him all over again, with the same dark hair, olive-toned skin and dimple in his chin.

"He's very *busy*," Jenny said, sounding frazzled.

Ever since George started walking, he'd been a wild man. He was running them ragged trying to keep up with him, but they loved every minute of it.

"Our son is full of beans like his daddy," Jenny said.

"That's right," Alex said, kissing George's neck and making him squeal with laughter. That was Alex's favorite sound. Was there anything quite like a toddler belly laugh? Alex held him until George began to squirm, wanting to be free to roam. They'd fully childproofed the house so he could have the run of the place, and thanks to some well-placed gates, they kept him somewhat contained.

Alex went to Jenny, who was at the sink washing breakfast dishes, and put his arms around her from behind. When he kissed her neck, she pushed back against him. Just that quickly, he wanted her.

"Down, boy," she said, even as she pressed her ass against his erection.

"Don't send him mixed messages. It confuses him."

"Are we talking about your precious package in the third person now?"

With his hands on her hips, he breathed in the familiar, comforting scent of her hair. "So what if we are? And he is very, *very* precious."

Jenny's laughter was right up there with George's on Alex's list of his favorite things. She turned around, kissed him and put her arms around his neck as she glanced over his shoulder to check on George. "How's the storm prep going?"

"Getting there."

"You look tired."

"I'm beat."

"How much more do you have to do?"

"A few more hours and we should be set. We've done what we can. We just hope it's enough."

"My parents and sisters have been calling every thirty minutes or so, it seems. They're stressed out about us being here during the storm."

"I'd rather be here than worrying about what was happening here from the mainland."

"Me, too." She swallowed hard. "I think."

"Don't worry. We'll be fine. This is why I included the whole-home generator when we built this place, and don't forget we built it to withstand hurricane-force winds. If we lose power, Paul and Hope and the kids will come over. It'll be fun."

"My hero." She kissed him again. "Thank you for planning for every possibility."

"We'll have lots of time for storm snuggling, too."

"Is that a thing?" she asked. "Storm snuggling?"

"If not, it should be."

"I'm kinda scared."

"Don't be. We'll get through it like we get through everything else—together. I swear we'll be fine." As he held her tighter, he hoped he was right about that.

PAUL FOUND Hope stretched out on their bed, napping with baby Scarlet. Since he could use a quick nap much more than he wanted lunch, he shed his dirty clothes, washed up and then settled next to his wife and daughter for some shut-eye.

He was about to doze off when he decided he should set an alarm on his phone so he wouldn't sleep the rest of the day away.

"I didn't expect you to be home so soon," Hope whispered.

"Alex and I are taking a break before we head out to finish up."

"I'm glad you're here."

He put his arm around her and nuzzled the soft skin of her shoulder. "I'm always glad to be here."

"They've already canceled school for tomorrow," she said.

"Ethan will be thrilled."

"Snow days and hurricane days. Only in New England."

"I remember both from my childhood. Best days ever until I found you and Ethan and Miss Scarlet." He would forever marvel at the best thing in his life coming from one of the worst things. He'd met Hope and Ethan when they hired her to be Marian's private-duty nurse in a last-ditch effort to keep her at home awhile longer.

"We're so glad we found you, too."

As THE FERRY backed into port, Piper stood on wobbly legs and nearly fell over. Only Jack's quick move to put his arms around her kept her from toppling.

"Easy," he said. "Get your bearings."

"Wow, I'm all out of whack."

"That was one of the roughest rides I've ever had, and I've been coming here for years."

"Glad it wasn't just me who thought so."

"Definitely not. They'll probably have to hose down the boat after that."

"Gross."

"So gross." Jack kept his arm around her as they walked toward the rear of the boat to disembark.

A faint whiff of vomit filled the air, making Piper fear that she might yet lose her lunch even as she enjoyed his closeness.

"Breathe through your mouth," Jack said.

"Good advice."

"Almost to fresh air."

"Can't come soon enough."

The cool air coming in through the open door was a welcome relief.

She kept waiting for him to release her, but he held her close the whole way down the steps and off the boat.

"I usually feel better the minute I step onto land," he said, "but I have a feeling this one will linger."

"I'm right there with you. It's gonna linger."

"Where you headed?" he asked.

"To the Sand & Surf."

"I'll walk you home."

"You don't have to."

"I know. I want to."

"Okay, then…"

"Okay, then."

As they walked the short distance from the ferry landing to the hotel, the usually bustling downtown area was deserted and most of the storefronts were boarded up. Someone had spray-painted FUCK OFF ETHEL in red on the plywood that covered windows on one of the restaurants.

"That's funny," Jack said.

"I don't think Ethel is listening."

"Nope. Isn't it weird to see the downtown so quiet?"

"It's creepy. I don't like it."

"I don't either, but I must confess that it's nice to know we won't be dealing with drunk and disorderly people this weekend."

"There is that."

"Give me a hurricane over that any day."

"Stop! You don't mean that."

"I kinda do," Jack said with a sheepish grin, "but don't tell anyone I said that. You'll get me run out of town."

Piper laughed. "It's nice to have blackmail material on a state police officer."

"Blackmailing a police officer is a felony."

"It is not."

"Is, too! Ask Blaine."

"I'll do that."

"Can I tell you another secret?"

"Oh, more blackmail. Let's hear it."

"I missed you when I was on the mainland."

The statement had the effect of sucking all the air from her lungs. "No, you didn't."

"Yes, I did!"

"Why didn't you text me?"

"I wasn't sure you'd want me to."

"I did want you to. I was disappointed when you didn't."

The noise he made sounded like he'd been punched or something. "Ouch. I'm sorry. I wasn't sure how long the trial would drag on, and I didn't want to be, you know, sending smoke signals I couldn't do anything about."

"I'm sure you had plenty of ladies on the mainland to keep you warm while the trial dragged on."

Jack stopped walking so abruptly that Piper nearly stumbled.

Once again, he stopped her by taking hold of her arm. "I wasn't with anyone over there."

"You don't have to tell me what you think I want to hear. It's fine. It's not like we were seeing each other or anything."

"There hasn't been anyone since I lost my wife."

Shocked, she stared up at him. "You lost your wife?"

"Three years ago. Fucking breast cancer."

"Oh God, Jack. I'm sorry. She must've been so young."

"Diagnosed at twenty-eight, two years after we got married. She died at thirty-two. That was three years ago."

Piper's heart ached for him and the woman he'd loved. "I'm so, so sorry."

"Thank you. I'm doing better than I was. The first year or two after was… It was rough."

"I can't imagine. I'm sorry if I made it sound like you're a player. That was rude of me. I had no idea."

"It's fine," he said with the charming smile that had gotten her attention on the day they met, even when she was dealing with a nightmare of her own. "You didn't know." He offered his arm, and she curled her hand around his elbow as they continued toward the hotel. "You also couldn't have known that you're the first woman I've had any sort of flirtation with, if you want to call it that, since…"

"Huh. Well, I'm, uh…" Piper released a nervous laugh. "I don't know what to say to that."

"You say, 'Wow, Jack, that's a pretty big deal, and it ought to be treated as such.'"

"Um, okay… What you said."

"Next, you might ask what we should do to treat this as the very big deal it is."

"I'm afraid to ask."

He tossed his head back and laughed, and oh damn, was he sexy.

She'd been wildly attracted to him from the get-go, but after hearing what he'd been through, she was even more intrigued—and a little unnerved.

"First of all, we should hang out during the storm. And second, after that nonsense over, you ought to let me take you to dinner."

"I can do both those things."

"You'll be at the hotel during the storm?"

"That's the plan, unless we have to leave for some reason."

"If you do, I'll find you."

"You have my number," she reminded him.

"I know."

"Don't be afraid to use it." As they approached the stairs to the front porch of the Sand & Surf, Piper turned to face him. "Thanks for getting me through the ride from hell. The ginger ale and crackers saved me."

"Thanks for getting me through it."

"I didn't do anything for you."

"You kept me company. That's not nothing."

Piper glanced up at the front door to the hotel. "Well, I'd better get to work. Laura sounded so frazzled when she asked me to come back early."

"Blaine is waiting for me, too. I'll check in later?"

"I'll be here."

He shocked the shit out of her when he kissed her cheek before he walked away.

Piper stood there for a full minute after he left, her head spinning even more than it had on the rough ferry ride. She placed her hand over the spot on her cheek where he'd kissed her as she thought about what he'd shared with her.

Funny how you could think you knew someone, but you didn't. Not really. Not until they wanted you to know them. And what, exactly, did it mean that he wanted her to know him?

CHAPTER 5

"*P*iper? I thought that was you! Thank goodness you're back."
She turned to find Laura standing at the door and went up the stairs.

Laura hugged her like they hadn't seen each other in years rather than two weeks. "I've never been so happy to see anyone in my entire life."

"That can't possibly be true."

"It is true. I've got sick kids with Sarah and Charlie in Italy with Russ and Adele, and all my summer help gone back to school. I'm dying, and now there's Ethel to contend with."

"Piper is here to make it all better."

"And Laura is delighted to have her back. Thanks for cutting your vacation short."

"It was fine. My mother was driving me crazy asking me what I plan to do with my life now that I let Ben get away, so I was glad to have a reason to come back early. The ferry ride, however… Barf."

"I saw the boat coming toward South Harbor, and it made me sick just looking at it."

"You ought to have been on it. They're cleaning it with fire hoses."

"Ew."

"Yep. I ran into a friend who helped me get through it."

"Anyone I know?"

"In fact, it was. Jack Downing."

"Oh," Laura said with a big smile. She knew how dazzled Piper had been over him for months now. "Is that right? And how is our favorite hot cop?"

"He's quite lovely and back on the island to stay now that the trial he was working on has ended."

"Isn't that a fun development? That you both came back to stay on the same day. You're back to stay, aren't you?"

"For as long as you need me."

"Girl, that's apt to be ten to fifteen years."

Piper laughed at the face Laura made to go along with the statement. "I'm here for you."

Laura hugged her again. "Thanks."

"What can I do?"

"Take over the desk for me so I can check on Owen and the kids?"

"You got it."

"Excellent."

"Hey, Laura…"

"Yes?"

"Did you know Jack was a widower?"

"What? No!"

"Don't say anything about it to anyone, okay? I wasn't sure if that was public info, and I guess it isn't."

"I only know him to say hi to. Wow. That's so sad."

"His wife died of breast cancer three years ago. She was only thirty-two."

"Oh, that's awful."

"Yeah, for sure. I had him pegged as a world-class player, but he said he hasn't dated anyone since he lost her."

"Huh. How do you feel about that?"

"I feel sad for him that he lost her and intrigued because he told me I'm his first so-called flirtation since that happened."

"Ohhhh, well… Isn't that interesting?"

"It is. He makes me all… fluttery inside."

"Is there any better feeling than that?" Laura asked with a sigh and a smile. "Owen still makes me feel fluttery, even after three kids have done their best to kill our romance."

"Nothing can kill your romance with Owen."

"Aw, you're sweet to say so. We're muddling through somehow. I'm pulling for you to get your happy ending, too."

"Thanks. It's good to be back."

"We're so glad to have you. I'll be down to relieve you shortly so you can settle in."

"No rush. Do what you need to. I've got you covered."

"Bless you," Laura said as she took off for the stairs, heading for the apartment she and Owen shared with their kids on the third floor.

When she was alone at the front desk, Piper fired up the computer and immediately felt guilty when she googled Jack Downing and Rhode Island state police. The third item on the list was a newspaper article about Jack's late wife, Ruby Downing, who'd chronicled her four-year battle with breast cancer on Instagram and had more than one million followers at the time of her death.

Piper clicked on the link to Ruby's account and then on her last post, in which she announced that she and her sweet husband had made the difficult decision to end treatment.

She'd quoted Saint Timothy. "I have fought the good fight. I have finished the race." She thanked her doctors, nurses, extended family and friends who'd stood by her and Jack through the highs and many lows of her illness. "But most of all, I thank my love, Jack, without whom I would've given up a long time ago. Make the most of every day, y'all. You never know how long you have. Peace out."

Piper scrolled through the photos Ruby had attached to the post. The one from their wedding took her breath away. What a beautiful couple they'd been, and obviously so in love. Time ceased to exist as Piper scrolled back to earlier posts that told the story of a happy life until cancer upended everything. She read about harrowing treatments, setbacks, infections and the leave of absence Ruby had taken from her teaching job, hoping it would be temporary. In between the cancer updates were sunrises, sunsets, flowers, the babies of friends and family and a black dog named Scout, who'd belonged to her parents.

"Whatcha looking at?" Laura asked, startling Piper.

She felt like she'd been caught watching porn at work, or something equally embarrassing. "I've done a bad, bad thing and looked up Jack and his late wife, Ruby. This is her Insta account." Piper moved over so Laura could see the photos. "She was so brave and inspiring. She fought so hard."

"She was lovely."

"Check out the wedding photo." Piper clicked on the post that included it.

"Wow. Stunning."

Piper clicked on the red box in the corner to exit out of the browser. "Sorry. I didn't mean to fall into such a rabbit hole. How long were you upstairs?"

"An hour."

"Jeez."

"It's normal to be curious, Piper."

"I know."

"But?"

Piper took a moment to try to get her thoughts together before she answered Laura's question. "I was starting to get a little excited about the thing between us, whatever it might be. But now…"

"It's okay. You can tell me. No judgment."

"How could I ever compete with her and what was obviously a very big love, you know?"

"I see what you mean, but I think it's significant that he told you he hasn't been with anyone since she died."

"Is it too big of a deal? Don't they say the first big relationship after a huge loss is always a disaster? Would I be setting myself up for another heartbreak by letting this go any further? I've had enough of that to last me a lifetime, and I'm sure he has, too."

Laura seemed to give her questions considerable thought. "Those are important things to think about, but here's another perspective. Would you be sad if you never got a chance to find out what you might have with him?"

Piper recalled the immediate spark of attraction at a time when she was in no place to be attracted to anyone, as well as the way he'd come to her rescue on the ferry. She'd thought about him endlessly during the weeks he'd been off the island.

"I missed him while he was gone," she said, "and I thought that was odd since I don't really know him all that well. A few conversations, a couple of laughs, some low-key flirting. That kind of thing. So it was weird that I missed him, right?"

"Not at all," Laura said. "You like him. He likes you. There's a spark of something there, and you were hoping to find out what that might be."

"And now I just don't know." She glanced at Laura, who'd been like a big sister to her since she showed up on the island in rough shape after a horrible breakup and then was assaulted the first time she ventured out. "What would you do?"

"The curiosity would have me wanting to spend more time with him."

"Even knowing what I do now?"

"I think so, but I'd proceed with caution."

"Thank you for listening."

"No problem. We old married people live vicariously through people like you who are still dating."

"Not that long ago," Piper said, "I thought I was done with dating, and now I'm back to square one."

"Don't forget, I've been right where you are." Laura had shared how she'd found out her new husband was still on dating apps and meeting women after their wedding. "It totally sucks to have to start over, but trust me, it's worth it when you get it just right." Laura squeezed Piper's shoulder. "I have a good feeling about you and Jack, for whatever that's worth."

"It's worth a lot."

The phone on the desk rang. "I've got it," Piper said. "Sand & Surf, this is Piper. How can I help you?"

"Hi, Piper, this is Dara Watson, the lighthouse keeper?"

"Of course. Hi, Dara. What can I do for you?"

"Oliver and I are wondering if you have any rooms available. We're a little unsettled about riding out the hurricane at the lighthouse."

"I just got back to the island, so hang on for one second and let me check with Laura."

"Sounds good, thanks."

Piper put her on hold. "Dara Watson is asking whether we have rooms. She and Oliver don't want to ride out the storm at the lighthouse."

"I don't blame them. Tell them to come over. We've got plenty of room after just about everyone left and our reservations canceled for this weekend."

Piper pressed the flashing button. "Dara? We've got rooms, and Laura said to come over."

"Oh, great. Tell her thanks. We'll be there soon."

"Sounds good."

Piper had no sooner put down the phone than it rang again with a call from Slim Jackson, asking the same question.

"Erin and I aren't sure our summer shack is up for a hurricane," Slim said.

"We've got rooms, and you're more than welcome to come," Piper told him.

"Excellent. Erin will be glad to hear that. We're on our way into town."

"See you when you get here."

"Don't charge anyone who comes in today," Laura said after Piper hung up with Slim. "We're happy to provide shelter for those who need it, although I sure do hope this old girl will still be standing when it's over." Laura took a tentative look around the nearly one-hundred-year-old building. "She creaks and moans during a Nor'easter. I can't fathom what a hurricane will be like."

Piper was truly nervous about what was coming their way and hoped the grand old hotel that'd begun to feel like home would survive the storm.

IN THE WANING daylight over North Harbor, Big Mac McCarthy stood at the sliding glass door that led to the deck and looked down over his "kingdom," such as it was—the marina and hotel that had been their life's work. He and his wife, Linda, had put everything they had into making their businesses a success and had recently branched out with other endeavors, including the Wayfarer in South Harbor and the old alpaca farm that was being turned into a "shabby chic" wedding venue.

Whatever that was.

The kids told him it would be a hit, and he'd learned to trust their judgment. Having his six grown children and seven grandchildren—with six more babies on the way—living on the island was a dream come true, except for at times like this when five of them were in the line of a monster storm and the sixth one was melting down in Ohio, worried about her family on the island.

And then there was Joe and Seamus and their plan to take the ferries to sea to "ride out the storm." It was no wonder his princess was on the verge of an epic panic attack thinking about her beloved husband at sea in a hurricane while her children were on the island that sat in the bull's-eye of the storm.

Who could blame Janey for being so upset? When he'd heard about Joe and Seamus's plan, he'd felt a bit of panic himself. Of course he understood the need to protect the boats, but good Lord, the idea of being out on the ocean in a hurricane made his knees weak. And Big Mac McCarthy had seen his share of rough seas while living on an island for more than forty years.

He'd tried telling Janey that Joe and Seamus would be fine, but he had his doubts. Not that he'd ever say that to her when she was half a country away trying to keep it together.

From his vantage point looking down at the harbor, Big Mac could see that "the boys," as he referred to his son Mac and their business partner, Luke, had done a great job of preparing the marina and hotel for the storm. They'd refused to allow him to help after he'd had an episode of vertigo a couple of weeks ago that was later tied to an ear infection.

"No ladders for you," Mac had declared, and that had been that.

As he got closer to seventy, that sort of thing happened more often. Time marched on with a relentlessness that never failed to amaze him.

"It's looking wild out there, love," Linda said when she joined him at the window.

He put his arm around her. "Sure is, and the storm isn't even here yet."

"Are you feeling all right?"

She'd asked him that a hundred times since the vertigo, but he understood that he'd worried her, so he answered the question the same way every time. "I'm feeling great, except for this bitch Ethel threatening my island."

"She's got nothing on Gansett Islanders."

"Let's hope so. Have you talked to Janey again?"

"Just now," she said with a sigh. "She's distraught."

"Poor kid."

A knock on the door preceded an invasion of adults, kids and a dog named Burpee.

His grandson PJ ran to him, and Big Mac lifted him into his arms. "What's the good word, my man?"

"Sleepover with Grammy L and Papa!"

"That's right."

His little eyebrows furrowed with concern. "Daddy going to sea."

Big Mac kissed the top of his head. "He'll be just fine. Don't you worry." He put him down and picked up his sister to give her some love. Being a grandfather was the best thing since ice cream. Viv rested her head on his shoulder. He wondered if she understood what was going on or if she was just too young.

Carolina came in on crutches, with Seamus carrying bags behind her. "Thanks for having us, guys," Caro said.

Linda kissed and hugged their longtime friend. They'd first met Carolina and Joe when he and Mac were in second grade and had been the best of friends ever since. That they now shared grandchildren with

Carolina was one of life's sweeter developments. "No problem at all," Linda said.

"Yes, it is a problem," Carolina said. "But we appreciate it anyway."

"Aye," Seamus said. "I'll feel much better knowing my family is with you."

Jackson and Kyle came in carrying backpacks and pulling suitcases, their expressions grave. They were certainly old enough to understand what was happening, and after having lost their mother to lung cancer not that long ago, they were understandably worried about Seamus.

Watching the four of them form a family bond had been among the most satisfying things Big Mac had witnessed in his life. He ached for the boys—and for Seamus, who'd be worried sick about them while he was gone.

"Could I have a word?" Seamus asked Big Mac in the lilting Irish accent that had become so familiar to him since Seamus came to work for Joe and fell in love with Joe's mother.

Big Mac kissed Viv and put her down to run around with her brother. He gestured for Seamus to follow him into the study while Linda got Carolina and her broken leg settled in a recliner.

Seamus closed the door. "I wanted to say thank you for having my family while I'm gone, and if..." He took a deep breath. "If anything happens, I was hoping I could count on you to... well, take care of them."

Big Mac saw tears in the other man's eyes, and his heart went out to him. "You'll be fine, and we're always here for you and your family. You know that."

"I do, and I take great comfort in it all the time, not just at times like this. It's a strange thing for a man who lived his entire life without responsibility for others to find himself in a spot like this, loving other people more than he loves himself."

"Trust me. I get it. When you have a family, your heart walks around outside your body."

"Aye, that it does. It helps to have friends like family that you can count on." Seamus extended his hand to Big Mac.

He shook the younger man's hand and then hugged him. "Try not to worry. We'll take care of your family. Just be safe out there."

"That's the plan."

When they rejoined the others in the living room, Seamus went to Carolina and bent over to whisper something that made her tear up as she hooked a hand around his neck and kissed him.

Then he turned to the boys and held out his arms to them. "Be good lads while I'm gone, you hear me?"

"We will," Jackson said as he and Kyle clung to Seamus.

"It'll be okay," Seamus told them. "Don't worry. Take good care of Caro, okay? She still needs lots of help."

It was a heartbreaking scene to witness, Big Mac thought as he watched Seamus and Joe talking to their loved ones.

PJ and Viv were in tears saying goodbye to their daddy.

"You guys should just go," Linda said. "This won't get better with time."

"She's right, mate," Seamus said to Joe. "Let's get to it."

"Please come back to us," Carolina said when Joe leaned over to kiss his mother.

"We will," Joe said. "Don't worry."

"Hahahaha, right." Carolina wiped away tears. "What do we have to worry about?"

Joe took Seamus by the arm to lead him out of the house. "Let's go."

Seamus looked back at Carolina as Joe moved them toward the door.

Linda huddled with PJ and Viv. "Now, now, loves. Daddy will be back before you know it. And in the meantime, Grammy has ice cream and s'mores and new games and lots of fun stuff planned."

"Ice cream," Viv said, immediately brightening.

Linda laughed. "I thought that might get your attention. Come on, boys," she said to Jackson and Kyle. "Let's have dessert before dinner."

Leave it to his Linda to come up with the perfect distraction for four kids who desperately needed it, Big Mac thought.

"Still the best mom there is," Carolina said to Big Mac as Linda led the kids into the kitchen.

"Indeed she is."

"They'll be all right, won't they?"

"I'm sure of it. Do you know anyone better qualified for a mission like this than the two of them?"

"No, I don't, but I can't understand why they didn't just take the boats over to North Harbor and anchor them."

"Because the anchors wouldn't hold them with the wind predicted, and they needed the boats for last-minute runs, so it's too late to run them up the river. This is the best plan to protect the assets."

"Who will protect the two men I love with all my heart?"

"That's in God's hands."

CHAPTER 6

"Tell me we're doing the right thing here," Seamus said as Joe drove them to the ferry landing in town.

"We are," Joe said. "Without those two boats, we're out of business, and you know that."

"I do, but we're risking our lives to protect a business when we both have so much to live for."

"The first couple of hours will be bad, but after we get outside the cone, we'll be fine."

Leaving his family behind with a monster storm bearing down on them went against everything Seamus believed in as a husband, father and man, but protecting the business that provided for all of them was critical, too.

"I've never been so torn between what I needed to do and what I wanted to do."

"I feel you," Joe said. "Poor Janey is in Ohio having a stroke about this."

"Tough place to be with a storm coming toward everyone she loves."

"Yeah, for sure," Joe said. "How bad do you think it's going to be afterward?"

"Hard to tell. The power grid is old and limited, as we learned during the blackout, so we might be without power for quite some time."

"Thank God for generators."

"I'm glad I let Mac talk me into getting one at the house after the blackout," Seamus said.

"Same, but we can't ever tell him he was right."

"Understood," Seamus said with a chuckle.

At the ferry landing, Joe parked in the employee lot. They grabbed their bags from the back of the truck. They'd packed clothes and enough food and water to last three days. Hopefully, they'd be back within a day or two, but they'd prepared for a variety of scenarios.

Seamus's cousin Shannon came out of the office with three of the other mates who worked on the boats, each of them carrying multiple bags.

"What're you doing here?" Seamus asked them.

"We're going with you," Shannon said.

"No," Joe said. "We don't want to risk anyone else."

"What's your plan for throwing off lines and such?" Shannon asked in the familiar cadence of home. "We've already decided you're not going alone, and we've packed everything we need, so let's do this."

The four men walked toward the two vessels that were backed into port.

"What do you think?" Seamus asked Joe.

"I'd rather have the company than not, and they seem determined."

"Then let's get this show on the road."

They boarded the boats, fired up the engines and cast off the lines, all within ten minutes.

Seamus had to admit that Shannon was right. It would've been tricky to leave without help, especially with the wind blowing as hard as it was.

Joe signaled for Seamus to take the lead, so he put the engines into gear and pointed the helm toward the breakwater. After they left the pier, Shannon and Danny, the other mate, came up to the wheelhouse.

"Hold on, boys," Seamus said.

As they cleared the breakwater, the boat rolled hard to the right and then the left.

"Holy *shit*," Shannon said, laughing. "This is awesome."

Damned fool, Seamus thought. None of this was awesome or fun or exciting. It felt wrong to be leaving his loved ones behind. He cast a glance out the window behind him, watching as Joe took the same wild ride out of the harbor, and breathed a sigh of relief when the other boat had righted itself.

Seamus estimated the seas at about eight feet, which made for a wild, roller-coaster ride as they headed east toward Martha's Vineyard. "If you guys leave the wheelhouse, I want you tethered," Seamus said.

"We're one step ahead of you," Shannon said, raising his sweatshirt to show Seamus that he'd already donned the harness. "Don't worry, boss man. We've got this."

Seamus hoped he was right about that.

OLIVER WATKINS MOVED through their bedroom in the top floor of the lighthouse, tossing clothes into bags and gathering what they needed for their dog, Maisy. Hopefully, Laura wouldn't mind having her at the hotel. He hadn't thought to remind Dara to ask when she called. Gansett Island was the most dog-friendly place he'd ever lived. It was a safe bet that they'd welcome Maisy.

At least he hoped so.

It was strange, even years later, not to be packing for the little boy they'd lost tragically. Oliver still felt like there was something he was supposed to be doing, someone he should be caring for who wasn't there anymore but who was always with them.

Grief was strange that way, resurfacing at the oddest times to remind you that life would never be the same without the person you'd lost. But he and Dara had learned over the last few months that life could be sweet again and there was still joy to be found even as they would mourn their son for the rest of their lives.

They'd been watching the storm for days, hoping it would change course and miss the island. Depending on which model they believed, anything could still happen. He wasn't taking any chances with Dara and the baby she was carrying. But with things looking more dire by the hour, they'd decided to get out of the lighthouse and move into town before the worst of the storm hit during the night.

"I can hear you moving around up here like a caged tiger," Dara said as she came up the spiral staircase to the bedroom. "You need to chill out. The storm is still hours away."

"I want you somewhere safe."

She put her arms around him and rested her head on his chest. "We'll be fine."

"You seem quite sure of that."

"When you've been through what we have, what's a Category 2 hurricane to us?" Taking the lighthouse keeper job on Gansett had been the best thing they could've done for themselves. Being on the island, among new friends, had helped them find their way back to each other.

"When you put it like that…"

"Everything else is minor compared to losing Lewis."

It'd taken tremendous courage to decide to try for another child. As the weeks passed, they got more excited to meet their new little one. The next seven months would seem like an eternity, but Oliver was determined to enjoy the time alone while they could, starting with a night or two in a hotel.

"Are you ready?" he asked her.

"Whenever you are."

"I hope this place will still be here after."

"It's withstood big storms before," she said. "I'm sure it'll be fine, but I'm glad we don't have to stay here to find out."

"I am, too. Even though the Surf is right on the coast, at least we won't be completely alone there."

"That's my thinking as well, although I'm looking forward to some storm snuggling."

"That sounds perfect to me."

Oliver carried their bags down the two flights of stairs and out to their SUV. Then he went back for the bag of food she'd packed to share with their hosts, as they fully expected to lose power during the storm.

Dara followed him to the car, with Maisy on a leash. "I can't believe I forgot to ask if it's okay to bring her."

"I'm sure it's fine," Oliver said. "Gansett is so dog-friendly."

"I hope Laura doesn't mind."

As they left the lighthouse property, Oliver put the car in Park and went back to shut and lock the gate. The grounds would remain closed until after the storm had passed. Over the last couple of days, they'd watched the seas get progressively rougher as the surf crashed against the rocky shoreline below.

"I'm glad not to be on the ferry today," Dara said.

"I saw the last one coming in when I was in town. It was rocking and rolling."

"I feel sick just thinking about it."

"It's strange to realize that there's no way on or off the island for the next little while."

"Don't remind me. My parents and sister are having a fit over us being stuck here. They've been calling and texting all morning. Monique said she should've stayed for the parties."

Oliver grunted out a laugh. "She would focus on that."

"My sister is nothing if not consistent."

"Did she ever say whether she hooked up with that Coast Guard guy? What was his name?"

"Linc, and no, she didn't say anything, which is odd. She usually kisses and tells."

"Do you?"

"Of course not," she said with a laugh.

"Even to her?"

"Even to her."

"I mean, I wouldn't care if you did. It's not like we're big news anymore."

"Yes, we are."

He looked over at her. "How so?"

"For a long time, everyone was very concerned about whether we would hold it together. I was concerned about that."

"I know," he said with a sigh. "I was, too."

"So the fact that we seem to have answered that question somewhat definitively is big news all around."

"I suppose so. It's crazy..."

"What is?" she asked.

"Before we lost Lewis, if someone had asked me if there was anything in this world that could tear us apart, I would've said no way."

"Same."

"Life certainly has a way of showing us who's boss, huh?" he asked.

"For sure. But what matters is that we somehow managed to hang on to each other despite the worst possible thing. That makes me so thankful, because I couldn't imagine losing you, too."

"I'm glad that's behind us, but it's a reminder that we need to keep our eye on the ball—always."

"My eye is on the ball," she said, reaching over to give him an intimate squeeze.

Since he hadn't seen that coming, he nearly swerved off the road. "Cripes, woman! A little warning would be nice."

Dara laughed so hard, she snorted. "What fun would a warning have been?"

After he'd parked in the Surf lot, he leaned across the center console to kiss her. "This is what I missed the most. The easy fun. The silliness."

"Me, too. I'm glad it came back."

"I'm glad it all came back. Let's try hard to never lose it again, okay?"

"Deal."

He insisted on carrying all their bags through increasingly stronger wind to the main entrance to the hotel.

Piper greeted them at the check-in desk. "Hi there! How's the weather?"

"Sporty," Oliver said as Dara tried to straighten her hair after the wind had messed it up. "And getting more so by the minute, or so it seems."

"Yikes. Well, let's get you guys checked in."

"We hope it's okay we brought Maisy," Oliver said.

"No problem at all." Piper handed over a key to room 210. "That's second floor to the left. Please let us know if there's anything you need. Laura also said to tell you she and Owen are making dinner tonight and to come down around seven if you're interested."

"We brought some stuff to contribute." Dara handed her the bag of food. "And we'd love to do dinner. Tell them thanks for us."

"Sounds good," Piper said.

Oliver withdrew a credit card from his wallet.

"Oh, there's no charge during the storm. Please make yourselves at home."

"No way," Oliver said. "We want to pay."

"Boss's orders. You don't want to get me in trouble, now do you?"

"That's very nice of you guys," Dara said. "Thank you so much."

"Our pleasure. We'll see you at dinner."

As they went upstairs, Oliver said, "There's no other place on earth like Gansett Island."

"I was thinking the same thing. Everyone on here is so nice and welcoming."

"We need to talk about what we're going to do when our lighthouse tenure ends."

"I want to stay."

"I do, too."

"That was easy."

Oliver inserted the key in the door to room 210, which was on the town side of the building. That was probably intentional, as the oceanfront rooms would take the brunt of the storm. "If there's anything left after Ethel has her way with us, we should look at some houses."

"Isn't Ned Saunders the one to talk to about that?"

"He is. I'll ask him the next time we have coffee at the marina, if we get to do that again this season. Big Mac said they might not reopen after the storm."

"That'd be a bummer."

"It would." Oliver had come to look forward to starting his days with Big Mac, Ned, Mac, Luke, Big Mac's brothers, Frank and Kevin, and the other guys who gathered at the marina each morning for coffee, doughnuts and bullshit. There was a lot of the latter, and he enjoyed every minute with them. They also included him any time they decided to spend an afternoon fishing or doing whatever fun thing they got up to. When Big Mac was involved, there was always fun to be had.

"Mac said his dad always says that when they have a big storm in September, and they usually reopen."

"I hope they do, and by the way, this room is gorgeous."

"It is."

"Laura told me a while ago that when they redecorated, they tried to bring back a lot of the original charm that'd been muted over the years."

"They did a great job." Oliver noted the shining wood trim, wallpaper that had been made to look vintage and inviting white bedding on a king-size bed. "How about a nap before dinner for my baby mama?"

"Your baby mama wouldn't say no to that."

They kicked off their shoes and slid into soft cotton sheets.

"This is lovely," Dara said. "It feels like a vacation."

"Everything on this island is like a vacation."

"That's why we love it so much."

When she snuggled up to him and rested her head on his chest, he put his arm around her and kissed the top of her head. "Best hurricane ever."

CHAPTER 7

On the hotel's third floor, Laura rocked her baby daughter, Jo, to sleep, hoping the poor little thing could get some relief from the relentless flu that had made her, her brothers—and their parents— miserable for days now. Laura remembered the time she and her brother, Shane, had gotten the chicken pox at the same time after their mother had died. She didn't know how her dad had handled that on his own.

As always, Laura gave thanks to her husband, Owen, who was her greatest source of daily support, but especially when the shit hit the fan like it had lately. First, Holden had come down with the flu, then Jon and now Jo. Owen and Laura were holding their collective breath, hoping they didn't get it, too.

"Is she asleep?" Owen whispered when he ducked his head inside the room Jo shared with her twin, Jon. They'd been talking again about finally looking for a bigger home, but they couldn't seem to bring themselves to make the move away from the hotel they ran together. They loved *living above the store*, as Owen said.

Laura shifted, trying to see Jo's cute little face. "I think so."

"Want me to take her?"

"Sure." Laura's arms had pins and needles from holding her daughter for so long.

Like the expert he was, Owen lifted Jo off Laura's lap and laid her in the crib. They tiptoed out of the room, hoping for the best as Laura shook her arms to get the blood flowing again.

"Are all three of them asleep at the same time, or am I dreaming?" Owen asked as he kneaded the tension from Laura's shoulders.

She turned to face him. "Don't jinx us."

His grin was one of her favorite things in life, especially when he directed it at her. "Whatever shall we do with this unexpected break?"

"I need sleep, and I need it now." She hadn't gotten more than two or three hours at a time over the last few days.

"Whatever my queen requires is what she gets."

Owen took her hand and led her into their room. He turned down the bed and waited for her to get in before pulling the covers up and kissing her cheek.

"Come nap with me."

"I still have some storm prep to do." He kissed her again. "You get some rest. I'll be back in a bit. Text me if anyone wakes up."

"Set me an alarm for an hour, will you? I need to start dinner."

"I'll take care of dinner. What were you planning to make?"

"Pasta to use up the sauce Stephanie made, meatballs, salad, garlic bread."

"I got it. You sleep."

Laura crooked her finger to bring him in for a better kiss. "Thank you for all you do. You're the best."

"No, you are," he said, kissing her again.

"Sometimes, especially during weeks like this one, I wonder if you don't regret not taking that last boat off the island way back when."

"I have never once, not for a single second, regretted that decision."

"Even when kids are puking and pooping on you?"

"Even then. I love every second of our life together, and you know that."

"I'm the luckiest girl ever."

"I'm the luckiest."

She shook her head.

He kissed her forehead and then her lips one more time. "Rest while you can, love. I'll be back soon."

"I'll be here."

"Call if all hell breaks loose again."

"You'll be the first to know."

Laura woke much later to darkness and the low hum of voices in the next room. It was almost eight o'clock, and she'd been asleep for three hours. *What the hell?* She dragged herself out of bed and emerged from the bedroom to find all three kids sitting at the table eating spaghetti as if they hadn't been as sick as dogs as recently as the day before. "What goes on out here?"

"We hungry, Mommy." Holden spoke for his siblings, as usual. They joked that Jon and Jo would never get around to talking because Holden did it for them.

"This is a wonderful development," Laura said, kissing the tops of three little heads before going to hug Owen. "Does this mean we've turned the corner?"

"Let's hope so, or we're gonna have some colorful vomit later."

"Ew."

Chuckling, he said, "Are you hungry?"

"I could eat something."

"Have a seat."

"Some kind of service in this restaurant," she said to the kids, who giggled at the face she made.

"It's nawt a restront, Mommy," Holden said.

"I think it is, because we have a very handsome waiter serving us."

"That's Daddy!" he said with the belly laugh she loved so much.

Laura acted surprised to realize Owen was their waiter. "So it is."

That sparked more laughter from all three of them. If Holden laughed, the other two did, too. They copied everything he did, which he loved. Most of the time, anyway. Every so often, he got annoyed by them, but he was a good sport for the most part. It was hard to believe he'd soon be three.

Which reminded her that she needed to plan his party once they got past the hurricane. One thing at a time.

"What's the latest on the storm?" Laura asked Owen when he brought his plate to the table and sat next to her.

"No change. But the good news is the ocean side of the hotel is boarded up, along with the first floor on the street side, and everything is either tied down or brought in. We're ready for whatever Ethel has in store for us."

"I hope she takes a hard turn away from us."

"Me, too, but that's not looking likely."

Laura ate the spaghetti, meatballs, bread and salad Owen had made. "This is good. Thanks for cooking." She gasped. "What about the guests?"

"Made the same for them, and they're enjoying it downstairs."

"I don't deserve you," she said with a sigh.

"Quit that nonsense."

"I won't quit it. While I slept for *three hours*, you cooked for a dozen people and took care of three little kids."

"They helped me, didn't you, guys?"

Holden nodded. "We helped."

Laura gave Owen a skeptical look. "I'm sure they were a big help."

"We was, Mommy. I carried the bread. Jon took the salad, and Jo took... What did she take, Daddy?"

"Dessert," Owen said.

All three kids perked up at the mention of one of their favorite things.

"And what's for dessert?" Laura asked.

"Brownies."

"Daddy made them!"

"Daddy is Superman."

That led Holden to jump up and "fly" around the room like Superman.

Jo and Jon got up to chase after him, and just that quickly, mayhem ensued.

"Glad to see them feeling better," Laura said as she sipped from a glass of red wine Owen had poured for them.

"Me, too. I hate when they're sick, even if I love all the sleeping."

"Right?" she asked with a laugh. "I fear they're so well rested that they're going to be up all night."

"I hope not. The storm will scare them."

"Hell, it scares me. Did you talk to your mom earlier?"

"I did. She's frantic. With all of us here except for Josh, she's hardly enjoying the trip with worrying about us. I tried to reassure her, but you can imagine how that went."

"I feel for her. I wouldn't want to be so far away when everyone I loved was staring down a monster storm."

"Me either."

SARAH FELT frantic as she watched the weather forecast that was in Italian but showed the huge storm barreling toward tiny Gansett Island. That image required no translation. How was she supposed to think of anything else when six of her seven children, their partners, her three

49

grandchildren and Charlie's pregnant daughter and her husband were on that island, not to mention countless friends?

She took a deep breath and released it, the apprehension reminding her of the horrible years she'd spent in a bad marriage. Now that she was happily remarried to Charlie, she tried never to think of those awful years, but the anxiety currently gripping her was eerily reminiscent.

They were in a gorgeous suite in a sumptuous hotel in Rome, with her parents in an adjoining suite. This was a trip she'd dreamed about for most of her life, and she couldn't enjoy it while her loved ones were in peril.

She startled when Charlie's hands landed on her shoulders. She'd thought he was asleep, like she should've been. As if that was going to happen.

"Easy, love. It's just me."

"Sorry. I'm so on edge, I feel like I might break."

"I won't let that happen." He continued to knead the tension from her muscles, but even he couldn't make her relax, and that was saying something. He had a magic touch where she was concerned. "Do you want to go home?"

"We couldn't get there at this point."

"We could get much closer."

"You went to so much trouble—and expense—to plan this beautiful trip. I'm so sorry I'm such a wreck."

"Don't be sorry. I'm nervous, too. Steph is pregnant. All I can think about is what I'd do if anything ever happened to her or the baby or any of your kids. It's tough to be so far away when they're going through this."

"What'll we do if we don't hear from them after?"

"It's apt to be a day or two if the cell towers are affected."

"I can't deal with this. I just cannot."

"Call Owen and talk to him. He always makes you feel better."

"He's probably busy getting ready."

Charlie checked his watch. "By now, he's probably done."

Thankfully, he was good at calculating the time zones, because she stank at it. "I'll try him."

Her eldest answered on the second ring. "Were your ears ringing? We were just talking about you."

"What about me?"

"That we feel bad that you're worrying about us and this storm while you're supposed to be enjoying Italy."

"I'm a wreck!"

"That's what we figured, but we're all fine, Mom. We've done what we can, and now we're waiting to see what happens."

"That's the part I'm afraid of."

"We'll be okay. I know there's no point in telling you not to worry, but we'll get through it. It's going to take more than a storm to defeat this place."

"Owen," she said on a sob.

"I know, Mom."

"We might come home."

"Don't do that. There's nothing you can do here. You couldn't even get here. The last boat arrived earlier, and by all accounts, it was a hellish ride. Seamus and Joe are taking the two biggest boats out to sea to ride out the storm. Planes have been grounded."

"I haven't felt this helpless in a long time," Sarah said, recalling the nightmare years when she'd felt powerless against an abusive husband who thought nothing of hurting their babies physically and emotionally. That they each carried emotional baggage from those years was something that weighed heavily on her.

"I wish there was something I could say to make you feel better," Owen said. "We've done everything we can think of to prepare. I think we're in good shape."

"I guess we'll find out."

"Try to enjoy the trip, Mom. We'll keep you posted. If, for whatever reason, you can't get through to us afterward, contact the Coast Guard. They'll have word from the island."

The possibility of not being able to reach them by phone didn't bear thinking about. "Will do. I assume you've checked in with the others?"

"I have, and Grant, Jeff and I were at your house earlier, boarding up windows and bringing in your deck furniture and grill."

"Thank you for doing that."

"Of course. We may end up over there if we lose power."

"Please," Sarah said. "Feel free. Charlie said the same thing. That's why he had the generator installed—for times like this. Our home is your home. Tell the others that, too."

"I will, Mom. Now go try to enjoy Italy."

As if that was going to happen until after this storm was over. "Take care, Owen. Love you all."

"We love you, too. Hang in there, and tell Charlie, Grandma and Grandpa the same thing."

After she promised to give the others his message, Sarah ended the call and put down the phone. She'd already sent texts to Julia, Katie, Cindy, Jeff and John, checking on them, and would hear back from them when they had a chance.

"Let's go back to bed, sweetheart," Charlie said. "There's nothing more we can do now."

"We can pray."

"Already done that." He gave her hand a gentle tug and helped her up. As he walked backward to the bedroom, he gazed at her with the sweet love that now filled her days and nights. "No matter what, we have each other, and we'll get through this and everything else."

"Having you makes everything bearable, even this kind of awful worry."

They got into bed and curled up to each other.

"I was so happy to have most of them on the island with me," Sarah said tearfully. "I never imagined anything like this."

"Gansett and its citizens are a hardy stock. They'll take a hard hit, but they'll be fine."

"And if they aren't?"

"Then we'll deal with that when or if it happens, but there's no sense expecting the worst when they've done everything they can to safely prepare."

She clung to his reassurances as she tried to relax her heart and mind so she could sleep, but she wouldn't rest easy until she knew her loved ones were safe.

JULIA LAWRY PACED the length of the dock a hundred times, her dog, Pupwell, following her as she waited and hoped that Deacon would return soon. The chop in the basin was getting stronger all the time, with the splashing water making the dock slippery as she made another loop. If she kept moving, she wouldn't go into complete panic about why he was still out on the churning water long after dark. The wind whipped through the basin, making her worry about being blown off the dock as rain lashed her face.

Pupwell let out a soft whine.

"I know, baby. Mama is worried, too. Where is he, and why isn't he answering his phone?"

Julia debated whether she should call Deacon's brother, Blaine, the chief of police. Technically, Blaine was Deacon's boss, but they tried not to let that get in the way of the sibling relationship they'd worked hard to repair since Deacon had relocated permanently to Gansett Island.

Would he want her to call Blaine? Probably not. But what if he was in trouble and needed help? She had no idea what to do, and when that happened, if Deacon wasn't available, she called Owen.

"Hey, Jules, what's up?" her older brother asked when he took her call.

"I'm worried about Deacon. He's not in yet, and it's dark. The seas are huge, and he's in that little boat. I'm not sure if I should call Blaine or if he'd want me not to."

"Whoa, take a breath. I'm sure he's fine."

"It's really bad out there, Owen. The seas are hitting the breakwater and sending spray twenty feet into the air. He's on that small boat... I'm worried."

"I take it he's not answering his phone."

"No. Not for a few hours now."

"Hmmm."

Julia wanted Owen to tell her that Deacon was fine, that she had nothing to worry about, but that *hmmm* said it all. "I should call Blaine, right?"

"I think so."

Her stomach dropped when he said that. "I'm scared, O. He's been out all day, and he's never this late."

"It's not a usual kind of day, but it can't hurt to let Blaine know he's overdue. Where are you? I'll come and wait with you."

"That's okay. I'm sure you've got your own stuff going on."

"I'm coming, Julia. Are you at the dock?"

"Yeah."

"I'll be right there."

"In case I forget to tell you..."

"I know, hon. Be right there."

He and Julia and her twin, Katie, had always been there for one another, in the best and worst of times growing up with an abusive, narcissistic father who was now in prison for assaulting their mother. Julia tried hard to never think of the man they referred to as "the general," but he was inside them all, whether they wanted him there or not. They most definitely did *not* want him there.

Thinking about *him* was better than wondering where Deacon was and if he was okay.

Only because it was so unlike him to be out of touch with her for this long, she pulled out her phone and called his brother.

"Hey, Julia." Blaine sounded rushed and stressed. Who could blame him with a Category 2 hurricane bearing down on his island? "What's up?"

"Um, so, Deacon isn't in yet."

"What?"

"I'm at the dock. There's no sign of him or the boat, and he's not answering his phone."

"Let me try to raise him on the radio. Hang on."

In the background, she could hear Blaine saying, "Base to harbor master. Come in, harbor master." She heard him say the same thing three more times with no reply.

Julia tried not to panic, but it wasn't easy.

Blaine picked up the phone again. "I'll call Linc at the Coast Guard to ask for his assistance. They can send a boat out to look for him."

"Blaine…"

"Try not to think the worst. He's highly experienced and can handle just about anything."

She wanted to ask if he could handle a ten-foot storm surge in a twenty-foot boat, but the words were stuck behind the massive lump in her throat.

"Come over to the station. We'll monitor things from here. Okay?"

"Yeah, sure. Okay."

"Keep breathing."

"I'm trying to. Be right there."

Before she left the dock, she scanned the blackness outside the breakwater, looking for even the faintest of lights, but saw nothing. As she walked up the ramp, Owen approached her.

"Anything?" he asked.

She shook her head. "Blaine is calling the Coast Guard. He said to come to the station."

Owen put his arm around her, and she leaned into him, taking comfort from him the way she had all her life. "I'm sure he's fine. He knows what he's doing out there."

Julia nodded so he'd know she'd heard him, but again, her throat was too tight for words. The feeling reminded her of the many times in her life that panic had made it difficult for her to talk or eat or do anything other than wallow in fear.

Deacon was the brightest light in her world, the undisputed love of her life. If she lost him…

No, she couldn't think about that. She simply could not.

She forced herself to breathe and to put one foot in front of the other while praying as hard as she had in years for the safety of the man she loved.

CHAPTER 8

*B*laine boiled with tension in his office as he waited to talk to Linc Mercier, the Coast Guard commander who ran the Gansett Island station. He'd been on hold for two minutes and was about to lose his mind when he finally heard a click.

"Hey, Blaine, how's it going on your end?"

"Not great. My brother is overdue and isn't answering his phone or the radio."

"Oh shit. It's mean out there. I just came in from a patrol. We didn't see him, but we weren't looking for him. I'll send a boat out and keep you posted."

"Thanks, Linc."

"You got it. I'll be back to you soon."

"Appreciate it."

As Blaine ended the call, he slumped into his office chair, thinking of his brother and hoping he was just busy and unable to get to the phone or radio. The twinge of anxiety in his gut forced him to acknowledge that it wasn't like Deacon to be out of touch while on the water.

Blaine had to give his younger brother credit for having matured into a responsible, dependable colleague, friend and sibling. Their relationship had recently evolved into true friendship after years of driving each other crazy. Watching him fall madly in love with Julia Lawry had been fun and rewarding. The two of them were great together.

If anything happened to Deacon...

Because he couldn't sit still, Blaine jumped up again and went to the big picture window that overlooked downtown and the harbor. He scanned the horizon, looking for any sign of a boat, but couldn't see anything other than churning seas and whipping wind that had the rain coming down sideways. The massive seas only added to his agitation, so he did what always made him feel better when he was anxious or upset.

He called his wife.

"Hey, babe," she said. "How're things at hurricane central?"

The sound of her husky, sexy voice was all it took to calm the storm raging inside him. "Deacon's late coming in. I just sent the Coast Guard to look for him."

"What? No... He's fine. Of course he is."

"That's what I said to Julia, but it's not like him to be so late, off the radio and not answering his phone. She hasn't talked to him in hours."

"Oh my God, Blaine. Are you worried about him?"

"Trying not to be, but..."

"What can I do for you?"

"I just needed to hear your voice."

"I can come there and bring the girls."

"No, don't disrupt them at bedtime. I'm sure he's fine, and we'll hear something any minute."

"Will you keep me posted?"

"Of course, and I'll stop at home to see you if I can."

"I'll be here."

"That's all I need to know, babe."

"Love you. Love Deacon."

"Love you, too."

"If there's anything I can do..."

"You've already done it. I'll let you know what's going on."

"I'm saying a prayer."

"Thanks, love."

Blaine ended the call reluctantly. He wished he had nothing to do but snuggle with her for the next few days, but his community was counting on him and other leaders to get them through this crisis, and that's what he'd do.

Mason Johns, his counterpart at the fire department, appeared at the door to Blaine's office. "What's this about Deacon?"

"No sign of him. Linc is sending a boat out to look for him."

"Shit."

"Yeah."

"I can send our boat out, too."

"Let's give the Coasties a chance to do a search before we put more people in danger."

"Any of my people would be glad to go look for Deacon. We think the world of him. You know that."

"I do, and I appreciate the offer. I don't want to send more people into harm's way just because he's my brother and I'm worried." Blaine prided himself on professionalism and always keeping his emotions in check on the job. That was easier said than done at times like this. "I can't imagine why he's not responding to the radio."

"He might've had an electrical failure of some sort," Mason said.

"Yeah, possibly." But that wouldn't explain why he wasn't answering the handheld radio he always carried in addition to the radio hardwired into the boat.

"Let me ask you this… If he was anyone else, would you ask me to send out my boat?" Mason asked.

Blaine thought about that. "Yeah, I guess I would."

"Then let me do it."

"All right. Thanks."

"Of course. Can I do anything else for you?"

"No, thank you. Just hoping for the best."

The radio Mason wore on his hip came to life with a call about a tree down on Glen Forest Road.

"I'll send people to help with that," Blaine said.

"I'll deploy our rescue boat and keep you posted. Let me know if you hear anything."

"Will do. Thanks again."

Blaine followed Mason out, asking the dispatcher to send a car to Glen Forest Road to assist with a downed tree.

Owen and Julia came into the lobby with Pupwell trotting alongside her, as always.

"Any word?" she asked, her face pale and her eyes big. She was soaking wet, and her dark hair was plastered to her head, despite the raincoat she wore.

"Nothing yet. Come in. Warm up." Blaine led them into his office, took their coats and hung them on the tree in the corner. "Wyatt, get some fresh coffee for my guests, and hurry up about it."

"Yes, sir, Chief," the young patrolman said. "Coming right up."

Julia's lips were blue, and her body trembled, probably from fear as much as the chill. "I don't know what to do. What should I do, Blaine?"

"We're doing everything we can. Coast Guard and fire department boats are looking for him, and the Coast Guard will issue a distress call that'll go out to mariners in the area." Not that Blaine expected there to be many boats out, but you never knew who might see something. "I'd tell you not to worry, but I know that's pointless."

She placed her hand over her mouth to muffle a sob.

Owen was right there to put an arm around her, to hug her close and offer comfort.

"I'm sorry," Julia said. "I don't mean to be emotional. It's just not like him to be out of touch. I'm so scared something happened to him."

Blaine was, too, but he'd never say that to her. "Deacon is one of the most highly trained people on the water around here, and if anyone can get himself through a tricky situation, it's him."

"I know." Julia wiped tears from her face. "It's just so rough out there and about to get much worse. What'll we do if we can't find him?"

"We're doing everything we can to find him," Blaine assured her, but even that wasn't true. If the storm wasn't a factor, Linc would have choppers and planes assisting in the search, but that wasn't possible in the current conditions. He also didn't want to tell her that time was critical at a moment like this. The longer Deacon was missing, the less likely they were to find him. She didn't need to know any of that.

Hell, he wished *he* didn't know that stuff.

After he sent Julia and Owen home to wait for news, he decided to call Seamus O'Grady, who had taken the ferries to sea with Joe Cantrell. From his vantage point, Blaine couldn't quite see the ferry landing, so he wasn't sure if they'd left yet.

"What's up, Blaine?" Seamus asked.

"Are you still taking the boats out?"

"We're already gone. Why?"

"My brother is missing. Hasn't come back from his afternoon patrol. Coast Guard and fire department are looking for him, but I was hoping you would keep an eye out, too."

"Oh my God," Seamus said. "Of course we will."

"We can't raise him on the phone or radio," Blaine added, "and Julia tried tracking his phone, but it wasn't available. The Coasties have a boat out looking for him, and the fire department has their boat out, but they'll have to come in as the storm gets closer."

What Blaine didn't need to tell them was that at some point, it would become illogical to risk multiple lives to save one.

"We'll be on the lookout," Seamus said. "And we'll keep in touch on the radio."

"Appreciate it." Blaine cast an eye toward the roiling seas that sent spray twenty feet into the air when waves collided with the breakwater. "Be safe out there."

"Will do."

Grant McCarthy helped his brother Evan carry the heavy wrought-iron furniture from the deck at Evan's house into the basement. "This shit weighs a ton," Grant said as they carried a chair down the stairs from the deck to the yard, the wind and rain making everything more complicated.

"Why do you think I needed help?" Evan asked, panting from exertion.

"Why'd you have to get such heavy shit?"

"Came with the house, and Grace likes it."

"I see."

"Is your house ready for the storm?"

"Yeah, we didn't have to do much. We're much more inland compared to you, so I didn't board windows or anything like that."

"I debated whether I should, but I figured it'd be a major hassle to replace them."

"For sure. Did Mac bust your balls when you asked for plywood?"

"What do you think?"

Grant grunted out a laugh as he set the chair down in the basement. "One down. Ten to go."

"I wasn't going to move them, but they're saying the wind could be over a hundred miles an hour."

"What did you think of when you heard the storm was named Ethel?" Grant asked.

"Oh my God! All I could think of was Ethel from the hotel!"

"Right?" Grant imitated Ethel's smoker's voice when he said, "Grant McCarthy, you're never going to amount to anything if you don't stop being a smart aleck."

Evan bent in half with laughter. "That's so spot-on. She's probably off in some retirement village in Florida cracking up about a storm named for her bearing down on Gansett."

"No doubt. I'm glad you guys got home ahead of Ethel's arrival."

"Grace is still sick from the flight. It was the worst one I've ever been on."

Grant cringed. "I hate flying on a good day."

"Yesterday was most definitely not a good day. We were so worried about the house, we decided to go for it."

Thanks to the success of the "My Amazing Grace" song Evan had written for his wife, they'd bought a massive home right on the coast.

"We would've taken care of it for you," Grant said.

"You guys had your own homes to think about, plus the marina, the hotel, the Wayfarer. You didn't need to deal with my house, too."

"We would've."

"I know, and I appreciate it."

They hefted and hauled, swearing and laughing, until all the furniture was stored inside.

"What goes down must come back up after the storm," Evan said.

"Call Adam to help with that."

"Mac says he's insane right now, worrying about being stranded here during a hurricane with Abby expecting quads. He's of no use to anyone, according to our big brother."

Grant followed Evan up the interior stairs from the basement to the wide-open first floor that had incredible views of the angry ocean through the one small window Evan hadn't boarded. "Abby's not due for months. He needs to calm down."

Evan opened two beers and handed one to Grant. "Can't say I blame him with the way babies arrive in our family. One niece on the ferry, two more in a helicopter, another born during a tropical storm."

"There's a history. I'll give you that."

"How's Steph feeling?"

"Great. Pregnancy agrees with her—and me. It's made her super horny."

Evan laughed. "Lucky you. Grace feels like crap almost all the time."

"Aw, that's rough. Sorry to hear it."

"She keeps saying it'll be worth it, but I'd like to move the clock forward so she can be through it."

Grant downed the last of the beer and put the bottle in the recycling bin under the counter. "Our babies will be here before we know it."

"I still can't believe Adam and Abby are having *four*. What a couple of overachievers."

"No kidding. I'd better get home and make sure Steph isn't doing more than she should. She's full of energy. I'm apt to find her swinging a sledgehammer at a wall."

Evan laughed. "Good thing you pulled the trigger on buying the place, huh?"

"Right? 'Cause our damage deposit would be long gone by now."

Evan walked his brother to the door. "Thanks again for the help."

"Any time."

"If we end up without power, come over. We've got a generator."

Grant gave Evan a bro hug. "We'll be here. Be safe."

"You, too."

Evan waved from the door as Grant drove off and then went upstairs to find Grace. As usual these days, she was sound asleep. He stroked her hair and kissed her cheek, but she didn't stir. He couldn't wait for their baby to arrive so she could get back to her usual routine of having fun with him. No matter where they were—on the road or at home—they always had fun together. That's what he missed more than anything since pregnancy had made her so tired, she could barely function.

Evan went back downstairs to look out of the small window to the ocean. He thought of Joe and Seamus taking the ferries out to sea in the storm and shuddered.

You couldn't pay him to be out in this, but he didn't blame them for wanting to protect the boats they relied upon to make a living.

Evan was startled out of his thoughts when Grace wrapped her arms around him from behind.

"What're you thinking about?" she asked.

"Joe and Seamus taking the boats out to sea."

"I'm sick just thinking about it."

"I know. Me, too. My dad said there hasn't been a storm like this in all his forty years on the island."

"I'm trying not to be scared, but..."

"Nothing to worry about, babe. We'll be fine. This house was built to withstand a Category 5 storm, and we're too high up to be worried about storm surge."

"I would've preferred to live here forever and not test that."

"Same, but here we go. How're you feeling?"

"Better after a nap."

"Glad to hear it."

"They say this kid will be worth it..."

"That's what I'm told."

"Was someone here? I thought I heard voices."

"Grant came over to help me move the heavy-as-fuck furniture off the deck."

"Ah, okay. Are they ready for the storm over there?"

"Yep. He said he needed to get home because Steph might get a big idea to take down a wall while he's gone."

"It's not fair that she got all the pregnancy energy and I got none."

"You'll feel better soon. I'm sure the third trimester will be your jam."

"God, I hope so. I wanted to go back to work while we're home, but how can I do that when I can't stay awake for more than a couple of hours?"

"Fiona has everything under control at the pharmacy, so don't worry."

"I know she does, but I miss being there."

As he turned to face her, Evan felt terrible about that. She'd turned her pharmacy over to Fiona to run while they were on the road, promoting his exploding career while hers took a back seat. "I've been thinking about staying home for a year or two. I can write and record some new music while you tend to the pharmacy and we enjoy our new little one. What do you say?"

The immediate brightening of her expression told him everything he needed to know about her true feelings about traveling all over the country, from one concert to the next. "I'd really love to be home for a while, but only if you're sure it won't hurt your momentum."

He held her close, thankful every day to have found her in this crazy world. "My momentum is just fine, and I'm tired of the schlepping, too. Let's stay home for a couple of years and finally make this place our home."

"Yes, Evan," she said on an exhale that sounded a lot like relief. "Let's do that."

CHAPTER 9

*O*ver at Adam and Abby's house, Abby was trying to get comfortable with four babies sitting on her bladder and other important organs. She had months to go and couldn't fathom getting any bigger than she already was.

Be careful what you wish for had become their slogan.

All she'd wanted was to be pregnant. Her wish had come true four times over, which would've been amazing if they'd come one at a time. But no, she'd had to be an overachiever with quadruplets.

Four boys, no less.

She was going to be the mother of five boys under the age of two.

Five.

Four babies.

All at the same time.

Even weeks after getting the news about the quads, she was still reeling, and if she was being honest, she was scared. Not even the raging hurricane could overtake the storm inside her, where panic was ever-present as she contemplated the next few months.

Adam came into the living room, carrying their son, Liam.

"Mama!"

Abby held out her arms to the child who'd made her a mother through adoption. They'd been told their chances of conceiving were infinitely small due to her polycystic ovary syndrome. Her doctors had been as shocked as she was that she'd not only conceived naturally, but she was carrying two sets of identical twins, a result so rare as to be considered a miracle.

She was a marvel, or so they all said.

As Liam snuggled into her embrace, she pushed aside her troubling thoughts so she could focus on her little boy. "Did you take a good nap, buddy?"

"He did," Adam said. "Two whole hours." Adam had been working in his office upstairs while Liam napped, and Abby tried to get some rest downstairs. She'd fallen into the habit of coming downstairs in the morning and staying there until bedtime. Stairs had become a problem already, and it was frightening to think that everything she was feeling now was only going to get much worse before the babies arrived.

"How are things down here?" Adam asked.

"Just fine, as you know because you texted ten minutes ago to check on me."

She loved his sexy grin, his handsome face, his thick dark hair and those dreamy McCarthy blue eyes. Would their babies look like him? She hoped so.

"Can I get you anything?" he asked.

"A hand up so I can use the bathroom would be great."

"We can do that, can't we, Liam?"

The child nodded and got up to pull one of her hands while Adam pulled the other.

As she rose to her feet, the pressure on her bladder was so intense, she nearly wet her pants. She walked as quickly as she could to the half bath and made it just in time. There was no doubt in her mind that she'd be forced to wear diapers before this pregnancy was finished. Something else to look forward to.

She emerged from the bathroom to find Adam waiting to give her an escort back to the sofa. "My hero," she said, smiling at him.

"Sure I am. After I knocked you up with four babies, I'm lucky you even speak to me." Adam was taking much more pleasure in this pregnancy than she was, bragging to his brothers every chance he got that his boys were the most potent of all because he'd made four babies at once.

"Yes, you are, but I've decided to forgive you."

"Thank goodness for that."

"I'm scared of how bad things will get before they arrive."

He sat next to her and took her hand. "Don't be, love. Whatever you need, we'll get it for you."

"I need a bigger body, skin that stretches, a bladder that doesn't need to be emptied every three minutes... To begin with."

"I'll get right on that list." He helped her back to her spot on the sofa, where she spent most of her time. She worried about gaining massive amounts of weight from being inactive, but what choice did she have? She couldn't do much of anything. Her doctor had told her to take it easy, and Victoria was coming to the house every other day to check her blood pressure and other vitals.

They were doing everything they could to ensure a safe delivery, but she was still unnerved by the challenges that lay ahead.

"Mama! Truck!" Liam held up the new truck she'd ordered for him in the last inventory she'd purchased for her Abby's Attic store in town. Two employees were now running the store, while she helped from the sidelines with ordering, payroll and other paperwork.

"That's the best truck ever," Abby said.

"Best truck. Ever!"

"He's becoming a regular chatterbox," Adam said.

"What are you hearing about the storm?" Abby asked, casting a concerned glance toward boarded windows.

"It's still a Cat 2, but the wind and storm surge will be a problem. We'll probably lose power overnight, if not before."

"Thank God Mac told us to get that generator."

"I would've thought of it," Adam said indignantly.

"Whatever you say."

"I would've!"

"You guys are so ridiculous with your posturing."

"It's what brothers do. You'd better get used to it. We're going to have five of them."

"Five more McCarthy boys. Just what this world needs."

Adam leaned over to kiss her. "It's exactly what this world needs."

LILY HARRIS WAS VERY unhappy about the storm. She hadn't stopped crying for more than an hour as the wind got louder and the rain beat down on the roof, making a sound like a hundred boots stomping.

"Shhhh, my angel," Sydney said as she walked her around the living room. "Everything is just fine. Mama is here, Daddy is on the way home, and poor Buddy is sad that you're sad."

The golden retriever who'd once been so protective of Syd's late children, Max and Malena, had transferred all his love to Lily, and seeing her upset had him agitated, too.

Syd had never been so happy to hear the door open along with Luke's nightly whistle for Buddy, who went running to him.

"What's going on, family?" Luke asked.

Lily shuddered from an hour of sobs.

"Our little darling is not enjoying the storm," Syd said.

"I'm filthy, so let me grab the quickest shower ever, and then I'll take over."

"We'll be here."

Hearing Luke's voice had had the magical effect of calming their daughter. It never failed. He walked in and whatever was going on was forgotten so she could give him her full attention.

"Dada."

"He's taking a shower, and then he'll be right here."

"Want Dada."

Smiling, Syd cuddled her closer. "I know, baby girl. I do, too."

Buddy seemed relieved that Lily had stopped crying and had settled in his dog bed, eyes still vigilantly watching his favorite person.

Even when her daughter cried for an hour, Sydney was so thankful for this new life she and Buddy had found with Luke and Lily. The first boy she'd ever loved, and their baby daughter, had helped heal her broken heart after losing her first husband and children to a drunk driver. There'd been a time when Sydney was certain she wouldn't survive the loss of her family, and now, several years later, she'd been blessed with a second chance that she never took for granted.

That was especially true since the accident she and Lily had had at the marina earlier in the summer when Syd's foot had slipped off the brake, and they'd ended up in the water inside the car. She hoped to never again experience the terror of the few minutes that had followed before Luke and others had come to their rescue.

She couldn't even think about that without breaking into a cold sweat, so she tried very, very hard never to think of it.

Easier said than done.

Sydney held Lily a little closer, eternally thankful for her and Luke and the joy they'd brought back into her life.

Luke emerged from the bedroom in the back of the house, wearing only a pair of basketball shorts. "Where's my best girl?"

"Dada!"

Sydney handed Lily over to Luke and then shook out her tired arms. Their little one was getting bigger and not as easy to tote around as she'd once been. She thought of something she'd read once, a long time ago, about how there would be a last time you pick up your child, but you wouldn't know in that specific moment that it was the last time. The message had been to appreciate every time you held that precious baby in your arms, because the time would come when they were too big for such things.

She wanted to slow down the passage of time to keep Lily small for a while longer, but she already knew how time marched forward, and babies grew quickly into little people with minds of their own.

Yesterday, she'd received the most exciting news possible from Victoria, who'd confirmed Sydney's suspicions that she was expecting again. Luke had been working nonstop and had gotten home after she and Lily were in bed the night before, so Sydney hadn't yet gotten to share the news with him. She couldn't wait to tell him as soon as Lily was down for the night.

"Dada to the rescue," Syd said when she sat on the sofa next to them.

Lily had her head on Luke's chest and her thumb in her mouth, her eyes heavy the way they got this time of day, especially when she hadn't had a good nap and hadn't been able to watch Dora, due to the power flickering. The storm had thoroughly disrupted their lives, and Sydney would be thankful to see the last of Ethel.

"How was everything today?" she asked Luke.

"Not too bad. Just a lot of running around and trying to make sure we've thought of everything."

"I'm sure you guys did a great job getting ready. And you're doing the usual great job of settling our baby girl. Nothing Mommy did worked this afternoon. She was so unsettled by the storm."

"It's loud. Probably scared her."

The lights flickered again, and then the room went dark.

"Welp, there it goes," Luke said. "I'll get the generator out for the fridge once she's down for the night."

They worked together to get Lily down, and then Sydney cooked burgers on the grill while Luke got the generator hooked up on the deck. He ran an extension cord into the house and connected it to the fridge.

"How long will that cover us?"

"I've got enough gas for a few days."

"After this, we need to pull the trigger on the whole-home thing Mac told us to get."

"He was reminding me of that earlier today."

Sydney laughed. "I have no doubt."

"He said to come to his house if we need to."

"That's nice of him."

When they sat down to dinner, Luke brought the wine she enjoyed at the end of the day to the table. "None for me, thanks."

He stopped short and stared at her. "Why?"

Laughing, she said, "I skip some nights."

"Only when you're pregnant. Are you? Pregnant?"

"Damn it, I had a whole plan to tell you, and you ruined it by guessing!"

"You're pregnant. For real?"

"Yes, Luke," she said, amused by his stunned expression. "As real as it gets."

He came to where she was seated at the table and extended his hand to her.

When she took hold of it, he gave a gentle tug to bring her up and into his arms. He held her so tightly, it almost hurt, but in the best possible way.

"Just when I think I have it all, there's more," he said gruffly.

"Are you happy?"

"So, so, *so* happy. I never knew happy like this was even possible. Do we need to have Vic confirm it?"

"She did, yesterday, but you've been so busy. I wanted a minute to ourselves to share the news."

"You've been holding out on me."

"Only because you were completely exhausted when you got home last night."

"If it's a girl, we have to name her Ethel."

"We're not naming her Ethel!"

"Why not? I'll never forget when I found out about her—smack in the middle of Ethel."

"Not happening."

"You're no fun."

"Is that so?"

"Well," he said, pulling back to smile at her. "You're fun sometimes."

Sydney kissed him. "Like now?"

"I need another sample to decide for sure."

She kissed him again, tossing a little tongue action into the mix.

"You are, without a doubt, the most fun I've ever had in my entire life, and I love you more than you'll ever know."

"Nice save, Mr. Harris."

"Nice life, Mrs. Harris."

"Thank you for that."

He squeezed her tightly again. "Thank *you* for that."

PIPER SERVED the meal Owen had made for the guests in the hotel's first-floor dining room. She'd set a table for four to include Oliver, Dara, Slim and Erin, the only guests currently in residence. Owen had cooked for them because the in-house restaurant, Stephanie's Bistro, was closed due to the storm.

"Why don't you join us, Piper?" Erin asked.

"Oh, that's all right. I can eat in the kitchen."

"Don't be silly."

They started moving things to make room for Piper at the round table.

"Please join us," Dara said with a warm smile. "No need to eat alone when you can be among friends."

That was what Piper loved about Gansett—how inclusive people were. Everyone was a friend, even if you didn't know them well. "I'd love to. Thank you."

She went into the kitchen to make a plate for herself and brought it and a wineglass back to the table to join them.

"This is so cozy," Erin said of the softly lit room with a fire burning in the hearth and the wind howling outside. "It's good of you guys to have us."

"That's all thanks to Laura and Owen," Piper said. "She told me to put up anyone who needed lodging for the storm, and dinner is compliments of him."

"It's delicious," Slim said. "And it's a huge relief to be here. Our place out here is basically a shack."

"Ours is a lighthouse located at the end of the island expected to get the biggest hit," Oliver said, grinning at Slim.

"You win," Slim said with a laugh. "I wouldn't want to be there either."

"Yeah, it felt a bit… exposed," Oliver said. "We're very happy to be hunkered down at the Sand & Surf."

"Likewise," Erin said. "What brought you guys to the island and the lighthouse?"

Dara glanced at Oliver, who nodded, seeming to encourage her. "Our three-year-old son was killed in an accident almost three years ago."

"Oh God," Erin said. "I'm so sorry."

"I am, too," Piper said.

"It was brutal, and we were floundering for a long time after," Dara said. "When Ollie saw the lighthouse keeper job advertisement, it just seemed like a lifeline. It's been that and so much more than we ever could've imagined."

Oliver reached for her hand. "We recently found out we're expecting again, which is exciting and terrifying."

"Congratulations," Slim said. "We've got a baby on the way, too."

"That's wonderful." Dara raised her wineglass full of ice water. "To new babies."

They touched glasses in honor of their new lives.

"What brought you to Gansett?" Dara asked them.

"I've been flying in and out of here for years," Slim said, "but it's gotten a lot more interesting since I met Erin a few years ago."

She smiled at her husband. "My should've-been sister-in-law, Jenny, was the lighthouse keeper once upon a time."

"We've met Jenny," Oliver said, "and her delightful little George."

"Did she tell you what brought her to Gansett?" Erin asked.

"She did. We were so sorry to hear she'd lost her fiancé on 9/11."

"He was my twin brother," Erin said.

"Oh, Erin," Dara said. "I'm so sorry."

"Thank you. It was rough after we lost Toby. But Jenny loved it so much here and talked me into taking over the lighthouse after she moved in with Alex." She glanced at Slim. "Best thing I ever did, for more reasons than I could possibly list."

"We feel the same way," Oliver said. "Like we've found ourselves again here, as crazy as that might sound."

"I get that," Erin said. "From the first day I arrived, I felt like I could breathe again."

"Same," Oliver said. "In many ways, this place has saved our lives—and our marriage."

"I feel the same way about being here," Piper said, sobered by the things the others had said. A broken engagement seemed trivial next to their losses. "A bad breakup sent me looking for somewhere else to be. I came for a vacation and ended up staying when I found the same things you all did. A warm, welcoming place with the nicest people I've ever met. It felt like home right away."

"Cheers to Gansett Island." Erin raised her glass of water. "And prayers that Ethel goes easy on us."

"I'll drink to that," Oliver said as they touched glasses again.

CHAPTER 10

*A*fter the others had enjoyed the brownies Owen had baked and then gone upstairs to their rooms, Piper loaded the dishwasher and wiped down the kitchen counters. As she worked, she thought about the things her dinner companions had shared. Their stories, coupled with what she'd learned about Jack and his late wife, had her feeling contemplative about life and its many twists and turns.

You just never knew what was coming—good, bad, ugly, painful, devastating, exhilarating. It was all possible. Learning to roll with whatever came her way was something she was working toward. The breakup with Ben had left her reeling, as if a rug had been pulled out from under her. Then she'd been attacked by a man she met on the island. Only recently had she begun to feel settled again, mostly due to the time she'd spent on Gansett, working at the Surf with Laura, Owen, Sarah, Charlie and Adele. Their friendship, and that of other people she'd met on the island, had helped to put her back together after the attack.

Everyone had been through something. Like Laura finding out that her new husband was still on dating sites and meeting other women shortly after their wedding. She'd left him, come to Gansett for her cousin Janey's wedding, met Owen and found her destiny.

Piper had never met a more happily married couple than the two of them. They and many other couples she'd met on the island gave her hope that she could someday find her "one." Not that she needed a man to make her life complete, but she'd enjoyed being part of a couple when she was with Ben and had missed that since he'd ended their relationship and called off their wedding.

The shock of the breakup she hadn't seen coming had resonated for months afterward. Only lately had she reached the point where she didn't think about him every day anymore or pick through the rubble of their relationship trying to figure out where it had gone so wrong. What did that matter now? It didn't. She was looking ahead, not backward, and lately, she found herself thinking much more about Jack than Ben.

As if she'd conjured him, Jack said, "Knock, knock."

Piper turned to find him standing in the kitchen doorway. "Hi there." Her heart gave a happy lift at the sight of his wind-tousled reddish-brown hair and ruddy cheeks covered with late-day whiskers.

He looked tired, windblown and soaked. "I was hoping I'd find you still here. We decided to take a break while we could."

"I'm cleaning up after dinner. Did you eat?"

"Not yet."

"Would you like some spaghetti and meatballs?"

"That sounds great, if you have enough."

"We do."

While he took off his foul-weather gear and hung it to dry by the fire in the salon, Piper got out the containers she'd just put in the fridge and fixed him a plate that she microwaved. "Salad?"

"Sure. Thank you."

"No problem. How are things going out there?"

"The harbor master is missing after a routine patrol, so that's got us all on edge."

Piper gasped. "Deacon? *Julia's* Deacon?" She'd gotten to know Julia quite well as she performed almost every day at Stephanie's Bistro.

"Yeah."

"Oh God. She's a friend. They're madly in love. I hope he's okay."

"From what Blaine says, if anyone can survive a hurricane stranded at sea, it's Deacon. The Coast Guard has a boat out, and the fire department sent one, too, but they'll have to come in when the conditions worsen. This is the calm before the storm."

Piper gestured toward a window where the white froth on the sea was visible even in the dark. "This is considered *calm*?"

"Compared to what's coming."

"Gulp." Piper filled a bowl with salad and set it in front of him on the island, along with several kinds of salad dressing. "Laura is afraid this place won't be able to withstand the storm."

"It's built like a brick shithouse." He put ranch dressing on the salad, information Piper filed away with the other things she now knew about him. "It'll be fine."

"How can you be so certain?"

"These old hotels were built to withstand the test of time. This one is a hundred years old. It's gotten through storms like this before."

"I thought there'd never been a storm this big on Gansett?"

"I'm sure there've been many that came close."

"Probably."

"Try not to worry," he said. "We'll get through it together."

"As in all of us or me and you?"

The grin that stretched across his handsome face was the most sinfully sexy thing she'd ever seen. "That depends on you."

"How so?" Piper took the plate from the microwave and the garlic bread from the toaster oven and put the meal in front of him. She went to the fridge and returned with Parmesan cheese. "What can I get you to drink?"

"Water is fine. I'm on call. Thank you. This looks amazing."

"Owen made it."

"I can't believe he and Laura run this place while chasing three toddlers and cook for everyone, too."

"They're the ultimate power couple."

"Seems like it. They must be glad you're back."

"Owen told me Laura immediately took a three-hour nap, the first time she's slept that much in days since the kids have been sick."

"Glad she got some rest."

"Me, too. She's the best. I love working with her and being here."

"And she must love having someone she can trust when she needs a break."

"It works out well for both of us. Laura is the only reason I was on that boat today. She's done a lot for me since everything happened earlier this summer. She was such a great friend when I needed one."

"I'm glad you had her to lean on. I thought about you a lot after the day we first met and kept coming back to how strong you were to report the assault and give us the info we needed to arrest him."

"I didn't feel strong at all," Piper said. "I was quaking on the inside at how close I came to complete disaster."

"I'm sorry that happened to you."

"I am, too, but at least he's in jail where he belongs, and I didn't have to testify against him."

"I was very glad for your sake when he took the plea and didn't drag things out."

"Enough about that. Can I get you more of anything?"

"No, this is great. Thanks again." He looked up from his plate, seeming a bit uncertain. "I was hoping I'd still be welcome to visit after what I told you earlier."

Piper furrowed her brows. "Why wouldn't you be?"

"It's just… a lot… to drop on someone. Tell me the truth… Did you look us up?"

"Maybe?" she said, feeling her face heat with embarrassment.

"It's okay. That's what I would've done."

"Your Ruby was beautiful and so courageous. Her posts touched me deeply."

"She was incredible."

"You must miss her so much."

"I do. I had a rough couple of years after I lost her. Kind of went through the motions to stay employed. Otherwise, I was a mess, even though I'd had ample warning it was coming. Nothing can really prepare you…"

Piper leaned across the counter and placed her hand on top of his. "I'm so, so sorry."

"Thanks. I'm doing better now. They assigned me to Gansett to take some of the pressure off after everything happened. It's been good for me to be here, to have a fresh start away from where everyone knows my sad story."

"I'm so glad you're doing better, and I know all about going somewhere that no one knows your story."

"What are you running from?"

"Nothing quite like your story. Just a broken engagement and a canceled wedding."

"Ouch."

"Yeah, those were some good times. Let me tell you."

"Sounds like it."

"Again, not the end of the world in the grand scheme of things."

"But it was the end of the world you expected to live in for the rest of your life, so still a loss."

"Yes, but not like yours."

"Loss is loss, Piper. Don't downplay yours because you think mine was so much worse."

"But it was. Ruby died. That's so much worse than a bad breakup and a wedding that didn't happen."

"All right. I'll give you that, but your thing was bad, too."

Piper shrugged. "It happened. I've moved on, and I've decided I'm better off without him."

"How come?"

"After it all blew up and the wedding was canceled, I felt oddly relieved. Bizarre, right?"

"Did you ever figure out why?"

"I think it was because I'd come to realize that maybe we weren't as well matched as I'd thought, but the train had left the station with the wedding, money had been spent, invitations printed, but thankfully not sent… I didn't see a way out of it. Despite that, I was still blindsided when he said he didn't think we should go through with it. It was unexpected, to say the least."

She refilled Jack's ice water. "I guess he was having the same second thoughts I was, so it's for the best that we didn't get married. Although you can't tell my mother that. She loved him and was far more devastated than I was that the wedding was canceled."

"Thank you." He raised the glass in a toast to her before he took a sip. "My parents loved Ruby more than me. That was our joke."

"It helps when they approve."

"They told me from the beginning that she was special and not to fuck it up."

Piper sputtered with laughter. "They said it like that?"

"Just like that."

"Were you known for fucking things up before that?"

"My dating track record was a bit spotty. My parents eventually told me not to bring anyone home unless I was planning to keep them. Dad said I had to quit getting my mother's hopes up."

"I think I'd like your parents."

"They'd like you, too."

The compliment went straight to Piper's overcommitted heart. After everything she'd learned about him that day, she liked him even more than she had before. She no sooner had that thought than she had the wild urge to pull back and run away from him.

"What's the matter?" he asked, picking right up on her change of mood.

"Other than a hurricane aiming for us? Not a thing."

"Don't do that. Something just upset you. Tell me what it was so I won't do it again."

"Oh, your Ruby taught you well, didn't she?"

He grinned, which once again transformed his face from ruggedly handsome to sinfully sexy in a flash. "I used to like to tell her I could be trained. Tell me what just happened."

"When you said your parents would like me, it just hit me in a weird place."

"Tell me more about this weird place."

"After the bad breakup and the incident here earlier this summer, I sort of decided I was going to stay away from guys for a while. I need to figure out who I am without a partner, but then I met you, and staying single didn't seem quite as appealing."

"Ah, I see." His dark eyes twinkled with mirth. "This is a concerning development."

"Don't make fun of me."

"I would never do that."

"Yes, you would."

He shook his head, but his expression was full of the devil—and he was one handsome devil. "I really missed seeing you when I was stuck on the mainland."

"So you said."

"I mean it, and that's kind of a big deal for me."

"Is it?"

"Uh-huh. Like I said, I haven't dated at all since Ruby died. I haven't wanted to. Until now, that is."

"I, um... Well... Oh."

She loved the way laughter looked on him. "Articulate, Piper. Very articulate."

"It's your fault. You come in here looking all..."

"What? How do I look?"

"Good. Really, really good, even windblown and soaked to the skin. And you scramble my brain with compliments and blunt honesty, and I'm not sure what to do with that."

"You can agree to spend some time with me. I know my situation is a lot to take on—"

"It's not. I mean, it is, but what I'm trying to say is…" She sighed. "See what I mean about you scrambling my brain?"

Again with that sexy grin that made her heart skip a beat and had all her girl parts standing up to check him out. They liked what they saw. And now she was making her body parts into people. This was bad and getting worse all the time, but for some reason, that didn't concern her the way it probably should have.

"Does that mean you'll hang out with me?"

"Yes, I think I will."

"Excellent."

GETTING five kids to go to sleep when the wind was howling and the rain was beating against the windows would've been a hard enough job. But add to it that their dad and favorite person was late getting home, and Maddie McCarthy was feeling as miserable as her kids. Thomas refused to go to sleep until Daddy got home, Hailey and Baby Mac wouldn't stop crying, and the twins were upset because their older siblings were. Desperation had her calling Mac to find out where he was and when he'd be home.

"Just finishing up at the alpaca farm." He sounded stressed and exhausted. "I'll be there soon."

"The storm has everyone on edge."

"Mommy! The house is rocking! It's gonna fall down!"

Thomas's proclamation had Hailey and Mac crying even harder than they'd been before.

"I won't ask how it's going there."

"Thomas is afraid the house will fall down."

"Tell him I said it won't."

"And you're sure of this?"

"Sure-ish."

"Mac…"

"I'm coming, babe. Getting in the truck now."

"Please drive carefully. It's so awful out. Now the lights are flickering."

"If we lose power, the generator will come on."

"Thank you for thinking of everything we need before we need it."

"Don't worry about anything. I'm coming."

"See you soon."

Maddie put down the phone and picked up baby Emma, hoping to console her. Evie was in the swing and seemed content for the moment. Contentment was a minute-to-minute thing with twins. Hell, it was a minute-to-minute thing with all five of them, especially on a day like this, when the older ones had been cooped up inside while the storm intensified.

"Mommy! The house is shaking again!"

She looked up at the top of the stairs, where Thomas was standing at the gate they used to keep little people from tumbling down the stairs if they got up during the night. "Daddy said the house is fine, and he'll be home in a few minutes."

"I want Daddy," Hailey said on a sob when she joined Thomas at the top of the stairs.

"Everyone needs to get in bed if they want to see Daddy. He's only coming to see kids in bed."

The two of them went rushing back to their rooms.

That Daddy was their favorite was a constant source of amusement to him. Maddie spent all day every day with them, and he came riding in like the conquering hero at the end of a long day and made everyone happy. She didn't hold it against him, though, because he made her happy, too.

She'd been anxious all day about the storm, about the possibility of something happening to Mac that would keep him from getting home to them, about the damage the island might sustain and how that would affect their family and friends. So much to worry about as the storm got more intense with every passing hour. When she'd declined an invite to stay, Maddie had sent their nanny, Kelsea, home so she'd be safe before the storm arrived in full force.

With Emma still in her arms, Maddie went to the window that faced the driveway to watch for Mac. He'd boarded up the windows on the lower level the night before, but had left the second-floor windows uncovered so they could watch the storm.

Before she met him, she would've laughed at the notion that she'd one day be standing in a window, baby in her arms, waiting for her man to come home. She'd been there and done that as a child after her father left her, her mother and sister, jumped on a ferry and disappeared from their lives. For years, Maddie had sat in the window of their South Harbor apartment, watching the people disembark from the ferries, looking for someone who wasn't coming back.

Mac would always come back. He was as different from the man who'd fathered her as a man could be, and he'd restored her faith in the concepts of love and family and loyalty and devotion. He would, quite literally, claw his way through fire to get to her and their children. Of that, she had no doubt whatsoever.

She wanted so badly to see him coming toward them that she thought she might be hallucinating when she saw headlights at the end of the lane that led to their house. But as the lights got closer, she exhaled for the first time in hours when she realized it was him.

He was home, and just that simply, she felt a thousand times better.

That's what he'd done for her since the day they'd met. He made everything better. Before him, she'd thought the last thing she needed was a man complicating her life. But when it was the *right* man, that wasn't how it worked. And Mac McCarthy was definitely the right man for her. Even after years together, her heart still skipped a crazy beat when he came through the sliding door, soaked, windblown and obviously exhausted.

She went to him, as fiercely drawn to him today as she'd been that first day, when she'd tried so hard to push him away after they'd collided, him accidentally knocking her off her bike. How silly it seemed with hindsight that she'd ever tried to push him away.

"I'm soaked," he said as she approached him.

"I don't care."

He dropped his raincoat onto the floor and wrapped his arms around her and Emma, smelling of fresh air and hard work.

"Very happy to see you," she said.

"Likewise, babe. It was a long-ass day."

"Here, too."

He kissed Emma's soft head and then Maddie's lips. "I'm sure it was."

"Did you get it all done?"

"Everything we could. The rest is out of our hands."

"Is everyone safe?" Maddie asked.

His deep sigh set her on edge. "Deacon Taylor hasn't returned from a routine patrol, and Seamus and Joe have taken the ferries to sea to protect them from the storm."

"What?" she asked on a whisper. "They did *what?*"

"I'm surprised Janey didn't call you. She's called everyone else trying to get someone to talk them out of it, but they weren't hearing it."

"And Deacon... My God, his boat is so small."

"It is, but like Blaine said, he knows how to handle himself out there, and if anyone can survive this, he can."

"Poor Julia. She must be out of her mind."

"She is, but she's with Katie and Shane."

"And Joe and Seamus… They'll be all right, won't they?"

"God, I hope so."

CHAPTER 11

*K*atie brought Julia a cup of the hot tea she liked, with a shot of bourbon and a squeeze of lemon added in deference to the circumstances.

She took the mug from her twin. "Thank you."

Katie sat next to her on the sofa, where Pupwell was curled up in Julia's lap. He'd refused to even go outside to pee unless she went with him, seeming to know she needed him more than usual.

As she ran her fingers through the dog's silky hair, she took comfort from him and the knowledge that Deacon would do whatever it took to get home to them.

"I wish there was more I could do," Katie said.

"It helps to be here with you and Shane."

"Mom called again. She was worried when she couldn't reach you, but I told her you were napping."

"You didn't say anything about Deacon, did you?"

"No, I didn't see the point in getting them more upset than they already are."

"That's good."

Julia's phone rang, and she grabbed it to check the caller ID. "It's Deacon's mother." She pressed the green button to take the call. "Hi."

"Oh, Julia. Blaine just called us. I'm out of my mind with worry. I can only imagine how you must feel."

Hearing that Blaine had informed their parents that Deacon was missing only made her more nervous than she already was. "I'm trying to stay calm, but it's not easy."

"Blaine reminded us that Deacon is very well qualified and knows how to handle just about anything out there."

"I'm clinging to that."

"I won't keep you. If you hear anything…"

"I'll call you right away. And you'll call me?"

"Of course, honey. I just want you to know… Seeing my Deacon in love with you has just been so wonderful."

"Thank you," Julia said softly. "He's the best thing to ever happen to me. I can't bear to think about what I'd do without him."

"Don't do that. He'll be home soon. I know it."

They agreed to keep in touch and ended the call.

Julia checked the phone and found there were no messages. "I wish we'd hear *something*."

"I'm sure the Coast Guard will find him soon."

"They're probably close to calling off the search as the storm gets closer. They won't want to endanger a bunch of people looking for one." But that one… He was one in a million, the man who'd stolen her heart and changed her mind about true love and happily ever after. He was the other half of her soul.

"I know you're thinking the worst and probably trying to prepare yourself for it, but I'm betting on Deacon. He loves you so much, Jules. He'd swim back to shore to get to you if that's what it takes."

Thinking of him swimming in the turbulent ocean broke her.

With Katie's arms around her, she sobbed her heart out.

Pupwell whined and nudged her leg.

Julia pulled back from Katie to tend to her sweet boy. "I'm okay, buddy."

He licked the tears from her face.

"He's trying to remind you that he was found swimming, and Daddy will be found, too," Katie said.

For the first time in hours, Julia laughed. "Thanks for that, sweet boy. Mama needed to hear that."

Shane came into the living room, carrying a tray that he put on the coffee table. "I thought it seemed like a soup-and-grilled-cheese kind of night."

Julia's mouth watered when the scent of the soup wafted toward her.

"Thank you, Shane. It smells delicious." She hoped she could eat it. At times like this, her throat closed, making it nearly impossible to eat. Eating disorders had been the legacy she'd brought from her violent childhood. It'd been a long time since she'd had trouble eating, long enough that she'd nearly forgotten what it was like to be so upset that she couldn't eat.

She leaned in to take a sip of the soup, hoping she'd be able to swallow it. The savory flavors exploded on her tongue as her stomach growled with interest. "This is delicious, Shane. Thank you again."

He sat on the floor on the other side of the coffee table and reached for the third bowl of soup on the tray. "You're welcome. I wish there was more I could do."

"It helps to be here with you guys, and thank you for going to get Pupwell's food and toys. We'd be going crazy by ourselves." After she heard that Deacon was missing, Katie had invited Julia to come to their house. They'd sent Owen home to be with his own family, with promises to keep him posted on the search for Deacon.

"You'll never be alone in our family," Katie said. "Everyone is texting to ask how you are and if there's any news."

It was so surreal. She expected to get a call from him any second telling her it'd been a big misunderstanding, that he'd been working and hadn't heard the phone or radio calls. But deep in her heart, she knew he'd never be out of touch with her this long unless something terrible had happened.

Julia shuddered when she tried to imagine what that terrible thing might be. When she pictured him alone on that small boat, bobbing in huge waves with no way to contact anyone… She put down her spoon and wiped her mouth with a napkin.

"We can heat it up later." No one knew more about the challenges Julia faced when it came to eating during stressful times than Katie did. When they were children, Katie used to sneak food into their shared bedroom and beg Julia to eat something. But that damned lump in her throat often made it impossible, no matter how hungry she might've been.

She was always hungry, or so it had seemed, until one day she just… wasn't. That'd been the start of a years-long struggle with maintaining a healthy weight. She'd come so far from there that she'd nearly forgotten how it had felt to be unwell.

"Do you want to lie down?" Katie asked.

"Maybe we could watch TV or something. I'm afraid I'll just spin if I go to bed."

"Sure, we can do that." Katie reached for the remote and turned on the TV, which was set to one of the Providence stations providing coverage of the storm. Katie quickly changed the channel. Three channels later and there was only storm coverage. "Let's try Netflix."

Katie found a movie that looked good, but Julia just stared at the screen, unable to focus on anything other than wondering where Deacon was and if he was still alive.

The possibility that he wasn't was just too big to process.

JOE HAD to admit that the ride was much rougher than he'd expected. It was wilder than anything he'd ever experienced in more than twenty years as a ferryboat captain and during a lifetime of rides to and from the island with his grandfather while growing up on the island. It took all his skill to navigate seas that topped fifteen feet by his estimation. The roller-coaster ride was making him queasy, which rarely happened.

He glanced over his shoulder to make sure Seamus's boat was still right behind them, and then he picked up the radio to call his colleague or stepfather or whatever the hell the Irishman was to him. "How you doing?" he asked.

"Hanging in. You?"

They had to be careful what they said, knowing Carolina was monitoring the radio and would read between the lines to get the true story. "Same. Should be through the worst of it any time now."

"That's what the radar says."

When they got far enough east of the storm, the plan was to basically float at sea until it was safe to return to port, all the while trying not to make himself sick with worry about his children, mother and extended family on the island with a monster storm heading toward them. Protecting the two primary assets of the company that supported them all was the right thing to do. But leaving them on the island had been excruciating.

As soon as they reached calmer waters, he'd call home to see how they were doing. He took a sip of the coffee one of the mates had gone downstairs to make and scanned the seas in front of them, lit by the massive spotlight on the bow. He thought his eyes were playing tricks on him when he saw an upside-down boat with a man on top of it waving to him.

"Seamus, I've got an overturned boat in front of me with a guy on top."

Attempting a rescue in seas this large would be ludicrous, but they had to try. It was too dark to be able to tell if it was Deacon Taylor. Because the boat was upside down, there were no distinguishing marks to tell him who it might be.

"What's the plan?" Seamus asked.

"We have to at least try to get him."

The ferries were huge compared to the small boat the man was clinging to. Getting close to him would be next to impossible.

"Toss him a ring," Seamus said.

Joe looked to his mates, Colin and Keith. "I'm not going to require you to do this."

"We'll do it," Colin said. "Of course we will."

Keith nodded in agreement.

"Put on your survival suits first."

As they were two of the company's more experienced deckhands, he had faith in their abilities.

Joe slowed the vessel to a crawl while the three of them donned the suits that would keep them alive if they went overboard. But that wasn't going to happen. Or so he hoped. He put on the tether harness and clipped a line to the hook on the front. "I'll head to the aft controls so I can see you." Before he left the wheelhouse, he said, "Listen, use your judgment. If it can't be done, it can't be done."

"We'll get him," Keith said. "We can't leave him out here to die."

Joe felt the same way, but as the big ferry bobbed in the huge seas, he had no idea if they could do this. "Bring a handheld radio and help me get close enough."

Seamus positioned his boat behind them, casting additional light on the stranded boater.

Joe put up the hood of his foul-weather jacket and followed the others out of the wheelhouse. The other two men went downstairs to the lowest deck while Joe made his way to the back of the boat, clinging to the rail as the wind and rain beat down on him. The conditions were so intense, he could barely see five feet in front of him, let alone maneuver the ferry close enough to rescue the man. Seamus's light was helpful, but Joe kept losing sight of their target.

After he secured his tether to the metal rail, he opened the aft controls and edged the ferry toward the boat, hoping he was heading in the right direction. He pulled the handheld radio out of his pocket. "Help me out, Seamus. I can't see shit."

"You're about twenty feet from him." Seamus calmly conveyed directions that helped Joe bring the ferry within a few yards of the disabled vessel. Over the loudspeaker on his boat, Seamus said, "Let it rip, boys. You might not get any closer."

"Keep talking to me, Seamus. I can't see them."

"They missed on the first throw. They're bringing it back."

Damn it, Joe thought. Holding the position was next to impossible as they rocked from side to side.

Seamus directed him back into position. "They're trying again."

"Come on, come on, come on," Joe said under his breath as he fought to stay standing on the deck.

"They got him," Seamus said. "They're hauling him in."

Joe decided he was probably needed more downstairs than he was at the controls, so he closed the cover, unclipped the tether and headed for the stairwell, nearly falling twice as he held on tightly to the metal railing. The stairway was somewhat protected from the elements, so he quickly descended the two flights that got him to the lower deck, where Keith and Colin were in an epic struggle to pull the man toward the ferry as the seas swelled to heights Joe had never experienced before.

After he clipped his tether to a chain on the deck, Joe grabbed the line and added his weight and strength to the effort while Seamus kept the light on the man with the life ring around his body. The wild movement of the ferry bouncing in the seas made it difficult to stay upright as they pulled with all their might.

"He's getting closer," Colin yelled.

Joe could barely hear him over the roar of the wind. He doubled down, pulled as hard as he could, every muscle in his body telling him he needed to get back to the gym. Fatherhood had messed with his fitness routine, and he was feeling his age.

Time lost all meaning as they pulled the man closer to the ferry.

Colin edged his way forward, rope in hand, keeping his tether clipped to a metal loop. He dropped so he was lying facedown on the deck.

Keith followed, holding Colin's feet.

Joe wrapped a line around Keith and secured it to a cleat. Later, he would try to recall the details, but he wouldn't be able to say exactly how they'd managed to drag the man on board. But they did. Somehow.

The four men pulled one another to safety in the wide-open bay that normally housed cars and trucks. They crashed onto the deck, gasping from exertion and sweating despite the chill of the rain.

Joe wasn't too concerned about immediately returning to the helm, because there was nothing out there to hit, and Seamus had an eye on them.

The man they'd rescued turned onto his back and removed the hood of his survival suit.

Deacon Taylor.

"Are we ever glad to see you, mate," Joe said.

"Not half as glad as I am to see you," Deacon said, gasping for air. "'Thank you' seems rather inadequate, but it's all I've got."

"What the hell happened?"

"I got swamped by a massive wave that swept away my phone, my handheld radio and shorted out everything else." He wiped water off his face. "The boat filled with water that I tried to bail after the bilge pump failed, but I overturned about three hours ago and was running out of strength to hang on when I saw you guys coming. Thought I was hallucinating because what kind of crazy bastards would be out in this shit?"

Joe laughed. "Blame it on the Irishman. It was his big idea."

Speaking of the Irishman... The radio crackled to life. "Everyone all right over there?"

"Yep," Joe replied. "We've got Deacon, if you want to get word back to shore."

"A lot of people are going to be very happy to hear that news."

"Anyone got a phone I can borrow?" Deacon asked.

Joe pulled the Velcro on his pocket, removed his phone, checked to see that they still had service even several miles offshore, entered the code and handed it to Deacon.

He punched in a number and closed his eyes as he waited for the call to go through. "Hey, baby. It's me."

From several feet away, Joe could hear Julia's piercing scream and smiled, thinking of the relief Deacon's loved ones would feel once word got out that he'd been found.

"Good work, guys," he said to Colin and Keith. "Very good work."

CHAPTER 12

$\mathcal{B}$laine was at home for a brief dinner break when his phone rang with a call from dispatch. He was almost afraid to take it. He'd been on edge all day, worrying about Deacon and the storm and, well, everything.

Tiffany stepped up behind him and massaged his shoulders. "Aren't you going to get that?"

"Yeah." He grabbed the phone because he never ignored a call from work. Ever. That'd caused him some consternation with his wife, who didn't appreciate intimate moments being interrupted by a phone call he had to take. "Taylor."

"Chief, they found your brother." Clara, the dispatcher, spoke so fast that Blaine had to struggle to keep up. "They hauled him onto one of the ferries. He's safe."

"That's great news." Filled with relief, he looked up at Tiffany. "They've got Deacon."

"Oh, thank God," she said.

"Everyone here is so happy to hear the news," Clara said. "We've been sick with worry."

Blaine wasn't surprised they were celebrating at the public safety building. His brother had become very popular with their colleagues. "Any word on what happened?"

"Not yet, but I'm sure you'll hear from him."

"Thanks for the call. I'll be back soon."

"See you then."

Blaine ended the call and exhaled a deep breath.

"Thank God," Tiffany said again.

"You said it, baby." The words sounded gruff, even to him, due to the emotion clogging his throat. He and his brother had formed a deep bond in the months they'd been working together, a deeper bond than they'd ever had before, and the thought of losing him had been impossible to bear. "I need to call my mom."

While he did that, Tiffany continued to knead his shoulders, which felt so fucking good. She knew just what he needed without him ever having to tell her. "Mom, Deacon is safe."

She let out a sharp cry of happiness and then called to his dad with the news.

"They were taking the ferries out to sea for the storm, and they spotted him. I don't know anything more than that yet."

"This is the best news ever. Did someone tell Julia?"

"I assume Deacon called her, but I'll call her to make sure."

"I'll call your sisters," she said, sounding tearful. "Thank you for this news, Blaine."

"Best call I ever made. Talk soon."

"Love you."

"Love you, too."

Blaine dialed Julia's number.

"Oh, Blaine," she said, sounding tearful. "He just called. He's on one of the ferries."

"I'm so glad you heard from him."

"He said he'll call you when he can."

"I'll look forward to that."

"Thanks for all the support."

"Of course. We both love him. See you soon."

Blaine put down the phone and dropped his head into his hands, trying to let go of the stress and anxiety of a hellish few hours so he could enjoy the brief respite with Tiffany. "Are the girls asleep?" he asked.

"For a while now."

"I'm sorry I missed them."

"They know you're busy dealing with the storm."

"I'd rather be here with you guys."

"We'll be waiting for you when you're done."

"I'm going to do one more patrol of the island and then pack it in. I've got to get some sleep at some point." He and Mason had worked out a schedule to provide coverage during the storm, although they'd told island residents who'd chosen to stay that they might not be able to get to them during the storm if they needed help.

"I'll wait up for you."

"You don't have to do that."

"I want to." She kissed his neck, which was all it took to fire him up. "I've been missing you these last few days."

Blaine groaned. "Why you gotta do that to me when I just said I have to go back to work?"

Her giggle only added to the pressure in his lap. He loved her laugh. Hell, he loved every single fucking thing about her. He reached for her hand and brought her around to sit on his lap. With his arms around her, he buried his face in her hair and breathed in the strawberry scent that drove him wild. "I keep thinking that one of these days, I'm going to get over this crazy fever I have for you."

"Please don't *ever* get over it."

His low chuckle rumbled through his chest. "No chance of that happening."

"I worry about that sometimes."

He pulled back so he could see her gorgeous face and tucked her dark, silky hair behind her ear. "What do you worry about?"

She shook her head. "Never mind. It's nothing."

"Tell me."

"I worry sometimes that you might fall out of love with me."

He could only imagine that his entire expression went flat with shock. "You worry about me falling out of love with you."

"I mean… Not really. It's just that it happened to me before, so—"

Because he couldn't bear to hear another word about her son of bitch first husband, he kissed her. He kissed her until she was wrapped around him, limp in his arms. "I will never, ever, ever, for the rest of my life, fall out of love with you. Not for one second."

"I'm sorry," she replied. "I shouldn't have said that. It's pregnancy hormones making me crazy. I know I have nothing to worry about where you're concerned."

"You don't. I couldn't live a minute without knowing you love me as much as I love you. I couldn't bear to come home and not have you here making everything better just by breathing the same air as me. I can't sleep unless you're next to me. I don't care what I'm doing, I'm always thinking of you and wishing I was with you and counting the minutes until I can come home to you." He kissed her again and then once more for good measure. "Don't *ever* be worried about me falling out of love with you."

"Okay." She laughed as she wiped away tears. "I'm sorry I even said that. I know better."

"Yes, you do, but don't be sorry. I get where it's coming from." He nuzzled her cheek. "That was *so* then, and this… this is now and forever."

She hugged him tightly. "I love you so, so much."

"That's all I need, baby. You and our girls and this little one you're cooking up… You guys are everything to me."

They held each other until another call interrupted the moment.

"Sometimes I fucking hate my job."

"I hate it a lot of the time."

Smiling, he reached around her for the phone on the table. Goddamned dispatch. Again. "Taylor."

"We've got a big tree down on the west side," Clara said. "I'm sending some officers, but you wanted me to keep you in the loop."

"I'll head out there. Thanks."

"No problem."

Blaine put down the phone. "Duty calls, but I'll be home in an hour or two to continue this conversation."

"I'll look forward to that."

He kissed her as tenderly as he possibly could because she deserved all the love and tenderness he could give her. "So will I."

At the Beachcomber, Jace Carson had a big crowd, mostly made up of the employees from the massage and tattoo studios, which had closed early due to the storm. The employees from both establishments had decamped to his bar. He'd expected a slow night, but thanks to them, he'd been hopping for hours. When his girlfriend, Cindy Lawry, came in and took the seat he held for her every night he worked at the bar, he used his chin to say hello as he typed food orders into the computer. The management had decided to stay open while they could since no one knew what to expect after the storm.

He'd heard from Seamus that the boys and Carolina were with Big Mac and Linda while Seamus took the ferries to sea with Joe. The thought of that made Jace sick to his stomach, but he assumed Seamus and Joe knew what the hell they were doing. At least he hoped so. Jace had become rather fond of the crazy Irishman who was raising his sons and appreciated that Seamus and Carolina had made him part of their family. After learning his ex-wife, Lisa, had died of cancer while he was in prison, Jace had come to the island to figure out what'd become of their sons.

Things on Gansett had worked out way better than Jace ever could've hoped for, and the woman at the center of his new life had quickly become an essential part of his days and nights. He brought her an ice water with a lemon and placed it on a Beachcomber cocktail napkin in front of her. Because of the migraines that plagued her, she avoided alcohol. "Evening, pretty lady. You come here often?"

"Every chance I get. The bartender is hot."

Jace narrowed his gaze. "You'd better be talking about me and not Casey over there."

"Haha, you know exactly who I'm talking about."

Smiling the way he did any time she was nearby, he said, "Are you hungry?"

"I could eat a little something. Surprise me."

"I love to surprise you. Stand by." He went to the computer and typed in an order for the clam chowder she loved and the baked cod dinner that others had been raving about all night, putting her meal on his tab.

When he returned to her, she was laughing at something Duke, the owner of the tattoo studio, had said. He'd been trying to talk her into some ink for a while now.

"I see gorgeous flowers on that pretty arm," Duke said, subtly flirting with her the way he always did.

"I've told you a hundred times," Cindy said, "I'm scared of needles."

"You won't feel a thing."

"*Right.*"

"I mean it. I'm so smooth that you won't even know what's happening."

"If it sounds too good to be true," Jace said, "it probably is."

"Don't listen to him," Duke said. "What does he know?"

"Um, he has a ton of ink, so he knows what it feels like," Cindy said.

"And it hurts like a mother effer," Jace said.

"There you have it," Cindy said. "Tattoos are not for me."

"You break my heart with this constant rejection," Duke said mournfully.

"She loves our stuff," Sierra, owner of the massage studio, said to taunt Duke. She had spikey dark hair and brown eyes and a killer body that had the guys in the bar flocking around her whenever she came in. "She lets me put my hands *all over* her."

"As often as I can," Cindy added.

"Can I watch sometime?" Duke asked, teasing.

"Absolutely not," Jace said, leaving no room for further debate.

Duke affected a crushed expression. "He's absolutely no fun."

"She knows otherwise," Jace said with a smile and a wink for Cindy, who turned bright red. God, he loved that blush.

"I should've been a massage therapist." Duke held up his hands. "I have the hands for it."

"If you say so," Sierra said, rolling her eyes.

"Let me ask you something," Duke said. "What do you do when a client farts during a massage?"

Everyone around him lost it laughing.

Jace shook his head. Leave it to Duke. He had tattoos on every square inch of skin, right up to his jawline, where he seemed to have come to his senses just in time. The art was colorful and interesting. Jace had to give him that much.

"You act like it didn't happen," Sierra said, responding to Duke's question.

"So it happens a lot?" Duke asked.

"From time to time. It's no biggie. Everyone farts." Sierra leaned across Cindy, lowering her voice. "You want to hear the craziest thing that's ever happened?"

"Uh, yeah?" Duke said, brows raised.

"I once had a guy who was so relaxed, he crapped himself right on the table."

"Stop it!" Cindy sputtered with laughter. "No way."

"True story."

"What'd you do?" Duke asked, wide-eyed.

"I had to nudge him to let him know something had happened. He was mortified and apologized profusely. I gave him towels to clean himself up and then rolled up the bedclothes and threw them in the dumpster. Shockingly, he never came back."

"I would literally *die* of embarrassment," Cindy said as she rocked with laughter.

"It was pretty funny," Sierra said. "We laughed about it for weeks."

"I'm sticking with tats," Duke said. "Ain't never had anyone crap themselves in my chair."

"Yet," Sierra said.

"Don't jinx me, woman!"

Jace loved this bar and the people who came in to keep his evenings entertaining. Not even a looming hurricane could dampen the fun at the Beachcomber. He delivered chowder to Cindy as Sierra moved over to talk to Duke and the guys with him. "That was hilarious," he said.

"I'm dying just thinking about it. I may have to give up my massage habit."

"Don't do that. You enjoy it too much."

"Still... I can't believe that can even happen."

"Sierra said it's happened once in what I assume has been a long career."

"She's been doing massage for twelve years."

"There you have it. Once in twelve years. I think you're safe to continue getting massages." He placed a rolled napkin containing silverware for the rest of her meal in front of her. "Any word on Deacon?"

"Not yet."

"How's Julia?"

"Not good. She's with Katie and Shane. I asked Katie if I should go over there, but she said they're trying to encourage Julia to get some rest."

"That's probably not going to happen."

"That's what I thought, too. I feel so bad for her. She's so, so happy with him. If anything happens..."

"He'll be fine. I'm sure of it."

Cindy's phone chimed with a text. "It's from Katie. They found him. Oh my God. Joe and Seamus spotted him floating at sea on his upside-down boat."

"Wow. He got lucky."

"Thank goodness. Julia must be sick with relief." Cindy typed a response to her sister. "Katie says Julia can't stop crying since Deacon called her."

"I'm so glad he's okay."

"Me, too." Cindy released a deep breath. "All I could think about was what would happen to Julia if he didn't come home."

Jace put his hand over hers. "It's okay to exhale. Everything is okay."

"When these things happen... It's sort of triggering for us."

"I understand, but Deacon is okay, and Julia will be, too."

She nodded and took a sip from the fresh glass of water he handed to her. "Thank you."

"No problem. I hate to see you worried or upset about anything."

"It helps to have someone to lean on at times like this."

"I'm happy to have you lean on me any time you need to."

"That's apt to be a lot."

"I'm not going anywhere."

"I'm worried about what's to become of our island after this storm."

"Whatever happens, we'll rebuild better than before. That's what Mac told us at work earlier. He said there's nothing that can't be fixed except loss of life. He said to stay safe and to keep the faith."

"Good advice."

"I was comforted by it. I hope you are, too."

"I am. It's true. If we're all safe, we can fix what's broken after the fact."

"That's right."

He no sooner said those words than one of the large plate-glass windows rattled from a particularly strong gust of wind. The rain was coming down so hard, he could barely see through it.

Matilda, the Beachcomber's night manager, came into the bar. "Let's start to shut down, Jace. The storm is getting closer, and we need everyone to get home safely."

"Will do," Jace said. "You heard the boss. Last call."

Much moaning and groaning greeted that announcement.

Jace was busy for the next few minutes, pouring refills and settling tabs. He made multiple runs to the kitchen and delivered food to Cindy and several others.

"Oh, that looks good," she said. "Thank you."

"My pleasure. Enjoy."

While she ate, he moved quickly to get the bar cleaned up and more tabs settled as the crowd started to thin out.

"Go with God, y'all," Duke said when he stood to leave. "And come in afterward for your 'Fuck Ethel' tats."

"We'll run right over," Jace said, grinning.

Thirty minutes after the last call, everyone was gone except for Cindy.

Jace cleared her plate and pushed her credit card back toward her. "All set, love."

"You can't keep paying my tab!"

"Says who?"

"Says me. You're working to make money, not spend it."

"I'm making plenty working for Mac. I still do this gig one night a week for fun, as you know."

"Still… You shouldn't be paying for me all the time."

"Why?"

"Because!"

"You're gonna have to do better than that." He grabbed the cash bag and shut off the lights over the bar. "Let's go home and continue this argument naked."

"We *will* continue it," she said when he came around the bar and took her hand.

"I can't wait."

CHAPTER 13

*S*ince receiving Deacon's call, Julia couldn't stop crying. The relief was so overwhelming that it needed a way out through the tears. The agony of hours spent fearing he might be gone forever would stay with her long after he was safely back on shore.

Katie tiptoed into the guest room, where Julia was attempting to sleep with Pupwell curled up beside her.

He raised his head when he sensed Katie coming, but seeing it was her, he relaxed again.

"Are you okay?" Katie asked.

"I'm trying to be, but I can't stop the damned tears."

"That's understandable. He had a very close call."

"It's unbearable to realize he was in so much danger for hours."

He'd explained how the boat had been swamped by a massive wave that swept away his handheld radio and cell phone, and shorted out every other piece of electronic equipment, including the ship-to-shore radio and bilge pump. Then the boat had rolled over, leaving him adrift on top of it until Joe had thankfully spotted him bobbing in the violent seas. From what he'd said, the rescue had been a heroic operation that could've gone either way.

"I can't stop shaking over how easily I could've lost him."

Katie got in bed with her and put her arms around Julia. "Hang on to me until you can hang on to him."

"Thank you for being there for me."

"Always. You would've done the same for me."

"I hope I never have to."

"You were right by my side when I lost the baby. That's just how it goes for us Lawrys. We stick together in good times and bad."

"There's been a lot more good than bad lately. I've gotten used to it."

"I know," Katie said with a laugh. "Everything is so good that when it isn't, it sends us spiraling into the past."

"I hate that for all of us."

"I do, too, but that's just how it goes."

"Loving someone like I love Deacon… It's terrifying."

"Most of the time, it's wonderful. Stay focused on the good and don't dwell in the darkness. You know who wins when we do that."

"Yeah, I do know." They'd never give their father that kind of easy victory. "And we can't let that happen."

"No, we can't. So you stay focused on the positive and let go of the negative now that you know he's safe."

"He's still on a boat in a hurricane."

"But he's not alone, and he's on a much bigger boat than he was, with a highly skilled captain at the helm. He'll be fine."

"I can't wait to see him."

"I bet he can't wait to see you, too."

As THE FERRY bobbed in the stormy seas, Deacon stretched out on one of the benches and tried to relax after changing into dry clothes loaned to him by the other guys. He'd drawn the line on underwear, choosing to go commando under the sweats that Colin had given him. They'd insisted on sharing their food and water with him, too, which had been a welcome relief after drinking rainwater to stay hydrated during his ordeal.

All he'd thought about after the boat rolled over and cast him adrift was Julia and how upset she must be to not be able to reach him. Hearing her voice on the other end of the phone had been a huge relief. Just as he'd suspected, she'd been frantic with worry, and he hated having done that to her, Blaine, his parents, family and friends.

Fearing you might die made you think about all sorts of stuff, especially the things you hadn't done yet—like marry the love of your life and have lots of babies with her. He'd be rectifying that as soon as he possibly could. Until then, he was content to close his eyes and think of her and the love of this and all other lifetimes he'd found with her. She was every-thing to him, and all he needed for the rest of his life was more of every-thing with her.

Colin came down the stairs to check on Deacon. "You doing all right?"

"I'm fine, thanks."

"The cap says we should be out of the worst of it within an hour."

"Sounds good." Thankfully, rough seas had never bothered Deacon, until he'd thought he might die in them. "Do we still have cell service out here?"

"Amazingly, we do."

"Could I borrow your phone for a minute?"

"Sure." Colin handed it over. "Heard you've got a fiancée back on the hard," he said, using the nautical term for land.

"Yeah."

"I'll let you talk to your lady. Take your time. We're able to charge on board."

"Thanks, Colin. For everything. You guys saved my life."

"We're glad it worked out."

After Colin went back upstairs, Deacon called Julia again. She answered on the first ring, sounding uncertain and congested, probably from crying.

"Hey, baby, it's me again."

"Deacon..."

"I'll let you guys talk," he heard Katie say in the background.

"I'm glad you're with Katie and Shane."

"They insisted on bringing me home and keeping me sane."

"Did you eat something?" He knew how hard it was for her to eat during times of stress and had spent quite a lot of time worrying about that while fought to stay alive in monster seas.

"I had some soup and part of a grilled cheese that Shane made for me."

"Good."

"Deacon..."

"What, honey?"

"I thought I knew how much I loved you, but I found out today it's way more than I thought."

"You were all I could think about out there. I just wanted to get home to you and our furry little boy."

"You're safe on the ferry, right?" she asked, sounding tearful and exhausted.

"Absolutely. Joe says we're about an hour from smoother seas."

"I feel sick just thinking about how rough it must be."

"You wouldn't like it."

"Blaine called and your mom. Everyone was so sweet to me today."

"I'm glad you were well supported. I'm so sorry I put you through such an ordeal."

"I'd say it was okay, but…"

Deacon laughed softly. "I'll try to never do that again."

"Yes, please."

"My sweet, sweet Julia. I love you more than life."

"I love you more than that."

"No way."

"Way!"

Chuckling, he said, "How's our little boy?"

"He's worried about Daddy, but he feels better now that he knows you're safe."

"Tell me the truth. Is he snoring?"

"So loud. I'm surprised you can't hear him."

Deacon laughed hard. "I knew it."

"He was great today. He knew something was wrong and never left my side. I had to go out with him to the yard, or he wouldn't have peed."

"That's my boy, taking good care of Mommy when I'm not there."

"We can't wait to see you and hug you and kiss you."

"Same, love. I can't wait."

"I hope you can come home soon."

"Probably be at least another day, depending on what the storm does."

"I can hold it together for that long, I suppose. Did you talk to Blaine?"

"Not yet. I'll call him after this."

"You should go do that. He was eager to speak to you."

"And I'm eager to speak with you, in addition to some other things."

"Like what?" she asked softly.

"I can't wait to hold you and taste you and breathe you in and make love to you and have everything with you. Why are we waiting to get married? That was all I could think about out there when I wasn't sure I'd ever see you again. Why haven't I married you?"

"Deacon…"

"Let's do that soon, okay?"

"Okay."

He could hear the tears in that single word. "Don't cry, baby. Everything's all right, and we're going to have it all. I promise."

"As long as I have you, I have it all."

"I wish I was there with you and Pupwell."

"We wish that, too."

"You're going to stay with Katie and Shane during the storm?"

"Yes."

"Good. I don't want you to be alone."

"We're not alone, but we're lonely for you."

He groaned. "I'd give anything to be there with you guys. Soon enough."

"You should call Blaine."

"Yeah," he said but made no move to end the connection to her. "Did I mention that I love you?"

"A few times, but I never get tired of hearing that."

"I never get tired of saying it or feeling it or living it."

"I hope you never do."

"I won't. You're really going to marry me?"

"I really am. As soon as I can."

"I can't wait for that, for everything."

"Me, too. Now go call your brother."

"Are you trying to get rid of me?"

"Not even kinda."

He laughed at the emphatic way she said that. "I'll call you again in the morning."

"I'll look forward to that. Will you be able to get some sleep?"

"I think so. I'm exhausted."

"Close your eyes and dream of me."

"I don't have to close my eyes to dream of you."

"Near-death Deacon is very romantic."

"Near-death Deacon had a lot of hours to think out there, and it all just kept coming back to you." He heard her yawn. "Go get some rest, baby. I'll see you soon."

"Hurry home."

"Will do." Deacon reluctantly ended the call when he'd much rather listen to her breathe all night long. Then he dialed Blaine's number, which he'd memorized when they started working together.

"Taylor."

"Hey, it's me."

"Jesus, Deacon. Way to take five years off my life."

"Sorry about that."

"What the hell happened?"

"A huge wave swamped the boat, swept my handheld and cell phone over the side and shorted out the rest of the electronics. Another wave flipped the boat over, but I was able to stay with it, and that's how Joe found me."

"Thank God he spotted you and that you're all right."

"Sorry about the boat."

"That's what insurance is for."

"Have you seen Julia?"

"I was with her earlier. You'd have been proud of her. She was upset, but held up admirably."

"We're getting married as soon as we possibly can."

"That's great. I'm happy for you guys."

"You'll be my best man, right?"

"I'd love to."

Once upon a time, not that long ago, his older brother would've been the last person Deacon would've asked to stand up for him. Now, he couldn't imagine asking anyone else. "She's at Shane and Katie's. Check on her for me, will you?"

"Yeah, brother. I will."

As HE DROVE the outer perimeter of the island, Blaine ended the call with Deacon and returned his full focus to navigating the road, with the wind and rain rocking the SUV and making it difficult to see anything.

He was so thankful to hear from his brother—and honored to be asked to be his best man. That never would've happened only a few months ago, but they'd traveled light-years from when Blaine first insisted Deacon come to the island after he was arrested in a bar fight defending the honor of a female friend. He'd always thought of Deacon as a fuckup, but he'd become a friend and valued colleague. While Blaine wasn't looking, his little brother had grown into a fine man and an outstanding police officer. He'd been a great addition to Blaine's team.

Even though Deacon was Blaine's most recent hire, the younger guys looked up to Deacon, who'd done ten years with the Boston Police Department before a knee injury had forced his early retirement. Boston's loss was now Gansett's gain. Deacon had a level of experience that even

Blaine would be hard-pressed to match, which was why Blaine had put him in charge of training as well as being the harbor master. Those things didn't usually tax Deacon's injured knee.

It'd been a long few hours, filled with worry since Julia first informed Blaine that Deacon was overdue. Getting the call that he'd been found by Joe and Seamus had been one of the best calls of Blaine's life. He slowed the vehicle to a crawl as visibility became more impaired by the second. The storm was nearly upon them, and the rain was coming down harder than he'd ever seen on the island. After having grown up there, he'd seen his share of storms.

As he crept along, he kept a careful eye out for fallen trees and power lines. It'd taken them more than two hours in the pouring rain to deal with the massive tree that'd been blocking the road on the north end. Even in a hurricane, they had to keep the roads open so emergency vehicles could respond if needed. Only because he was driving so slowly did he spot something by the side of the road.

What the hell was that?

He turned on his emergency lights and pulled off the road, keeping his headlights trained on the object. After tugging the hood to his foul-weather coat over his head, he got out of the truck and fought the elements as he made his way toward the thing he'd spotted. As he got closer, he realized it was moving.

"Hello?" he called, speaking loudly to be heard over the roar of wind and rain.

The person startled and looked up at Blaine.

A woman sitting hunched over. And was that a child tucked up against her body?

"What're you doing out here in the storm?"

"I… We were staying in a cottage, but the wind… The whole place was shaking and then the roof blew off. I was frightened, so I decided to leave, hoping I'd find someone to give us a ride into town." Her teeth were chattering so hard, she could barely speak.

"Let's get you into my SUV and warm you up."

"I… I don't think so."

"You can't stay out here in a hurricane." He was shouting to be heard in the storm and noted that she recoiled from him.

"It's a *hurricane*?"

He nodded. How could anyone not know that? "I'm Blaine Taylor, the chief of police on the island. I can take you somewhere safe. Please let me help you. If you stay out here, you and your child are apt to be killed."

"C-could I see your b-badge?"

Blaine fished it out of his pocket and used his flashlight to light it up for her.

"O-okay."

As she kept a tight hold on the sleeping child, he helped her up and put an arm around her when her legs wobbled under her. Once she was steady on her feet, she stepped away from him, but followed him to the vehicle. He held the passenger door for her, suspecting she wouldn't release the child for any reason, even to secure him or her in the back seat.

After he got in, Blaine shut off the passenger air bag and helped her buckle the two of them in. Under normal circumstances, he'd insist she properly secure the child, but he wasn't about to argue with an obviously traumatized mother during a hurricane.

Since he didn't want to have to come out this way again until the storm had passed, he continued the long way around the island on the way back to town while trying to think about where he could take his passengers. He kept coming back to one place—home with him. He and Tiffany could give them a safe place to stay until the storm passed. Then they could figure out next steps.

"Do either of you need medical attention?" he asked.

"I… I don't think so."

"With the storm raging, there aren't a lot of options for shelter. I could bring you to my home. My wife and I can provide a safe place for you and your child to stay during the storm."

"I-I wouldn't want to b-be a b-burden."

"You wouldn't be. We'd be happy to have you."

"I-if… If you're sure."

"I am." He had so many other questions to ask her, but now was not the time. They needed to get her and her child somewhere warm and safe before the worst of the storm hit. Blaine put a call in to Officer Wyatt Abrams, who'd volunteered to stay at the public safety building during the storm so the others could be home with their families to get some rest after days of frantic storm prep. The entire department would remain on call via handheld radios in case they lost cell service.

"What's up, Chief?" Wyatt asked.

"I've just done a final patrol and am heading home. Call me if anything comes up."

"Will do. Be safe."

"You do the same. Don't leave there without calling me first, you hear?"

"Yes, sir."

"Thanks for taking one for the team. This'll be remembered at evaluation time."

"Why do you think I volunteered?"

He laughed as he pressed the button to end the call. Cheeky bastard. Blaine hadn't mentioned the passengers he'd picked up. For now, he'd tend to them himself until he knew more about where they'd come from and what they needed. As he drove home, he called Tiffany on the Bluetooth.

"Hi," she said, her voice having the usual effect of raising his spirits.

"Hi there. I wanted to let you know I'm on the way home with a couple of guests who got caught in the storm. I thought they could use our guest room."

"Sure, no problem. I'll make the bed."

"Thanks, honey. Be there shortly."

"See you soon."

As he headed for home, he couldn't wait to see Tiffany and to hunker down with her for the storm. He hoped the addition of houseguests wouldn't complicate things, but he had no regrets about offering up their home to people in need.

"I'm surprised you hadn't heard about the storm," he said tentatively, hoping he didn't come across as harsh in any way.

"We were staying in a house without television or internet, and I couldn't get a good signal for my phone." Her teeth had stopped chattering once the heat in the SUV had kicked in. "I had no idea a hurricane was coming until the roof blew off, and I was afraid it would fall down around us. I thought it would be better to leave, but that didn't work out so well. Thank you for stopping when you saw us."

"I'm glad I spotted you and didn't drive right past."

She shuddered, as if thinking about what could've happened if he hadn't seen them. "I feel so stupid."

"You didn't know. I can see how that would've happened." Although it'd be a cold day in hell before he was ever cut off from the outside world for any reason. As chief of police, he was always reachable. He'd heard other high-ranking police officers say they had a hard time unplugging even after retirement. He'd be the same way. Maybe it was time to insist that rental houses on the island have landlines for when cell service was interrupted.

The thought of how many other island residents might be cut off from help during and after the storm made him anxious. He would send officers to every home on the island after the storm.

He could feel the wind increasing as he drove through the deserted downtown area on the way home, relieved to see the outside light on when he pulled into his driveway a few minutes later. "What's your name?" From what he could see in the faint light, she had dark hair that was plastered to her head from the rain.

"McKenzie, and this is Jax."

"How old is he?"

"Nine months."

"We have two daughters. One is six, and the other is about his age."

"I'm sorry to be a bother. I'd go to a hotel, but I can't afford it. I used the last of my savings to get to the island."

Everything she said left him with more questions to be dealt with another time. "Let's get you inside and warmed up. I'll come around for you." He got out of the SUV and battled ferocious wind as he rounded the front of the vehicle on his way to the passenger door, which was nearly ripped off when the wind tried to take it. He held out a hand to McKenzie, who kept an arm tightly around her son as they made their way up the stairs to the back deck.

Tiffany opened the door for them and then stepped back to let them in.

Wind and rain followed them in before Blaine could wrestle the door closed.

"It's getting wild out there," Tiffany said.

"Wilder by the minute," Blaine said. "Tiffany, this is McKenzie and her son, Jax. McKenzie, my wife, Tiffany."

"Welcome to our home," Tiffany said.

"Thank you for having us."

Blaine stepped aside to let Tiffany assist McKenzie and the baby, while hoping he'd done the right thing by bringing strangers into their home.

CHAPTER 14

*P*iper had expected Jack to leave after dinner, but when he checked in with work, he learned everyone was headed home to ride out the storm, knowing they could be called back at any time. They moved from the kitchen into the salon and sat in front of the fire. He settled in, legs crossed at the ankles, glass of ice water in hand while he entertained her with stories from his career as a state police officer after she'd asked him to tell her about his job.

"Local cops refer to us as Triple A," he said with a grin. "They think all we do is help stranded motorists, but it's a lot more than that. We assist in all sorts of cases, including the investigations of cops gone bad."

"Does that happen a lot?"

"More often than you'd think. Some of them start to get a god complex. They think they can do whatever they want and get away with it. We get called in when a department wants an impartial investigation of one of their own. We oversee all sorts of investigations—everything from homicide to gaming to computer crimes, and we patrol all the state's roads and highways."

"Wow. That's a lot."

"It can be. It was when I was a detective. They moved me to admin when Ruby was sick, which took some of the pressure off. I'm still dealing with cases I had as a detective, though. Like the trial that just wrapped up after more delays than I could count."

"Congratulations on the conviction."

"Thanks. It was my case from the beginning, and I stayed on it all this time."

"You must feel very satisfied now that it's over."

"I am. It was a grind from the start. I'll never forget that crime scene. It was brutal."

"I can't imagine. I give you guys so much credit for being the ones to deal with stuff that the rest of us couldn't bear to look at."

"Police get a bad rap because of the criminal misbehavior of some, but most of us get into this business because we want to help people. At least that's why I became a cop. But enough about me. Tell me more about you."

"Your stuff is far more interesting."

"I'll be the judge of that."

"Well, let's see," Piper said. "I'm the youngest of five kids."

"That must've been fun."

"It was, for the most part. They're all quite a bit older than me, so they treated me like a baby until I was, like, fifteen and begged them to knock off the baby stuff. My brothers wanted to kill my ex when he called off the wedding, which was kind of funny. I'd never seen them so mad on my behalf. They're all married with kids and great careers, and then there's me, still trying to figure out what I want to be when I grow up. I've started more careers than anyone I know, but nothing sticks. I've been a retail manager, a restaurant manager, an office manager, and now I'm trying on hotel management for size."

"How's it fitting?"

"So far, so good, but mostly because I love working with Laura, Owen and Sarah so much, and I like being here on Gansett."

"What do you like the best about the island?"

"The people. Everyone is so nice and friendly and welcoming. I've made so many friends here, more than I've ever had in my whole life. I've always been content with one or two good friends. I didn't need to be the life of the party, but here… Everyone is so nice that I can't help wanting to get to know them all."

"I agree. It's a very welcoming place. It's been like that for me, too. I've become very good friends with Blaine and Deacon Taylor, Mason Johns, Mallory and Quinn James, to name a few."

"I don't know Mallory and Quinn except to say hello, but I've met all the others, and they seem great."

"They are, and they invite me to join them in whatever they're doing, even though I'm single and they're not. They don't care."

"Do they know about Ruby?"

He shook his head. "You're the only one I've told about her out here."

Piper was incredibly honored to hear that. "Why is that, do you suppose?"

Jack shrugged. "I was looking for a fresh start when I came here. It didn't seem wise to clue them in to my great tragedy. I didn't want to become a pity case for everyone, like I was at home."

"I can understand that, but they all seem like good people. They'd probably want to know you better."

"Maybe. We'll see. It's not something I talk about much anymore. It overtook our lives for four years, and when it was over, I continued my leave of absence for a few months until I felt ready to get back in the game. When I went back to work, I wanted a fresh start."

"How'd that go?"

"Good days. Bad days. Everything in between. I've learned that you can't just power your way through a loss like that. You have to give it the time and attention it demands. I'm still a work in progress on that front. I'll think I'm doing much better, and then it'll be our anniversary or her birthday, or some other memory will pop into my head out of nowhere, and it sets me back."

Piper put her hand on his arm. "I keep saying I'm sorry, but I really am. I can't possibly know how hard that must be or the courage it takes to keep moving forward after such a painful loss."

He covered her hand with his much bigger one. "Thank you. Life can be a bitch sometimes, but it's also full of good stuff, too. Like this… with you. It's good stuff, or at least it feels good to me."

"It feels good to me, too."

Their gazes collided and held. The wind and rain pinging against the windows combined with the cozy glow of the fireplace made Piper feel like she was inside a snow globe with only Jack for company, which was fine with her. He was very good company.

"Oh, sorry," Owen said when he came into the room. "I didn't mean to interrupt."

Feeling as if she'd been caught doing something naughty, Piper pulled back her hand, cleared her throat and shifted her gaze toward Owen. "You didn't. We were just talking."

"How're you doing, Jack?" Owen asked.

"Better now that I'm back on Gansett, and by the way, your spaghetti was excellent."

"Oh good. Glad you enjoyed it."

"Everyone did," Piper said. "They said to pass along their thanks."

"No problem." Owen moved toward the one small window that wasn't boarded to look outside. "It's getting worse by the minute, or so it seems."

"It's definitely getting louder," Jack said.

"You feeling any shaking down here?" Owen asked.

"Nope."

"That's good. I'm worried the roof will blow off."

"Nah," Jack said. "This place is solid."

"From your lips to God's ears," Owen said, still sounding concerned.

"We'll make sure the fire is out before we go to bed," Piper said, earning her an intrigued glance from Jack. "Or, I should say, before *I* go to bed."

Jack's low chuckle was greeted by a playful glare from her.

"The Sand & Surf is a no-judgment zone," Owen said, grinning. "What happens on Gansett stays on Gansett."

"What happens on Gansett is all over Gansett before it happens," Piper said.

"That's also true. I'm going up to attempt to get some sleep. Call if you need anything."

"Will do," Piper said. "Good night."

"Night," Owen said. "Jack, feel free to grab a room if you don't want to go out in the storm."

"I might do that. Thanks, Owen."

"Sure thing."

"He's such a nice guy," Jack said when they were alone.

"They're the best bosses I've ever had. They're making me want to put down some roots here."

"Are you staying here at the hotel?"

"Yes, I have one of the tiny rooms on the third floor, which works out perfectly for what I need. I think about getting an apartment or something, but it's so expensive to live here, even in the off-season."

"It is. I'm lucky to have accommodations provided by the department."

"Where?"

"Next door to the Coast Guard station in North Harbor. It's a two-bedroom apartment that I share with whomever is sent out on any given week. I'm the only one permanently assigned here right now. In the summer, there're two of us."

"Like Owen said, you're welcome to stay here if you'd rather not venture out."

"I think I might take you up on that. If I get called in during the storm, it'd be easier to already be in town."

"I can set you up with a room."

"Are you eager to get to bed?"

"Not particularly. Why?"

"I was kinda enjoying talking to you and was hoping you might keep talking to me for a while longer."

Piper melted at the way he looked at her when he said that. For a girl who'd planned to stay unattached after her most recent romantic disaster, she was getting awfully involved with a handsome man who enjoyed talking to her and made her breathless when he looked at her that way. "I can do that."

AT EASTWARD LOOK, the wind made the house shake. Nikki Stokes was comforted by the presence of her fiancé, Riley McCarthy, his brother, Finn, and Finn's fiancée, Chloe, as well as Riley and Finn's dad, Kevin, his wife, Chelsea, and their baby daughter, Summer. Her grandmother, Evelyn, was also there, and being with her always made Nikki calmer than she would be otherwise.

But damn, this storm was scary.

They had the TV tuned to the local Providence station. A weatherman was positioned on the beach in Narragansett, which was the closest town to Gansett. The wind and rain were so strong that the man could barely remain standing as he reported on the approaching storm.

"As Ethel bears down on the southern coast of Rhode Island, she has tiny Gansett Island in her crosshairs," he shouted over the roar of the storm. "The latest models are showing the storm coming ashore on Gansett overnight as a strong Category 3 with wind gusts topping one hundred twenty miles per hour and a storm surge expected to top ten feet."

The in-studio anchor thanked the weatherman for his report and urged him to get to safer ground. "We spoke with Gansett Island Fire Chief Mason Johns a short time ago. He provided an update on the situation on the island."

Mason's face was shown on a computer screen. "We've done everything we can think of to prepare for what promises to be one of the worst storms the island has ever seen."

"Island residents were encouraged to evacuate over the last few days," the anchor said. "Do you have a sense of how many people heeded that warning?"

"Most of our year-round residents chose to stay and ride out the storm so they can do whatever they can to protect their homes and businesses."

"Do you have a count of how many people are currently on the island?" the reporter asked.

"Not a complete count, but we average about seven hundred off-season residents. We've encouraged a buddy system of sorts among the island residents that would have people checking on each other before and after the storm. We know of island residents who've abandoned summer cottages and moved to hotels in town or are staying with family and friends."

"Without ferries or planes, the island is cut off from the mainland. What special steps have you taken to provide emergency support to those who need it?"

"We've got our medical team hunkered down at the clinic," Mason said, "and most of my department is at the public safety offices for the duration of the storm. In addition, we have on-call support from the police department, state police and the Coast Guard. We've encouraged island residents to call only for legitimate medical emergencies during the storm."

"When do you reach the point where it's too risky for your team to answer a call?"

"We're already there. We'd try our best to get out to a resident in need, but we told people if they stayed, they might be on their own during the storm."

Nikki swallowed hard.

"Bad time to have a heart attack on Gansett," Kevin said.

"Good thing we have you, a sorta doctor," Finn said, drawing a snort of laughter from his brother. They loved to tease their psychiatrist father about not being a "real" doctor.

"I could save you in a pinch, but after that jab, I might not bother," Kevin said.

"Right," Riley said. "As if."

Anyone who knew Kevin McCarthy even a little bit had no doubt he'd jump in front of a speeding train if one of his children was in danger.

"That's an empty threat if I've ever heard one, Kev," Chelsea said.

"What've I told you about ganging up on me with them?"

She smiled at her husband. "That it's fun?"

"That is not at all what I told you."

Everyone else laughed.

Nikki tuned back into what Mason was saying as they wrapped up the interview.

"My department stands ready to assist the Gansett Island community," he said, "as we recover from the storm and get back to business as usual."

Nikki's stomach hurt at the thought of wide-scale damage, loss of life and property.

Riley came up behind her and slid his arms around her. "You're not stressing out, are you?"

"Maybe a little. I'm afraid we made the wrong call by staying when they recommended evacuation."

"It's not the wrong call to stay with our home so we're here if anything happens."

"I'm scared."

He turned her so she was facing him. "Don't be, honey. We'll be fine. Soon enough, the storm will be gone, and we can get back to normal around here."

Nikki looked up at him. "I finally have everything I've ever wanted. You, this house that we've made our own, a job I love at the Wayfarer, our family and friends nearby. The thought of something threatening any of that is just so overwhelming."

"Most of the people we love best are here. Gigi and Coop are safe in LA. Jordan and Mason are safe at the public safety building. Try not to worry. It's going to be fine."

She exhaled and tried to get her nerves to chill the hell out. If anyone could help her with that, Riley could.

"What do you say we turn in early and try to get some sleep while we can?"

Since nothing made her feel better than snuggling with Riley, she nodded in agreement.

"We're going to bed," Riley said. "Are you guys all set with everything you need?"

Every bedroom in the big house would be full that night, as they'd decided to hunker down together.

"We're good," Kevin said for all of them. "Thanks for having us."

"We're so glad you're here," Nikki said. A full house sure did beat worrying about their loved ones during the storm.

"Make sure that fire is out," Riley said to Finn.

"I've got it," he said. "Night."

Nikki followed Riley upstairs to the bedroom they'd decorated together in soothing neutral tones. It was her favorite room in the house because it was theirs, a place they could rest, relax and love each other after long days at work. In two short months, they'd be getting married. She couldn't wait for forever with him, but she was also worried about how The Chesterfield, their wedding venue, would handle the storm.

After they took turns in the bathroom, they met in bed, snuggling up to each other like they did every night. The second his arms were around her, she felt calmer, even if the wind made the old house shake and the windows rattle ominously.

"Hurricanes are loud."

"Very," Riley said with a chuckle.

"I'll never take a quiet night for granted again."

"I put the roof on this place myself. It's solid, and it'll hold. I promise."

"Since that roof is the reason we met, it's good to know it'll hold."

"It'll hold, and so will we. We'll ride out every storm that comes our way together."

Nikki closed her eyes and gave thanks for him and everything he'd brought to her life. Before she met him, she'd had no idea what was possible when you were in love with the right man. She lifted herself onto her elbow and gazed down at him in the glow of a nightlight.

"What's up?" he asked, twirling a length of her hair around his finger.

"You're very good at making me feel better when I'm stressed."

"That's my job."

"You do it very well."

"If you're going to do something, you should do it as well as you can," he said.

"That sounds like a Kevin-ism," she said. That was what he and Finn called their father's words of wisdom.

"Every so often, he's right about something," Riley said.

Nikki leaned in to kiss him. "He's right about a lot of things."

"No, he isn't."

Smiling, she nodded.

He hooked his arm around her and drew her into another kiss, knowing full well that she couldn't think of anything other than him when they were together this way. It was his antidote to any worries she had, and with a massive storm bearing down on them, she was more than happy to let him work his magic.

Was there any other word for what it was like to love Riley McCarthy? No, *magic* was the best word to describe it.

He removed the T-shirt she'd worn to bed and kissed a path to her breasts, giving each nipple his undivided attention for long enough that she was squirming under him, immediately wanting more.

"Patience, my love. I can't get you completely relaxed in five minutes."

"Yes, you actually can."

His low chuckle made her smile as he moved down to kiss her abdomen. "My love is the sexiest woman on the planet."

"You're biased."

"No, I'm not. It's true. There's no one sexier than my Nikki."

"If you say so."

"I say so, and you'd better not argue with me, or I won't give you want you want." He pressed his face between her legs and seemed to breathe her in through the silk of her panties.

"You don't hear me arguing," she said, breathless with anticipation.

Riley had many skills, but his oral game was a particular favorite of hers, and he knew it. Her panties slid down over her legs, his fingertip sliding over her skin giving her goose bumps everywhere.

Then he kissed his way up the inside of her leg, and the goose bumps quadrupled as she held her breath, waiting for him to reach his destination. At least she wasn't stressing out about the storm anymore, which he knew, and that was why he was dragging this out as long as he could. He didn't want her worrying. He wanted her *feeling*.

"Riley..."

"Hmm?"

"Don't hmm me! You know what I want!"

"All in good time, love. These things can't be rushed."

"Why not?"

He looked up at her, a devilish expression on his unreasonably handsome face. "Are we gonna argue right now, or do we have better things to do?"

"We have better things to do, so get on with it."

His shoulders shook with laugher as he started kissing his way back down her legs, drawing a moan of frustration from her. "Patience, my love."

Nikki hoped her growl conveyed her feelings about her lack of patience. Since he was determined to do things his way, she closed her eyes and floated on a sea of sensation as he used his lips and hands on her legs. By the time, he got to the main event, she was so aroused that the first stroke of his tongue over her clit was all it took to make her come.

"That was easy," he whispered as he slid his fingers into her to ride the waves of her orgasm.

Nikki reached for him, bringing him up so their bodies were aligned as he pushed his cock into her, filling her the way only he could do.

"Hi," he said, smiling down at her as he brushed hair back from her face.

"Hi there."

"What's new?" he asked as he pressed deep inside her.

She bit her lip to keep from crying out the way she would have if they'd been alone in the house. "Nothing much."

"What's that you say? Nothing *much*?" He withdrew almost completely before filling her completely again. "How's that for nothing much?"

Nikki couldn't believe the way he made her laugh during sex, almost every time.

"I'll give you nothing much," he muttered.

She rubbed circles over his back. "My poor baby. I didn't mean to insult your manhood."

"Well, you did, and now you're going to have to make it up to him."

"Isn't that what I'm doing?"

"This is just phase one of the makeup tour."

"Oh, so it's a tour, is it?"

"A full-on tour."

"I'll have to give this some considerable thought."

"Good thing we have plenty of time with a hurricane day out of work tomorrow. It might take all day for you to properly atone for your sins." His hips pivoted with a deep thrust that touched the spot deep inside that almost always led to a screaming orgasm.

Again, she bit her lip to stay silent as she rode wave after wave of intense pleasure.

He gripped her shoulder and hip as he found his own release, expelling a gasp before he landed on top of her. "What do we think of hurricane sex?"

"It's right up there with any-given-Tuesday sex."

"I'd better up my game, then, because this was supposed to have been special."

"It's always special with you, Ri. Every time."

"Same, sweetheart." He kissed her and rested his forehead on hers. "Love you to infinity and beyond."

"Love you even further than that."

"No way."

"Yes way."

Outside, the storm frothed and boiled with rage. Inside, safe in the arms of her love, Nikki slept.

CHAPTER 15

"What do you say we hit the hay?" Finn asked Chloe after his dad and Chelsea had followed Evelyn up to bed. Baby Summer had been asleep in Chelsea's arms for an hour by the time they finally took her up to the portable crib they'd brought for her.

"I'm ready when you are," Chloe said.

Finn went to tend to the fire, making sure every ember was extinguished before he closed the flue and the glass doors. Then he went to the sofa and held out his hands to carefully help her up.

She winced as she stood upright.

Finn hated to see her in pain from the rheumatoid arthritis that plagued her, especially during weather events like the current storm. The dampness seemed to make everything worse. "Are you okay?"

She thought he couldn't see how she battled through the pain to give him a reassuring smile, but he saw it. He saw it all with her, and he ached for her when the pain was bad.

Finn offered his arm, and she curled her hand around his bent elbow. As always, he let her set the pace as they made their way slowly up the stairs with their dog, Ranger, following them at the same slow pace.

"I hate this," she whispered, sounding tearful.

"You hate what?"

"Feeling and moving like I'm eighty when I'm only thirty. You should be having hot hurricane sex on a night like this, and instead, you're helping me up the stairs."

It made him mad when she said things like that, but he kept the anger to himself since it was directed at her condition, never at her. "There's no one in this entire world I'd rather snuggle with during a hurricane than you, and you know that, so quit trying to get rid of me."

"I'm sorry. I know you don't like when I say stuff like that."

He dropped her off at the bathroom in the hallway and went into the room they used whenever they stayed with Riley and Nikki at Eastward Look. The big old house had become like a second home to them, and they loved being there. After he turned down the bed, he went to check on Chloe.

The bathroom door opened, and she came out wearing nothing more than a tank and the boy shorts that did wondrous things for her ass. On the way by, he gave that wondrous ass a squeeze, while wishing there was a way he could take away her pain.

"Go get comfy," he said, kissing her cheek. "Be right there."

Finn had brought the foam mattress topper from their bed at home because she was so much more comfortable with it than without it. When she'd caught him rolling it up earlier, she'd told him he didn't have to bring that. "Yes, I do," he'd said. "You need it, so we'll bring it. Besides, I've gotten used to it, too, and now I'm spoiled."

She'd frowned but hadn't said anything else about it.

He took a leak and brushed his teeth, then crossed the hall to their room and closed the door. The roar of the storm had gotten much louder in the last few hours, and he wondered how much worse it would get before it was over.

Finn joined Chloe in the bed but left the bedside light on so he could see her as he turned on his side to face her. "Hi."

"Hi yourself."

"What's up?"

"Other than the hurricane?"

"Yes, other than that."

"Not much."

"Don't lie to your fiancé. It's poor form. You're stewing about something, and you know it's easier to just tell me than to make me kiss it out of you."

"But kissing you is my favorite thing ever."

Smiling, he moved close enough to kiss her. "Talk to me."

"It's the same old thing." Her lovely violet eyes went shiny with unshed tears as she touched the engagement necklace he'd given her because her hands were too swollen for rings. "I hate this body I'm stuck with, how it limits me and you and how it's gotten worse rather than better with the new meds, and I can't stand being such a sad sack all the time. I miss cutting hair, and I want you to have everything—"

He kissed her again, before she could say something that could never be unsaid. "If I have you, I have everything I've ever wanted and more than I could've ever hoped for. I wish more than anything that you didn't have to deal with pain and frustration, but please don't include me on the list of things you hate."

"Finn... Of course you're not on that list. You're at the very top of the list of things I love with all my heart."

"That's the only thing that truly matters to me. That and your comfort, your happiness, anything you need. I've told you before that I don't want you to worry about me or dwell on things you think I'm missing out on by being with you. If you're near me, I'm content. I don't care what we're doing." He put his arm around her and kissed her cheek. "I just need you, Chloe. That's all."

"I'm very lucky to be loved by you."

"And I'm lucky to be loved by you. Let's stay focused on the positives, okay? Such as our wedding, which I can't wait for. How much longer?"

"You know exactly how long."

"Nine months, fourteen days, twelve hours."

Her laughter made him happy because she spent so much of her life in terrible pain. "Can you remind me again why we're waiting so damned long?"

"Because that was the soonest we could book the Wayfarer."

"We own the joint." Each of the McCarthys owned a piece of the business they'd purchased as a group, and their first season had been a smashing success until the hurricane had forced them to shut down, losing a precious September weekend.

"And it's booked until the end of June, as you know."

"You'd think my future sister-in-law could've gotten us in sooner," Finn grumbled.

"Nikki did what she could for us, and you know that, too, so quit being grumpy."

"You know what would be cool?"

"What's that?"

"A hurricane wedding."

"No one in the history of weddings has ever said a hurricane wedding would be cool."

"Then I guess I'm making history by saying why don't we just do it this weekend? My uncle Frank would come over and the rest of the family. No one is doing anything else."

"Except cleaning up after a major storm."

"Eh, it'll all get done, and people need to eat. So we invite them over for food and throw a wedding in the mix."

"We don't have a license."

"We can take care of the legalities after the fact. I don't want to wait nine more months to be married to you, Chlo. I want you to be my wife now."

"Because you're afraid I'll change my mind."

The fact that she said that as a statement and not a question struck fear in his heart. "No, that's not why."

"Yes, it is, Finn, so don't pretend otherwise."

"It's really not. I know how much you love me even if you worry about burdening me and other silly things that don't warrant discussion."

"They do warrant discussion."

"Don't."

"Do."

"So you'll marry me this weekend?"

"Finn..."

"It's a simple yes-or-no question. Shall we have a hurricane wedding and then party it up next June as planned?"

"You really want this?"

"I really do. I want all the questions answered once and for all, so you can't suddenly decide you're sick of me and show me the door."

"That's not going to happen," she said with a resigned expression. "You've made yourself completely essential to me."

"Then my work here is nearly finished."

"It's just getting started, mister."

"Yes, it is. That's what I've been trying to tell you."

"You're sure about shackling yourself to this situation for life?" she asked tentatively.

"All I know is that you and your situation make my life complete, so yes, I'm sure."

"Then let's have a hurricane wedding."

MARIE FORCE

He fist-pumped the air. "She said yes!"

"Don't sprain something. What good will you be to me then?"

"Baby, I'll always be so good to you."

She drew him into a deep, soulful kiss. "I love you more than anything in this entire world."

"I love you all the way around the world and back again. We're going to be the happiest married people in the history of married people."

"You make me believe that."

"It's safe to believe it because we both know it's true." As he held her close, he shortened the countdown to their wedding to two days. He liked that number much better than the other one.

"Is she the cutest baby girl ever, or am I biased?" Kevin asked Chelsea as they watched Summer sleep on the bed between them.

"I think you might be biased, but I do have to agree that she's the cutest baby ever."

He was completely besotted by his little girl, with hair and eyebrows so blonde, they were nearly white. She had big blue eyes and the cutest pink lips. Her tiny fingers and toes were the source of endless fascination to him, as if he'd never had a baby in his life before. With Riley and Finn close to thirty, it felt like a lifetime ago since he'd been equally obsessed with them.

"Thank you for giving her to me." Kevin ran a finger lightly over her arm. She had the softest skin he'd ever felt. "I would've said my life was complete before, but she's the frosting on the cake."

"She's perfection, and I should be the one thanking you for taking a second spin on fatherhood when your sons are already grown men."

"A couple of years ago, I would've laughed if someone told me I'd be remarried with a new baby. I had no idea what was missing from my life until I found you and Summer."

"I'm so glad you feel that way. I was worried it might be too much for you."

"It's too much in the best possible way. I can't believe how perfect she is or how much I love her, like she's always been here. It's hard to explain."

"I get what you mean. I feel the same way."

"We're having another one, right?" he asked. "She really shouldn't grow up alone."

"I wasn't sure you'd want to."

"I want to. ASAP."

"I'm ready when you are, Doc. How about I put Miss Summer in her crib, and we get to work on a brother or sister for her?"

"Um, do you have to ask? You want me to move her?"

"Sure."

Kevin was careful not to disturb his sleeping princess as he moved her from their bed to the portable crib that had humbled him earlier when he tried to set it up without the directions. Chelsea had come to his rescue once again. As he gently placed the baby on the crib mattress and removed his hands, she never stirred. She was a wonderful sleeper in addition to her many other attributes.

He got back in bed and reached for his wife. "Do we want another girl or a boy?"

"We'll be happy with whatever we get."

As he kissed her, he rolled her under him and settled between her legs, immediately ready for baby-making activities. "Yes, we certainly will."

"Can I get you anything else?" Tiffany asked from the doorway of the guest room.

McKenzie was on the bed in pajamas Tiffany had loaned her, breast-feeding her little boy. "I don't think so but thank you so much for everything. I don't know what we would've done if your husband hadn't found us and brought us to your lovely home."

"We're very happy to have you."

"I was so scared out there with no info about what was happening."

"That must've been terrifying."

"It was."

"Is there anyone you need to notify that you're safe? You're more than welcome to use my phone."

"No, there's no one."

Tiffany wanted to ask how that was possible, but she kept the thought to herself. Whatever was going on would only be made worse by probing questions from strangers. "I showed you where our room is. Please come get me if you need anything during the night."

"You're so kind. Thank you again."

"Our pleasure. I'll see you in the morning, if not before."

"Sleep well."

"You, too."

Tiffany checked on her sleeping girls, recovered Addie, and then joined Blaine in their room, where he was already in bed. After he'd worked thirty-six hours straight, she was glad he was finally getting some rest.

"Everything all right?" he asked.

"Yep. They're settled into the guest room."

"Thank you for having them. I didn't know where else to bring them."

"Of course they're welcome here. I asked if there was anyone she wanted to call to tell them they were safe, and she said there was no one. How does she have no one?"

"I don't know, but we've done what we can for them tonight, so come to bed and snuggle with your husband."

"My husband needs sleep more than snuggling."

"There's nothing your husband needs more than snuggling."

After she brushed her teeth, she got into bed with him and gave him what he said he needed most.

"Now, that's what I'm talking about," he said when he was wrapped up in her, breathing her in the way he always did, as if she was his only source of oxygen. Being loved by him was the best thing to ever happen to her, right up there with her two beautiful girls and the baby on the way. Everything about this pregnancy felt different from her first two, so she thought she might be expecting a son this time. Either way, she'd be delighted, and so would Blaine. He loved being a girl dad.

Blaine's hands never stopped moving, caressing her and making her shiver with the desire he aroused in her so easily. When she was married to Jim, she'd often made herself go through the motions in bed because she thought that was what a wife should do. Blaine had shown her something else entirely, and she loved him madly.

"What're you thinking?" he asked, his voice gruff and sexy.

"I'm thinking about you and how much I love you."

He gave her breast a light squeeze that drew a shiver of pleasure from her. "That's how I want you thinking. Not worrying like you were earlier."

"I don't really worry. I'm not sure where those insecurities come from."

"I know where they come from, but he's ancient history, and I'm right here and not going anywhere ever."

"Keep reminding me of that, okay?"

"Any time you need to hear it."

She turned to him and placed her hand on his face. "I was thinking earlier about the first time I ever saw you at the clinic and how I was immediately interested, even though I was still married and had no business being interested in anyone."

"Same, babe. I took one look and was completely sunk in the best possible way."

"Remember that time on Luke and Syd's deck?"

"I remember everything, especially the longing I felt for you while I was waiting for you to be free of him."

"I also had no business jumping right into something with you, but I couldn't resist you. And I still can't."

"I thought I'd go mad watching you prance around outside the store in the sexiest lingerie I'd ever seen, with every other guy on the island panting over the woman I already thought of as mine." He squeezed her ass and pressed his erection against her belly. "You made me into a raving lunatic."

Tiffany laughed at the way he practically growled as he said that.

"You did, and you enjoyed torturing me."

"It was kind of fun."

He gave her a light tap on the ass that made her laugh.

"You need to sleep, Blaine."

"I need you more than I need sleep."

"That's not true."

"It's very true."

She used her fingertips to close his eyes. "Sleep now. We'll have lots of time after the storm passes for other stuff."

"Don't wanna sleep," he said, but he kept his eyes closed.

She kissed him. "Shhhhh."

He whimpered, but still, his eyes remained closed.

Five minutes later, his breathing had shifted into sleep.

Tiffany smiled as she watched him, as captivated by him as she'd been the first time she ever saw him.

CHAPTER 16

*A*t the public safety building, Jordan was reading a book on the sofa in Mason's office while he gave yet another interview to one of the Providence news stations. He was far more interesting than the book. She was so proud of him and how he'd stayed cool even with constant requests for interviews from local and national news while juggling questions from colleagues and calls from Gansett citizens. He'd been going nonstop for hours.

She'd planned to stay at their place for the storm, but he'd arrived around five o'clock in his department SUV and insisted she pack up and come to the station with him, so he'd know she was safe while he focused on work. Her sister, Nikki, and grandmother, Evelyn, had sided with Mason and were relieved that she wasn't alone for the storm. They'd invited her to come to Eastward Look, but she was happy to be with Mason, even if they were "camping" in his office.

Mason had brought an air mattress from home that he blew up with air compressor from the garage where they kept the fire engines. He'd set it up on the floor for when she wanted to rest. The first trimester of her pregnancy had been rough. She was tired all the time and nauseated a good portion of every day, but still elated to be expecting her first child. The baby had come as a surprise to them, but it had been the best surprise of their lives, and they couldn't wait to meet their little person next spring.

In a few weeks, they'd be leaving the island to head to LA to film the next season of her reality show with her best friend, Gigi Gibson. Mason would take a leave of absence from the department for the time it took to film, and they'd come back long before the summer tourist season kicked in.

Sometimes still she couldn't believe the way it had worked out for them to be together despite jobs they loved on opposite coasts. Mason and Gigi's boyfriend, Cooper, would appear in the new season of the show that would focus on Jordan and Gigi shifting into long-term relationships and, in Jordan's case, starting a family.

As she watched Mason conduct an interview with CNN, she wondered if he was ready to be famous. They'd talked some about that, and he said he didn't care about that if he got to be with her. It amused her to think of him being stalked next summer by tourists who'd come to the island looking for the hot fire chief.

They couldn't have him. He was all hers.

When he finished the interview, he stood and stretched.

"My hero," Jordan said from her perch on the sofa.

"Stop."

"I won't stop. You're a very sexy fire chief all the time, but especially in crisis mode."

He took a seat next to her and reached for her hand. "You're making me blush."

Jordan laughed as she curled her fingers around his hand. "You don't blush."

"I do with you. All the time."

"When?"

"Right now."

She studied the face that had become as familiar to her as her own in recent months. "I see no sign of a blush."

"I'm blushing on the inside."

"Well, that's no fun."

Smiling, he leaned in to kiss her. "How's my baby mama feeling?"

"I'm fine and secretly glad you convinced me to come to work with you."

"I wouldn't have been able to think of anything but you alone in that cabin during the storm, so thank you for agreeing to come with me."

"Like you gave me a choice."

"The choice is always yours, my love, but I'm glad you made the right one."

She appreciated he said that, knowing what she'd been through with her ex-husband trying to control her. "You know I'd rather be with you than anywhere else without you."

"And that, right there, makes me the luckiest guy who ever lived."

Jordan leaned her head on his shoulder. "We're both lucky."

"I'm luckier than you are because you're way out of my league, but you love me anyway."

"Don't say that. It's not true."

"Jordan, sweetheart," he said with a laugh, "it's absolutely true."

"No."

"Yes."

"Have you seen you?"

"Have you seen *you?*"

"We'll have to agree to disagree on this topic," he said, stroking her hand and arm.

"What else do you have to do tonight?"

"More interviews for the eleven o'clock news, and then I guess we wait to see what happens with the storm."

"Do you have time to rest for a bit?"

"I suppose I do. Let me just check in with the others first."

He kissed her cheek and got up to leave the room.

She watched him go, admiring the way his navy uniform pants clung to his muscular legs and backside. She'd never had a thing for men in uniform until she met him after he saved her life. Now that uniform and the man who wore it were at the center of her life, and she couldn't be happier to have found him in this big, crazy world.

While he was checking in with his team, she used the bathroom attached to his office to change into pajama pants and a tank top and brush her teeth. When he returned to the office, she was waiting for him in the bed he'd made for them on the floor. If they had to camp out, he'd said, she was going to be comfortable.

He was always thinking of her first and foremost, which was such a welcome change from her ex-husband, who'd always thought of himself first and her a distant second. She'd put up with that crap far too long, and now that she had someone who had made her the most important part of his life, she would never let him go.

"Can you change into something more comfortable?" she asked him.

"I suppose so." Mason disappeared into the bathroom and came out wearing a T-shirt and sweats. He tossed his uniform over a chair, so it'd be handy if he needed it, and got into bed with her. "Fancy meeting you on an air mattress in my office," he said when she snuggled up to him.

"Have you ever slept with someone in your office before?"

"Not ever."

She ran her hand over his chest and down to cup his cock. "Oh, I get to take your office virginity."

"You're not taking anything in my office."

"Why not? You locked the door, right?"

"Yes, but—"

She pounced. Before he could finish his sentence, she was on top of him, kissing him and moving in a way she knew he couldn't resist. The moan that came from deep inside his chest had her struggling not to laugh as she used her body to let him know how this was going to go.

When he raised his hands to cup her breasts, she knew she had him, but she didn't let up. Rather, she doubled down, grinding against his rock-hard cock as she kissed him with unrelenting fervor.

And then he took over, wrapping his arms around her and rolling them so he was on top. He broke the kiss, his expression conveying a sort of stunned amusement that gave her great pleasure. "You little vixen."

"What did I do?" she asked, blinking innocently.

His low growl made her laugh when he bent his head to bite her neck.

"Don't leave marks, Chief. We wouldn't want anyone to know what you were doing in your office."

"I'm going to spank your ass and leave some marks."

"Oh," she said breathlessly, "*when?*"

Like someone had flipped a switch in him, he was all hands as he quickly removed her pajama pants and his sweats. He was inside her so quickly, she barely had a second to prepare before he was stretching her to the absolute limit the way he always did.

Jordan clawed at his back and wrapped her legs around him to keep him buried to the hilt.

"Fucking hell, Jord," he said on a gasp. "Let me move."

"Not yet," she said. "I just need a minute to catch up."

He raised himself up to look at her. "I didn't hurt you, did I?"

"Not at all."

"Are you going to let me move?"

"In a minute." She tightened her internal muscles around him. "Or two."

"I'm not going to last that long if you keep that up."

"What? This?"

He gasped. "Yes, that," he said through gritted teeth.

"Okay, you can move now," she said, dropping her legs.

He was like a man possessed as he hammered into her with unrestrained passion. But he was always careful not to put too much weight on her abdomen or to hurt her in any way. And he knew just where and how to touch her to give her the kind of pleasure she'd thought only happened in fairy tales before he showed her otherwise.

With him, she never had a problem having an orgasm. In fact, he often got two or three out of her when one had been a miracle in the past. She'd learned that being with the right man made all the difference, and this man... This man was absolutely perfect for her, which he proved again as he brought them both to silent, straining climaxes that had them shaking from the effort to stay quiet.

"Did you hear that popping sound?" she whispered when she'd caught her breath.

"What popping sound?"

"Your office cherry."

He shook with laughter. "Vixen. That's my story, and I'm sticking with it."

"I can live with that as long as I get to live with you."

"You've got me, baby. Forever and ever."

She tightened her arms around him. "That might not be long enough."

IN LOS ANGELES, Gigi Gibson anxiously watched the news about the storm bearing down on the island where the only other people she loved lived. Jordan, Nikki and Evelyn had been her family until Cooper James came storming into her life and changed everything. But oh, how she loved those ladies.

"They'll be fine," Coop said when he joined her on the sofa after a shower.

"How can you be so certain?"

"Gansett Islanders are tough. They know how to work together to get through anything that comes their way. Jared and Quinn were out all day helping wherever they could. They said everyone was doing what needed to be done. That's how they are there. Everyone pitches in."

"I saw that myself when I was there, but a storm like this... I can't bear to think of that beautiful place in shambles."

Cooper put his arm around her. "If that happens, they'll rebuild."

She rested her head on his chest, unable to look away from the storm coverage.

"Maybe we should watch something else," he said.

"I need to watch this, so I know what's happening."

"Have you talked to Jordan?"

"About an hour ago. She's camped out with Mason at the public safety building. He didn't want her to be alone at his place during the storm."

"I'm surprised she didn't go to Nikki's."

"She said she wanted to be home in case Mason got to take a break."

"I'm glad she's with him at the station and not alone."

"Me, too. Do you think Eastward Look will be okay?"

"I'm sure it will be fine. That place has withstood all kinds of storms for decades, and remember, Riley and Nikki met when he replaced the roof, so you know that's solid."

"I guess so. I just want it to be over and to hear that everyone is okay."

"It'll be over soon."

"Can't happen fast enough for me."

CHAPTER 17

*P*iper walked Jack to the second floor of the Sand & Surf just after midnight and handed him a key to one of the empty rooms on the street side. "We're leaving the ocean-view rooms empty during the storm," she told him.

"Probably for the best."

As they stood in the hallway, the hotel creaked and moaned as the storm got closer.

She glanced up at him, feeling incredibly anxious. "That doesn't sound good."

"I'm sure it'll be fine."

Piper wrapped her arms around her middle, suddenly as anxious as she'd been in a long time. The feeling reminded her of the day she'd been attacked, making her shudder.

"Are you all right?"

"Just scared."

"Why don't you sleep here with me, so neither of us has to be alone during the storm?"

"I... uh..."

"Just sleep." He flashed that lethal grin as he tucked a strand of hair behind her ear. "I promise you'll be safe with me."

"Will I, though?"

His brows furrowed. "You're not afraid of me, are you?"

"Not physically."

"How, then?"

"My heart's been through a lot. Not as much as yours, but it's been a lot for me." She forced herself to look up at him, to make eye contact. "I'm not sure I'm prepared for you."

"I didn't think I was prepared for you either, until I was gone for a couple of weeks and thought about you every day."

The confession left her breathless. "Every day, huh? That's a lot."

"Yeah, it was, and now that you're standing right in front of me, so sweet and beautiful, I can't seem to think of *anything* but you."

"Oh. Well…"

"Yeah, so, I was hoping you might hang out with me during the storm since there's no reason for you to be scared or alone when I'm right here."

He was asking her to trust him, to put her faith in him, to take a chance on him. Was she ready for that? Probably not, but he was standing right there, strong and sexy and obviously as interested in her as she was in him.

The building took that moment to let out a particularly loud groan that had her stepping forward into Jack's waiting embrace. As his chin rested on top of her head, she couldn't help but note how perfectly they fit together, like two pieces of a puzzle that had somehow managed to find each other in the great jigsaw of life.

As soon as that thought registered, Piper nearly laughed at the direction her thoughts had taken. He'd offered her comfort during a storm, not a white picket fence and happily ever after.

"You want to come in?" he asked softly as he ran his hand over her back in a soothing caress that made her knees weak.

"I'd like to get changed first."

"You know where to find me," he said, seeming reluctant to release her.

"Yes, I do."

"I'll be right here waiting for you. Will you come back?"

She held his gaze for a moment so charged, she wondered if he felt the powerful attraction simmering between them as keenly as she did. "Yes, I'll be back."

"DAN IS STEALING FROM THE BANK," Grant said. "That's the only possible explanation for how he's beating all of us so badly."

"Is that what you think?" Dan sipped from a glass of whiskey as he surveyed his kingdom on the Monopoly board. "I hate to break it to you, chump, but what you see before you is raw skill and financial wizardry."

"More like chicanery," Grant muttered.

"Oh my *God*," his wife, Kara, said on a moan. "Will you listen to him? How does he come up with such bullshit?"

"I only speak the truth, my love."

"Whatever," she said, throwing her shoe token at him.

It hit him square in the forehead, which set off a wave of hysterical laughter among Grant, Stephanie and Kara.

Dan frowned as he rubbed the red spot on his forehead. "That hurt."

"Boo-hoo, ya big baby," Grant said.

"This is the worst hurricane party I've ever been to," Dan said indignantly.

"This is the only hurricane party you've ever been to," Grant reminded him.

"Well, they're overrated if this is how it goes."

"I quit," Stephanie said, standing to stretch and peek out the window at the storm.

Grant came over to put his hands on her shoulders to knead out the tension that gathered there any time she was worried or upset.

"Are you sure this place won't fall down around us?" she asked for the umpteenth time that day.

"I'm sure. We're well protected this far inland. Nothing to worry about, except for maybe you took down too many walls."

"I only took down two."

"We'll find out if that was two too many." He kissed her neck. "Just kidding. We had the house surveyed before we bought it, don't forget. They said it was solid as a rock." Despite his reassurances, her shoulders were still tight with knots. "Do you want to try to get some rest?"

"I guess."

He didn't think either of them would sleep much with the wind making the house shake and the rain coming down so hard it sounded like a freight train coming for them.

"We're going to turn in," Grant said to Dan and Kara. "Do you guys have everything you need?"

"We do," Kara said. "Thanks again for taking us in for the storm."

"Happy to have you," Grant said. "Him? Not so much."

"Hey!" Dan said, sputtering. "You wouldn't even know her if it wasn't for me!"

"And you would've blown it with her if it wasn't for me."

"That's hurtful but true."

"Don't leave me alone with him," Kara said pleadingly. "We've got enough problems with wind without the windbag making it worse."

"You love me," Dan said, grinning at his wife.

"On that note, see you in the morning," Grant said.

"Night, guys," Stephanie added.

"Hope you can get some sleep," Kara called after her.

"You, too."

When Grant slid into bed with Stephanie a few minutes later, he reached for her and made her comfortable in his embrace, picking up where he'd left off with the massage of her tight shoulders. "I don't like all these knots in my love's shoulders."

"Can't help it. This shit is scary."

"I know, but we'll be fine."

"I keep thinking about Joe and Seamus out to sea, and my stomach starts to ache."

"They're fine, too. Janey said he called her a little while ago, and everything is fine. They're east of the storm now and riding it out."

"Still. They're *out to sea*. In a *hurricane*."

"If they hadn't gone, we might never have seen Deacon again."

"I keep thinking of him and Julia, too, and all our family and friends, and my dad and Sarah in Italy while this is happening. He's frantic with worry for us. I hate that for him, for both of them, when they've so looked forward to the trip."

"I know, but hopefully by tomorrow, we'll be able to reassure him and Sarah and Janey and everyone else who's worried about us that we're just fine."

"I really hope so."

"HAVE YOU EVER HAD HURRICANE SEX?" Dan asked Kara when they were alone in the living room with only the candles Stephanie had lit earlier for atmosphere.

"What if I say I have?"

His brows lifted almost to his hairline. "Who is he, and how do I have him killed?"

Kara laughed helplessly. She did that a lot with him. It was the thing she loved best about their relationship. Well, that and the great sex and the tender love and his total devotion to her. That last one had annoyed the hell out of her at first. Now she wondered how she'd ever lived without him and his kind of devotion for the first thirty years of her life.

"I'm serious. Who is he, and more important, *where* is he?"

"You don't know him, and I have no idea where he is."

"But you shagged him during a hurricane?"

"I did."

"This is truly shocking news. How old were you?"

"Eighteen."

"Where did your parents think you were when you were shagging some limp dick during a hurricane?"

"At my grandmother's. I told a lot of lies in those days."

"So you're a liar *and* a charlatan. I want my money back on this marriage."

"You do not, and PS, his dick wasn't limp."

"This is an outrage!"

Again, she laughed so hard, she made no sound. Had she ever had more fun than she did pushing his buttons? Nope. Never. "Does this mean you don't want hurricane sex?"

"When did I say that?"

"You only seemed interested when you thought it was my first go-round with hurricane sex."

"I'm always interested, as you well know."

"But you asked for a refund. How am I supposed to know you're still interested?"

"The refund has been canceled."

"I see how it is."

Smiling, he said, "I love you, Kara Torrington."

"For some strange reason, I love you, too, Dan Torrington."

"Nice how that works out, huh?"

"Very, very nice."

"Nicest thing ever," he said, kissing her. "Why don't you take me to bed and have your wicked way with me?"

"We can't do that here."

"Uh, yes, we can."

"They'll hear us."

"We don't hear them, and PS, if I'd known that hurricane sex was off the table if we came to stay with them, we'd still be at the cabin. And PPS, this is further proof that we need to buy a real house here."

"PPPS, stop with the PS."

"I've got a lot of postscripts to share with you."

A particularly strong gust of wind had the house shaking and groaning, the rain beating against the roof sounding like a million marching feet.

Dan put his arm around her. "Let's go to bed."

"You heard that, right?"

"Heard what?"

Kara elbowed his ribs as they blew out the candles and walked toward the bedroom and bathroom on the opposite side of the house from Grant and Stephanie's room. She elbowed him so often, it was a wonder he didn't have a permanent bruise on his ribs. Not that he would mind if he did. Being with her, teasing her, was worth the bruises.

Her phone chimed with a text. "It's my mother again, wanting to make sure we're okay."

"Tell her your big, strong, heroic husband is taking very good care of you."

"I will not tell her that."

"You want me to?"

"That's okay." She typed her reply and then plugged the phone in to charge on the bedside table. "Did you charge your phone and laptop?"

"Yes, ma'am. Grant said if we lose power, we can go to Big Mac and Linda's. They've got a generator."

"I'm sure they've also got a full house. They don't need more people."

"We're not just people. We're family."

Kara rolled her eyes at him. "Last time I checked, your name wasn't McCarthy."

"I'm a McCarthy by osmosis."

"Meaning you've ingratiated yourself to the point that you consider them family, but they've probably had more than enough of you."

"Baby, they love me. What's not to love?"

"Well, there's your propensity to speak of yourself in the third person. There's your enormous ego. There's your—"

"Enormous penis?"

Kara lost it laughing. She laughed so hard, she had tears in her eyes. "I can't even with you. I just cannot."

"That's what you were going to say, right?"

"Stuff it, Torrington."

"*Oh*, I'd *love* to stuff my enormous penis in your—"

She kissed him and pinched his lips closed. "Shut it."

"If I shut it," he said, wiggling out of her grip, "then I can't lick you in that place you like so much."

"I swear to God, if you don't shut up, I'm gonna..."

"What?" he asked, his eyes glittering.

"Forget it. You'd like that too much."

He walked her backward toward the guest room bed and came down on top of her, mindful not to put too much weight on their baby. "Now you have to tell me."

"Nope."

"Yup."

She pulled him into an openmouthed, tongue-twisting kiss that was one of the few truly effective ways of shutting him up.

His hand landed on her face as he kissed her with hours' worth of desire. As he pulled back, he kept his lips moving lightly over hers. "Before you made me fall in love with you, I thought the most exciting thing in the world was arguing a case I knew I would win before I even arrived at the courthouse."

"*I* made *you* fall in love with *me*? Are you rewriting history now, Counselor?"

He shook his head. "Nope. You gave me no choice but to fall in love with you. But as I was saying, arguing a slam-dunk case has nothing on hanging out with my gorgeous wife."

"Just when you're on the verge of becoming completely insufferable, you go and say something sweet. And PS, you made me fall in love with you by being a relentless pain in my ass."

He pinched her ass for emphasis. "I'm so glad you fell in love with me. I'm not sure what I would've done with myself if you hadn't."

"I'm sure your insufferableness would've gotten even worse without me around to keep you humble."

"No doubt." He caressed her face and gazed into her eyes. "Now, about that hurricane sex you promised me."

"When did I promise you that?"

"Earlier. I heard you."

"Can you prove that?"

"I'll have the stenographer read back the transcript."

Again, she rolled her eyes.

"It would be easier to have the sex than to argue about it."

"Easier for whom?"

"Oh, I love when you're all proper with me."

"You love when I breathe."

"That's true. I need to keep you breathing. So, about the sex you promised me…"

"Once again, you're wearing me down in a desperate effort to make you stop talking."

"That's what I do best. Made a whole career out of it, in fact."

"It's a good thing you married me, because anyone else would've stabbed you in the eye by now."

"Aw, baby, I'm so lucky you love me so much."

Kara pulled him into a kiss, and as the wind howled and the rain beat down on the roof, he showed her that hurricane sex with him was much different from what she'd experienced in the past. She had to bite her lip to keep from screaming more than once, especially when he buried his face between her legs and brought her to a quick, sharp orgasm with his tongue and fingers.

Lord have mercy, the man was good at that, not that she could ever, ever, *ever* tell him so.

He moved up, dropping kisses on her abdomen and breasts as he slid into her in one deep stroke that had her gasping from the impact. "Tell me the truth… Was it this good with Limp Dick?"

"Shut up, Dan."

"Tell me, Kara." He moved in her as his lips slid over her neck, electrifying her from head to toe with sensation. "This is way better, right?"

"No comment."

He stopped moving and withdrew from her so suddenly that she was left gasping. "What the hell?"

"Is it better than Limp Dick or not?"

"Honestly, Dan, you've lost your ever-loving mind."

"I need to know."

"Yes, it's better! Everything is better with you than it's ever been with anyone. You already know that, so why are you making such a big deal out of this?"

Grinning, he entered her again, holding still for a long time, so long that she started to squirm from wanting him to move. "Just making sure."

"You're so ridiculous."

"This is what you do to me. You make me into a lunatic."

"You were a lunatic long before you ever met me."

"You took me to a whole other level."

"Is that a compliment?"

"Of course it is."

"Now how about you finish what you started while we're both still young?"

"Was that a complaint?"

"Absolutely not."

"I didn't think so." He reached beneath her and cupped her ass to hold her tighter against him as he picked up the pace and had them both straining to reach the peak at the same instant. "Ah… Yes, Kara. *Yes.*"

As he came down on top of her, she kept her arms around him, making soothing circles on his back. A minute or two later, he rolled to his side, bringing her with him, their legs intertwined. "Best hurricane sex ever."

"It's right up there in the top ten."

His laughter rocked them both. "You love to drive me crazy."

"It's so easy."

"I love you anyway."

"Thank goodness for that."

CHAPTER 18

*L*ong after the rest of his family was asleep, Mac was still awake, thinking and rethinking everything they'd done to prepare for the storm and hoping it had been enough. Would the plywood covering the massive plate-glass windows at the Wayfarer hold? Would his parents' home withstand the brutal wind and rain, exposed as it was at the top of the hill above North Harbor?

And were Joe, Seamus and their crews safe at sea on the ferries?

He'd spoken to Janey again before bed, and she was nearly delirious with worry, but who could blame her? Even knowing Joe and Seamus were far to the east of the storm, they were still a long way from home during a huge storm targeting an island where everyone else she loved was stranded.

If they lost power, how long would it be out? Did they have enough gas for the generators? Had he done everything he could to care for his family, home and businesses? What if there was an emergency on the island that they couldn't handle with the resources available?

This storm was reminiscent of Tropical Storm Hailey, which their daughter was named for. She'd arrived in the middle of the storm when the island's only doctor had been on the mainland. Thank God David Lawrence had been home at the time. He'd saved Hailey's life when she was born blue and unresponsive.

Mac shuddered as he thought of that night and the sheer terror of realizing Maddie was in labor on a remote island in the middle of a storm. Thank God she wasn't pregnant for this one, but plenty of other people they cared about were—Stephanie, Abby, Grace, Tiffany, Kara, Daisy…

His stomach churned as he pondered the million-and-one things that could go wrong during a storm of this magnitude and whether their tiny island community would be able to cope with the fallout.

"Why are you awake?" Maddie asked. "Did something happen?"

"Nothing other than a hurricane."

"Is everything all right?"

"So far." Mac turned toward her and put his arm around her waist. "Go back to sleep, love." She'd been so tired since the twins arrived. He wanted her to sleep while she could.

"It sounds pretty bad." Maddie burrowed into his chest. "I'm scared."

He tightened his grip on her shoulder. "Don't be. Nothing to worry about."

"How do you know that?"

"I just do." He told her what she needed to hear even though his anxiety was through the roof as the storm got louder and closer.

"I keep thinking about Joe and Seamus and the others out at sea during this…"

"They're fine. They're well east of it by now."

"I'm sick just thinking about what they must've gone through."

"They did the right thing getting the boats out of here."

"Tell that to Janey and Carolina. They're both senseless with worry. I was texting with them earlier. I didn't even know what to say."

"Everyone is doing what they can to minimize the damage." The day before yesterday, he'd helped Kara take her launches out of the water and stash them inland, where they'd be protected. They'd pulled his father's boats out of the water. They'd boarded up everything they could. Food, water and fuel had been stockpiled some time ago, in anticipation of a hurricane or blizzard.

"Then why are you buzzing with anxiety?"

"Am I?"

"You are."

Most of the time, he loved that she knew him better than anyone. At times like this, however, he wished he could better hide his worries from her. "I'm thinking about whether we did everything we could to protect lives, homes, businesses."

"Mac, you did everything and then some. Because of you, the island had enough plywood for everyone who needed it. You installed all those whole-home generators for most of our loved ones. You ordered an entire fuel truck for storm prep. What more could you have done?"

"I don't know what I don't know."

She placed her hand on his face and urged him to look at her. "You did more than anyone to make sure the island was as ready as it could be. You've worked twenty hours a day for a week to get us ready."

"I just hope it was enough."

"It was more than enough. The rest is out of your hands. Believe it or not, there're some things that even the mighty Mac McCarthy can't control."

"I don't like that."

"Believe me," she said on a laugh, "I know." Maddie pushed herself up on an elbow. "Do I need to bring out the big guns to relax you?"

"What would these big guns you speak of entail?"

"It would go something like this…" She leaned over to kiss the center of his bare chest and then moved down to trace the outline of his ab muscles with her tongue, heading down until she was nuzzling his hard cock through the boxer briefs he'd worn to bed. "Are you relaxing yet?"

"Does that feel relaxed?" he asked.

"Not at all, so let's see what we can do about that, shall we?"

"Maddie… You don't have to…" All the air left his body in one exhale as she bared his cock and took it into her mouth.

"What were you saying?" she asked.

"Not a thing."

Chuckling, she took him in again, adding some tongue this time, which brought him to the brink of release in a matter of seconds. After a complicated pregnancy and the arrival of the twins, they'd barely had time for a kiss every day, let alone anything like… *Oh damn.* "Maddie, honey… Wait."

"Don't wanna wait."

The combination of lips, tongue and suction, coupled with her hand tight around the base, was all it took to take him right over the edge. "Holy *shit*," he said when he could speak again.

"Do you feel better?"

"Hell yes, I feel better."

"I want you relaxed so you can get some sleep."

"Mission accomplished. How about I return the favor?"

"You don't have to."

"What if I want to?"

"Oh, um, well… If you must."

Grinning, Mac said, "Oh, I must. I absolutely must." He moved so he was kneeling between her legs and ran his hands up over her calves and thighs, taking her nightgown up as he went. "Are you still sore, love?"

"Not like I was."

"My baby mama is such a Wonder Woman."

"Right," she said with a laugh. "That's me. Wonder Woman."

"You're my Wonder Woman."

"I'm one big stretch mark, and I'll never get my waist back and—"

He stopped her rant when he ran his tongue over her most sensitive flesh. "Don't talk shit about my wife. You know I don't like that." When he had her attention, he sucked on her clit, running his tongue back and forth as he reached up to pinch her nipple.

She gasped and raised her hips, silently asking for more, which he was happy to give her.

He pushed two fingers into her, moving carefully so he wouldn't hurt her in any way. "Okay?"

"Mmm, yes, very okay. Don't stop."

"Not gonna ever stop." He teased her and stroked her until she was thrashing and arching and moaning almost louder than the storm. And then she broke, her internal muscles clutching his fingers so tightly that his cock was hard again like he hadn't just come.

"Maaaaaaac."

Best sound ever was his name uttered on her long gasp of pleasure.

He had to give her credit. He was no longer thinking or worrying about the storm. "Do you think we could do more?" Her six-week appointment was that coming week, so they were close enough as far as he was concerned. But it wasn't up to him.

"We can try."

Mac moved up to align their bodies. "Tell me to stop if it hurts."

"You'll be the first to know."

As he started to push into her, she froze. "Mac! Condom."

"I'm snipped."

"You're not getting that thing anywhere near the promised land ungloved until we're sure it took." His appointment to test whether the vasectomy worked was in two weeks.

"That *thing* is offended."

146

"Too bad. Glove up or no nookie."

Groaning, he pulled back and went into the bathroom to get a condom, rolling it on as he returned to the bed. "After everything we went through getting snipped, my boys and I would like to formally register our objection to the condom."

"So noted." She held out her arms to him. "Go slow, okay?"

"Tell me if anything hurts. I don't ever want to hurt you."

"I think it'll be okay."

"Will Victoria be able to tell that we jumped the gun?" he asked of her midwife.

"No," she said, laughing. "It's not like something grows back."

"Ew, don't be gross."

"I'm not!"

"You know I have a weak stomach when it comes to girl things."

"Are you going to talk or act?"

"I'm definitely going to act." He went as slowly as he possibly could as he began to enter her in the tiniest possible increments. "Okay?"

"Uh-huh."

Mac could tell she was tenser than usual, probably anticipating pain that hopefully wouldn't materialize. "There're no words to tell you how much I've missed this." It'd been months since they were able to do anything.

"Me, too."

"This might be quick."

"Even though I took the edge off?"

"Even though. As much as I love that, there's nothing better than this."

"No, there isn't." She held him close as he moved slowly and carefully. "Still okay down there?"

"Still okay. If you want to go a little faster, I think it's fine."

Her words sparked a fire in him, but he was still cautious, even as he went up on his arms and picked up the pace a bit. "Touch yourself," he whispered. "I want to watch you come."

She bit her lip and reached down to caress herself as he watched and tried to wait for her to get there before she shredded his self-control. A few minutes later, he felt the telltale signs of her impending release and held off until the last possible second so they could do it together.

"So hot," he whispered in her ear as they came down from the incredible high.

"Yes, you are."

"You're the hottest mommy in the whole wide world, and I love you endlessly."

"I love you infinitely."

"I love you unendingly," he said.

"Limitlessly."

"Unceasingly."

"Perpetually."

"I can't think of another way to say forever."

She squeezed him tightly, and he finally relaxed for the first time in days. If they had each other, everything would be fine.

He'd make sure of it.

PIPER WENT UP to the third floor to shower and change into pajamas. She brushed her hair and teeth and stared at her reflection in the mirror as she picked through everything that'd happened since she stepped onto the ferry to return to Gansett. After weeks of thinking about Jack and wondering if anything would come of their subtle flirtation, he'd come storming back into her life, providing information about himself that had sent her spinning into an online rabbit hole.

What she'd learned about his life had only made her interested in knowing more. But it had also made her wary of wading into the emotional minefield of his tremendous loss. Was she equipped to handle everything that came along with possibly dating a widower? Her stomach fluttered with nerves that had nothing to do with the huge storm and everything to do with him.

She really liked him.

A lot.

Her phone chimed with a text from Jack. *Are you coming back? I'm scared of the storm.*

Smiling, she responded. *Yep, coming down now.*

Yay.

How did he do that with just a few short texts? How did he get her so flustered and excited to spend more time with him? She needed to go slowly with this guy, for his sake as well as her own, and as she went downstairs to spend the night with him, she wondered how that counted as going slowly.

"Special circumstances," she muttered as she landed on the second floor, where the howl of the wind was even louder than it was upstairs. "This wouldn't be happening without the storm."

You just keep telling yourself that, girl.

She wanted her inner voice to shut up and leave her alone to enjoy whatever might happen with the hot guy who'd captured her attention months ago—and held her attention ever since, even when he was off-island for weeks at a time.

As she walked along the corridor toward his room, the door opened, and he stepped out, smiling when he saw her coming.

All thoughts of not being ready or worried about emotional baggage were blown to bits when she saw him standing, shirtless, in the doorway, smiling warmly at her, seeming glad that she'd come back. She'd never experienced the concept of "walking on air" until that very moment.

And then he held out a hand to her, and she was sunk.

Whatever this was with him, she wanted it. She wanted *him*. The things she'd learned about him earlier only made him more attractive to her, even as her heart ached for him and what he'd lost.

"You had me worried for a second there," he said as he led her into the room, closing the door and locking it behind them.

"How come?"

"I thought you changed your mind about coming back."

"I didn't."

"I wouldn't blame you if you had. This… Me… It's a lot to take on."

She tipped her head as she looked up at him, trying not to be overly dazzled by his gorgeous face. "Am I taking you on by coming back?"

"I don't know." He looked so cute and maybe a bit vulnerable as he pondered the question. "Are you?"

She'd been so caught up in the way he was looking at her that she hadn't realized he was still holding her hand until he gave it a squeeze.

Piper swallowed, hoping to rid herself of the huge lump in her throat. "I think I'd like to."

"But you're not a hundred percent sure, right?"

"I'm about ninety-nine percent sure."

"What's holding back that last one percent?"

"You… You've been through a lot, and this would be…"

"The first time I've been taken on since then," he said, in keeping with his earlier comment.

"Yes."

"If you're wondering if I'm ready, like really and truly ready, it's hard to say that for certain. I think I am. I want to be. But the grief is always part of my picture now, and it complicates everything."

"I understand that as much as I can without having experienced a loss like yours."

"I don't mean to make it part of everything, but it is whether I want it to be or not."

"You don't have to explain yourself to me, Jack."

"But I do… You're not only taking me on, but you're taking on my late wife and my grief and my ongoing journey to figure out my life without her. It's a lot to ask of anyone."

"You're not asking it of me. I'm giving it willingly." As she said those words, she was aware that she'd crossed some sort of threshold, going from uncertain to committed in a matter of minutes.

He released her hand and placed both his hands on her hips, guiding her closer to him as he lowered his head until his lips were poised just above hers, so close, she could nearly taste him. "Tell me this is what you want."

"It is. You are."

His lips found hers in a kiss that went from slow to fire in a flash of heat that nearly knocked her off her feet. Holy *shit*, the man could *kiss*. Being on the receiving end of years of pent-up desire pouring forth into one all-consuming kiss for the ages was something she wouldn't soon forget.

Piper had never been kissed so thoroughly, as if she was the only oxygen available in all the world, and he was desperate for what only she could give him. Kissing in the past had been pleasant and arousing. It had never been so intense.

The sound of something crashing outside had them pulling apart to stare at each other, him looking as stunned as she felt.

He rubbed a hand over his mouth. "We, uh… What was that noise outside?"

Piper forced her legs to move toward the window. She raised the blinds to look down at the street. "Something fell off one of the buildings and smashed in the street. I can't tell what it is from up here."

Jack came up behind her, put his arms around her waist and kissed her neck, making her legs and every other part of her tremble with a rush of desire that left her breathless. "You have no idea how long I've wanted to hold you and kiss you and talk to you like we did today. Or I guess it was yesterday now."

"Time flies when you're having fun during a hurricane."

"It certainly does."

Piper nudged him back so she could turn to face him.

He drew her in close, nuzzling her nose before giving her a sweet, gentle kiss.

"Is this difficult for you?" she asked softly.

"Not as difficult as it would be if it wasn't you here with me."

As far as compliments went, that was a pretty good one.

"I've had some time these last few weeks," he said, "to bring myself around to being ready for this, for you."

"Is that what you were doing over there on the mainland?"

"When I wasn't dealing with work, I was thinking of you and hoping you might be thinking of me."

"I had myself convinced I wasn't on your radar when I didn't hear much from you while you were gone."

"You were very much on my radar, but I wanted the chance to talk to you in person about the stuff I shared earlier. I wanted you to know..." He shrugged and then sighed. "I was so glad to see you on the ferry."

"I was glad to see you, too."

He kissed her again.

Piper curled her arms around his neck to keep him from getting away as he leaned into her, pressing his erection against her abdomen.

"When I invited you to stay with me," he said, "I meant to keep you company during the storm. I don't want you to think I'm expecting anything."

She rubbed against him suggestively. "You're not expecting *anything?*"

He gasped, his fingertips digging into her hips. "I, uh... It's been a while for me, Piper. It might be over before it begins."

"I don't know if you've heard," she whispered, "but it's a regenerating organ."

A choked laugh escaped his lips. "I actually knew that."

"So then there's nothing to worry about."

CHAPTER 19

*J*aney Cantrell had worn a path in the carpet in her living
room from pacing for hours as she kept one eye on the
Weather Channel and the other glued to her phone, hoping
for updates from home. Since it was after midnight, the texts from family
and friends had tapered off, and the last time she heard from Joe, he'd told
her about rescuing Deacon Taylor and how they were now far enough
east of the storm that the seas had calmed considerably.

That had been a huge relief.

Her mom had reported that the kids went to bed without a fuss. They
were worn out from playing with Kyle and Jackson, who'd been "great"
with Janey's little ones, according to Linda. Everything was fine, but still
she paced, stopping only to watch a live shot from the Gansett bluffs,
where the wind was so strong, the reporter could barely remain standing.

Janey felt nauseated as she watched the wind and rain batter her
beloved home, the place where her two children, parents, four brothers,
their wives, her mother-in-law, nieces, nephews and so many other loved
ones were taking shelter from the massive storm.

It was unbearable to be so far from them at a time like this. She
wanted to get in her car and start driving toward them, but that would
mean missing classes, labs, exams. If she walked away from school again,
she wouldn't come back. With one semester to go until she graduated,
walking away wasn't an option.

So she stayed and she paced and she worried and she drank wine.

A lot of wine.

When the phone rang, she startled and nearly spilled the wine all over herself. She fumbled with the phone and took the call from Joe.

"Hi."

"Hey, hon." He sounded as tired as she felt. "How's it going?"

"Never been better. You?"

He laughed. "I'm looking at the moonlight reflecting on calm seas."

"That must be a relief."

"It's much better than it was."

"Will you get to sleep?"

"I can't. I'm the only licensed captain on board, so I have to stay at the helm. But the guys are keeping an eye out while I catnap."

"I'm glad you're not alone out there."

"Me, too. It's been good to have them along. I couldn't have saved Deacon on my own, that's for sure."

"Thank God you spotted him."

"No kidding. That was a lucky break. I thought I was seeing things for a minute there."

"Julia and his family must be so relieved."

"They are. What're you hearing from our family?"

She updated him on the report on the kids from her mother. "I'm sure they're having a great time with the older kids."

"They were before the storm. Jackson and Kyle are so good with them. Very patient. PJ follows them around like Burpee the dog does."

"That's so cute. I wish I could see that."

"Soon enough, my love. Everything will be back to normal."

"Not soon enough for me. I miss home and everyone, and this storm is so scary."

"I know it's pointless to tell you not to worry, so I won't, but we're all fine, and the kids are safe with your parents. My mom is there, doing what she can. Mac is right down the road if they need anything, and the others are also nearby. They're in the best possible hands if they can't be with us."

"And whose hands are you in?"

"The god of the sea is always with me."

Only he could make her laugh when she was as tightly wound as she'd ever been. "Leave it to you, Joseph."

"What?"

"To make me laugh when nothing about this situation is funny."

"Go try to get some sleep. You don't want to fall behind this early in the semester."

"I can't even think about school right now."

"You have to think about it. The sooner you finish, the sooner we're back where we belong."

"I can't wait to be back where we belong. I just hope the island is still standing after this storm."

"It's going to take a lot more than a little old storm to break Gansett. You know that. No matter what happens, we'll fix it and get on with it."

"And then you and my kids will come home to me, right?"

"As soon as we possibly can."

AT THE ISLAND'S only medical clinic, Victoria Stevens, nurse practitioner/midwife, was locked in a fierce Yahtzee game with Dr. David Lawrence and his wife, Daisy. They'd spent hours glued to the TV news coverage of the storm and had learned the storm had been upgraded to a Category 3, packing nearly one-hundred-twenty-mile-per-hour winds and a ten-foot storm surge that threatened Gansett's pristine coastline.

An hour earlier, the clinic had lost power, and rather than deploy the full-facility generator, they'd chosen to use a portable generator only for the refrigerator where they kept perishable medications. Since they had no idea how long they'd be without power, they were keeping the main generator available for after the storm.

"He cheats," Victoria said bluntly as candles flickered. "That's the only possible explanation for how he rolls exactly what he needs every time."

"It's pure skill, my friend," David said smugly after he notched his third straight win.

"Cheater."

"I wouldn't even know how to cheat at Yahtzee. The dice are what they are."

"And why is it called Yahtzee, anyway?" Victoria muttered as she tossed her pencil on the table in defeat. "Such a dumb game."

Daisy giggled at their banter. "My husband doesn't cheat."

"Not anymore, that is," David said dryly.

The two women laughed at the grimace he made.

"We don't joke about that," Daisy reminded him.

"Sorry, dear."

"Those days are long behind you now."

He took her hand and kissed her palm. "They certainly are."

Everyone knew that he'd once cheated on island golden girl Janey McCarthy when they were engaged, and he'd been stricken with lymphoma. Life had moved on for all of them. Janey was happily married to Joe Cantrell. David was in remission and married the love of his life, but the journey from then to now had been difficult and fraught.

"If you two are getting romantical, I'm outta here," Victoria said, bitter to be riding out the storm without her own love, Shannon O'Grady, to snuggle with. He'd decided to go to sea with his cousin, Seamus, over her strenuous objections. She'd been overruled and would be sleeping alone tonight.

"We'll try to control ourselves," David said.

"Do that." Victoria checked her phone, hoping for something from Shannon, but she hadn't heard anything for a couple of hours. Hopefully, he was getting some sleep, which was what she ought to be doing, too. Who knew what would be needed from them tomorrow after the storm hit the island?

"No word from Shannon?" David asked.

"Not for a while, but I'm sure they're fine. They were well to the east of the storm the last time we talked."

She was far more worried about whether the wedding they'd planned for the following weekend would be able to go forward. They were getting married at Seamus and Carolina's, but that would depend on whether they had power and water and everything else they needed— including Shannon's family, coming from Ireland—to go forth.

There were so many unknowns at this point that she could drive herself crazy worrying about whether it would happen or if his family could even get to the island. Who knew what they'd be left with after Ethel ran roughshod over the place?

"Are you thinking about the wedding?" Daisy asked.

"I'm trying not to because I know there're much bigger things to be worried about." Such as her future groom at sea on a ferry during a hurricane. Not to mention the potential for power outages, massive damage and possible loss of life.

Daisy put her hand on Victoria's arm. "It's perfectly understandable to be concerned about something you've been looking forward to."

"It makes me feel like a selfish cow to be concerned about a wedding at a time like this."

The clinic's windows were rattling louder by the hour as the storm got closer. She hoped they would hold when the worst of it hit overnight.

"You're not a selfish cow, Vic," David said. "Anyone who knows you would say you're anything but."

"You have to say that. You're my maid of dishonor."

David frowned. "I thought we'd agreed on best man."

"I like maid of dishonor better."

"You would."

He was her best friend in the world, and there was no one else she would've asked to stand up for her when she married Shannon, but oh, how she loved to poke at him. They had a brother-and-sister relationship they both enjoyed, and she adored Daisy, who was a bridesmaid.

Shannon's parents and aunt were due to come for the wedding, and she'd been fielding texts for days about whether they ought to cancel their plans. Because she knew how badly Shannon wanted them there for his big day, she'd pleaded with them to hold off on making any decisions until after the storm passed and they had a chance to assess the damage.

Getting married was stressful enough without a major hurricane disrupting everything. Again, she tried to calm her racing mind and focus on the much bigger concerns facing the island and community than whether Victoria Stevens's wedding would go off as scheduled.

"I'm going to turn in," she said to David and Daisy. "Let me know if you need me."

"Sleep well," Daisy said.

"You, too."

They'd decided to stay at the clinic in case they were needed during the storm, but so far, things had been quiet. She was thankful for that, but with nothing to keep her busy, she had too much time to fret about wedding disasters and to worry about Shannon out to sea with Seamus.

Her stomach was a churning mess as she went to lie down in one of the exam rooms. David and Daisy were sleeping on the pull-out sofa in his office. Before she tried to power down her overactive mind, she sent a text to Shannon. *Are you awake?*

He responded by calling her.

"Hey," she said.

"Hi, love. How're you holding up?"

The delightful notes of his Irish accent put her at ease, as always. "Better now. How about you?"

"I'm missing you."

"For the record, I hate hurricanes."

"Me, too. Anything that takes me away from my Vic is to be despised."

There'd been a time, not that long ago, when she'd wondered if they had any chance of a future together with the ghost of his murdered girl-friend hanging over him. Victoria had been forced to almost leave him to get him to commit fully to her, and since then, he'd been all in with a level of devotion she could've only dreamed about before him.

"Are you all right?" he asked after a long silence.

"Just thinking about you and us and everything and hoping we get to have our big day next weekend."

"If, for whatever reason, it doesn't happen then, it *will* happen. I promise."

"I know." She wanted to wail at the possibility of it not happening as planned, because she knew how important it was to him to have his family there. It'd been a massive operation to get them all scheduled to come, and she couldn't conceive of having to cancel or postpone their plans.

"You don't sound convinced."

"I'm trying not to make a massive, threatening storm all about me."

"Of course it's about you, love. You're the bride."

"It's not about me, Shannon. It's about getting the island and the community through this. Our wedding is an afterthought compared to that."

"It's not an afterthought for us, and you're the least selfish person I've ever met. Don't be hard on yourself for being disappointed by the possi-bility of our wedding getting messed up."

"I'll try not to be."

"That's my girl."

"Thank you for always trying to make me feel better."

"That's what I'm here for."

"I need you to get back here safely."

"We will. The worst is behind us. Now we're just floating until the storm goes by. Hopefully, I'll see you sometime later today."

"I hope so."

"In the meantime, I want you to close your eyes and have sweet dreams about the wonderful life we're going to have together and not worry about the formalities. It'll all work out the way it's meant to."

"Thanks for the reminder."

"Any time. You good now?"

"I'm much better than I was."

"I love you."

"I love you, too."

"Rest, my love. All is well."

The rattling of the windows and the roar of the wind and rain would say otherwise, but Victoria decided to listen to the man she loved with all her heart and try to get some much-needed rest.

DAVID KEPT an arm around Daisy as they snuggled on the sofa bed. "Our mattress at home has spoiled me for all others," he said.

"This one is a bit thin compared to that beauty you insisted we needed from the mainland."

"I was right, wasn't I?"

"You're always right, dear."

He pinched her bum.

"What?" she asked, laughing. "Most of the time, you're right. I've learned to trust your gut about most things, including mattresses."

"And I trust yours about all the important stuff, such as what we're going to name Peanut."

Since they'd decided not to find out what they were having, they were considering names for both possibilities and calling the baby Peanut in the meantime.

"I'm stuck on Helen for a girl," Daisy said.

"I'm not sold on that. It reminds me of an old woman."

"Everything old is new again. And besides, I had a great-aunt named Helen who was one of my favorite people."

"And I love that, but still… Helen. I don't know. What are my other choices?"

"Helen?"

David laughed. "I see how it is. How about for a boy?"

"I have no idea. Nothing stands out to me."

"I like Myron."

"*What?* Myron?"

"Myron and Helen. That'd be a perfect little family."

Daisy turned over and used her cell phone flashlight to light up his face. "Are you playing with me?"

David winced from the bright light. "Would I do that?"

"Yes, I think you would. *Myron?*"

"Helen?"

"Fine." She stuck her lip out in a dramatic pout. "If my Helen cancels out your Myron, then we're back to the drawing board."

"Excellent."

"You did that on purpose, and I'm gonna tell Vic that you *do* cheat at Yahtzee."

David rocked with laughter. "I did not, and I do not."

"Did and do."

"How does one cheat at Yahtzee?"

"I have no clue, but you've figured it out."

"No way. You can't figure out what the dice are going to do, and I like the name Myron."

"I'm reconsidering this entire thing."

"What entire thing?"

"Being married to you and procreating with you."

Hearing her say that struck a note of fear in him, even if he knew she was joking. He tightened his arm around her. "You know you can't ever leave me, because I'd die."

"I'm not going anywhere, and you know it, even if you cheat at Yahtzee."

"Do not."

"Do, too."

David was still smiling as he drifted off to sleep, wrapped up in his beloved wife, thinking of a blonde little girl named Helen and wondering what the morning would bring to their little island.

CHAPTER 20

*P*iper wondered if it was possible to kiss so much, her lips could become injured. If so, she and Jack had crossed the threshold for lip injury quite some time ago and were heading into surgical-repair territory, a thought that made her giggle.

"What's so funny?" Jack asked, keeping his lips close to hers.

"I was wondering if you can overuse your lips to the point of injury."

"If so, we must be nearly there."

"I think 'there' was passed about an hour ago."

"Sorry."

"I'm not, so you shouldn't be either." She reached up to comb her fingers through his hair. "You want to know something funny?"

"Yep."

"The first thing I liked about you was your hair."

"My hair?"

"Uh-huh. Hair is very important to me."

"So if I lose it, is that game over?"

"Are you losing it?"

"Nah," he said, grinning. "All the men in my family have lots of hair. On my mother's side, too. I should be good to go."

"Oh, phew. That's a big relief."

He bit his lip as he smiled at her and then winced. "Wow, my lips actually hurt."

"Told you." She continued to play with his hair now that she was allowed to touch him any way she wanted. "There're other things we can do besides kiss, you know."

"Are there?"

"I know it's been a while for you…"

He laughed. "Don't worry. I remember how."

She dropped her hand to his face, caressing his cheek and rubbing his whiskers with her thumb. "Do you feel ready for that?"

"I think so?"

"You're not sure?"

"There's no way to be entirely sure about something like that, except to do it and hope for the best."

"I see."

"I want you to know… When I'm with you, I'm not thinking about her or wishing you were her or anything like that. But all the time, *always*, I wish she was still here."

"Oddly enough, I understand what you mean."

"It's a lot," he said, frowning. "I know it is, and if it's too much for you, I get it."

"It's not, or at least I think it's not. If you're open with me and talk to me about what you're feeling, I think maybe we can try to figure it out together."

"I can do that, or at least I can try." He played with a strand of her curly hair. "It's just that I worry about where the line is between you being understanding and my sad past interfering with our very nice present."

"It's not interfering. It's part of who you are, and in case you haven't noticed, I like who you are."

"I noticed." He dragged a fingertip gently over her bottom lip. "I want to be ready for you, Piper. I really, really do."

"I'm right here." Before she'd run into him on the ferry, she would've said she wasn't ready for any of this, but after seeing him again, learning more about how he'd cared for his sick wife and kissing him, all she wanted was more.

They'd lost power at some point, but the streetlights must've been on auxiliary power, because they cast a faint glow into the room.

Piper sat up in the bed and peeled the tank over her head and tossed it aside. Then she returned to his embrace, pressing her bare breasts against his chest and smiling when he sucked in a sharp deep breath.

"Damn, that feels good," he said. "*You* feel so good." His hands seemed to be everywhere as he explored the flesh she'd bared to him. Then he replaced his hands with his lips, and she had to remind herself to be quiet so they wouldn't be overheard.

Once he started touching and kissing her body, it was like he couldn't stop until he'd touched her everywhere. Kissed her everywhere. Her shorts and panties were removed in an impatient tug, and then his tongue was between her legs, and her fingers were buried in his hair.

Good Christ Almighty, he was good at that and had her rushing toward release before she had the chance to worry about all the things she usually did when this was happening. Jack didn't leave a single brain cell left for worrying, as they were all cheering him on and sending her flying toward the kind of climax she'd read about in books but had never experienced for herself.

Holy. *Shitballs.*

She came so hard, she might've passed out for a second. Before she had a second to regroup and prepare for the next part of the program, he was ripping open a condom and rolling it onto his impressive erection. Everything about this was different from what she'd had before, including the sheer size of him. For a hot second, she panicked, thinking she couldn't do it, but then he slid home, stretching her to the point of pleasurable pain and touching her in places she hadn't known existed until he showed her.

He was ruining her for all other men, one deep stroke at a time, and she was there for it. Ruination had never felt better.

"THANK you so much for coming over to keep me company," Kelsey said as she let Jeff Lawry into the apartment she called home on the island. The converted barn was shaking so hard, she was afraid it might collapse. And when she'd lost power just before midnight, she'd immediately called Jeff.

"I'm glad you called." He glanced up at the high ceiling over the big open room she called home. "I can see why you were worried," he said as the building creaked and groaned. "We could go to my mom's house."

"How was the driving?"

"Kind of scary. The wind was pushing the car all over the road."

"I'm so glad you got here safely. Maybe we should stay put and hope for the best?"

"Whatever you want to do is fine with me."

"Mr. McCarthy brought me these battery-powered lanterns in case we lost power. I'm so thankful to have them. It was scary dark for a minute there after the power went out."

"I heard it's out all over the island. That's another thing we have at my mom's—a generator."

"Can we go there tomorrow? After the storm passes?"

"Sure. We can do that."

She realized she'd just asked him to spend the night, but she sort of hoped he'd planned for that when he came over. "In case I haven't told you, I hate hurricanes. My parents are calling every thirty minutes to check on me. They wanted me to come home before the storm, but I couldn't leave Maddie to care for five kids, including infant twins, while Mac was working twenty hours a day."

"I'm sure she appreciated you sticking around."

"She did, but she sent me home early so I wouldn't be driving in the storm."

"That was nice of her."

"It was, especially since she had no idea what time Mac would make it home." Kelsey went to the sofa and took a seat, curling her legs under her. "I could've stayed there or with Mr. and Mrs. McCarthy. They also invited me. But it's been a long week with the kids, and I was ready for some downtime."

"Can't say I blame you. I'm exhausted after this week. Mac had us going from sunup until nine o'clock some nights."

"Were you asleep when I called you?"

"Nope."

"Are you lying?"

"Maybe?"

"Jeff! You shouldn't have taken the call."

He linked his fingers with hers. "Don't you know by now that when you call, I'll always take it?"

She still couldn't believe he'd given up an apartment and a perfectly good job in Florida—in his field of computer science—to stay on Gansett Island with her and to work with Mac. "You need to sleep."

"I assume you're planning to sleep at some point?"

She nodded. "I'm cooked after this week."

"If you want to go to bed, I can make myself comfy right here," he said of the sofa.

Kelsey appreciated that, even after the sacrifices he'd made to stay with her, he never pressured her for more than she was ready for. "There's no sense in you sleeping on the sofa when there's plenty of room in my bed."

"I love this hurricane," he said with a smile.

"Stop! It's terrible."

"There's nothing terrible about getting to sleep with you." He got up and gave her hand a gentle tug. "Lead the way."

She crossed the wide-open room to the screened-off area in the back corner.

"Do you have a pillow fetish I need to know about?" he asked as he took in the huge assortment on her bed.

"I like pillows."

"I see that. What do we do with them when we want to actually sleep in the bed?"

"We move them," she said indignantly. Her pillows were nonnegotiable.

"I like this one." He held up the pillow that was in the shape of Gansett Island with the saying "Living on Island Time" embroidered on it.

"That was ridiculously expensive in town, but I wanted something to remember my time here, so I spent the money."

"You'll have me to help you remember your time here."

"I know, but the pillow was calling my name."

"I'm not sure how I feel about this pillow situation."

"You get me, you get my pillows."

"Hmm." He sat on the edge of the bed. "I'm going to need to think about this."

She stopped what she was doing with the pillows. "Really?"

"I'm done thinking." He stood to help her finish clearing the pillows off the bed.

"Don't throw them," she said. "Some of them are delicate. That one belonged to my grandmother." She pointed to a lacy pillow with an embroidered pattern.

"Are there other pillow rules I need to be aware of?"

"Nope. That's it. Be gentle with them."

With a huge stack of pillows sitting on both sides of the bed, Jeff stretched out on top of the down comforter that she slept with year-round because she was always cold.

Kelsey got under the covers and turned to face him.

"Hey there, what's up?"

"There's a boy in my bed."

"Scandal."

The building creaked and groaned as the wind beat against it.

Kelsey glanced up at the ceiling. Had that water spot been there before? She wasn't certain. "Storms freak me out. They always have."

"I'm here to keep you safe."

She looked over at him. "I'm so glad you're here, and not just because I was scared of the storm."

"I'm glad to be here, too. This is much better than sleeping alone."

Kelsey had something else she wanted to say to him, but now that the moment was upon her, she was nervous. "I... I wanted to tell you... that I, um... I appreciate that you haven't been pressuring me for, you know..."

"Sex?"

Was it possible for an entire body to blush? If so, hers just did. "Yes. That."

"I told you... Whatever happens between us will be on your timetable. I'm here for the long haul."

"I had planned to wait until I got married."

"I know, and if you want to get married, we can do that whenever you want."

"Jeff, be serious."

"Kelsey, I'm as serious about you as I've been about anything in my life."

"You're twenty-two. I'm twenty. We're too young to talk about getting married."

"Who says? We're both legal adults, and we want to be together forever. At least that's what I want."

"I want that, too, but it just seems... We only met a few months ago."

"Are you going to feel differently about me a year from now or two years from now?"

"Well, no, but..."

"Marry me, Kelsey. Let's figure life out together."

She shook her head.

"Are you saying no?" he asked, sounding hurt and surprised.

"I'm not saying no. I don't know what to say."

He took her hand and kissed the inside of her wrist.

She wondered if he could feel the way her heart was pounding. "What if..."

"Ask me anything. I love you. I want to be with you forever."

"What if we get married and the sex is, you know, not good? And then you're stuck with me... Are you laughing? Seriously?"

"I'm sorry. It's just that you're so damned cute."

"I'm not cute. Babies are cute. Grown women are not cute."

"You're adorable. The sex will be great because it's you and me, and we love each other."

"Don't you want to be certain before you take me on for life?"

"It's important to you that we wait, so that's what we'll do."

"It was important to me to wait. Before."

"Before what?"

"Before I met you. And now..."

"What, Kels? Tell me what you're thinking."

"That maybe we shouldn't wait."

"Oh, I see."

"Do you want to?"

"Yes, Kelsey, I want to, but I'll still want to marry you whether we do that or not. I wasn't just asking you to marry me so we could get to the good stuff. I asked you because I want to be with you always."

"How can you know that for sure at twenty-two?"

"I feel like I've already lived four lifetimes with what I've been through." He'd told her about being raised by an abusive father, his struggles with drug addiction and a suicide attempt. "All I know is that when I first met you and spent time with you, I felt calm, settled and at peace for the first time ever. It was like someone whispered in my ear, 'There she is. She's what you need.' When you've endured what I have and find what you need, you don't let it go, not for anything."

Her eyes flooded with tears that she wiped away with the back of her hand.

"Don't cry. I'm not good with girl tears."

She laughed as she brushed away more tears. "That was a lovely thing to say."

"I mean it."

"I know you do." Kelsey would've thought she'd need a stiff drink and a dark room for what she was about to do, but with him, she didn't need either of those things as she reached for the hem of her T-shirt and pulled it up and over her head.

His sharp inhale was his only reaction while he waited to see what she might do next.

She tugged at his shirt. "Your turn."

166

Jeff whipped the shirt up and over his head, tossing it aside as his greedy gaze traveled over her, seeming to like what he saw. "Come here," he said gruffly, holding out his arms to her.

Kelsey scooted across the mattress on her knees to meet him in the middle.

He put his arms around her.

She nearly fainted at the feel of his chest hair against her tight nipples.

"Feels good, right?"

"God, so good."

"I want this to be as special for you as you are to me."

"It will be, because it's you."

He brushed the hair back from her face. "You know it hurts the first time, right?"

"Yes."

"I'll try to make it so it doesn't hurt too badly."

"I'm sure it'll be fine."

"I never want to hurt you." His hands moved in soothing strokes over her back, making her shiver from the excitement and anticipation.

They were really going to do this, and she didn't feel the slightest bit hesitant. Now that she'd made up her mind, she wanted to hurry and get to the main event.

But he had other ideas as he eased her back onto the bed. "I need to make sure you're good and ready, so it doesn't hurt."

"I am ready."

"Not yet, love, but you will be. Do you trust me?"

"Yes, of course I do."

"Then I want you to relax and just feel. Okay?"

"Okay." She wasn't exactly sure what she was agreeing to, but she had faith in him, that he would take good care of her.

"Are you comfortable?" he asked.

"Um, well, I've never been topless in front of anyone before, so…"

He touched his tongue to the tip of her left nipple, and she nearly launched off the bed. Only his weight on top of her kept her in place. "You should be topless in front of me as often as possible. You're so, so beautiful."

She wanted to ask him to do that tongue thing again, but she didn't have to ask.

He cupped both her breasts and teased her nipples with his thumbs and tongue, but when he sucked the right one into his mouth, she cried out from the sharp spike of desire she felt everywhere. The ache between her legs made her feel needy and desperate for relief.

"Jeff."

"What, honey?"

"I'm ready."

"Not yet. Trust me on this." He continued to play with her breasts until she was half out of her mind with need. The storm raging outside had nothing on the one happening inside her. If he didn't do something to ease the tension soon…

He tugged on the pajama pants and had them and her panties off in a matter of seconds. As he knelt between her legs, Kelsey tried not to be embarrassed or self-conscious or anything other than in the moment, but that was easier said than done.

"Look at me," he said.

She forced her eyes open to look up at him as she trembled.

"Are you okay?"

Nodding, she said, "I'm trying to be."

"You're doing great. Are you still sure this is what you want?"

"I'm so sure."

She was in no way prepared for what he did next, using his shoulders to push her legs apart so he could… Oh my *God*. Was that his tongue? Her first thought was to try to get away from him, but he had his arm across her hips, keeping her anchored to the bed as he… And then his fingers were inside her, touching and stroking as the urgency grew to the point that she felt like she'd shatter if he didn't…

The sound that came from her was one she wouldn't have recognized as herself if she'd heard it anywhere else.

"Yes, love, just like that. Let it happen."

As if she had a choice. The orgasm crashed down on her like the biggest wave ever, pulling her up so high, she wondered how she didn't crash into the ceiling. She felt like all the doors had opened to her, and she finally understood why people made such a big deal about—

"Oh." The sudden, intense pressure between her legs brought her crashing back to reality. She opened her eyes to find him poised above her, held up on muscular arms as he moved slowly and carefully.

"We'll go nice and easy, okay?"

She bit her lip and nodded, until another thought occurred to her. "Condom?"

"All set, love. I told you you'll always be safe with me, and I meant that."

"Tell me what I should do. I don't know what to do."

"Your job is to relax and breathe. Can you do that?"

"I... I think so."

"Breathe, sweetheart. It's all good. Just close your eyes and breathe. It's going to hurt, but only for a second. Are you ready for that?"

"Um... I guess?" The words came out on a squeaky exhale.

He pushed hard, and the pain ripped through her, taking her breath and pulling a sharp cry from deep inside her.

As he continued to whisper to her to breathe, that he loved her and wanted to make her feel so good, he pushed deeper into her.

Kelsey gripped his biceps, her fingers sinking into his flesh.

"Does it hurt?"

She shook her head because she couldn't speak.

"I'm sorry, love. It'll only hurt like that once, and then it'll feel so good. I promise."

Kelsey was shaking so hard, she could barely think, but as quickly as it had come, the pain receded.

He kissed her face, her lips, her neck. "Talk to me, love. Are you all right?"

"Yes. I'm fine." It had hurt more than she'd expected it to. "You... You can move if you want to."

"I want to, but only if it feels good for you, too."

"It does, or it will. I'm okay."

He began to move again, slowly, tentatively, and he was right, it did feel good.

"God, Kels, nothing is better than this. Nothing in the whole world is better than you. I can't wait to have this and you forever."

As she held on tight to him, the big barnlike structure above them creaked and groaned as the hurricane-force winds intensified. Safe in the embrace of her love, the storm might have been a million miles away for all she cared about it.

CHAPTER 21

"This is the stupidest thing I've ever done," John Lawry said to his friend Niall Fitzgerald as Niall drove them to the parking lot at the island's southernmost point.

"Really?" Niall asked. "This is the stupidest thing? Then you ain't been living right."

"I was a cop. Remember?"

"Eh, that was so last month. Now, you're a civilian, and it's time to do stupid shit like stand in a hurricane and show it who's boss."

"What if it shows *us* who's boss?"

"You're not afraid, are you?"

"Kinda? I mean, there's a perfectly safe house with a generator where we could be riding out the biggest storm to ever threaten this island."

"What fun would that be? Let's go check it out."

"Are you sure this is a good idea?"

"Absolutely not, and that's what makes it fun. Come on!"

While everyone else on the island was taking shelter, John had let Niall talk him into this foolish outing to see just how bad the storm really was. On the ride out there, the rain had been falling so hard, they couldn't exceed fifteen miles per hour, and they'd been the only fools on the road.

When Niall opened the car door, the wind pulled it right out of his hand, nearly ripping it off. "Whoa!"

"Maybe that's a sign that this is a dumb idea!" John had to yell to be heard above the roar of the storm.

"Nah, it's fine."

Despite his reservations, he didn't want to be seen as a wimp by the man he had a massive crush on, so John used both hands to open the door and still nearly lost control to the wind. He had zero desire to be out in this hellscape, but he stepped out of the car nonetheless and was almost immediately knocked off his feet by the sheer power of the wind.

Niall was facing into it, arms out and face lifted into the rain like a god of weather or some such thing.

John made his way around the car and wrapped an arm around Niall's waist, hoping their combined weight might make it less likely that they'd be swept away. They were standing about ten feet back from the new fencing that had recently been erected after several near-miss disasters on the bluffs.

He hoped they weren't going to be the next disaster as it took every ounce of strength he had to remain standing when the wind was strong enough to easily knock them off their feet. "Okay, we did it. Can we go now?"

Niall put an arm around him. "Not yet. It's just getting good."

They had to scream to be heard over the storm. "Uh, this isn't good! This is insanity!"

"Feel the power of it? It's awesome!"

John was about to disagree when Niall suddenly kissed him.

They were so caught up in the kiss that the storm nearly succeeded in toppling them.

Niall laughed and kissed him again. "Now do you feel it?"

"I feel it." He felt so many things for the talented Irishman who'd captured his attention at the Beachcomber, where Niall was a regular performer. "But can we take this somewhere less dangerous?"

"If we must."

"We must."

As John released his tight hold on Niall's coat, the strongest gust of wind yet succeeded in knocking them to the ground.

While John would've panicked, Niall laughed.

He stretched his arms and legs out like he was making a snow angel and laughed his ass off.

"We need to go, you crazy bastard!" John screamed at him.

"Not yet. It's just getting good." He grasped John's hand as the rain beat down on them, and the wind roared. "I've never felt more alive than I do right now."

John couldn't deny he felt the same way. Maybe he'd spent too much of his life playing it safe, and it was time to take some chances. Meeting Niall had been the best thing to happen to him in a very long time, if ever, and he was looking forward to whatever adventures they would have together.

One thing was for certain, he'd never forget Hurricane Ethel and the first time he kissed Niall.

THE FULL STRENGTH of Hurricane Ethel roared ashore on Gansett Island at 2:10 in the morning, with sustained winds topping a hundred miles per hour. More than three inches of rain fell the first hour, and the storm surge brought the ocean inland, flooding many of the lower-lying streets, including Ocean Avenue.

Despite being exhausted from a relentless week, Blaine was awake listening to the intensifying storm while Tiffany and the girls slept through it.

The wind and rain had gotten louder as he'd lain awake waiting. For what? He couldn't say for certain, but it felt like they were in the middle of Armageddon. All he thought about every day was protecting his family and community from anything that would threaten their safety. So he felt particularly helpless at a time like this, when there was nothing he could do but hope for the best.

A loud crash outside had him sitting up and then bolting out of bed to investigate what'd happened. He ran downstairs to the back door and flipped on the floodlights that illuminated the backyard.

Shit. A tree had come down on Tiffany's red VW Bug. The car was crushed under the weight of the tree. That would break her heart. She loved that silly little car.

"What is it?" she asked from behind him.

"Your car just met a tree."

"No! Not my Bug!"

"I'm so sorry, love. We'll get you a new one."

"I hate this storm!"

Blaine put his arms around her. "A car is replaceable."

"I know, but I'm still allowed to be pissed at Ethel for squishing my Bug."

"Yes, you are. Let's go back to bed for a bit." His alarm was set for six so he could get a jump on assessing the damage. While he was up, he decided to check in with Wyatt.

"Hey, boss. How's it going?"

"That's what I wanted to ask you."

"Very quiet. Not hearing much of anything."

"How about next door?" he asked of the fire department.

"Same. No calls."

"I guess no news is good news. Let me know if anything comes up."

"Will do. Get some rest."

Blaine ended the call before he could retort that rest was hard to come by when his island was under attack by Mother Nature.

"Would you feel better if you were at work?" Tiffany asked.

"No, I want to be here with you guys in case anything else happens." He needed to be in both places, but *nothing* was more important than the safety of his wife and children. With his hand on her lower back, he guided her toward the stairs to go back to bed.

"It sounds like a tornado," Tiffany said warily.

Ashleigh appeared in the hallway. "I'm scared, Mommy."

"It's okay, baby." Tiffany went to her daughter and picked her up, bringing her into their room, where she settled her between them.

The baby monitor on Tiffany's bedside table crackled to life when Addie started to cry.

"I've got her," Blaine said, getting up to retrieve their other daughter. He went into Addie's room and lifted her from the crib. "It's okay, love. Daddy's here."

She snuggled into the crook of his neck, the way she always did, and like always, his heart nearly exploded with love for her. He'd had no idea fatherhood would be like that, love on top of love on top of more love.

He returned to their room, keeping Addie snuggled in his arms.

Tiffany had Ashleigh tucked in against her.

As the storm raged outside, the people he loved best were safe. He only hoped that everyone else they loved was, too.

NED SAUNDERS STOOD at the sliding door to his deck and watched the storm batter the trees he and Francine had planted last spring—with the help of their sons-in-law, Mac and Blaine. They'd done most of the work while Ned had supervised. He was good at that. Supervising, that was. He wasn't good at being patient as a monster storm beat the crap outta his island. He couldn't believe they still hadn't invented a way to blow up a hurricane or tornado to keep it from menacing people and property.

Surely there must be a way by now to make these storms go away, and if there wasn't, there ought to be.

"What're you doing up?" Francine asked when she came out of their bedroom.

"Just checkin' things."

"And is everything the same as it was a few hours ago?"

"Looks like it."

"Then come back to bed. You'll find out soon enough how bad it was."

Because there was nowhere Ned would rather be than in bed with his lovely wife, he let her lead him back to the bedroom, where she gave him a not-so-gentle push toward his side of the bed. "Don't be pushin' me around, woman."

"Someone's gotta keep you in line."

"And you think that oughta be you?"

"Who else would you prefer?"

"No one, doll, as ya well know."

"All right, then. Can we go back to sleep now?"

"I ain't the one doin' all the talkin'."

"Are you calling me a big mouth?"

"Now, would I do somethin' stupid like that?"

"I don't know. Would you?"

"Fighting" with her was the most fun he'd ever had in his life. There were days—most days, in fact—when he wondered how he'd survived for more than thirty years without her, after falling for her when he was young and dumb. If only he'd tried harder to keep her attention after that charmer Bobby Chester came to town and wooed her away from him.

"Hello? Are you there? Come in, Ned."

He chuckled at her saucy tone.

"What're you thinking about?"

"Why I didn't fight for ya way back when."

"What? You're thinking about *that* in the middle of a hurricane?"

"I think about that all the damned time."

"Ned, don't dwell on the past. It's over and done with. And isn't the present sort of nice?"

"Sorta nice," he said with a laugh. "It's the nicest darned thing ta ever happen to me."

"Focus on the here and now and forget the rest. I was so stupid back then, so full of myself. I would've made a mess of things with you the same as I did with him."

"It wasn't you who messed that up."

"It takes two to mess up a marriage, and I was just as much at fault as he was."

"I don't believe that, and I never will."

"Believe it. I didn't give him any slack. I was on him all the time about everything he said and did. I was a total pain in the ass, and I would've been to you, too. You probably would've ended up hating me, same as he did."

"Never. I could never hate ya."

"Yes, you could've, and you would've if you'd been married to that version of me. I'm different now. Life has humbled me and made me appreciate the good things, like what we have now."

"We'll hafta agree ta disagree on whether we woulda stayed married. I say we woulda 'cause I never woulda let ya go fer anything, and I don't wanna hear ya blaming yerself for what the sumabitch did to you and the girls."

"I don't blame myself for that, but I take my share of the blame for the marriage not working out."

"He was damned lucky ta have ya, no matter what ya say, and he shoulda known that." He looked over at her. "Are ya laughing at me?"

"I'm laughing with you."

"Except I ain't laughing."

That only made her laugh harder.

"What in tarnation sakes is so damn funny?"

"You are. You're very sweet and cute with your certainty that we would've gotten through anything and still be going strong all these years later."

"We woulda, and I don't see why that's so funny."

"I was a bitch, Ned. A stone-cold bitch. I thought I was the shit, with men falling all over themselves to be with me. The way I treated you, the sweetest, nicest man I ever knew, was unconscionable. You always deserved better than me. You still do."

"Donchu dare say that ta me. Donchu dare." He was rarely ever angry with her but hearing her say that lit a fuse in him. "Yer the only one I ever wanted, and ya damned well know that, too."

"I do, and I feel very lucky to have you."

"No more a that shit 'bout what I deserve, or ya'll make me mad."

"Yes, dear."

"Get ova here and make up with me. And do a good job of it."

She moved over to him and propped herself up on her elbow. "What would count as a good job?"

"Use yer imagination."

She leaned in to press her lips to his. "I'm very sorry for saying I didn't deserve you. Do you forgive me?"

"Not yet."

He felt her smile as she kissed him again. "Now?"

"Nope."

More kisses. "Getting warmer?"

"Yep, I sure am."

She laughed as she kissed him again. "That ought to settle us up."

He hooked an arm around her to keep her close to him. "Don't never let me hear ya say that again 'bout deserving me, ya got me?"

"Yes, Ned, I've got you."

"Good."

CHAPTER 22

*D*aisy woke from a sound sleep, startled by a crashing sound outside and a sharp pain in her side. What the heck was that? She knew she shouldn't have eaten the pizza David had ordered from Mario's. It always gave her heartburn, even more so since she'd been pregnant.

Another pain slashed through her, making her gasp. Shit, that hurt.

"What's the matter?" David asked sleepily.

"I'm not sure. I think I have heartburn."

"Does something hurt?" he asked, sitting up.

"A weird pain."

"Where?"

She pointed to her abdomen.

"For how long?"

"About half an hour, I guess."

"Let's go to one of the exam rooms so we can make sure everything is okay with the baby."

"It's not the baby." It couldn't be that. "It's heartburn from the pizza."

"That would hurt up here." David pointed to her chest. "Not down there."

"It's gas. It must be."

"Let's make sure, okay?"

She didn't want to go with him and find out that anything was wrong with their baby, so she resisted when he tried to help her up from the bed.

"Daisy, please."

"It can't be the baby," she said, wincing as another pain sliced through her.

He gave her hand a gentle tug.

Reluctantly, she let him help her up and followed him across the hall to an empty exam room.

"Have a seat. I'll get Vic."

"Do you have to disturb her? Can't you check me?"

"You don't want me doing a pelvic exam."

"Why do I need that?"

"Just hang on, sweetheart. I'll be right back."

In the two minutes he was gone, the pain got much worse. So bad, she was bent in half when he returned with Vic.

"Daisy!" David reached for her and held her as the pain got progressively worse.

"I can't lose this baby," she whispered. "Please…"

They moved quickly to help her out of the T-shirt and pajama pants and into a gown.

David practically lifted her onto the exam table, and Victoria had a heart monitor for the baby on her in a matter of seconds. The sound of the baby's heartbeat was one of the best things Daisy had ever heard.

"Whatever this is," Vic said, "it's not the baby."

"As long as he or she is fine, I don't care what it is," she said, gripping David's hand.

"I want to do a quick exam and see if we can figure out what's going on," Vic said.

Daisy wanted to object, to tell her there was nothing wrong, but the pain said otherwise.

As always, Vic was quick but thorough while Daisy gritted her teeth and prayed for a simple explanation that had nothing to do with the baby.

David stood by her side, holding her hand as he watched everything Vic was doing, his cheek pulsing with tension that indicated he was as nervous as she was. Knowing that didn't help her stress level. While Vic poked and prodded, Daisy tried to stay focused on the steady beat of her baby's heart, which, other than the noise from the storm, was the only sound in the room. It was the only sound that mattered.

"I want to do a vaginal ultrasound," Vic said.

"What do you think it is?" David asked.

"I'm not sure yet. I'll be right back."

While she got the equipment needed, Daisy glanced up at David. "What's happening?"

"I don't know, love, but Vic will figure it out. She's the best."

"Are you scared?"

"I'm sure it's nothing serious. Let's try not to worry too much."

Victoria returned, rolling the ultrasound machine into the exam room. "This won't hurt at all, but I'll need you to stay still so we get good images, okay?"

Daisy was trembling so hard, she wondered how she'd ever manage to stay still. "I'll try."

After Victoria inserted the wand, David leaned in for a closer look at the screen. "Look, Daisy. There's our baby."

"Do you want to know the sex?" Victoria asked.

Daisy looked up at David, who shrugged. "That's up to you," he said. "I want to know."

"You're having a girl," Victoria said.

"Hello, Helen," Daisy said.

David cracked the first smile she'd seen since the pain started.

"Oh, I love that name!" Vic said. "It's gorgeous. Helen Lawrence sounds like a movie star."

Daisy gave David an I-told-you-so look.

"Everything looks perfectly normal," Victoria said. "I think what you might be feeling is ligament pain, which happens as your body stretches to accommodate the baby as she grows. You're so petite, Daisy, that you're apt to feel that pain more acutely."

"Well, that's a huge relief," David said.

"What can I do about the pain?" Daisy said.

"You can take some Tylenol, but only if it's completely unbearable."

"I can stand it as long as I know it's nothing terrible."

"Just growing pains."

Daisy gripped David's hand. "We're having a baby girl."

"Yes, we are," he said, bending to kiss her.

"I'll leave you guys to celebrate."

"Thanks for getting up for us in the middle of the night, Vic," Daisy said.

"Anything for you guys. I'm so glad everything is all right."

"We are, too," David said. "Thanks again."

"You got it."

He helped Daisy to sit up and change back into her PJs, and then lifted her off the table, surprising her.

"Put me down before you throw your back out!"

"You heard what Vic said. My baby mama is very petite and easy to carry."

Since there was nowhere else she'd rather be than in his arms, she wrapped herself around him for the ride back to bed.

"How's the pain?"

"A little better than it was."

"I'm sorry you have to deal with that."

"Whatever it takes to have a healthy baby."

David put her down on the bed and tucked her in. When he got in next to her, she reached for him. "It's a *girl*. A baby girl!"

"I think her middle name ought to be Myron."

Daisy swatted him. "That's not happening."

"Oh, come on. I compromised on Helen."

"When you can give birth to the babies, you can name one of them Helen Myron. Until such time, the answer is a big, fat no."

"It's not fair. You couldn't birth the babies without my contributions."

"Nice try. The answer is still no."

"I love you, Daisy Lawrence, even when you're mean to me."

"I love you, too, David Lawrence, even when you're delusional."

"Helen Myron Lawrence has a nice ring to it."

"Go to sleep, David."

THE SLOW-MOVING storm hammered the island relentlessly, flooding roads as the wind downed trees and power lines, sometimes both at the same time. Power was out to the entire island, according to the early news.

Big Mac was standing at the door to the deck at six o'clock Friday morning when he received a call from a neighbor.

"Mac, your barn next to the hotel collapsed in the storm."

His first thought was for Kelsey, their current tenant and Mac and Maddie's nanny. He couldn't see that building from his vantage point. "Thanks for letting me know."

"You got people living there?"

"I do."

"I'll be out to help."

"Thanks, Bud. Appreciate it."

Big Mac hung up and called the fire department to report that the building had fallen with a tenant inside and then ran upstairs to get dressed.

"What's wrong?" Linda asked.

"The barn collapsed."

"Oh my God! Kelsey..."

"I'm on my way, and so's the fire department."

"Call Mac, too. He'd want to help."

"I'll call him from the truck." Mac gave his wife a quick kiss. "Try to get a little more rest before the babies are up."

"I won't rest until I know Kelsey is okay."

"I'll keep you posted."

"Be careful. Leave the heroics to the younger men."

He scowled at her. "Love you, even when you're being insulting."

"Love you, too, even when you think you're younger than you are."

"I'll remember this," he said over his shoulder as he headed out the door, praying that Kelsey was all right.

Big Mac moved a large tree branch that had fallen across his driveway and got in the truck to call his son.

"What's up?" Mac asked, sounding sleepy.

"The barn collapsed."

"Kelsey..."

"I'm on my way, and I called the fire department."

"I'll be right there."

Big Mac drove down the hill toward the hotel and marina, fighting wind and rain and puddles so deep, he feared ruining his truck. A huge tree was down, blocking the road. He pulled over and put the flashers on and grabbed the work gloves he kept in the truck.

With both hands on the door, he opened it slowly against the wind that could've ripped off the door and stepped out into shin-deep water. The hood on his foul-weather jacket was no match for Ethel, and he was soaked in seconds as he ran toward the pile of rubble where the barn used to be. Kelsey's car was parked outside, as was a pickup truck Big Mac didn't recognize.

"Kelsey!"

He couldn't hear much over the storm as he started pulling at pieces of wood. "Kelsey!"

In the lingering darkness, it was hard to see much beyond the pile of debris.

Mac arrived a few minutes later, running across the yard behind the hotel. "Anything?" he asked Big Mac, who shook his head.

"I doubt the fire department will be able to get here," Mac said. "The roads are nearly impassable."

Big Mac's heart sank at realizing he and Mac were probably Kelsey's only hope.

His neighbor Bud materialized out of the gloom. "What can I do to help?"

"Start pulling debris away, but be careful you don't get hurt yourself," Big Mac said.

"No worries. I've got it."

As the three men worked, they continued to call for Kelsey, but didn't hear anything from inside.

"That's Jeff Lawry's truck," Mac told his father.

"Aw, God, are they both in there?"

"Probably," Mac said, his expression grim.

"I wish she'd come to stay at the house," Big Mac said as he helped Mac move a huge piece of splintered wood.

"Maddie tried to get her to stay with us, too."

Mason Johns and his firefighters came running toward them. "Couldn't get the trucks here, so we came on foot."

"Thanks for coming," Big Mac said. "We believe there're two people inside."

"Let's get them out," Mason said.

KELSEY THOUGHT she heard voices but couldn't be sure. The storm was so loud, and the ringing in her ears was even louder. They'd had about two seconds' warning that the building was coming down, and Jeff had dived on top of her, taking the full brunt of the collapse on top of him. He was unconscious and bleeding.

She could feel his blood dripping onto her. "Jeff, please... Wake up."

Her right arm was pinned, so she used her left arm to caress his hair, hoping to get a reaction from him. The only thing she could tell for certain was that he was still breathing, but slowly. Very, very slowly.

Tears leaked from the corners of her eyes. "Jeff... You can't leave me right after you asked me to marry you. Wake up!" She gave his hair a pull, but even that did nothing to help.

"Kelsey!"

She turned her head toward Mac's voice. "Here! We're over here! Mac! Help!"

"We're coming. Just stay strong."

Hearing his voice had her sobbing with relief and fear and so much love for the man who'd saved her life. If that act cost his life… She couldn't let her mind go there, or she'd lose what was left of her sanity. "You can't die on me, Jeff Lawry. I need you too much. I love you. Please don't leave me."

She could hear her rescuers getting closer, but as they disturbed the rubble pile, things shifted and fell.

"Keep your eyes closed Kelsey," Mac called to her.

"Okay."

"Is Jeff with you?"

"Yes, he's hurt bad. Hurry."

"We're hurrying. Are you hurt?"

"I don't know. My right arm is pinned by something, and there's all kinds of stuff on top of us."

"Try not to move too much, just in case," Mac called back to her.

Kelsey wanted to ask in case of what, but she didn't want to know. Her right arm and hand had lost feeling a while ago, and the weight of Jeff's body on top of her made it difficult to breathe.

As her rescuers got closer, she started to see flashes of daylight and felt rain leaking in.

"Please hurry," she whispered, noting that Jeff's breathing had gotten even slower.

She lost track of time while she waited and hoped and prayed for herself and Jeff, but mostly for him. They'd had such a beautiful night together, the most beautiful night of her life, and it was just the start for them.

It couldn't be the end.

It just couldn't.

"I'm not sure if you can hear me," she said with tears rolling down her face, "but if you can, I want you to remember that I love you. We're getting married. We're going to do everything together. But you have to stay with me. I need you to stay with me. I love you. I love you. I love you."

If, God forbid, he died, she wanted those to be the last words he heard.

She kept saying it until the light came flooding in, along with rain that quickly soaked them.

"I'm here, Kels," Mac said. "We're going to get you guys out of there."

She'd never been so happy to see him. "Jeff is hurt bad, Mac."

"We'll get him out." A cut on Mac's face was bleeding, but he didn't seem to care. "We'll get you both out."

He continued to toss aside the wreckage of the building as he made his way closer to them.

"I've got them right here," Mac called to others. "There's a beam on top of them. I need more people over here! Hurry!"

Things began to move more quickly then, with people suddenly crawling over the pile of wreckage that had once been her home.

Kelsey curled her left arm around Jeff's head, wanting to protect him in any way she could, not that it would make much difference.

Their rescuers pushed through the rubble until people were on both sides of them, the rain pouring down on them, the wind whipping and howling like it had all night. She could hear them discussing the best way to remove the beam that had landed on them. At some point, she must've lost consciousness or fallen asleep, because she startled when a weight was lifted from around them.

"We've got the beam off you," Mac said. "The paramedics are coming in now."

It took what felt like forever for them to get Jeff strapped onto a backboard—upside down. They mobilized his neck and then carefully lifted him off Kelsey and then rotated the board, so he was face up. Thankfully, they'd put on clothes after they had sex because she'd been cold.

"Is he going to be okay?" she asked as two men worked on freeing her arm from whatever was holding it down.

"We'll do everything we can for him," one of the firefighters said.

By the time they lifted her out of the building on a backboard, sensation was returning painfully to her arm. She'd heard one of them say it was broken.

Mac ran with the paramedics through the storm toward an ambulance. "I'm here, Kelsey."

"Jeff."

"The paramedics have him, and they'll take care of him."

"Is there a truck?" one of the men asked. "The ambulance is gone with him."

"We'll take mine," she heard Big Mac McCarthy say.

She was placed in the back of Big Mac's pickup truck and covered with a blanket because she was suddenly shivering uncontrollably, and her arm hurt bad.

Mac and two of the paramedics got in the back with her, using their coats to shield her face from the rain. He knocked on the back window, and the truck lurched forward, did a U-turn and headed for town.

"I'm so sorry this happened, Kelsey," Mac said.

"It's not your fault." Her teeth chattered. "Blame Ethel."

"She's a nasty bitch."

Kelsey grunted out a laugh that was followed by more tears. "Is Jeff going to die?"

"I really hope not."

CHAPTER 23

*B*laine got the call about the collapse of the McCarthys' barn and headed to the public safety building to provide coverage while the fire department worked the scene.

He'd barely had time to pour a cup of coffee when Duke from the tattoo shop came in, looking terrified. He had colorful ink that stopped right below his jawline, long dark blond hair, brown eyes and a goatee.

"What's up, Duke?"

"There was a woman and baby next door to me. I went over to check on them, and they're gone. She was there yesterday after the ferries stopped running, and now she's gone. They're gone."

"They're at my house."

"What?"

"I picked them up last night. The roof blew off and she was afraid, so she decided to walk into town."

"In a hurricane?" Duke asked, incredulous. "With a baby?"

"She had no TV, and her cell phone had died. She didn't know a storm was coming until it was here."

"Huh." Duke ran his hand through his rain-soaked hair. "She's at your place, you said."

"Yes."

"Okay. Okay, then."

"How'd you get here with all the roads closed?"

186

"I rode my bike," he said, referring to his vintage Harley-Davidson.

Blaine raised a brow. "In a hurricane?"

"I was worried about her. And the baby. I saw them over there the last week or so, and then they were gone."

"It was good of you to check on her. I'll let her know you did."

"Oh, um... Tell her if she needs anything, I'm next door."

"I'll do that."

"Did you, um, catch her name?"

"McKenzie, and the baby is Jax."

"Thank you."

"Thanks for coming in, Duke."

"No problem."

After Duke left, Blaine got sucked into what seemed like a thousand things over the next few hours. They got calls about trees down, cars crushed, boats aground, power out, sand covering the roads by the beaches. The list went on and on, but other than the collapse of the barn in North Harbor, he hadn't heard of any other serious injuries and was hoping their luck would hold until the storm had finally moved on from Gansett.

OWEN GOT a call from Daisy Lawrence, letting him know his brother Jeff had been brought to the clinic in critical condition. David had asked her to notify Jeff's family.

"I'll be right there," Owen said, wondering how Jeff had gotten critically injured.

"What is it?" Laura asked.

"Jeff got hurt somehow. He's in the clinic. They said..."

She crossed the room to him. "What did they say?"

"He's in critical condition."

"What happened?"

"Daisy didn't say. She just said David asked her to call me."

"You need to tell the others."

"Yeah, right. Okay."

Laura took his phone from him.

"Don't tell my mom. Not yet."

"I won't."

While he stood over her shoulder watching, she sent a text to Julia, Katie, Cindy, John and Josh, letting them know Jeff had been injured and that Owen was heading to the clinic to check on him. She also told them they'd decided not to tell Sarah, since there was nothing she could do from afar but worry. "Should we tell Steph, too?" As the Lawry's stepsibling, she'd become part of their family since Sarah married Charlie.

"Yes, of course," Owen said. "Thank you."

"I'm sure he'll be fine," Laura said after she'd texted Stephanie and handed his phone back to him. "He's young and strong."

Owen nodded, but his heart was in his throat.

"Call me if you need anything." She went up on tiptoes to kiss him. "Go to your brother. Love you."

"Love you, too." As he went downstairs, he thought about how his siblings would look to him to guide them through whatever level of crisis this turned out to be, and he had the time it took to walk to the clinic to get himself together to be strong for them. He battled the wind and rain as he walked through the deserted downtown area. It was so strange for there to be no ferries in port, no cars on the streets, no people anywhere.

The sidewalk and street were littered with sand, seaweed, shells and other debris that had washed ashore overnight. He was relieved to see that the storm drains seemed to be keeping up with the massive influx of water, and other than a few large puddles, there didn't seem to be much flooding. Thinking about water and drainage was better than wondering what he was going to hear about his youngest sibling at the clinic.

Jeff had come so far from the hellish years of drug abuse that had been capped by a suicide attempt when he was a teen. Like all the Lawry siblings, growing up with their asshole father had left a mark on Jeff, who'd been stuck at home by himself after the others had moved out. They'd done what they could for him, but they couldn't protect him from being the sole focus of the general's attention.

The suicide attempt had blown the lid off the entire situation, with their grandparents finally learning the truth about their home life and intervening to get Jeff out of there. They'd saved his life by moving him to Florida, where he got the treatment he needed to overcome the addiction and the intensive therapy that had helped to restore his mental health.

Jeff had recently graduated from college with honors and had fallen in love with Kelsey over the summer. His life was just starting. A sob erupted from Owen's chest. *Please let him be okay.*

When Owen walked through the automatic doors to the clinic, Mac was the first person he saw. He looked rough and had a nasty cut on his face. "What're you hearing?" Owen asked.

"Nothing yet." Mac ran his hands through soaking-wet hair. "We just got them here a few minutes ago."

"What happened?"

"They were at Kelsey's place in the barn, and it collapsed. Took us an hour and a half to get to them. A beam had come down on top of them."

"Oh my God," Owen said on a long exhale. "Were they conscious?"

"Kelsey was."

The implications hit Owen like a ton of bricks. He didn't know what to do with himself as he stood there processing the information and feeling helpless to do anything for his youngest sibling.

Julia and Katie came running into the clinic and hugged Owen.

"How is he?" Julia asked.

"Don't know yet."

"I'll see what I can find out," Katie said over her shoulder as she headed for the double doors that led to the exam rooms. She worked as a nurse practitioner at the clinic.

Cindy arrived with Jace, Johnny with Niall, and their stepsister, Stephanie, and her husband, Grant. Josh called, asking for an update Owen didn't have. "I'll let you know as soon as we hear anything. We're not telling Mom for now."

"If it's bad," Josh said, "get her home."

"I will."

"Tell him…" Josh sounded like he was crying. "Tell him I love him."

"We will. The others are all here. We'll take care of him."

"Thanks, O, for always holding us together."

"I just wish I could do something."

"You're doing it, just by being there for the rest of us."

Owen feared losing control of his emotions. "I'll keep you posted. Love you."

"Love you, too."

Cindy and Johnny went right to Owen. He knew they were looking for reassurances that he couldn't give them, so he held them close, giving and taking the support they all needed.

Maddie McCarthy arrived and hugged her husband. "I came as soon as Mom and Ned could get there to stay with the kids. How are they?"

"We don't know," Mac said, putting an arm around his wife.

"Should we call Kelsey's parents?"

"Let's ask her what she wants us to do when we see her."

"You're bleeding," Maddie said.

"It's nothing."

An anxious hour passed before David Lawrence came to talk to them, bringing Katie with him. Owen, Mac, Maddie and the other Lawry siblings swarmed him.

"How are they?" Mac asked.

"Kelsey has a badly broken arm that'll require surgery. Jeff's pelvis was broken, and we're concerned about internal bleeding, lumbar involvement that can lead to further complications, blood clots, among other things. We've got him stabilized for the moment, but we need to get him to a level-one trauma center as soon as the helicopters can fly again."

"When will that be?" Julia asked, her eyes wide with fear.

"It could be tomorrow."

Owen moaned at hearing that news. "David…"

"We'll do everything we can to keep him stable, but I won't lie to you. We're in no way equipped for injuries of this magnitude."

Julia let out a cry of distress.

Cindy hugged her as they wept.

"What about his spine?" Julia asked.

"From what we can tell from the X-rays, it appears his hips and pelvis bore the brunt of what landed on him. But we won't know anything for sure without further testing that we can't do here."

The weight of despair sat on Owen's chest like a cement block. They could lose Jeff because they couldn't get him off the island for the care he needed.

"Should we call Mom?" Johnny asked.

"No," Owen said without hesitation. "She can't get here, so there's no point in calling her." He felt very strongly that was the right thing to do, but who knew what the right thing was in a situation like this?

"I agree with Owen," Katie said. "There's nothing she can do except panic, and that won't change the outcome for Jeff."

"Will you stay with him, Katie?" Cindy asked tearfully.

"Of course, and I'll keep you posted."

"What can we do for him?" Julia asked.

"Pray," Katie said.

PIPER WAS at the front desk when Laura came downstairs with the kids, which was a comical sight to behold as she tried to keep three little ones from falling. Jack had been called into work before dawn and had promised to check in with her later. She couldn't wait.

Last night had been... spectacular. That was the only word she could think of to describe it.

She went to the stairs in case one of the kids tripped and looked up to say good morning to Laura. That's when she noticed her friend's pinched expression. "What's wrong?"

"Owen's brother Jeff was badly injured when a roof fell on him."

"Oh no." She picked up Jo while Laura reached for Jon. "Where was he?"

"At Kelsey's in North Harbor. She's hurt, too, but not as badly as he is. Owen just called. They need to get Jeff to a level-one trauma center, but the helicopters can't fly yet."

"Oh God," Piper said.

"David and Vic are doing everything they can for him, but they're not equipped for something like this."

"What can I do?"

"I came down to make breakfast for the guests."

"I'll do that. Go relax with the kids in the sitting room. I'll take care of the guests."

"Thank you, Piper. My head is all over the place right now. I can't focus on anything."

"I'm sure. I've got you covered."

Laura used her free arm to hug her. "I'm so glad you're here."

"I am, too." The more time she spent at the Surf, on Gansett and with Laura, the more she felt at home. "I'll take care of everything. Don't worry."

JULIA SENT a text to the number Deacon had called from. *This is Deacon's fiancée, Julia. I wanted to tell him my brother Jeff has been hurt pretty badly...*

She wasn't sure if she would hear from him, but she wanted him to know what was going on.

After she sent the message, she put her head back against the wall and closed her eyes, exhausted from the emotional onslaught of the last two days. If she never lived through another hurricane, that'd be fine with her.

All she could think about was Jeff, so grievously injured that the doctor was worried about him surviving until they could get him off the island, which wasn't going to happen any time soon with the storm still sitting on top of them.

That also meant that Deacon couldn't come home yet either.

She wanted to wail from the agony of it all.

Her phone rang, and she pounced on the call from the same unknown number that Deacon had called from before. "Hey."

"What happened to Jeff?"

Julia shared what she knew. "It's bad, Deacon. They aren't saying much more than that, and with no one flying and no boats... There's no way to get him to Providence."

"I can talk to Joe about coming back into port so we can get him there."

"It's not safe yet for you guys to come back."

"Let me check with Joe. It might be okay."

"Deacon, please don't do anything dangerous. The storm is still bad."

"I'll call you back after I talk to Joe. If there's anything we can do, we'll do it."

"I miss you so much, it's crazy."

"I miss you just as much. Hang in there, love. The storm will be over soon, and things can get back to normal."

"I hope so."

"I'll call you back."

"Okay."

"Love you."

"Love you, too."

The line went dead, and Julia got up to ask the woman working at the clinic's reception desk if she could speak to Katie.

"I'll get her for you."

"Thank you."

Katie came out a few minutes later. The disturbed look on her sister's face took Julia right back to the time in their lives they tried very hard not to ever think about. Julia hadn't seen that expression on her sister's face in a long time and would like to never see it again.

"How is he?"

"Not good. His blood pressure is very low, and he still hasn't regained consciousness, which might be for the best. He'd be in a lot of pain, and there's not a lot we can do about that without narcotics." What she left unsaid was that as a recovering addict, his pain needed to be carefully managed.

That news hit Julia like a punch. "I talked to Deacon. He said they might be able to get back here with one of the ferries to transport Jeff to the mainland. He's talking to Joe about it now."

"I don't think that would work. The seas are still so rough, and he needs to be kept as still as possible, so we don't compound his injuries."

"Oh. Okay."

"It was nice of him to offer that, though. I'd spoken with David about whether the Coast Guard might be able to transport him, but he said the same thing. He's too fragile for a rigorous trip like that would be. We have to wait for a helicopter."

"Could he die?"

"It's possible, Jule. I won't lie to you guys. He's in very bad shape."

"Can I see him?"

"It might be too much for you."

Julia appreciated that Katie was always so protective of her. "He's my baby brother. I want to see him."

"Come with me."

"Let me just tell Deacon that the doctors don't want him on a boat." She sent the text to the number Deacon was using. *Dr. Lawrence says he's too unstable for a rough boat ride but thank you for trying.*

Julia sent the text and then followed Katie through the double doors that led to the exam rooms. Jeff was in the last one on the left, the largest of them all. The first thing Julia noticed was that his face was devoid of all color. Even his lips looked like they'd been bleached. He was attached to a bunch of beeping machines, and David Lawrence stood by his bed, watching the monitors with a worried look on his face.

"Oh," Julia said on a cry. "Oh my God."

Katie was there to hold her up. "He's fighting hard to stay with us," she whispered.

Julia moved closer to her brother and placed her hand on top of his, noting how cold he felt. "Jeff, sweetie, it's me, Julia. We're all here, and we love you so much. We need you to hang in there, okay?" She bent over the bed to kiss his forehead and stroke his hair. "Don't you give up. Please don't give up. Kelsey needs you. We all need you."

When she stood upright, she turned to hug Katie, who was also in tears. "Could I see Kelsey?"

"Sure. Right this way."

Kelsey was across the hall in a smaller room.

Outside the curtain, Katie said, "Kelsey, it's Katie and Julia. May we come in?"

"Yes, please."

Victoria was working on a computer next to Kelsey's bed.

Kelsey had her injured arm propped on a pillow. It was purple with painful-looking bruises.

"How are you doing?" Julia asked.

She'd met her brother's girlfriend a few times at dinners at their mother's home and loved her for Jeff.

"All I care about is Jeff, and no one will tell me anything," Kelsey said with tears streaming down her face. "Please tell me how he is."

Katie exchanged silent communication with Victoria and then sat gingerly on the edge of Kelsey's bed. "He's in very serious condition with a broken pelvis and other injuries."

Kelsey gasped. "He'll be all right, though, won't he?"

"We hope so. The thing is… He needs to be transported to the mainland, but we have no way to get him there with the storm."

"There has to be something we can do!"

"We're doing all we can for him here until the storm lets up enough to allow a chopper to come pick him up," Katie said.

"How long will that be?" Kelsey's gaze darted between Katie and Julia. She seemed to hope one of Jeff's older sisters would have the answers she needed.

"We just don't know," Katie said with a sigh. "In the meantime, is there anyone we can call for you?"

Kelsey seemed to think about that for a minute. "I suppose I should call my parents. They're probably frantic that they can't reach me, and they'll find out about this soon enough."

Julia held up her phone. "I can make the call for you."

"Does your mom know?" Kelsey asked.

Katie shook her head. "We've decided not to tell her because there's nothing she can do from Italy, and she'd be frantic."

"I love this island," Kelsey said tearfully. "I truly do. But right now? I hate it."

"We understand completely," Katie said.

CHAPTER 24

Mac hadn't felt this helpless since Maddie had gone into labor during a tropical storm with Cal Maitland, the clinic's only doctor at the time, off-island. Dr. David Lawrence, home on vacation, had come to their rescue then and again when Janey had nearly died giving birth to PJ. If anyone could figure out a way to keep Jeff Lawry alive under these circumstances, it was David. He figured he ought to share that thought with Jeff's siblings.

"You guys," Mac said to the Lawrys, who were huddled together in the waiting room. "Listen… David is the absolute best guy for this job. If anyone can save Jeff, it's him. Remember what he did for Maddie and Janey… I know it's a terrible situation, but David knows what he's doing. He'll do everything he can for Jeff."

"Thank you, Mac," Owen said. "We needed to hear that."

"I wish there was more we could do," Mac said.

"You did the most important thing getting them out of that building," Johnny said.

"Let me clean that wound on your face, Mac," Katie said.

"Don't worry about it."

"I worry it'll get infected, and cleaning it will give me something to do," Katie said.

"Go, Mac," Maddie said. "Let Katie clean you up."

"Would you like to come sit with Kelsey?" Katie asked Maddie.

"I'd love to."

They followed Katie through the double doors. She pointed Maddie to Kelsey's room.

"In here, Mac," Katie said. "Have a seat on the table."

He did as she asked, even though he felt like the proverbial cat on a hot tin roof. There were a million things he needed to do, but with Jeff and Kelsey in the clinic because of a building their family owned, he felt it imperative to stay close to them, to help if he could, even if he knew nothing about what they might need.

"It's not your fault, Mac," Katie said gently. "No one would ever blame you or your family."

"The building was ours."

Katie dabbed at his face with something that stung like a son of a bitch. "I've gotten to know her a little in the last few weeks. Jeff brought her to some family dinners at my mom's. She told us how much she loved having her own place for the first time ever. She said it made her feel like a real grown-up."

"She's the most delightful person," Mac said, his voice wavering. "I don't know what we would've done without her this summer, especially since the twins came."

"She wouldn't want you to blame yourself."

"I wish she'd stayed with us or my parents. We all invited her."

"They probably wanted to be alone. They're madly in love."

"I know."

"We remember what that was like, right?" Katie asked. "Those first early days, when you think you'll die if you can't be together all the time."

Mac loved to think about the day he met Maddie and every day since then. "Yeah, for sure."

"What you said about David is true. If anyone can save Jeff under these circumstances, he can."

"What if he can't, though?" Mac asked her.

"Then we'll have to accept that this was Jeff's time to go."

Mac refused to consider that possibility. "It can't be his time. It just can't. Not yet."

THE EYE of the storm passed over the island on Friday around noon, giving residents a brief respite from the wind and rain. Blaine looked up at the sky as he and Jack Downing surveyed the damage on the island's west side, which seemed to have taken the brunt of the storm. Trees were down, several of the summer cottages had been destroyed, and the road was covered with sand and shells and dead crabs and other crap.

"What a mess," Jack said.

"It'll take a while to come back from this."

"How long do you think the power will be out?"

"Took a few days to get it back during the blackout. Who knows how long it'll be after this? It's not over yet. The eye is the halfway point."

"I saw on the news that the second half of the storm is less potent. Let's hope that's true."

They went to each of the collapsed cottages to make sure no one was trapped. Blaine made a note of the address of each collapsed cottage so he could notify the owners.

A call from dispatch came over the radio. "Chief, we got a call from Sam Weyland that his brother Billy rode out the storm out on his boat in the Salt Pond. The boat is sunk, and there's no sign of his brother anywhere."

"Damn it," Blaine muttered. "That's Billy from the gym. Let's call Linc and the Coast Guard in to search the pond. We'll take the land. Let's also get our divers out there to check to make sure he's not inside the boat."

"Ten-four."

"What the hell was he thinking riding out a hurricane on a boat?" Jack asked.

"Deacon talked to him days ago about moving to shore, but he refused to leave the boat. Said she was his home, and he wasn't going anywhere."

"And now his boat is sunk, and he's probably dead."

Blaine's deep sigh answered for him. "All we can do is give people the warning. We can't make them heed it."

"True."

They got back into Blaine's SUV and continued to make their way around the outer ring of the island, documenting damage to personal property, downed power lines and stopping occasionally to take a chainsaw to a tree blocking the road.

Jack smothered a yawn that caught Blaine's attention. "Are you okay? You seem sluggish today."

"Didn't get much sleep."

"Me either. The storm is fucking loud."

"Seriously loud, but that's not what kept me up."

Blaine came to a stop in front of a huge piece of wood blocking the road. They got out to haul it to the brush that lined the road. When they were back in the car, Blaine glanced over at him as they continued their trek around the island. "What kept you up?"

"A friend."

"Ah, I see. Well, good for you."

"She is good for me." After a pause, Jack said, "I, ah, lost my wife a few years back."

"Oh damn, Jack. I'm so sorry to hear that."

"Thanks. It was rough."

"I can't imagine." Blaine shuddered. The thought of losing Tiffany was something he couldn't bear to consider. "I just can't."

"I hope you never have to go through it."

"What happened to her? If you don't mind me asking."

"I don't mind. She had breast cancer."

"Ah shit. I'm sorry, man. Truly."

"Thanks. I don't say much about it, but my new friend said maybe I ought to open up a bit to my friends out here."

"I'm honored to be considered a friend. And it goes both ways."

"Good to know."

"So the new friend... I take it that's a big deal."

"First new friend I've had since my wife passed."

After a quiet moment, Blaine said, "And it was okay? Being with your new friend?"

"It was great."

"I'm happy for you."

"I'm happy for me, too, which is kind of weird."

"How so?"

"As great as it is to have met someone, it's also sad because I never thought I'd go down this road again."

"I get that. It's bittersweet."

"Exactly that." Jack took a sip of the coffee Piper had made for him at the hotel. "Life goes marching on, regardless of us. Our choice is to either live or not, and once you choose to survive, you've got no choice but to get on with it."

Blaine was incredibly moved by Jack's words. "I give you a lot of credit, man." He wasn't sure he'd be capable of going on without Tiffany. The very thought of having to would have brought him to his knees if he'd been standing.

Jack shrugged. "What're you gonna do?"

"Thanks for telling me about what you've been through."

"I've wanted to for a while now, but it's not something you can just pop into a random conversation."

"I guess not. I'm glad you told me, but so, so sorry it happened."

"Me, too. I've been doing better since I've been out here. There's something about this place…"

"I know, and what's funny about that is when I was growing up here, I thought it was the seventh circle of hell. Nothing to do. Nowhere to go. It was so *confining*. And now…"

"It's paradise," Jack said.

"That it is, and it will be again once this goddamned storm goes away and leaves us alone."

TIFFANY HAD ONLY JUST GOTTEN up and started coffee for her guest when McKenzie appeared in the kitchen doorway with Jax in her arms. She had long dark hair that she wore in a ponytail and gorgeous brown eyes.

"How'd you guys sleep?" Tiffany asked.

"Very well, all things considered. Thank you again for taking us in."

"It was no problem. I'm just glad you're safe. Coffee?"

"I'd love some."

"What can I get for Jax?"

"You don't happen to have any baby food or cereal, do you?"

"In fact, I do."

"You really are a lifesaver."

Tiffany brought Addie's high chair to the table and removed the tray so McKenzie could get him settled. "Does he like Cheerios?"

"He loves them."

Tiffany sprinkled the dry cereal on the tray and laughed when Jax started grabbing the pieces with his chubby hands. "He's adorable." He had light blond hair and big blue eyes, which had Tiffany concluding that he looked like his father.

"Thank you. I'm quite fond of him."

"Such a cute age."

"How old are yours?"

"Ashleigh is six, and Addie is one."

"And you have another coming soon."

Tiffany rested her hands on her baby bump. "Not until the spring, but I'm huge with this one. I think it might a boy."

"I was huge with Jax."

"I'd love to have a boy, but another girl would be fine, too. As long as he or she is healthy."

"That's right."

"What brought you to the island?"

"I inherited my grandparents' summer cabin and came out a week or so ago to check on it. I've had one issue after another. No power, no TV, no Wi-Fi. That's how I didn't know about the storm coming until it was on top of us."

"Oh, that must've been so frightening."

"Especially when it made the house rock like it was going to collapse at any second. I figured we'd be safer leaving than trying to stay. I tried calling for a cab, but none were running, so I decided to walk into town, and we know how that turned out." She shuddered. "I thought we were going to die out there. Your husband saved our lives."

"I'm so glad he spotted you and brought you here."

"I'll be forever thankful to both of you."

Tiffany served cereal and fruit for their breakfast and then for the girls when they appeared together, holding hands like always. Ashleigh was the best big sister ever to Addie. "There're my baby girls. Ashleigh and Addie, this is Ms. McKenzie and her son, Jax. They're going to stay with us for a bit."

"Hi," Ashleigh said with a shy smile as Addie hid behind her sister.

"Addie is our shy one," Tiffany said, reaching for her.

Addie snuggled into Tiffany's embrace and popped her thumb into her mouth. "Daddy," she said over her thumb.

"He's gone to work, but he'll stop in to see you as soon as he can."

Addie was the biggest daddy's girl who'd ever lived, even if she looked just like Tiffany and Ashleigh, with dark hair and the most gorgeous face Blaine said he'd ever seen.

Ashleigh filled a bowl with cereal for Addie and pushed it across the table, knowing her sister preferred the cereal without milk.

"You have quite the helper," McKenzie said.

"She's the best." Tiffany smiled at Ash. "I don't know what I'd do without her." Tiffany took a sip of the decaf iced tea that she drank while pregnant. "Is there anyone you need to call to let them know you're safe? My phone is charged, and you're welcome to use it."

"I should call my mom," McKenzie said, sounding reluctant. Last night, she'd said there was no one to call, so Tiffany was surprised to hear her say she should call her mother.

Tiffany got up to retrieve her phone from the counter and handed it to McKenzie. "Jax is fine with us if you'd like some privacy. Make yourself at home."

"Thank you again, Tiffany. You'll never know what this means to me."

"I'm a mom, too. I get it."

McKenzie took the phone into Tiffany's living room and sat on the sofa to make the call to her mother.

"Hello?" her mother said, sounding guarded as she took the call from a number she didn't recognize.

"It's me."

"Oh, thank you, Jesus. Why haven't you answered your phone?"

"It died two days ago, and I had no way to charge it after we lost power."

"I've been senseless with worry for you and Jax."

"We're fine. The Gansett police chief brought us to his home to ride out the storm. They're taking very good care of us."

"Why couldn't you stay at the cabin?"

"The roof blew off, so we had to leave." She didn't tell her mother the part about trying to walk to town with an infant and how Blaine Taylor had saved their lives. Her mother didn't need to know how close they'd come to disaster, especially since she'd told McKenzie she was foolish for taking a baby to a remote island in the first place.

"That cottage was always a bit ramshackle. I can't imagine what it must be like now."

"It was raining harder inside than out," McKenzie told her.

"You ought to just sell the place and use the money to set yourself up in a whole new life."

"We'll see. I'm not ready to make any big decisions."

"Can I reach you at this number if needed?"

"For now. I'll let you know when my phone is charged again. The power is out on the entire island, so I'm not sure when I can charge."

"As long as I know you two are safe."

"Sorry to worry you."

"I'm thinking of you all the time and wishing I could do something to make things easier for you."

"There's nothing you or anyone can do. I've just got to get through this for Jax's sake, and that's what I'm going to do."

"I'm here if you need anything."

She had learned that her mother's "help" came with strings attached, which was what had sent her to Gansett in the first place. "Thank you. I'll check in soon."

"Sounds good."

McKenzie ended the call just as someone knocked loudly at the front door. Tiffany came into the living room, carrying Addie, and opened the door. "Hey, Duke. What's up?"

"I, um, I heard that you had taken in the woman and child who lived next to me out on the west side. I, um, I brought some of their things from the house."

"That's so nice of you," Tiffany said. "Come in."

Duke came in bearing two huge bags. One was full of toys, and the other had clothes.

McKenzie recognized him as the guy who lived next door. She'd seen him in his yard and had wondered about him. At first glance, he'd seemed like someone she ought to be afraid of. He had kind of a tough, menacing look to him. But it was so kind of him to bring things from their house.

"This is McKenzie," Tiffany said.

"Good to meet you. I was glad to hear you'd found somewhere safe to stay. The house collapsed. It's a total loss. I was so worried about you and the little one. I went to the police, and Blaine… He told me you were here. That was a big relief."

The man she'd once thought of as menacing seemed deeply rattled by the entire thing, which was so sweet. She was so amazed by his kindness that she almost didn't hear the part about her house being a total loss. "It's so kind of you to bring us our things."

"I got what I could find. The clothes are all wet. You'll need to wash them when the power comes back."

Ashleigh came into the living room, carrying Jax. "He was starting to fuss."

McKenzie took him from her. "Thank you, Ashleigh."

"I, uh, just wanted to make sure you're all right," Duke said.

"Thank you so, so much," McKenzie said. "I sincerely appreciate this."

"Least I can do. Let me know if you need some help at the house. I can get a group of guys together to clean up when you're ready."

"Oh wow. That'd be so nice of you. I inherited the cabin from my grandmother."

His brows lifted. "Rosemary was your grandmother? She was a great lady."

"Yes, she sure was. I miss her terribly. I was her only granddaughter. We were very close."

"I was very sad to hear she'd passed. She used to make banana bread for me and the guys at the studio."

McKenzie smiled. "I miss her banana bread almost as much as I miss her."

"Tried to talk her into some ink, but she wasn't having it. Read me the riot act when I did my neck. 'Duke,' she said, 'some day you might need to get a real job, and who's gonna hire you with that crap on your skin?'"

McKenzie sputtered with laughter. "I can hear her saying that! She hated tattoos and piercings. I thought she'd have a stroke when I had my nose pierced as a teen."

"Believe me, I know. She told me to quit using myself as a canvas and get a hobby. All the guys in the shop loved her."

"Thank you for sharing that with me. It's nice to hear that she was so well loved here."

"She was for sure. I looked forward to her arrival every summer. She came right over to hug me and see what a mess I'd made of myself while she was gone."

McKenzie laughed as she brushed away a tear. The memories of her grandmother were among the best in her life, and she missed her fiercely.

"Well, I won't take any more of your time. Let me know when you're ready for cleanup at the house. We'll get you squared away, and you'll want to talk to Mac McCarthy about rebuilding."

Unless the insurance came through for her, that probably wasn't an option, since there was no way she could afford to rebuild. But he didn't need to know that. "Good to know."

"All right, then. You ladies take care."

"Thank you again, Duke."

"No problem."

After he left, Tiffany said, "That was so nice of him."

"Very. He's not what I expected."

"How do you mean?"

"When I saw him next door, I was a little afraid of him, to be honest."

Tiffany put Addie down to toddle over to her toys. "I can see why. He comes off as gruff and intimidating, but he's just the nicest guy."

When Jax started squirming, McKenzie put him down to crawl over to Addie. "I see that now. I feel bad for judging him based on the ink and the ponytail. My grandmother used to talk about having the best neighbors out here. I wasn't sure if he was one of them."

"Now you know they were buddies."

"Which is so funny to me. I can't picture her in a tattoo studio."

"Anything is possible on Gansett Island," Tiffany said.

"I'm beginning to see that."

CHAPTER 25

$\mathcal{P}$iper floated on air, even as chaos reigned all around her. Her heart ached for Owen, Laura and all the Lawrys as they waited anxiously for word about Jeff's condition. The island was without power, the damage was extensive, the storm wasn't over yet, and still… she floated on air.

Her night with Jack had been right out of a dream. She ought to be sore and tired, but she was elated and a little freaked out to think she could've married the wrong man. As much as she'd loved Ben, and she'd truly loved him, he'd never rocked her world the way Jack had. Everything with Jack was on a whole other level from what she'd experienced in the past.

Was she getting ahead of herself to feel so *altered* by one night with a hot man? Probably, but it was hard to contain the abundance of emotions that made her feel like she was made of champagne bubbles or something equally ridiculous.

On the gas stove that was thankfully still working despite the power outage, she cooked omelets for their guests and made coffee by boiling water that she poured over grounds and then transferred to an insulated pitcher that she carried into the dining room, where the two couples in residence were enjoying fruit and juice.

"You're an angel, Piper," Slim said. "I was just asking Erin how she was going to manage me without coffee."

"It wouldn't have been pretty," Erin said.

"This is amazing," Oliver said when he saw the meal she'd prepared. "Thank you so much for feeding us."

"No problem." She went into the salon to let Laura know that breakfast was ready. "I made some pancakes for the kiddos."

"You're the best, Piper."

"Least I can do." She helped to corral the kids into the dining room, where they had two high chairs stashed in the corner for when the family dined downstairs. When the twins were secured in the high chairs and Holden in a booster seat, Piper went to get the pancakes, which she served with maple syrup and confectionary sugar.

Then she returned to the kitchen to make plates of eggs and toast for herself and Laura.

"What would I do without my Piper?" Laura asked the others as she buttered the toast and supervised the twins eating their pancakes.

"She's amazing," Dara said. "We so appreciate your hospitality during the storm."

"We're glad to have you," Laura said. "And all the hospitality is compliments of Piper."

"And Owen," Piper said. "He cooked dinner last night."

"Is there any word on how his brother is doing?" Oliver asked.

Laura shook her head. "Nothing new. Just that he's stable for now, and we're hoping to be able to evacuate him as soon as the choppers can fly again."

"I wish there was something we could do for you all other than pray," Erin said.

"We appreciate the prayers," Laura said. "Jeff is the sweetest guy, and he's already been through so much…"

Dara reached over to squeeze Laura's arm. "He's young and strong. That'll help."

"I really hope so. We're keeping the news from my mother-in-law, who's in Italy with her husband and parents. They were so looking forward to the trip, and they've been so worried about us and the storm. They can't get here, so we figure there's no point in telling them."

"It's the right thing for now," Slim said. "The minute we can fly again, I'll do whatever I can to get his mother to him."

"We appreciate that, Slim," Laura said. "When Owen called, we decided we'll tell her tomorrow so she can start to make her way home. Hopefully, by the time she gets here, we'll have gotten Jeff moved off the island to a hospital in Providence."

"Let me know what I can do to help," Slim said. "I can pick her up wherever she lands on the East Coast."

"That'd be a great help. I'll pass that on to Owen."

As Piper listened to the island's residents step up for one another, she was thankful to live in a place where people took care of their friends the way they did there. Gansett Island was a place where she could get comfortable and build a life for herself, surrounded by people who truly cared.

When she'd come to the island for a getaway earlier in the summer, she'd never expected to find the home of her heart there, but that's what'd happened, and now she knew for sure that she wanted to stay forever.

And if Jack Downing was part of that forever, well… She wouldn't object to that.

"Let's have everyone over later," Linda McCarthy suggested later that afternoon as the second half of the storm passed overhead. "We've got food and power and everything we need for a get-together."

"Is it appropriate to have a party with Jeff and Kelsey in the clinic?" Big Mac asked.

"Everything that can be done for them is being done," Linda said.

"I feel sick over one of our buildings falling on them."

"I do, too, love. Of course I do, but knowing Kelsey, she wouldn't want us to be beating ourselves up. How often did she tell us how much she loved that place?"

"All the time," he said. "But still…"

"I know." Linda hugged him. "It's awful but having people over who need to eat during a power outage isn't disrespectful to them. I promise."

He put his arms around her and rested his chin on the top of her head. "If you're sure about that…"

"I am."

"Then let's have people over."

Linda sent a text to the kids as well as their closest friends and told them to bring anyone who needed a meal. Then she got busy cooking and preparing for an invasion. Having all the kids local was the best thing ever, and she couldn't wait until Janey finished school in Ohio and could be back on the island where she belonged.

Linda's phone rang. "Speak of the devil." She took the call from her daughter. "Hi, honey. Did you sleep at all?"

"Not much. How are things there?"

"You heard about Kelsey and Jeff?"

"I did. It's horrible, but I'm glad David is taking care of them."

It seemed a million years ago now that Janey had been engaged to David Lawrence. "We're thankful for that, too, but we need to get him to Providence as soon as possible."

"Is the storm still bad?"

"Bad enough that the choppers can't fly yet."

"Ugh. How are my babies?"

"They're great. Kyle and Jackson have been amazing. They're playing in the family room and keeping Carolina company."

"How's she feeling?"

"She's doing okay. Anxious like you are for the guys to come back into port."

"I talked to Joe an hour ago. They're hoping to be back by tonight."

"I know you'll sleep better once he's back on the island."

"I'll sleep even better when he's back in Ohio with me."

"Soon enough, love."

"I really hope so. How's everyone else?"

"Mac and Maddie are at the clinic with Kelsey, and I've heard from everyone else that they're hanging in. Everyone is coming for dinner."

"Wish I could be there."

"We'll FaceTime you when they're here."

"Sounds good."

"Try to get some rest, Janey. Everyone is okay, and Joe will be back in soon enough."

"I'll try."

"Love you, baby girl."

"Love you, too, Mama."

Linda put down the phone and got to work cooking for her family and friends, which was still one of her favorite things to do. Since they had no idea how long the power would be out, and the generator would last only so long, she emptied the freezer of chicken, burgers and steak. Hopefully, the power would be back before they ran out of food.

She tried not to get too far ahead of herself. Island life was unpredictable at the best of times, and a Category 3 hurricane was hardly the best of times. It was scary to be "stuck" on a remote island in the middle of the ocean, cut off from mainland support and services.

Normally, she loved the "we're all in this together" spirit of island life, but situations like Jeff's were a reminder of the downside.

She went to the sliding door to check the conditions and saw that the calm of the eye had given way to more wild wind and rain.

"How much longer is it supposed to last?" she asked Big Mac.

"Another couple of hours."

They could only hope that wouldn't be too late for Jeff Lawry.

"SOMETHING IS WRONG," Sarah told Charlie as she moved around their suite, tossing clothes into suitcases and gathering phone chargers and other items they'd taken out of their bags. "We need to go home."

"If something was wrong," Charlie said, "they would've told you."

"No, they wouldn't have, because they know I'm too far away to do anything, but I could tell with one sentence from Owen that something isn't right."

"What did he say?"

"It was what he *didn't* say. I can't explain how I know. I just do."

Her mother, Adele, came through the door that adjoined their suites. "What's going on?"

"We need to go home. Something is wrong."

"Did you talk to the kids?"

"I spoke with Owen, and I could tell something is up. He said every-thing is fine, but it's not. I can feel it." She placed a hand on her gut. "I feel it here. I need to go. You all can stay and enjoy the rest of the trip, but I need to get to my kids."

"If you're leaving, I'm leaving," Charlie said.

"Us, too," Adele said. "If something is wrong, I want to be with the family."

"I'll call the airline and see what we can do," Charlie said.

"Thank you," Sarah said tearfully. "Thank you."

Charlie went to her and hugged her. "I'll get you home as fast as I can."

At times like these, Sarah wondered, as Charlie went into the bedroom to make the call, how she'd managed to live most of her life without him by her side. Her ex-husband would've told her to shut up about going home, they'd spent the money to come to Italy, and by God, they were going to enjoy the trip. That would've been the end of it. But Charlie... All he cared about was her and making her happy. If she was worried or distressed, so was he.

Adele poured coffee for them and brought a cup to Sarah. "What can I do?"

"I'm glad you're here," she told her mother. "I feel better whenever you're close."

"Then I'll stay close until we know what's going on."

Sarah tipped her head and rested it on her mother's shoulder while hoping and praying that whatever the kids were keeping from her wasn't anything serious.

"His blood pressure is dangerously low," Victoria said to David when he returned from a quick break to eat.

David's heart sank at that news. "Shit. We've got to get him out of here."

"Or..."

"What?"

"We could operate here."

"No."

"David..."

He shook his head. "We can't take the chance."

"If we don't, we'll lose him. He's bleeding inside. If we don't stop that —soon—it's game over. We've got to at least *try*."

David took a deep breath and blew it out as he scanned the monitors that painted a dire picture. Vic was right. If they didn't do something— right now—Jeff's chances of survival would be nil. "Let me talk to Owen and the others."

He walked to the waiting area, where the Lawry siblings were sprawled out in chairs, some of them dozing.

Owen jumped up when he saw David coming. "How is he?"

"Not great." David raised a hand to massage the tension from the back of his neck. "There's internal bleeding that needs to be addressed immediately." He forced himself to make eye contact with Owen. "The thing is... We're completely unequipped for something like this."

"Have you done anything like this before?" Owen asked.

"I've assisted during residency, but I've never done it by myself. I want to be honest with you. It's a huge gamble to do something like this here, but I'm afraid if we don't, he won't make it to the mainland."

Owen glanced at Katie, who'd been going back and forth between tending to Jeff and Kelsey and being with her family. "What do you think?"

"We need to ask Kelsey," Katie said. "Jeff proposed to her, and she accepted. She's his fiancée. It should be up to her."

"Could we see her, David?" Owen asked.

"Just a couple of you."

"Owen and Katie," Julia said. "You guys go. We'll support whatever you decide."

John and Cindy nodded in agreement.

"Before we decide to proceed, do any of you know your blood type or Jeff's?"

"I'm a universal donor," Cindy said. "Type O, Rh negative. I've been donating blood for years."

"That's great news," David said. "We're going to need to stock up ahead of the surgery."

"Whatever is needed," Cindy said.

"Let's go talk to Kelsey," Owen said.

Katie led the way for her brother, and David followed them.

When they appeared at the foot of her bed, Kelsey perked up. "What's going on?"

"Jeff needs surgery," Katie said.

"Are the helicopters flying again?"

"Not yet," Katie said.

Kelsey's eyes darted among the three of them before landing on David. "So, what's the plan?"

"I'd have to do it here," David said, "and soon. We believe he's bleeding internally, and that must be stopped. The thing is, Kelsey, we're not equipped for something like this, and having me operate on him isn't ideal. I've assisted on surgeries like this during my residency, but I've never done it myself before."

Kelsey whimpered.

"I'll do everything I can for him," David said. "You have my word on that. But we need to decide now."

Kelsey looked to Katie and Owen. "We have to, right?"

"We do," Owen said grimly.

"We'll get him prepped and keep you apprised," David said. "Katie, I hate to ask this of you, but can you assist?" She had more surgical experience than Victoria did.

"Of course."

"Please," Kelsey said softly as tears rolled down her cheeks. "Please save him. I love him so much."

"I'll do everything I can," David said before he left the room with Katie. They walked into Jeff's room, where Victoria was standing watch. "Let's get him prepped for surgery."

This reminded David far too much of the day that Janey had come in with a ruptured uterus. He'd had to perform emergency surgery to save her and her son. He'd pulled it off once before.

David prayed he could do it again.

CHAPTER 26

"*I*t's the right thing to do, isn't it?" Kelsey asked Owen when they were alone in her room.

"It's the only thing we can do. David said he'll die for sure if he doesn't at least try to stop the bleeding."

"I can't believe this is happening," she said on a sob. "We were so happy last night."

"I heard he proposed, and you accepted."

"He did, and I did. We were so excited, and now... He might die because of me. When we heard the loud crack before the building collapsed, he dove on top of me. He saved me, Owen."

"He loves you."

"And I love him."

"I'm sure that's why he's fighting so hard to stay here with you." He sat on the edge of her bed, careful not to jostle her. "I'm going to be honest with you. When he changed his plans, quit his job in Florida, gave up his new apartment to stay here with you, I thought he was making a big mistake. He'd worked so hard to get through college and to have this amazing opportunity, but he said the career would still be there when he was ready for it. 'All I want,' he said, 'is to be with Kelsey. She needs to be here for another year, so we're staying here. And then we'll see about my career.'"

She continued to sob as he spoke.

Owen handed her a tissue. "After seeing you guys together a few times, I understood why he'd done what he did. I could see that you two genuinely love each other. Maybe you're too young to be making such major life decisions, but you're both adults, and who was I to stand in the way of true love?"

"I love him so, so much. I never expected anything like this when I took the job with Mac and Maddie."

"Funny how that happens, huh?"

She nodded. "I can't lose him, Owen."

"He's going to fight so hard for you. I think maybe his love for you is what'll keep him alive."

"I really hope so."

PIPER WAITED until after lunch to text Jack to see how things were going. She chastised herself for feeling weird about texting him when she had no reason to feel that way. "For God's sake, girl, it's just a text."

"Did you say something?" Dara asked as she came into the kitchen to get ice water from the dispenser on the fridge.

"I was second-guessing my decision to text my new guy."

"Ah, I see."

"And of course I feel ridiculous for second-guessing myself."

"New relationships are such a minefield."

"Especially when he's a widower and this is his first foray since the tremendous loss. And please, keep that between us. He doesn't say much about it."

"Oh, yeah, for sure. That's a lot, and don't worry, I'd never breathe a word of it to anyone."

"Thank you." Her phone chimed with a text. "It's him." She scanned the words in which he said the island was a mess of downed trees and power lines, beached boats and several collapsed houses, but only two people had been seriously injured that they knew of so far, though another was possibly missing.

She responded to him. *One of the injured is Owen's brother Jeff.*

I heard he's in bad shape. I'll be by the hotel a little later. Will you be there?

Yes.

See you then. Can't wait.

"Oh wow," Dara said, "look at that smile."

"I'm seriously gone over him, even after I vowed I wasn't going to let that happen again for a while." She paused before she added, "My ex-fiancé called off our wedding earlier this year. It's way too soon, and yet…"

"And yet," Dara said with a knowing smile. "The best things happen when you least expect them."

"*Oh*, what're we talking about?" Erin asked when she joined them in the kitchen.

"Relationships that come out of nowhere," Dara said.

"That's one of my favorite subjects since it happened to me with Slim."

"How did you guys meet?" Dara asked.

"The first time was at a Tiki Bar gathering with a bunch of people there," Erin said. "The second time, he came to my rescue when I was riding my bike back to the lighthouse from town and got a flat tire—and then sprained my ankle when I was walking the bike. He gave me a ride home, and we've kind of been together ever since, even though we were apart a lot of the time at first. He works in Florida in the off-season, so we kept in touch by text and hours-long phone calls and FaceTime chats."

"I love that story," Dara said.

"How did you meet Oliver?" Piper asked.

"We met at Howard University during our sophomore year and have been together ever since."

"You were lucky to meet your 'one' so young," Piper said.

"We always felt lucky until, you know, life intervened."

"I'm so sorry about your son," Erin said.

"Thank you. We're doing much better since we've been here. Not sure what it is about this place…"

As Erin and Dara talked about how great Gansett had been for them in helping to put their lives back together after loss, Piper felt a burst of hope for herself—and Jack. Maybe this magical island would do the same for them as it had done for so many others.

"What's your story, Piper?" Erin asked.

"Well, I grew up in Western Connecticut, went to college in New York, graduated three years ago and have since held a progression of boring, unsatisfying jobs. I was about to get married earlier this year when my college boyfriend-slash-fiancé, Ben, decided he wasn't ready after all."

"Oh no," Erin said. "That's terrible. I'll never understand why men propose or women accept or vice versa if they aren't sure it's what they want."

"It was shocking, to say the least, but I'd had some doubts myself. I'd felt him pulling away for a while before he finally said the words. In a way, it was a relief, which was a sign that it wasn't the right thing for either of us."

"But it still must've been devastating," Erin said.

"It was. Especially for my mom. She *loved* him."

Dara and Erin laughed at the face Piper made as she poured ice water from a pitcher into their glasses.

"How did you end up on Gansett?" Dara asked.

"I came for a reset weekend, got attacked by a guy I met in a bar, came running back to the hotel, where Laura was such an incredible support to me as I reported the assault. Then she offered me a job, and here we are."

Erin stared at her with big eyes. "You got attacked..."

"Thankfully, I managed to escape before he got what he wanted, but it was a frightening episode, to say the least."

"I hope he's in jail," Dara said.

"He is. He took a plea, which saved me from having to testify. It's all over and done with now, but you know, that sort of thing tends to stay with you."

"It sure does," Erin said. "I had a near miss in college that haunted me for years."

"Same," Dara said. "Thank God for the self-defense classes my father insisted we take before we left home. My sister, Monique, said when it happened to her, the guy didn't walk right for months afterward."

"What is it about men who think they can just take what they want?" Piper asked.

"No kidding," Erin said. "It's revolting."

"In other news..." Piper felt like she was acquiring two new girl-friends, one confidence at a time. "I've met someone new."

Erin grinned at her. "Are we allowed to ask who he is?"

"It's Jack Downing, the state police officer."

"Oh, he's *yummy*," Erin said.

"Is he?" Piper asked. "I haven't noticed."

"Like hell you haven't," Dara said.

They shared a laugh.

"I don't think I've met Jack," Dara said.

Erin got busy on her phone and pulled up Jack's state police photo in a matter of seconds.

"Oh yes," Dara said emphatically. "I approve."

"Wow, I haven't seen that," Piper said. "That's a very good photo."

"A 'very good photo,'" Erin said with a snort. "Yes, it is."

Piper went to the door to the kitchen and looked to make sure they were truly alone. When she returned to the counter where the other two were seated on barstools, she leaned in, keeping her voice down. "Here's the thing. He lost his wife to breast cancer three years ago."

"She must've been so young," Dara said.

"She was thirty-two. Diagnosed at twenty-eight."

"So unfair," Erin said.

"Seriously," Dara said. To Erin, she added, "I promised Piper we wouldn't tell anyone about his loss, since he doesn't talk much about it."

"My lips are zipped," Erin said.

"I'm his first 'new friend' since she died," Piper added.

"That's a lot," Erin said. "How do you feel about it?"

"I feel pretty good, especially after last night."

"Oh?" Dara raised an expressive brow. "Do tell."

"We, uh, decided to ride out the storm together."

"Ride it out, huh?" Erin asked. "Is that a metaphor?"

They lost it laughing.

Laura walked into the kitchen and stopped when she encountered their laughter. "What'd I miss?"

"Piper was telling us how she rode out the storm," Erin said, waggling her brows.

"What's this?" Laura asked, laser-focused on Piper. "Has there been a development with Hot Cop?"

"You could say that. How's Jeff?"

"David is doing risky surgery, which I'm trying not to think about, so tell me everything about you and Hot Cop and give me something else to think about."

"It was pretty hot," Piper said as she processed the news about Jeff having risky surgery.

"Which we knew it would be," Laura said. "I was there when they met. There was a spark of something right from the start."

"It was so weird," Piper told Erin and Dara. "I'd just been through this awful experience with that creep, and when I saw Jack, I just felt better knowing he was helping to take care of the situation." Piper shook her head. "I can't explain it."

"You don't have to." Erin reached across the counter to put her hand over Piper's. "We get it. I don't know him well, but from everything I've heard, he's a great guy. Slim has played cards with him a few times and has nothing but good things to say."

"That's great to hear," Piper said. "I love that about Gansett. If you want to get the goods on someone, it doesn't take much effort." To Laura, she said, "I told them how he lost his wife and I'm the first person he's dated—or whatever you'd call it—since."

"Dated," Laura said with a snicker. "Is that what the kids are calling it these days?"

"Stop!" Piper said with a laugh. "We had a nice time."

"I'm glad you did," Laura said. "Sincerely."

"Thank you."

"Do you feel like this is the start of something important?" Erin asked.

Piper thought about that for a moment, reliving the pleasure she'd found in his arms and the effortless way they connected in bed and out. "I think it could be."

GEORGE MARTINEZ never napped this long, but since his mother could see him breathing thanks to the video monitor on her bedside table, she stayed in bed. She and Alex had grabbed a nap while they could after a mostly sleepless night listening to the storm.

Alex curled up to her back. "Let's hear it for low-pressure systems."

"Is that why he's sleeping so long?"

"Who knows? Whatever it is, it's a gift that shouldn't be squandered." To emphasize his statement, he pressed his erection against her back. "When was the last time we got to have afternoon nookie?"

"Before he was born?"

"That sounds about right. What do you say?"

"Let me brush my teeth first."

"Hurry. This might be the calm before the real storm of this day."

"I'm hurrying."

She rushed through a quick trip to the bathroom and returned to bed with minty-fresh breath.

Alex got out of bed. "I'll be right back. Get naked."

"Yes, dear," she said with a giggle.

He was so blunt, earthy, sexy and absolutely everything to her.

When he returned, she could tell he'd attempted to tame his dark hair with impatient fingers and had succeeded in making it more unruly. His late-day whiskers only added to his crazy sex appeal as he stalked into the room as naked as the day he was born, his cock hard and ready for business.

Alex plopped down on the bed and rolled toward her, kissing her with the red-hot desire she'd become used to in the years they'd been together. She kept thinking that surely it would start to wane, but it seemed to become only more intense as time went on.

He shifted so he was on top of her, gazing down at her with the gorgeous brown eyes their son had inherited. As he sank into her, he threw his head back, exposing his throat. "I never, ever, ever get enough of being inside you, Jenny Martinez."

And he said things like that, which only added to the heat they generated together.

"Hold on to me, babe."

She gripped his shoulders as he pumped into her, taking her on a wild ride that led to an orgasm that hit with almost no warning, in a flash of emotion and excitement that never failed to amaze her. How did he do that *every* time?

"I've missed afternoon nookie," he whispered in her ear, setting off goose bumps that made her shiver.

"Me, too."

To her amazement, he started moving again, pushing himself up on his arms so he was able to look down on her as he started the whole thing up again. "Is this okay?"

"Mmm, you have to ask?"

"Just making sure you're with me."

"Oh, I'm with you."

"Thank God for that. I don't know what I'd ever do without you."

After that, there were no more words, only gasps and sighs and pleasure that made her feel almost drunk in the aftermath.

"I mean that, you know," he said as she cradled his head on her chest. "I couldn't live without you."

"You could."

"No."

"You'd be surprised what you can survive." After having lost her fiancé, Toby, on 9/11, she'd thought for a time her life was over, too. And for a while, it had been. Then she answered an ad for a lighthouse keeper on Gansett Island and found a whole new life with Alex.

"I'd never survive losing you, so you'd better stay right here with me where you belong, forever and ever."

"That's the plan."

CHAPTER 27

By late afternoon, Ethel had begun to move away from the
island and headed toward mainland Rhode Island as a vastly
diminished Category 1 storm.

"Let's go home," Joe said over the radio to Seamus.

"I'm with you, boss man," Seamus replied.

While it was still remarkable to Joe that Seamus, who'd been hired to
run the company while Joe was in Ohio with Janey, was now married to
his mother, Joe appreciated that Seamus always deferred to him when he
was home. Not that he cared about being the boss, but he missed the
ferries and the routine of running the company when he was away, and it
was nice to slip back into his former role whenever he could.

Seamus knew how much that meant to him, which was another
reason to like and respect the Irishman who'd become such a big part of
their lives and their family. He'd seen Seamus step up for his mother big-
time since she'd slipped in the bathroom and badly broken her leg. She
was doing much better, but still had a long road ahead of her. He felt
better about going back to Ohio knowing that Seamus and the boys,
along with a wide circle of friends who'd pitched in to help, had things
under control.

Joe was dying to get back to Janey as soon as he possibly could. This
was the longest they'd been apart since they got married, and he missed
her fiercely. Even though he'd already talked to her multiple times that

day, he missed her so much that he decided to call her just so he could hear her voice as they steamed back to Gansett Island.

"Hey," she said. "Everything all right?"

"It is now that I'm talking to you."

"I miss you so much, it's not even funny."

"I was just thinking the same thing. That's why I called."

"You can never go anywhere without me again."

"That'd be fine with me. I hate being away from you."

"Where are you?"

"About twenty miles from Gansett."

"How long will it take you to get there?"

"Couple more hours."

"You must be so tired."

"I am, but I'm fine to get us home."

"Please be careful."

"I will. Don't worry. The guys are being great about letting me catnap while they keep an eye on things, so I've gotten some rest."

"I can't believe you and Seamus were going to go by yourselves."

"That does seem foolish in hindsight, but how could we ask other people to risk their lives to save our assets?"

Janey chuckled. "'Save our assets.' That's funny."

"Glad to entertain you. What're you hearing from the island?"

"David is operating on Jeff Lawry. Word is if he didn't, Jeff wouldn't survive the night."

"Wow. David sure does earn his keep around there, doesn't he?"

"Yes, he does. Where would we be without him?"

"Don't even want to think about it," Joe said with a shudder. He tried to never think about the day PJ was born. He preferred to think about the day after that, when he knew Janey and his son would survive.

"I'm praying for Jeff and Kelsey and their families."

"Me, too. And I'm praying this goddamned storm goes away so they can get him off the island as soon as possible."

"I hope that's not too late."

HOURS INTO THE SURGERY, David was doing everything he could to stay ahead of the game, but every time he took care of one bleeder, another one appeared. Katie wiped the sweat from his brow and handed him the instruments he needed before he needed them. Even though they'd never done anything like this before, they worked together like a well-oiled machine.

"Are you okay?" he asked her.

"Trying to be."

"If you need to step out, Vic can take over."

"I'll stay. I'd rather be in here than out there worrying about what's happening. At least this way, I know."

"And that's better?"

"Lesser of two evils. And by the way, you're doing a great job."

"I'm worried about the blood loss. We might need more than we have on hand, even with Cindy's donation."

"You've got five of his siblings in the building," Katie reminded him. "Do you want me to ask Vic to work on figuring out the best match?"

"Yeah, let's do that the next time she checks in."

Victoria had been popping her head in every fifteen to twenty minutes to ask if they needed anything and to get an update for Jeff's anxious fiancée and family members.

David kept up the pace of tying off bleeders and cleaning up the internal damage with the goal of not making anything worse than it already was.

Fifteen minutes later, when Victoria checked in, David had started to feel like he might be winning the war.

"Let's type and match the rest of Jeff's siblings just in case," David said to her.

"On it," Vic replied.

"I'll go last if the others don't match," Katie said. "I'm type B."

"We've already determined Jeff is type A," David said.

"Oh gosh," Katie said, realizing she couldn't donate to him. "I don't know what the others are, but they may know."

"We'll still have to confirm, of course," Vic said.

"Yes, please do," Katie said.

There was no room for error in these matters.

"I'll be back," Victoria said.

"I sure hope one of them is compatible," Katie said.

"Me, too."

. . .

VICTORIA WENT to the waiting room where the Lawry siblings awaited word on Jeff's condition. "Let's talk blood types, people. Do any of you know what you are?"

"I'm B," Owen said.

"I am, too," Julia replied.

That ruled them out, leaving Cindy and John as their only hope.

"I don't know what I am," John said.

"Let's get you tested right away in case we need it."

"Do you think you will?" Julia asked.

"David isn't sure we'll need it, but we want to be ready with more just in case."

"He's doing all right, though, isn't he?" Cindy asked.

"So far so good, but there's a long way to go." Victoria wanted to be careful not to give false hope. "Let's get you tested, John."

Victoria went through the motions to process the blood and determined that John was also type B. So Cindy was still the only one who could donate. "I can do more," she said.

"She's already donated a pint, but another half should be okay," Vic said.

"Should be?" Cindy's boyfriend Jace Carson asked. "Will she be okay if she donates more?"

"She'll be tired for a day or two," Vic said.

"That's fine," Cindy said. "Whatever it takes to save Jeff."

She stood to hug Jace and then followed Victoria to the exam room.

When she had Cindy set up to donate more blood, Victoria went to their tiny clinic kitchen and got a bottle of water and a protein bar for her.

"Thank you," Cindy said. "Jeff will be all right, won't he?"

"We're doing everything we can for him. Hopefully, we can get him to Providence tomorrow. Do you want me to get Jace to keep you company?"

"That would be great, thanks."

CINDY KEPT her gaze focused on the painting of sailboats on the far wall of the small room so she wouldn't be tempted to look at the blood pumping out of her body. She'd been known to faint at the sight of blood, and that was the last thing anyone needed with Jeff's life on the line.

Jace came into the room and pulled up a chair next to her, taking her hand and kissing the back of it. "Are you okay?"

She nodded. "Just trying to keep it together. It's all so upsetting."

"I know, babe. But he's tough, and he's been through worse and come out on top. We've got to stay hopeful."

"Trying. Thanks for being here."

"I wouldn't want to be anywhere else. You know that."

His sweetness nearly brought her to tears, but that wouldn't take much right about now. "Have you checked on the boys?" she asked of his sons, Jackson and Kyle.

"They're having fun at the McCarthys' house with PJ and Viv."

"I'm glad the storm is fun for them."

"It was fun for us, too, until we heard about Jeff and Kelsey."

"Yes," she said with a small smile, "it was." After he closed the bar, they'd gone home to the house they now shared and spent the night wrapped up in each other. "But every night with you is fun."

"Same for me. Being with you makes me feel peaceful in a way I never have before."

"I love to hear that. If anyone deserves some peace, you do."

"We all do, and I want that for you and your family, too."

"I keep thinking about my mom and grandparents and how upset they'd be about Jeff. Are we doing the right thing keeping it from them?"

"I think so, sweetheart. There's nothing they can do but worry."

"The knot in my stomach… Brings back memories I'd sooner forget."

"I'm sure."

She glanced fleetingly at her arm that was connected to the needle. "It feels good to be able to do something to help."

"You're our hero."

MADDIE SAT by Kelsey's bed and kept watch over her as she slept. She felt sick seeing their beloved Kelsey injured and upset about Jeff.

Mac came up behind her and massaged her shoulders. "Do you want to head home and get some rest? I'll stay with Kelsey."

"That's okay. I don't mind staying until the babies' next feeding. You should go home, though. Tomorrow will be busy for you, and you haven't slept much the last few days."

"I don't feel right leaving you here."

"I'll be fine, and I think Kelsey would rather have me. No offense, of course."

"I get it." He continued to work the kinks out of muscles gone tight with tension. "When I was a kid, I used to hate this place. I'd rail at being stuck here and always felt like I was missing out on what other kids were getting to do. Since I met you and we started a family and my siblings moved home, I've come to love it. But at times like this… I hate this place again."

"I understand that, but everyone who comes to live here knows the risks. We talked to Kelsey about that when we hired her."

"Knowing the risks doesn't prepare you for something like this."

"No," Maddie said with a sigh, "it doesn't. But they were so happy here. Anyone could see that. Kelsey was thrilled that Jeff decided to stay so they could be together."

"And now he might die because of that decision," Kelsey said as her eyes fluttered open and filled with tears. "It's my fault he was even here."

"No, sweetie," Maddie said, wiping the younger woman's tears with a tissue. "He's exactly where he wants to be. We could all see that."

"We're supposed to get married and have a life."

"You will, honey," Maddie said. "He's fighting so hard for that life he wants with you. I'm sure you're all he's thinking about."

"I want to go back to last night when everything was perfect."

"You'll get back there. You just have to hold on to hope."

"You really think he'll be okay?"

"I can't know for sure," Maddie said, "but if love can keep someone alive, Jeff will live forever because he loves you so much."

CHAPTER 28

*E*ven though it was possible she might be asleep, Seamus called Carolina just to hear her voice.

"Hey," she said in the sleepy, sexy voice that only he ever got to hear. "Everything okay?"

"It's much better now that I'm talking to you, love."

"How is it that you're still a charmer even when you're miles from me?"

"You inspire my charm no matter where I am."

Her low chuckle made him smile for the first time in hours.

"Where are you?"

"Steaming back toward you and the boys."

"I can't wait to have you back."

"I can't wait to be back. Been a long coupla days."

"Sure has."

"How're the boys?"

"Getting restless after being cooped up inside, but they've been such a big help with PJ and Viv."

"Are they taking good care of you, too?"

"Very. They bring me everything I need."

"They're good boys."

"Yes, they are. Jace has called a few times to check on us and said to let him know if we need anything."

"He's good people, too."

"I agree. I'm glad he's become part of our family."

"It's the right thing to have him be part of it. I'd hate to have the boys resent us someday for keeping him from them."

"Yes, for sure. And he's a wonderful guy. Can't hurt to have more people to love them."

"I'll admit it was hard for me at first, but like always, you made me see the way of it. More people to love them is indeed in their best interest."

"They adore you more than anyone, and they always will," Carolina said. "They know who was there for them at the most difficult time in their lives."

"That includes you."

"It does, but you… You're their true north."

"Maybe so, but you're right there next to me, making it all happen and giving me the family I never dreamed I might have."

"You were born for this."

"I was born to love you."

"Charmer."

He chuckled. "I just hope the place is still standing when we get home. Poor Shannon is trying not to think about the wedding, but I know it's on his mind."

"We'll make it work. Somehow."

"Yes, we will."

"How many more hours until you're home?"

"Just a few. I'll see you soon."

"I'll be counting the minutes."

"Me, too. Can't wait."

"Love you, my crazy Irishman."

"Love you more."

"No way."

"Yes way. We'll finish this argument when I get home."

"I can't wait."

EIGHT HOURS AFTER HE BEGAN, David completed the surgery. He felt like he'd done what he could to keep Jeff alive long enough to get him to the mainland. Without the surgery, he surely would've died from blood loss.

"He's still in critical condition and needs to be airlifted as soon as possible," David told Jeff's exhausted siblings. "But we bought him some time."

"Thank you so much, David," Owen said for all of them. "We're so thankful for you and Vic."

"And Katie," David said. "She was a rock star in there."

"And Katie," Owen said, putting an arm around her.

She leaned her head on her older brother's shoulder.

"You should go home and get some sleep. This'll be a long haul for Jeff, and he'll need you guys to be rested. I'll let you know as soon as we've arranged to get him off the island."

The siblings looked to Owen to decide what to do.

"David's right. This will be a marathon, and we need to keep ourselves healthy so we can help him."

"That's right," David said. "I'll call you if anything changes."

"Thank you again, David," Julia said.

"I wish I could do more."

"You did what you could," Cindy said. "And we'll never forget it."

After they had left, David went in to check on Kelsey, who'd been asleep when he looked in on her after the surgery. Vic had reported that Mac and Maddie had left because she had to go home to feed the babies, and he needed rest before the big cleanup began, but they planned to be back as soon as possible.

"Is the surgery over?" Kelsey asked him.

"It is, and Jeff did very well. We got him stabilized to make the trip to the mainland."

"When will that be?"

"We're hoping it'll be soon. The storm has started to move on."

"That's good news."

"He's hanging in there and fighting hard."

"I'm so scared."

"I wish I could tell you there was no reason to be, but he's not out of the woods yet. The sooner we can get him to Providence, the better. But the fact that he's made it this far is encouraging."

"Could I see him?" Kelsey asked.

"We could arrange that, but I have to warn you, it might be upsetting to see him hooked to machines."

"I can handle that if I get to see him."

"Okay. Let me get a chair for you."

With Victoria's help, they transferred Kelsey into a wheelchair and got her broken arm settled on a pillow on her lap.

"Are you comfortable?" Vic asked her.

"As much as I can be when everything hurts."

"We can give you something for that," David said.

"I want to stay awake, so I know what's going on with Jeff."

"I'll give you something that'll take the edge off without knocking you out."

"Thank you."

David carefully wheeled her across the hallway to the largest of the exam rooms, where the beep, beep, beep of monitors was the only sound.

Katie stood at her brother's bedside.

David got Kelsey as close as he could to the other side of Jeff's bed, close enough that she could put her hand on top of his.

"It's me, Kelsey, and I'm here, Jeff. I'm right here, and… I love you. Please stay with me. I need you."

David and Victoria both looked down at the floor in the same instant, moved to tears by the young woman's heartfelt words.

"Could I stay with him for a while?" Kelsey asked.

"If you feel up to it."

"I'm okay, and I'd rather be with him than not be."

"It's fine by me," David said. "It might make all the difference for him to hear your voice."

"I'll stay with them," Katie said. "Go get some rest, David. I'll come get you if anything changes."

Since he'd done all he could for Jeff until he could be airlifted, David left him in the hands of his sister and fiancée and went to sleep while he could.

CHAPTER 29

*D*eacon couldn't wait to get home. He stared at the horizon, trying to will the island to appear in the gloom that had his eyes watering from the effort to stay awake and on course. Never in his life had he been more eager to see anyone than he was to see Julia. If you'd told him a year ago that he'd be chomping at the bit to see any woman, he would've laughed.

Love and commitment and all that jazz were for other people. He would've said he was perfectly fine by himself and had no desire to go all in with anyone. Then he'd met Julia, and that was that.

He'd seen her for the first time at the clinic, after Finn McCarthy's ex-girlfriend had gone nuts and attacked him and Chloe with a knife. Then Deacon had "kidnapped" Julia from Shane and Katie's wedding, and that'd been the start of life as he knew it now. The sweetest life he'd ever known.

Since he was giving himself a headache staring at the horizon, he walked upstairs to the wheelhouse, where Joe was by himself at the helm. "How can you stare at gloom for hours on end?"

"I don't even notice it anymore."

"How close are we?"

"About fifteen to twenty miles to go."

"How long will that take?"

"A couple more hours."

He would die if he had to wait even that long to see Julia, a thought that instantly made him laugh.

"What's so funny?" Joe asked.

"I feel like I'm going to die if I can't see Julia right now."

"That's very sweet, and I know the feeling. Janey is in Ohio stressing out about her whole family dealing with a hurricane and her husband at sea."

"That's gotta suck for her."

"It does, but she feels better now that it's mostly passed and we're all fine."

"Is there any word on Jeff and Kelsey?" Deacon asked.

"Just that David did what he could to stop the bleeding for Jeff. They're hoping to evacuate them sooner than expected since the wind has died down."

"I really hope he'll be all right."

"Me, too. Also, do you know Billy, who owns the gym?" Joe asked.

"I do."

"He's missing. I guess he tried to ride it out on his boat in the Salt Pond. They found the boat, but no sign of him."

"Oh no. I told him two days ago that he needed to seek shelter on land, but he wasn't having it. He said the boat was home, and he was sticking with it."

"Why do people take such foolish chances?"

"I have no idea. I hope they find him safe." Deacon knew the odds of that were low, but he still had hope, especially after what he'd just survived. "How'd you meet your wife?"

"We grew up together here. Mac was my best friend since second grade."

"So you always had a thing for her?"

"I did, but I had to keep it to myself. She was with David Lawrence for thirteen years. We got together after they broke up in spectacular fashion. She caught him cheating on her while they were engaged."

"Damn."

"It was bad," Joe said. "Then her car broke down, she called me, and we've been together ever since."

"That's a great story. Do you ever wonder if you would've gotten together if her car hadn't broken down?"

Joe took a puff from a clove cigarette.

Deacon hadn't seen anyone smoke one of those in years.

"That's a good question. I'd like to think we would have, but I think the thing that really made the difference is that we were on the mainland, away from everything and everyone out here. That made it easier for us to figure things out without an audience, like we would've had here. You know?"

"Do I ever," Deacon said with a grunt of laughter. "When Julia and I started seeing each other, everyone was up in our grill—all her siblings, my buttinsky brother, Tiffany. Even my little nieces were involved."

"That's funny. I bet it was a circus."

"It was, but the truly funny thing was that I didn't care. I was so into her from the get-go that the whole world could've invaded, and all I would've seen was her."

"I get it. Those first days are the best."

"They really were. I keep waiting for that to subside, but it just gets better all the time."

"It doesn't subside when you're with the right person."

"Good to know. I can't wait to see her. Did I mention that?"

Joe laughed. "A time or two. I'm getting my ass back to Ohio as soon as I possibly can. This is the longest I've ever been away from Janey. It totally sucks."

"How does this even happen?" Deacon asked. "You're going along with your life, nothing holding you down, no one to account to, and then *bam*, there she is, and you can't live without her."

Joe shook with silent laughter. "That's about how it happened for me, except she was always there, and I always wanted her, and I'd resigned myself to being alone if I couldn't have her. There was no one else for me but her."

"How long had you known that before you got together?"

"Years. Decades."

"You didn't date anyone else in that time?"

"Here and there, but nothing serious. How could there be when I was in love with her?"

"And all that time, she was with David."

"Yep, and then he fucked it up, and the rest, as they say, is history. But he's redeemed himself with us. He saved Janey and our son when she suffered a very serious complication during his birth. I would've lost them both without him."

"Wow. That's crazy. You're indebted to your wife's ex."

"We owe him everything, and we never forget it. What he did that day with only the tools available to him at a remote clinic… He's a miracle worker."

"Sounds like he's doing the same for Julia's brother."

"Jeff is a lucky man to have David Lawrence with him at a time like this."

"Thank goodness for that, because I can't imagine their family without him."

JEFF CAME TO SLOWLY, blinking several times to bring the face standing above him into focus. He didn't recognize them, and why were the lights so freaking bright? His mouth was as dry as toast as he fought to say the only word that came to mind.

"Kelsey."

"She's okay. I'm Dr. David Lawrence, Jeff. Do you remember what happened at Kelsey's place?"

He searched his memory but couldn't come up with anything.

"The roof collapsed on the two of you, and you shielded her. Your pelvis was fractured, and you've had surgery to stop internal bleeding. We're hoping to evacuate you both to the mainland today."

"See… See her."

"Let us see if she's awake. She broke her arm and has been in a lot of pain."

Jeff winced hearing that. The low throb of pain from his midsection required his full attention when he wasn't trying to keep his eyes open. "Hurts."

"We've been giving you Tylenol and Ibuprofen, because Katie said you wouldn't want anything stronger."

"Right," Jeff said, grimacing.

David gave him a shot in the IV. "That'll bring some relief shortly."

"Thanks."

"Do you feel up to seeing Katie? She assisted me in surgery."

"Mmm." Jeff tried to nod, but his head felt like a cement block. "Yes."

The curtain parted, and Kelsey was wheeled into the room.

The first thing he noticed were the bruises and tears on her face. "Thank God you woke up," she whispered, covering his hand with hers. "I've been so worried."

"I'm okay," he said in a whisper that was all he was capable of. "Are you?"

"My arm hurts, but we're both alive. That's all that matters. You saved me. When we heard the roof collapsing, you jumped on top of me without even thinking."

"Love. You."

She broke down into sobs. "I love you, too."

"Gonna be okay. Promise."

Owen, Katie and Julia came rushing in and surrounded them. His eldest siblings looked like hell.

Julia and Katie wiped away tears when they heard him talking to Kelsey.

"You can't ever scare us like this again," Julia said.

"Sorry. Don't tell Mom."

"We didn't," Owen said. "But she's coming home anyway. She texted that they'd decided to come home because they can't enjoy the trip with everything happening here."

"Go home and sleep. I'm okay. You guys look like hell."

His siblings laughed.

"If only you knew what this has been like for us," Katie said.

"Safe to go home. I swear."

"We're hoping the chopper can get here in the next few hours now that the wind has died down," David said to the others. "I'll keep you posted."

"Johnny is going with you to the mainland," Owen said. "He volunteered."

"Doesn't have to," Jeff said as exhaustion threatened to drag him under.

"Yes, he does," Owen said. "Someone needs to be with you guys. It's all arranged."

"Let's let Jeff get some more rest," David said. "You guys should do what he said and get some sleep while you can. He's going to need you to be strong for him."

"Yeah," Jeff said, his eyes closed. "Kelsey."

She squeezed his hand. "I'm here, honey. I'm right here with you."

Hearing that, he drifted off again.

JACK SPENT all day assisting in the search for Billy Weyland, the only island resident known to be missing in the storm. While the rest of

Blaine's team answered other calls from island residents, he and Jack focused on the missing-person search, assisted by the Coast Guard.

"We're calling it for the night," Linc Mercier said when they came together on separate boats in the middle of the Salt Pond as the daylight began to fade. "We'll start again at zero eight hundred."

"We'll see you then," Blaine said, turning the police boat toward the New Harbor dock where it was kept.

Earlier, Blaine had mentioned the need to quickly acquire a new boat to replace the one lost in the accident that'd nearly killed Deacon.

As the day went on, Jack had gone through the motions of doing his job, but his mind was a million miles from Gansett Island as he'd realized, halfway through the day, that it was Ruby's birthday.

Her goddamned birthday, and he'd forgotten until he took a break to grab a quick bite to eat with Blaine, checked his phone and saw the texts from her family's group chat, celebrating what would've been Ruby's thirty-fifth birthday. Each of her siblings and her parents had shared memories from past birthdays and speculated about what she'd have to say about turning thirty-five. The messages had provoked laughter and tears from the others, while her husband hadn't given her a freaking thought all day. He'd been too busy wallowing in more recent memories, the ones he'd made with another woman.

He was disgusted with himself.

Sick to his stomach.

And heartbroken to have forgotten such an important date.

Sure, he could cut himself a break since the hurricane cleanup had kept them moving all day, but Ruby's birthday hadn't even been on his radar.

How was that possible?

The realization had sent him spiraling into thoughts and feelings he'd thought were long buried in the past. Grief, sharp and nasty, clawed at his guts with ruthless disregard for the progress he'd made, the journey he'd traveled for all the days he'd spent without her. The grief didn't care that he was feeling better, that he was moving on, that he had found someone else whom he might love.

None of that mattered.

"Jack?"

Blaine's call to him dragged him out of the emotional swamp and back to the present.

"What's the matter?"

"Nothing. Are we done here? I need to split."

"Yeah, we're good until zero eight hundred."

"See you then."

He was gone before Blaine could ask more questions he didn't want to answer. All day, he'd looked forward to when he'd be able to go find Piper at the hotel and pick up where they'd left off early that morning. But now... All he wanted was his solitary room in the building adjacent to the Coast Guard station where he could be alone with his memories and his recrimination.

"OH, BUMMER," Piper said.

She was in the salon with Laura, the kids, Dara, Oliver, Slim and Erin, all of whom had decided to stay for another night because they were having such a nice time together.

"What's up?" Dara asked.

"Jack texted that he won't make it over tonight. Something about having to stay late at work."

"That's too bad," Erin said.

"Oh well. Duty calls." Piper didn't share the fact that the text had come across as brusque. It had merely said, *Can't make it tonight.* That's it. She'd made up the part about having to stay late at work so the others wouldn't ask questions. She felt foolish for telling them how much she was looking forward to seeing him again.

"They're probably straight out cleaning up Ethel's mess," Slim said from his perch on the hearth where he was keeping the fire going.

"No doubt," Piper said.

She debated whether she should text him back, but in the end decided to go with something short and sweet to match the tone of his initial message. *Hope everything is okay.*

The text showed up as Read a few minutes later, but he didn't reply.

What was going on? Needing a minute to herself, she got up and left the salon.

Laura followed her to the lobby. "Everything okay?"

"It was," Piper said. "But something must've happened." She showed Laura the text she'd received. "The last time I talked to him, he said he couldn't wait to pick up where we left off."

"Hmm," Laura said. "That's odd."

"Maybe he's having second thoughts. Last night was a big deal to him. An even bigger deal to him than it was for me."

"That's possible. What will you do?"

"What can I do? He said he can't make it." She hadn't been this disappointed since Ben canceled their wedding, and for some ridiculous reason, this felt worse than that.

"My aunt and uncle are having everyone over tonight. Why don't you come with us and get a change of scenery?"

"I don't know if I'd be up for that."

"It'll be fun. The others are coming, too," she said of their guests.

"What time are you leaving?"

"Soon. Come on. There's no sense in hanging here by yourself. Let's go be with some fun people, get something to eat. You'll feel better after a night with my family. They're always a good time."

"All right," Piper said as a loud roar sounded outside.

"Oh, thank God!" Laura ran for the front door to watch the Life Flight chopper go over on the way to the clinic. "Thank God."

CHAPTER 30

*B*laine made sure the boat was secure and then headed for his SUV in the parking lot of the McCarthys' marina. When he reached the four-way stop sign, he considered his options. Straight ahead was home, but something had him hanging a right and heading for the Coast Guard station.

He'd gone about a mile when he spotted Jack Downing, head lowered, hands in pockets as he walked briskly.

Blaine pulled up next to him and put down the window. "Hey. Get in."

Jack kept moving as if Blaine hadn't said anything, so he laid on the horn, startling the other man.

"Get in the truck, Jack."

When Jack looked up at him, the despair he saw on his face broke Blaine's heart. Whatever was going on with him was bad.

"I'm all set. Thanks, Blaine."

"I'm not asking you. Get in the truck."

A flash of outrage replaced the despair, but only for a second. He could tell that Jack was dying to tell him that Blaine wasn't his boss, and he didn't have to do what he said.

"Get in, Jack."

Expelling a huff of indignation, Jack got in the passenger side and slammed the door.

"Where you going?"

"Home."

"What's wrong?"

"Nothing."

"I can sit here all night. Nothing better to do." That was the biggest lie he'd ever told. At the end of a hideously long day, all he wanted was his wife, his daughters and a cold beer—in that order. Any delay getting to them irritated him, but something had told him to take that right turn, and there he was.

Blaine pulled off the road, put the SUV in Park and activated the flashers. While he waited on Jack, he sent Tiffany a text. *On the way home but taking care of one more thing. Hope it's quick.*

Take your time, she wrote back. *We're fine but looking forward to Daddy coming home.*

Ah, he loved being Daddy to Ash and Addie. He could picture them at home, Tiffany curled up on the sofa while something mouthwatering cooked in the kitchen. She'd be overseeing Ashleigh and Addie's playtime, with McKenzie and Jax in the mix today. He hoped they were getting along okay. It was a lot to ask his wife to take in strangers, but he'd known she'd be as eager to help them as he'd been.

"You can just drop me at the barracks," Jack said after a long silence.

"We're not going anywhere until you tell me what happened between earlier, when you told me you were excited to be seeing someone after a terrible loss, and whatever went down an hour ago when your entire disposition changed."

"What're you, some sort of therapist now?"

"Nah, I'm just a friend wondering what's up with my buddy."

That seemed to take some of the starch out of Jack's posture. "I'm fine. Really. I just want to go back to my room and be alone."

"Hmm, see, I thought you'd be running right back to the lady you told me about, the one who had you smiling like I've never seen you smile."

"Please, Blaine. Just give me a ride home, will you?"

"Did she blow you off?"

"No."

Blaine sat for another minute before he abruptly threw the SUV into gear and made a U-turn, away from the barracks.

"What're you doing?" Jack asked. "Let me out."

"You're coming with me. Whatever's going on with you, you can figure it out at my place rather than off alone in a room somewhere."

"Goddamn it, Blaine. We're barely even friends. What right do you have to force your way into my life?"

"I have no right, but I've known you a couple of years now, and I've never seen you smile like you did earlier today. I wouldn't be doing my job as your friend if I didn't try to figure out what happened."

"You want to know what happened?"

"Yeah, I do."

"Fine. Here it is. I spent last night completely wrapped up in Piper, so wrapped up that I totally forgot that today was my wife's birthday. She would've been thirty-five today, and I didn't remember that until her family group chat, which still includes me, lit up with birthday wishes for her that I didn't see until this afternoon."

Blaine took a minute to think about what he should say next as he continued toward home.

"So could you please take me home like I asked you to?"

"Nah, you're coming with me."

Jack punched the passenger door hard enough to leave a dent. "For fuck's sake."

"And don't think about lunging for that door or any other stupid thing you might do."

"This is bullshit. I don't want or need your help. Just let me out."

"Let me ask you something."

Jack blew out a deep breath full of frustration. "What?"

"If it was me who was obviously dealing with something heavy, would you have left me out there on the side of the road, or would you have done what I did?"

Jack didn't reply, which said it all.

"I'll take you home later. After you eat something and have a minute to get your head together among friends."

"What friends?"

"Everyone is going to the McCarthys' later."

"I don't want to do that."

"It'll be good for you to be around people."

If it was possible to *hear* someone fuming, Blaine could tell Jack was about to blow a gasket.

"When was the last time you lost a wife?" Jack asked in a tight, pissed-off tone.

"Never, thank God, and I hope I never do."

"Then *how in the fuck* do you know what I need?"

"I don't. I just know that in your current state of mind, it might not be safe for you to be alone."

"What're you thinking I'm going to do?" Jack asked, incredulous. "If I were going to do *that*, it would've happened a long-ass time ago."

Blaine felt bad that he might've added to Jack's agitation, but he didn't regret picking him up or taking him home to his place rather than letting him go to a cold, lonely room when he was obviously upset. "You never know what'll drive someone over the edge."

"*You're* driving me over the edge."

"I'm driving you to my place, where Tiffany will have snacks and we'll have a cold one to take the edge off a rough day. And then we'll stop by the McCarthys' for dinner and some island gossip. After that, I'll take you home."

"I hope you don't expect me to put out at the end of this date you've arranged for us."

Blaine barked with laughter. "I'm good, but thanks for the offer."

"Fuck off. I wasn't offering."

LINDA HAD BEEN COOKING all day and had produced enough food to feed an army. Big Mac had said as much as he took a deviled egg off a platter and just missed getting his hand slapped by his beloved.

"Our family is an army," she'd said, "and when you add in friends, it's multiple battalions."

Big Mac was about to come back with a reply that would've been witty, but he was interrupted by the sound of a chopper going over the house. He ran for the sliding door and watched the Life Flight chopper speed overhead on the way to the mainland. "There they go," he said. "Thank goodness."

Linda put her arms around him from behind. "They're going to be okay. I know it."

"I told Mac to pay for anything they need."

"That's good. I know you feel terrible about this happening at a place we own, but it wasn't your fault."

"I still feel responsible for those two kids who were hurt at our place."

"That's why I love you. Because you take care of everyone."

"I try, and it breaks my heart that they were hurt."

"Mine, too, but we'll be there for them for the long haul."

"Yes, we will."

They were interrupted by a shout from PJ. "Grammy! When are my cousins coming?"

She turned from Big Mac to scoop up the little guy. "Very soon, my love."

"I can't wait! I want to see Thomas and Hailey and Mac!"

"They can't wait to see you, too."

PJ squirmed, wanting to get free.

She put him down, and he ran off to find Kyle and Jackson. "He's never going to be the same after being with those big boys," Linda said.

"He'll be asking for them for weeks."

"I can't wait to have them home to stay."

"Soon enough, love. Our Janey will be a doctor of veterinary medicine, at long last."

They'd been outraged when David Lawrence had discouraged Janey from going to vet school right out of college because, as he'd said at the time, island practices wouldn't cover the cost of two of them going to medical school. David had since earned their undying gratitude for delivering Hailey, saving Janey and PJ and for his devoted care to all the island's residents.

But back in the day…

"You're thinking about David," Big Mac said.

"I am, and today, I'm thankful he was there when Jeff and Kelsey needed him."

The front door opened, and Hailey, Thomas and baby Mac came rushing in, followed by their parents, who each had a baby in a car seat carrier.

"Grammy!" Hailey said. "The storm is finally over, and we can go back outside to play."

"Kelsey got hurt," Thomas said, his blond brows furrowing.

Linda picked up Mac and kissed the others. "I heard that. But she'll be okay."

"She broke her arm," Thomas said. "Mommy said she might not be able to play with us for a while."

"She'll be back with you very soon," Linda assured him. "Who's hungry?"

A shriek preceded PJ down the stairs to greet his cousins.

Thomas, always patient with the little ones, hugged PJ and Viv, who toddled after her brother.

With the kids occupied, Linda went to the kitchen to start putting out the food.

Adam and Abby arrived with Liam, followed by Stephanie, Grant, Kara and Dan.

"How's Jeff?" Linda asked Steph, who'd been at the clinic with her stepsiblings the night before.

"He was talking before the chopper came. Everyone is feeling more encouraged."

"I'm so glad to hear that. Poor Sarah must be beside herself with worry."

"They haven't told her," Steph said. "They figured there was nothing she could do, but she decided to come home anyway."

"Mother's intuition," Linda said. "She knows something is going on."

Evan and Grace arrived with Mallory, Quinn, Luke, Syd and Lily.

Linda was never happier than she was when surrounded by her family and closest friends. She made a plate of appetizers and poured a glass of Chardonnay that she took to Carolina.

"Thank you, friend."

"My pleasure."

"I owe you an entire senior citizenship full of me waiting on you after these last few days," Carolina said.

"You owe me nothing. After all we've been through together, we're surely even at this point."

"We're not even close to even, as you well know."

"Eh." Linda waved her hand as she took a seat next to her dearest friend. She and Caro had gone from the best of friends to family when her Joe married Janey. "Who's keeping score? Not me."

"Seamus just texted to say they're an hour out," Carolina said.

"Oh, good. You'll be so happy to have him back."

"Sometimes I still can't believe the way that man has taken over my life in the best possible way. I feel like a fool missing him so much when he was only gone for a couple of days."

"Remember how hard you tried to fight it with him?" Linda asked, smiling.

"He never lets me forget that."

"I'm sure he doesn't. You led him on a merry chase."

"I'm almost old enough to be his mother!"

Linda laughed the way she did every time Carolina said that. "You naughty cougar."

"I still feel that way sometimes, but oh, is he ever worth it."

"Yes, he is."

Jackson came over to where they were sitting together to ask if Carolina needed anything.

"I'm all set, my sweet boy, thanks to Auntie Linda."

"Let me know if you need water or something."

"I will, honey. Thank you." She watched him scamper off to join his brother and the other kids. "They're such good boys."

"They're delightful. I'm glad we had the chance to spend this time together and really get to know them."

"Never thought I'd be raising another family at my age."

"They'll keep you young. Them and your young stud of a husband."

"Stop!" Carolina said as she turned bright red.

Linda rocked with silent laughter.

"What is going on over here?" Maddie asked.

"Your mother-in-law is being outrageous," Carolina said.

"Not my mother-in-law. She's a respectable grandmother."

"Sure she is," Carolina said, rolling her eyes.

Ned and Francine arrived with a large, covered dish that Ned carried as he followed his wife inside.

"I made ziti," Francine said. "Boiled the water on the grill."

"I told you to get a generator," Mac said to Ned.

"Pshaw. Lived without one all these years, and I'm not gonna wimp out now."

"I'd like to get one," Francine said to Mac. "I'll call you when things calm down."

"I can hear ya," Ned said.

"Good, you old fool. You might be used to living without power for days on end, but I'm not into it if there's an alternative."

"Didn't I take good care a ya this mornin' with coffee and breakfast and everythin' ya needed?"

"You did, but there's no need to be without power if we don't have to be."

"What she said," Betsy said as she and Frank arrived with more food. "I want a generator, too."

"We'll ask Mac to order us one tomorrow, love," Frank said.

"Y'all are a buncha pampered babies," Ned muttered.

"Look at my hair, Ned," Betsy said. "This is what happens when it air-dries, and I don't have a straightener."

245

"I think your hair looks lovely," Frank said.

"You already know I'm a sure thing, so there's no point in lying," Betsy said to Frank as the others laughed.

"I'm not lying. I love your curls."

Finn and Chloe arrived with their dog, Ranger, as well as Kevin, Chelsea, Summer, Riley and Nikki, bringing even more food.

"Uncle Frank!" Finn said. "Just the man I'm looking for."

"What's up, son?" Frank asked his nephew.

"Chloe and I want to get married right now. We don't want to wait another day."

"I can help with that," Frank said. "Do you have a license?"

"We'll get one as soon as the town hall reopens and make it official," Finn said.

"That works for me," Frank said. "When do you want to do it?"

"Would now be okay?" Finn looked around. "Almost everyone is here except for Janey and Joe. Maybe we could FaceTime them?"

"What'd we miss?" Slim asked as he came in with Erin, Dara, Oliver, Piper, Laura, Owen, their kids, Shane and Katie.

"Now everyone is here," Finn said.

"Let's have a wedding," Frank replied, smiling.

CHAPTER 31

"I can't believe we're doing this," Chloe said to Nikki as they stood together in an upstairs bedroom at the McCarthys' home. Nikki had helped her change into the sexy white dress Chloe had bought months ago with her wedding in mind. They'd wrangled her purple-highlighted hair into a glamorous updo that Chloe orchestrated with help from Nik, who would be her maid of honor.

"It's very romantic."

"Finn is afraid I'll back out if he doesn't make it official soon."

"Would you?" Nikki asked, shocked.

"Part of me still thinks it's wrong to saddle him with my problems."

"You're not saddling him with anything. He loves you with all his heart. You'd ruin him if you ever left him."

"I know," Chloe said with a sigh, "and I love him with all of mine. Still… It's a lot to ask of anyone."

"Hey, Nicholas," Finn said from the doorway. "Can you give me a minute with my bride?"

"Of course. I'll see you downstairs."

"We'll be right there," Finn said, his gaze fixed on Chloe. "You look stunning, as always."

"Thank you, so do you."

He'd changed into a suit coat, dress shirt and the one pair of khaki pants he owned. She teased him about being a grown man with one pair of dress-up pants. "How many do I need?" he always asked in response to her ribbing.

"I couldn't help overhearing you and Nikki."

"I'm sorry. You weren't meant to hear that."

"It wasn't anything I don't already know, but it still breaks my heart to hear that you think I'd be better off without you, when you should know better by now."

"I do know better, but—"

"No buts, Chlo. You're everything I want and need. Will it always be easy? Hell no. Will there be hard times? I'm sure of it, but everyone has hard times. I'd rather go through the hard times with you than anyone else. You want to know why?" he asked, running a fingertip over her cheek.

"Why?"

"Because you're the only woman who's ever made me want forever with her. You're the only one I'll ever truly love. You're the only one I want to wake up to every day and go to sleep with every night. You're the only one I want to hold and kiss and make sweet love with. You're the only one for me, Chloe. Do I wish you didn't have to deal with so much pain and uncertainty? You bet I do, but I'm right here for all of it. The good, the bad, the painful. I'm here for it. I take you to be my wife because you're the only one I can picture spending the rest of my life with. Will you take me to be your husband?" He wiped away her tears with the gentle stroke of his thumb.

"Yes, Finn, I'll take you to be my husband."

His smile was a thing of absolute beauty.

She'd asked his dad to walk her downstairs. "Send Kev up."

Finn leaned in to kiss her. "See you down there."

"I'll be there." It had been, she realized now, inevitable from the start that they would take this next step together. He'd never wavered in his devotion to her or his willingness to roll with the uncertainties that came with rheumatoid arthritis. He'd shown her what true love was every day they'd been together, and even after she'd offered him multiple opportunities to choose an easier life for himself, he still chose her.

Kevin McCarthy appeared in the doorway, flashing the same irresistible grin both his sons had inherited from him. "You're a knockout."

"Aw, thanks."

"May I come in?"

"Please do. Thanks for the use of your arm."

"My arm is your arm."

"Before we go down there," Chloe said, battling an overload of emotion, "I just want to say thank you."

"For what, honey?"

"For your unconditional acceptance of me and my situation, and... for giving me the family I've always dreamed of but never had until I had you and your amazing sons and Nikki and Chelsea and Summer."

"We love you," Kevin said with poignant simplicity that touched her deeply. "And we love you with Finn, who's shown me sides of himself I never knew were there until he met you. He was always a good man. You've made him a great man."

"No, Kevin, you and your brothers made him a great man."

"Let's call it a draw." He kissed her cheek. "Welcome to the McCarthy family, Chloe. We're so, so happy to have you."

When he offered her his arm, she hooked her hand through the crook of his elbow.

"And thank you for the honor of escorting you."

Chloe looked up at the man who'd been like a father to her since she started seeing his son. "There was no one else I would've asked."

WITH RILEY BY HIS SIDE, Finn waited with tremendous anticipation for his bride to appear. The family that had given him so much was gathered around them, his cousin Janey on FaceTime. He'd decided to tell his mother after the fact, as she'd be annoyed to not be there—and rightfully so—but Finn hadn't wanted to wait another minute to make things official with Chloe. He would invite his mother to join them for the reception they'd hold next summer.

As wonderful as things had been with Chloe from the start, he'd begun to feel her pulling away since it became clear that her new medicine hadn't been the miracle they'd prayed it would be. The worse her condition became, the more she worried about the effect on him. He hoped that after today, she might never again be worried about something she couldn't change.

Her illness was part of who she was, and he loved everything about her, even her swollen knuckles. She would tell him he was nuts to think that way, but it was the truth. Did he wish with every fiber of his being that she could be spared the terrible pain? God yes, but if she had to live with that, at least he could be there to make everything else as easy for her as possible.

She feared that they wouldn't be able to have children.

He'd rather live without kids than live without her.

It was really that simple.

Finn glanced at Riley, who grinned at him.

"You ready for this?" Riley asked.

"Hell yes." He'd been born for this moment and this woman. He had no doubt of that.

When his father and Chloe appeared on the stairs, he saw only her smile. Her happiness and comfort were his only concerns, and from today on, they would be husband and wife, together forever, come what may. He was there for it all, as long as he got to spend his life with her.

Kevin delivered Chloe to him, kissing her cheek and then his as he joined their hands. "Love you both with all my heart," Kevin said with tears in his eyes.

"Love you, too, Dad."

"Thank you, Kevin."

"My pleasure, sweetheart." He stepped back to stand with Chelsea, who had Summer in her arms. Kevin put his arm around his wife and wiped away tears.

"Hi there," Finn said to Chloe. "You're gorgeous."

"So are you."

"I got nothing on you, babe."

"Are we ready to get married?" Frank asked.

"Let's do it," Finn said.

Chloe handed the small bouquet she'd put together earlier to Nikki.

Finn gently took hold of her hands, always careful not to cause her any more pain than she already had to deal with.

"Dearly beloved family and friends, we're gathered here today to celebrate the love of Finn McCarthy and Chloe Dennis, who are ready to pledge their lives and their love to each other. They've chosen to recite their own vows, so I'll turn it over to my nephew. Finn?"

"Sweet, sweet Chloe… The first time I ever saw you, I was dazzled. So dazzled that I managed to smack heads with you within a few minutes of meeting you." As they both smiled at the memory, Finn said, "The haircut you gave me that day was the most erotically charged thirty minutes of my life up to that point. You've topped that many times over since then."

"Finn! Stop."

He laughed at the blush that turned her face bright red. "I'm just saying. You're a smoking-hot woman, and I've been in your thrall since the second we met. And then I got to know you. I got to know your heart and your soul, and I was even more dazzled by what's on the inside. Your courage and resilience inspire me every day as you deal with challenges the rest of us can only imagine. I'm so, so happy that you're going to be my wife, that we have forever to spend together, that I get to wake up to your gorgeous face every day for the rest of my life. I, Finn McCarthy, take you, Chloe Dennis, to be my wife, to have and to hold, to love and honor every day of my life."

Finn wiped away Chloe's tears with the stroke of his thumb.

"I'll never forget you or your man bun or the first time you came into the shop and literally took my breath away—and nearly knocked me out."

Finn laughed. Would they ever forget that day? Nope. Not ever. He leaned in to kiss the spot on her forehead where they'd connected when they bent to pick something up from the floor at the same time. They'd connected in every possible way that day.

"Since then, you've shown me time and time again that I can count on you in the best and worst of times. You've never wavered in your devotion to me, even when I tried to talk you out of loving me."

"Can't be done."

"I've come to realize I'm stuck with you, and I'm a very lucky girl to be loved by you. I also want to thank you for giving me the family I've yearned for—Kevin, Chelsea, Summer, Riley, Nikki, Evelyn… All of you are so dear to me, as is the entire extended McCarthy family. You have no idea what you've done for me with your unconditional love and acceptance. I, Chloe Dennis, take you, Finn McCarthy, to be my husband, to have and to hold, to love and honor every day of my life."

"Finn and Chloe," Frank said, "you have stated your intentions before your family and friends. You have decided to forgo the exchange of rings, so it is now my pleasure to declare you husband and wife and to wish you a long and happy life together. Ladies and gentlemen, I give you Mr. and Mrs. Finn and Chloe McCarthy. Finn, you may kiss your bride."

Finn cradled her face in his hands and gazed at her for a breathless moment before he touched his lips to hers. "My wife," he whispered.

"My husband."

"Best day of my life."

"Mine, too."

. . .

JACK SAT between Ashleigh's and Addie's car seats in the back of Blaine's SUV.

"Why are you frowning?" Ashleigh asked him.

"I'm not frowning. That's my face."

"No, it isn't."

"Yes, it is."

"No."

"Yes." He made a face at her that made the little girl laugh.

"Your face is going to freeze like that, and then you'll be sorry."

Jack wouldn't have thought himself capable of laughing until Ashleigh showed him otherwise.

Then Addie joined in the laughter, and Jack couldn't deny that he felt lighter than he had in hours. He hated to say that Blaine might've been right but being with Tiffany and the girls had gotten his mind off his own troubles.

He'd planned to get out of the vehicle at the McCarthys' house and bug out to walk home until Ashleigh slipped her hand in his and made it impossible for him to escape without it getting messy. Reluctantly, he walked into the house with Blaine and his family, intending to stay for a few minutes before making his excuses.

"What'd we miss?" Blaine asked Mac.

"Finn and Chloe got hitched."

"Oh wow. That's awesome."

Jack hovered by the door, so Blaine gave him a not-so-subtle push forward. "Get a drink."

"I don't want one."

"Honestly, Blaine," Tiffany said. "If he wants to go home, take him home."

"Not yet," Blaine said.

"Do you want me to give you a ride home, Jack?" Tiffany asked.

"I can walk."

"That's not safe with the roads covered in sand and other debris," she said.

"I'll be fine."

"Hang for a bit before you go," Blaine said. "You can't help but have a good time in this crowd."

"I tried to tell you that I'm not in the mood for a good time tonight."

"And I tried to tell you that you shouldn't be alone."

Jack looked to Tiffany for help even as Ashleigh still held his hand.

"Blaine, you're being overbearing. Jack is a grown man and doesn't need you telling him what to do. It's the chief-of-police thing," Tiffany said to Jack. "It makes him think he's the boss of everyone."

Again, Jack laughed when he hadn't thought it would be possible.

Blaine scowled at his wife. "That is not true. I don't want my friend to be alone when he's obviously upset."

"Which is very nice of you," Jack said, "but I'm okay."

He no sooner spoke the words than Piper appeared in the kitchen, seeming stricken to see him there. Her gaze collided with his, full of hurt.

Damn it.

"Piper."

She turned away from him.

"I'll be right back." He released Ashleigh's hand and chased after Piper. "Wait. Please. Let me explain."

"No need to explain anything." In the kitchen, Piper poured herself a glass of iced tea from a pitcher and started to walk away. "You owe me nothing."

"Yes, I do. I owe you an explanation."

"Not here."

"Where, then?"

She shrugged. "I'm with my friends."

He watched her walk away and sit with a group of people in the living room. "Shit."

"What's wrong now?" Blaine asked.

"I told her I couldn't hang out tonight, and then I showed up here. So thanks for that."

"Sorry."

"Eh, it's fine. I'm going to leave, though." Before Blaine could protest, Jack added, "I appreciate you looking out for me. I really do. Thank you for being a friend."

"Sure. If you need anything…"

"I know where you are."

"Always."

"Thanks, Blaine." Jack hugged Tiffany, kissed Ashleigh's forehead and gave Addie an affectionate squeeze. "Thanks for having me."

"Any time," Tiffany said. "Are you sure we can't drive you home?"

"I'm all good. I promise."

"Be safe."

"I will."

Jack went out into the cool, damp air and took a deep breath. As he walked, he dictated a text to Piper into his phone. *I'm so sorry about tonight. Today was Ruby's birthday, and I forgot about it until I got some texts in her family's group chat. It threw me for a loop, to say the least. How could I forget her birthday? How? My issues tonight have nothing at all to do with you. I thought about our night together all day and was looking forward to tonight. I'm sorry. I'm leaving now, but I'll make it up to you.*

He sent the text before he could rethink every word and hoped he'd done the right thing by telling her he was melting down over his late wife the day after he slept with her for the first time. For some women, that would be an immediate deal breaker. He had no idea how it would be received with Piper, but he couldn't help how he felt.

He'd shared the truth with her.

That was all he could do.

CHAPTER 32

$\mathcal{P}$iper tried to shake off the sick feeling that had overtaken her the second she'd encountered Jack at a party after he said he couldn't hang out that night. Like she'd said, he didn't owe her anything, but damn, it smarted to realize he had blown her off to come to a party.

He could do whatever he wanted. It wasn't like they were in an exclusive relationship.

"Was that Hot Cop I saw?" Laura asked quietly.

"Yeah."

"What's going on?"

Piper shrugged. "He said he couldn't hang out tonight." Her phone buzzed with a text. She withdrew it from her pocket, read the message from Jack and then jumped up. "I have to go."

"Where?"

"To Jack. I have to go to him."

"Do you want me to drive you?"

"No, that's okay. He just left. I'll catch up to him."

"Please be careful out there. It's dark, and the roads are a mess."

"I will. I'll check in later."

Piper said thank you to Mr. and Mrs. McCarthy, wished the newly-weds the best of luck and rushed out the front door. She had a rough idea of where the Coast Guard station was, and Jack had said their barracks were located next door to the station. Piper hadn't done much running since high school track, but she took off at a sprint, determined to catch up to him.

It was dark, cool and damp, but the wind had finally died down, and the rain had stopped about an hour ago.

Her legs and lungs quickly protested the unexpected workout, reminding her of how long it had been since she'd been a runner.

She kept her eyes focused ahead, looking for him as she ran along the road that ringed the island's perimeter. About a mile from the McCarthys' home, she spotted him up ahead, walking quickly, head down, hands in pockets. "Jack!"

He stopped, turned and stared at her, incredulous. "What're you doing out here?"

"Looking for you."

"It's not safe, Piper. It's dark and... It's not safe."

She threw her arms around him and held him as tightly as she could.

It took him a minute to respond, but then his arms encircled her, as she tried to catch her breath after the mad sprint.

"You silly girl. What're you *doing?*"

"After I got your text, I wanted to hug you. I just wanted to hug you."

They stood there for a long time.

"I'm sorry," he said.

"Don't be. I understand."

"It's a lot, Piper. I'm a lot."

She pulled back so she could see his face. "It's not too much for me. I swear it isn't."

"I forgot her birthday."

"It's been a wild few days. Anyone could lose track of the date with everything that's been going on with the storm. You should be kinder to yourself. That's what she would've wanted for you, isn't it?"

"Yeah, but—"

"No buts, Jack. I didn't even know her, but I can't, for the life of me, think she'd want you doing this to yourself."

"She wouldn't."

"Then don't, okay? I'm sure you took beautiful care of her while she was here."

"I did what I could."

"I know you did." She pushed the damp hair back from his forehead. "I'm sorry you're hurting."

"I'm sorry I hurt you."

"You didn't."

He tipped his head as he studied her. "Not even a little bit?"

"I'm over it."

A horn tooted as a woody station wagon came to a halt next to them. "Heard you kids was walking home in the dark," Ned Saunders said. "Get in. I'll give ya a ride."

Jack smiled and shrugged and then followed Piper into Ned's cab.

"What the heck are ya doing out here in the dark anyway?" he asked when they were buckled into the back seat.

Jack reached across the seat for Piper's hand. "We were just heading back to my place at the barracks."

"Shouldn't be walking these roads in the dark. Gonna get yerselves killed."

"We won't do it again," Jack said with a smile for Piper.

Going after him had been the best thing she'd ever done, and she'd do it again in a hot second.

Ned dropped them at the barracks a few minutes later, refusing payment. "Be safe, ya hear?"

"Yes, sir," Jack said. "Thank you for the ride."

"Any time."

Jack took her hand and led her into the barracks. "This place is nothing special," he said.

"I'm sure it's fine."

They went up to the second floor, where Jack used a key to open the door. "After you."

Piper went ahead of him into a room that was nothing more than a double bed, a dresser and a desk.

"Bathroom's in there," he said, pointing to a door.

"It's nice," she said.

He laughed. "Sure it is."

"What else do you need?"

Jack put his hands on her shoulders. "Nothing now that you're here with me."

"I'm here, Jack." She looked up at him as she placed her hands on his hips. "I promise I won't run away when things get hard. What happened today is sure to happen again, and it's okay. I don't expect you to keep those feelings hidden from me because you think I don't want to hear about Ruby. I'll always want to hear about her because she's part of you."

Dropping his forehead to hers, he closed his eyes. "You have no idea how much that means to me."

"I can't know what you've been through, but what I see is a man who loves so deeply that even years after he lost his wife, he still loves her so much that he aches to realize he forgot something important."

"I never want to forget," he said gruffly.

"You never could. She's always with you."

"I want you with me, too."

"I'm right here."

"For how long?"

"As long as you want me to be."

"That could be a while."

"That's fine."

Jack tipped up her chin for a kiss. "Thank you."

"For what?"

"For being amazing. For being just what I need. For understanding. For all of it."

"No problem."

He kissed her again, and as she opened her mouth to caress his tongue with hers, she felt her heart open to accommodate the very real possibility that she might fall in love with this man. If she hadn't already.

THE FERRIES ARRIVED BACK in port shortly after nine p.m. Crewmembers moved quickly to secure the lines and get everything buttoned up so they could get home to their loved ones as quickly as possible. Deacon vibrated with tension and anticipation as he waited for permission to disembark.

"I'll never be able to thank you all enough," Deacon said as he shook hands with Joe, Keith and Colin. "You saved my life."

"Glad we were in the right place at the right time," Joe said. "Do you need a ride home?"

"No, thanks," Deacon said. "Julia is waiting for me."

"We'll see you around campus," Joe said as they walked off the boat together.

The other guys had backpacks and bags.

Deacon had the clothes on his back, all of which were borrowed, as well as a bag full of his wet clothes and his survival suit tossed over his shoulder. "I'll wash the clothes and get them back to you."

"No rush, man," Keith said.

Deacon Taylor, who'd loved being on the water his entire life, had never been so happy to step foot onto dry land. He walked directly to Julia, who was standing outside her car with Pupwell on a leash next to her.

He wrapped her into the tightest embrace in history, both in tears as they reunited.

"Shhh, love," he whispered, kissing the tears off her face. "Everything's all right now."

They kissed like they hadn't seen each other in years, with no care whatsoever for the guys whistling at them as they walked to their vehicles.

"You can never scare me like that again," she said, kissing him everywhere she could reach.

"I won't. I promise."

"I don't want to let you go even to drive home."

"Give me ten minutes in the car—and a shower—and then you can hold me all night long."

She held him for another five minutes before she released him. "I was so afraid I'd never see you again."

"I would've swum back to you if I had to. I was seriously thinking about it when the ferries showed up."

Julia trembled. "I'm so glad it didn't come to that."

"I am, too. Let's go home, love. We've got the rest of our lives, and I can't wait to enjoy every second of it."

Seamus and Joe arrived to a party at Big Mac and Linda's.

"Look at this, Joe. They threw us a welcome-home party."

PJ and Viv, seeing their dad, let out shrieks of excitement as they ran to him.

Seamus went right to Carolina, dropping to his knees next to her chair and extending his arms to her.

She embraced him tightly. "Thank goodness you're home safe."

"Aw, shucks. You're going to make me think you love me."

Carolina swatted him on the head. "Stop that nonsense."

"So you do love me?"

"Much to my dismay, I do."

He couldn't help but laugh at the testy way she said that. "I guess you're stuck with me."

"Looks that way."

Kyle and Jackson came running down the stairs and were on him before Seamus had a second to prepare for the attack. He wrestled them into submission and kissed their faces until they begged for mercy.

"I heard you lads were a big help while I was gone."

"We were," Kyle said. "We got everything Caro needed."

"Thank you for taking such good care of her."

"We had fun," Jackson said. "Was it super-duper crazy on the ferry?"

"So crazy. We had twenty-foot seas at one point."

"Dear Lord," Carolina said.

"It was *so* much fun," Seamus said, grinning at her.

"Crazy Irishman."

Seamus released the boys and went back on his knees to kiss her. "Missed you fiercely."

"Same."

He flashed his most satisfied grin and earned himself another bop to the head.

JOE CUDDLED with PJ and Viv, who clung to him in a way they hadn't in a long time. "Did you guys have fun with the Grammys and Pop?"

"So much fun," PJ said. "And with Kyle and Jackson."

"I'm glad you had fun. What do you say we give Mommy a call to let her know I'm back on the island?"

"She's been really worried," PJ said, his blond brows furrowed.

Joe pulled his phone from his back pocket and put through a Face-Time call to Janey, who answered on the first ring.

"Oh, look at you guys! Back together."

"Yep and heading home to you as soon as we can," Joe said.

Viv had her head on his shoulder and her thumb in her mouth, but she perked up at the sound of her mother's voice.

"Miss you guys so, so much. I'll never complain about the noise again."

"You hear that, kiddos?" Joe asked.

"Mommy has to study," PJ said. "Shhhh."

His parents laughed.

"We've got him well trained," Joe said.

"Puppies," Viv said.

"Hang on a second." Janey swapped the view on the phone so they could see the dogs on their beds in the living room. "They miss you guys."

"We miss them, too. I'll figure out our trip home tomorrow."

"I'll be waiting for you."

"Love you, Mommy," Joe said.

"Love you, Mommy," PJ said.

"Wuv you, Mama," Viv added.

"Love you, too. All of you. More than anything. Hurry home."

"We're coming."

CHAPTER 33

*M*ac stepped outside to take the call he'd been waiting for from John Lawry. "Hey. How's it going?"

"Good so far. They're settled in the same room, which made them happy."

"I'm sure it did. What are they saying about Jeff?"

"He's still being evaluated. Kelsey is scheduled for surgery on her arm in the morning. Her parents are on their way. And rumor has it my mom, Charlie and our grandparents are on their way home, too."

"Keep me posted on how they're doing?"

"I will. Hey, Mac?"

"Yeah?"

"They don't blame you or your family for this. You know that, right?"

"I do, but we still feel responsible."

"You're not responsible. Ethel did this. They don't want you guys beating yourselves up over it."

"Which is very kind of them, but we're here for them as long as they need us to be. Any bills, send our way."

"We'll worry about that later."

"I'm worried about it now, and we'll take care of it. Let them know that."

"I will."

"You've got the code to my uncle Frank's house, right?"

"All set. Tell him thanks for letting me stay there."

"He was happy to make it available to you."

"I'll text you with an update later."

"Thanks, John."

Mac ended the call feeling slightly better now that Jeff and Kelsey were on the mainland and receiving care at a level-one trauma center. He took a moment to compose a text to David. *Heard from John that the patients are settled at RI Hospital and scored the same room, which made them happy. Thank you again for all you did to get them stable enough to travel. We're lucky to have you as part of our community.*

Funny how life worked, Mac thought. Once upon a time, he'd wanted to kill David Lawrence for the way he'd treated Janey. Now… They owed him so much. So, so much.

So glad to hear they're safely settled. Glad I was here to do what I could, but at some point, we need to have a talk as a community about upgrading our capabilities here. We've had enough calamities to more than justify an investment.

Couldn't agree more. We'll talk after things settle down.

Sounds good.

Thanks again. Seriously. We're all so grateful.

You got it.

Big Mac came outside, looking for his eldest son. "Everything all right?"

"John just called to say that Jeff and Kelsey are settled in the same room. Jeff is being evaluated, and Kelsey will have surgery on her arm in the morning."

"Glad they're doing okay. Maybe we can take a deep breath now."

"John said no one blames us for this, but I still feel terrible about it."

"As do I, but we'll do all we can to make things right for them."

"Yes, we will."

Big Mac put his hand on Mac's shoulder. "Are you okay, son?"

"I'm better now that the storm has passed." He shifted his gaze toward the Salt Pond, which was illuminated by the moon. "It's easy to forget sometimes how isolated we are out here."

"I know what you mean. We go along our merry way until a Cat 3 hurricane shows up to remind us of how effed we are when things go sideways."

"David wants to beef up the clinic. He said we've had enough catastrophes to justify it."

"I agree. I'll bring it up with the council at our next meeting."

"It's probably time for another doctor out here, too. It's a lot for David, Vic and Katie to manage on their own."

"I'll add that to the conversation. I want you to know… You made it so everyone was ready for this storm, and I saw that. I saw your leadership and the ribbing you took when you urged everyone to stock up on plywood and generators. They're all singing your praises now."

"I did what I could to prepare us."

"You did more than anyone to ensure your family, friends and community were safe, and I'm proud of you for that. I really am."

"Thanks, Dad."

"But I also know how you fret when things go sideways."

Fret was a good way to describe the anxiety that caused him such distress. He worried about everything, to the point of madness. "I'm working on that."

"I hope you are, because at the end of the day, there's only so much we can do. The rest is out of our hands."

"That last part is what gives me nightmares."

"You do everything you can to keep us safe, and when you've done all you can, you have to let the rest go. Nothing is ever going to be perfect. Take poor Billy. We all tried to tell him he was crazy to try to ride out the storm on the boat. But he wouldn't hear it, and now he's probably gone." Despite intense searching, there'd been no sign of the missing man.

"I wish he'd listened to reason."

"We all do, but people make their own choices."

"I suppose we're lucky we only lost one person. Could've been much worse."

"It would've been much worse without the efforts of you, Blaine, Jack, Mason and a lot of other people who went all out to keep this community safe. It's time to release that deep breath you've been holding and celebrate a job very well done."

"Thanks, Dad. Appreciate the kind words. It's important to me that you're proud of me."

"Mac… My Lord. You're a son any man would be proud to call his own."

"The only man who matters is you."

Big Mac hugged him and released him when the door opened.

"There you are," Maddie said. "Everything all right?"

"Everything is just fine," Big Mac said. "I'll see you inside."

"We'll be right in, Dad." Mac held out his hand to Maddie. "Are the natives getting restless?"

"Not at the moment. The grandmothers have the babies, and the others are playing with cousins and friends. All is well."

Mac put his arms around her and held her close as he finally relaxed for the first time in days.

"Are you okay?"

"I'm great now that Ethel has gone away."

"We're all glad about that. What're you hearing about getting the power back?"

"Could be a week."

"Jeez."

"You gotta love island life."

"Thank goodness we really do love it."

"You know what I love best about island life?"

"What?"

He kissed her softly and sweetly. "That I get to live in this beautiful place with my beautiful wife and our five precious kids."

AFTER JOHN ENDED the call with Mac, he texted Niall. *Can you talk?*

Yep.

John made the call and smiled when Niall answered. Would he ever grow tired of that gorgeous Irish accent? Nope, never.

"How goes it?" Niall asked.

He gave him the same update he'd given Mac.

"I'm glad they're in the same room. That'll be good for them."

"Agreed."

"How're you holding up?" Niall asked.

"I'm fine if they are. My mom texted to say she'll be home by tonight and wants to know why no one is telling her what's going on. Owen told her to call him when she lands in New York. Slim offered to fly them home, but it'll probably be quicker to drive."

"It was the right thing to wait to tell her."

"I think so, too, but she'll be pissed we kept it from her."

"You were thinking of what was best for her when she was so far from home," Niall said. "Don't second-guess yourself."

John appreciated that Niall listened and offered helpful input. He'd never had someone like him in his life and was deeply appreciative to have him during such a difficult time. "Thanks for the support."

"Of course."

"It's not something I take for granted. That's been a problem for me in the past. Give, give, give. Get nothing back."

"Well, that's not how it's supposed to be."

"No, it isn't, but I'm preprogrammed to expect nothing, thanks to the way I grew up."

"That's in the past. In the present, you have friends who are there for you no matter what."

"You can't possibly know what that means to me."

"You don't think so? It hasn't been easy for me either. My parents still don't know I'm gay. I keep meaning to tell them, but before I can, they ask me when they can expect some grandchildren. I freeze up when they say that."

"There're other ways to have kids besides the usual path."

"I know, and hopefully, I'll get there someday and make all their dreams come true."

"I'm sure it'd matter to them that you're happy."

"It does, but I'm under no illusions about how they'll feel about me being gay."

"You're sure they don't already know? When I came out to my family, most of them weren't surprised, which surprised me."

"I don't think they do, but who knows? Maybe I'm not fooling them. I've never had a girlfriend. You'd think that'd be the first clue."

"Sometimes people don't want to see what's right in front of them."

"That's so true, but enough about that. You've got enough on your plate without worrying about me and my issues."

"I'm interested in you and your issues. I thought maybe you knew that by now."

"Oh, I know, and back atcha. You need to stay focused on your brother and Kelsey, your mom and grandparents when they arrive. I'll be here if you need to talk."

"That makes everything so much better."

They talked for a few more minutes before John said he needed to check on Jeff. He promised to be in touch with Niall later.

After spending the night at Frank McCarthy's, John arrived in Jeff's room to find the attending physician had come by for rounds.

"This is my brother Johnny," Jeff said.

The doctor shook hands with John. "Good to meet you. I was just telling your brother that we're going to do some scans and figure out a plan after we have the films."

"That sounds good."

"He's stable for now, thanks to your doctor on Gansett, who did a fine job and saved his life. Now we need to get him put back together. The ortho surgeon will be checking in shortly, too."

"Is there any word on Kelsey?" Jeff asked. "They said the surgery would be an hour, and it's already been two."

"She's in recovery. The surgery went well. They'll have her back here in a few hours."

"Oh good," Jeff said, visibly relieved. "That's great news."

"I'll see you after the scans," the doctor said.

After he left, John pulled up a chair to Jeff's bedside. "Owen will tell Mom what's going on when she lands in New York."

"Okay."

"You can expect an invasion shortly after that."

Jeff offered a faint grin that turned to a grimace due to the pain. "I can hardly wait."

"Are you sure you won't let them give you something stronger for the pain?"

"I'm very sure. I fought too hard to get free of that shit. I'm never going there again."

"In case I forget to tell you later, you're a badass."

"Whatever you say."

"I mean it. Even in immense pain, you've got an eye on your sobriety. I admire that."

"Got too much to live for these days to mess up like that again."

"Yes, you do."

"We all do." The nightmare of their childhood was in the past, their father was in jail where he belonged, and they were free to pursue their own joy, no matter where they found it.

"Absolutely."

OWEN WAS ON EDGE, waiting for his mother's call. He hated that he had to tell her that Jeff had been badly hurt, but she already sensed something was up, or she wouldn't have flown back to the States a week early.

The door opened, and Laura came into the apartment, smiling when she saw him sitting on the sofa.

Just that quickly, the tight knot of anxiety in his gut loosened some-what. That's what she did for him. And she still wondered why he'd stayed with her and her son rather than continuing his life as a traveling musician. Putting down roots with the exquisite Laura McCarthy had been the best thing he'd ever done.

He held out a hand to her, and she sat next to him on the sofa, curling up to him with her head on his chest and her arm around him.

"No call yet?"

"Not yet. They've got to clear Customs and all that."

"Right. That can take a while."

"And they're not allowed to use their phones until they get through." He played with her hair and took comfort in her presence. "I'm not sure how you do it."

"Do what?"

"Calm and settle me just by walking in the room and snuggling up to me. I forget every worry when I have you with me."

"You do the same for me, you know."

"How lucky are we?"

"The luckiest."

Owen lifted her chin for a kiss as his phone rang. "That's probably her." Keeping his arm around Laura, he reached for the phone on the coffee table and took the call from his mother. "Hey, Mom."

"What's going on, Owen? And don't say nothing because I know my children and—"

"Mom. Listen. Jeff was in a building that collapsed in the storm." She gasped.

"He and Kelsey were hurt. Jeff was hurt badly. His pelvis is broken, and it was touch and go at first. We were finally able to get them off the island last night, and they're at Rhode Island Hospital. Kelsey broke her arm and had surgery earlier. They're still figuring out what Jeff needs, but he's in the best possible place now—all thanks to David Lawrence, who saved his life by operating on him here. And before you get angry, we all decided it was best not to tell you since there was nothing you could do in Italy."

"Oh my goodness," Sarah said, sounding tearful. "He'll be all right, though?"

"We hope so, Mom, but it was bad. If David hadn't operated to stop the internal bleeding, he wouldn't have lived long enough to get him to Providence."

"Thank the Lord for David."

"We've been saying that for years now."

"What about the medication?"

"The doctors are aware of his addiction and are doing what they can to keep him comfortable without narcotics."

"That's a relief. You poor kids, having to go through such an awful thing."

"We're all right. Johnny is with him in Providence."

"We'll go right there from here. Charlie is saying we'll rent a car."

"Let me know when you're there. Johnny is staying at Frank's, and there's plenty of room for you guys, too."

"That's very helpful, honey. Tell him thanks for us."

"I will. You're not mad we kept it from you, are you?"

"No, you did the right thing. There was nothing I could've done but worry myself sick. The rest of you are all right?"

"We are. The island is a mess, but cleanup is under way. Power is out for who knows how long, and one man is missing. Billy from the gym. I don't think you know him."

"I don't, but Charlie certainly would know him."

"Yes, he would." Owen's stepfather went to the gym every day. "I'll let you know if we hear anything. He tried to ride out the storm on his boat. The boat was found sunk, but there's no sign of Billy."

"That's terrible. I'm sorry to hear it. Charlie has already got a car rented for us, so we'll hit the road to Providence. Keep me posted on anything you hear."

"I will."

"Thank you for taking care of everything while I was gone."

"We all pulled together. You should know that Deacon was also missing at sea for a brief time, but he was found by Joe Cantrell and Seamus O'Grady when they took the ferries out to sea to escape the storm."

"Thank God he was found. Poor Julia. I'll call her when I can."

"Sounds good."

"Love you, son."

"Love you, too, Mom."

Owen put down the phone. "Well, now she knows everything."

"You're such a good son, brother, husband, father. You take such good care of everyone."

He gave her shoulder a squeeze. "And you take such good care of me, which is what makes everything else possible."

CHAPTER 34

Seamus spent the night at Big Mac and Linda's with Carolina and the boys. The next morning, after breakfast, they thanked their hosts for having them during the storm and set out for home, uncertain of what they would find there.

When they rolled into the driveway, they saw that Shannon and Victoria were already there, surveying the damage, which was substantial. They had parked next to a downed tree that was blocking the driveway. Many trees were down, one of them having just barely missed smashing the house. The covered porch had been demolished, and the yard was a general disaster area.

"Damn," Seamus said on a long exhale when he emerged from the truck.

"Looks like a fine place for a wedding," Victoria said, her chin wobbling. "In less than a week."

"We'll get it cleaned up and right as rain," Seamus assured her. "Don't you worry."

"What? Me worry?"

"I told you that's what he'd say, love." Shannon put his arm around her. "We'll be ready."

"Will we have power?"

"Even if we don't, we'll figure something out," Carolina said from the front seat of Seamus's truck.

"Your job is to not worry," Seamus told Vic. "Leave the worrying to us." He went to the truck to lift Carolina out to carry her to the house, stepping over a tree trunk as they went. "Boys, get the bags and then go change into your work clothes. We've got a wedding to prepare for."

The boys and Burpee the dog charged inside, dragging bags and suitcases behind them while Seamus, holding Carolina, followed slowly behind them.

"You really think we can pull this together in time?" she asked.

"I'm sure of it."

"I'm glad you are..."

"We'll call for help and get everyone here to pitch in. We'll get it done."

By noon, he and Shannon had summoned a posse that included Jace Carson, Paul and Alex Martinez, Mac, Grant, Shane and Evan McCarthy, Dan Torrington, Luke Harris, Oliver Watson and Slim Jackson. The Martinez brothers had brought chainsaws and other equipment that was soon buzzing as trees were cut for firewood and debris hauled away.

Kyle, Jackson and Burpee were underfoot all day, helping where directed and generally adding to the chaos.

Carolina made sandwiches for everyone and then sat outside for a while to "supervise."

Seamus came over to check on her, wiping sweat from his face with his T-shirt. "How're you doing, love?"

"Much better now that you all have made such a big dent. I was worried when I first saw the mess."

"Me, too, but we'll be ready."

"I feel better about that than I did earlier."

He bent to kiss her nose. "Don't get too much sun."

"I've got sunscreen on. Are the boys being more trouble than they're worth?"

"Not at all. They're working hard."

"Really?" she asked, skeptical.

"Really. They're good boys."

"Yes, they are, but they're not workers."

"Not yet, but they will be. It's good for them to see everyone pulling together to get something done. Eventually, it'll sink in. I hope."

"It will. For sure. Joe called. He and the kids are coming by to see us before Slim flies them to Boston to catch a flight home."

"Janey will be glad to have them back."

"Yes, she will, but I'll miss them."

"Only for a little while longer, and then they'll be home for good."

"I can't wait for that."

He kissed her again. "Gotta get back to it."

The ferries would begin running again the next day, and he wanted to get most of the cleanup done before he had to go back to work. There would be a wedding here next weekend, come hell or high water. Well, hopefully no more high water. They'd had enough of that to last them awhile.

VICTORIA TRIED to manage the panic that had her spinning with wedding-disaster scenarios. She kept telling herself that in the grand scheme of things, it didn't matter if her wedding went off as planned next weekend. Everyone she loved was safe, Jeff and Kelsey were on the mend in Providence, none of her expectant mothers had gone into premature labor during the storm, and Shannon's family would arrive as scheduled on Thursday.

Everything was fine.

Yet she still felt like she was about to hyperventilate.

Her phone chimed with a text from Shannon. *Making big progress. Don't worry!*

He'd included pictures that made her feel a thousand times better. A few hours after they'd started the cleanup, she could see there were many fewer downed trees littering the yard where her wedding would be held. A huge pile of firewood had grown next to Seamus and Carolina's house.

David came into the break room to get coffee. "How's it going?"

"Better," she said, showing him the pictures.

When she'd arrived at the clinic in tears, her maid of dishonor had talked her down off the cliff of bridal madness so she could focus on work.

"Wow, they've gotten a ton done in a short time," David said. "Now you can focus on bride business and not worry about the location. You know Seamus and Shannon will move heaven and earth to be ready."

"They already are, even though they're exhausted from being at sea for days. Shannon said they didn't sleep much at all. He came home last night, hugged me, kissed me and crashed for nine hours. And he was still tired this morning."

"He'll be fine by next weekend."

"How's Daisy?"

"She's doing all right. I suggested she take a few days out of work at the hotel, which she decided to do because she's still having a lot of pain."

"Hopefully, that will stop before too long."

"I sure hope so," David said. "I hate to see her suffering."

"But pregnancy is the most natural thing, don't you know?"

"I've heard that nonsense somewhere before."

"From me. I wonder all the time how anyone survived it back before all the advancements we have now."

"Thank goodness for the advancements. Even with all I know, I still worry about her. She's so petite."

"She's a warrior, and she'll be fine."

"If you keep telling me that, I'll keep telling you the wedding will be fine, too."

"You've got a deal."

PIPER CAME AWAKE SLOWLY, uncertain for a moment where she was until the events of the previous evening came rushing back to remind her of coming to Jack's room at the barracks. His arm was around her, his naked body pressed against hers after a night of incredible pleasure.

She felt like she'd forgotten something as she tried to recall what day it was.

Sunday.

Her one day off at the hotel in season.

As far as she knew, Jack was off, too.

"What's wrong?" he asked.

"I was trying to remember what day it was and if I have to work."

"What's the verdict?"

"Sunday. My day off."

"Mine, too." He kissed her shoulder. "Nice how that works out, huh?"

"Very nice."

"What do you feel like doing?"

"I can't think of a single thing."

He pushed his erection against her backside. "I can think of a few things."

"I'm not sure I can after last night."

"Are you sore?"

"A little."

"Sorry about that."

"No, you're not."

"I am!" he said, laughing.

"It was worth it, but I might need some recovery time before we start that up again."

"Do you want me to kiss it better?"

"That's what started the thing that led to the soreness."

His low chuckle rumbled through his chest. After a long silence, he said, "Thank you for what you did last night, for coming after me, for what you said. It meant a lot."

"Do you feel better today?"

"I felt better the minute I realized you were running after me."

"I need to start running again. I quickly realized how out of shape I am."

He ran his hand down her arm over her ass to her leg. "You're in fine shape."

"I used to be an athlete, and now I'm winded after running for two minutes."

"I like to run. Maybe we can do that together?"

"I probably couldn't keep up with you."

"You keep up with me just fine."

"Are we still talking about running?"

His hand was now between her breasts, causing a tingle between her legs that she tried to ignore. "We're talking about everything."

Piper went still in his arms. "Everything?"

"Everything. That's what I want to have with you."

"Are you ready for that?"

"I want to be. Are you?"

"I think so."

"Are you over your ex-fiancé?"

"Very much so. I hardly think about him anymore, which is so strange. We were together for years before he backed out of the wedding. After that happened, it was like all the feelings just dried up."

"Wasn't meant to be."

"Definitely not. I'm glad now that he called off the wedding, even if it was traumatic at the time."

"I'm sure it was."

"He did the right thing for both of us."

"I'm very glad you were single when we met."

"I'm very glad of that, too. That first day, I was traumatized by what'd happened, and I still noticed you, which had me questioning my sanity."

"Is that when the nickname Hot Cop was born?"

"How do you know about that?" she asked, sputtering with laughter.

"I'm a cop. A hot cop, apparently. It's my job to know things."

"I can't believe you know about that." She couldn't stop laughing. "That's mortifying."

"I call you Hot Hotel Girl."

"You do not! You just made that up!"

"You have no way to know that." He shifted them so he was above her, gazing down at her with those gorgeous brown eyes. "It's fun to laugh again."

"Yes, it is. Laughter looks good on you."

"It feels good." He smoothed the hair back from her face. "Ruby would like you."

There was, she knew, no greater compliment he could pay her. "Do you think so?"

"I really do."

"I'm glad. I think I would've liked her, too."

"You would have. Everyone did."

"You're very handsome in the morning. Well, you're handsome all the time." She reached up to run her fingers through his hair, which was standing on end. "But I particularly like the morning look."

"I'll keep myself scruffy going forward, just for you." He gave her a gentle kiss on lips that were as sore as the rest of her. "Now that you've talked me into this, you're going to stick around, right?"

She raised a brow. "I talked you into it?"

"Very convincingly."

"I'm sticking around if you are."

"I'm not going anywhere as long as you're here."

DUKE HOPED he was doing the right thing when he pulled into Blaine and Tiffany's driveway and parked his truck. He grabbed the stuffed bear he'd rescued from the wreckage of McKenzie's house. The bear looked much better after the bath he'd given it last night.

Her name was McKenzie.

He'd noticed her and her son shortly after they'd arrived two weeks ago and had kept half an eye on them since. Not in a stalkerish way, of course. It was more in case they needed anything. He'd wondered what a young woman and baby were doing in the old Enders place that had fallen into disrepair in recent years. Was it safe for them to be there? Didn't they have anywhere else to go?

And yes, he'd noticed the woman was a stunner, but that wasn't why he was bringing the damned bear to her.

"Fuckin' liar," he muttered to himself as he went up the stairs to the back door, annoyed with himself for bothering with a stupid stuffed bear.

You could lie to some people, he thought. But it was damned hard to lie to yourself. What would a gorgeous woman see in a guy like him anyway? His own mother told him he looked like something the cat had dragged home from skid row, and that was when she was in a good mood.

He shoulda shaved or done something with his hair before he came over here, but it was too late now. Pissed with himself—and his mother— he knocked on the door. The smooshed red VB bug was the only car in the driveway. The SUV Blaine and Tiffany used when he was off duty was gone as was Blaine's police vehicle, so he wasn't sure if anyone would be there.

The door swung open, and there she was, holding her cute little guy on her hip the way mothers did. She wore a tank top and gym shorts that put miles of creamy white skin on display that made him want to swallow his tongue.

And then she smiled.

Was it possible to swallow a tongue?

She pushed open the storm door. "Hi, Duke. Come in."

Duke marveled at the warm welcome. Not a hint of hesitation. Probably because Tiffany had welcomed him into her home the day before. *See, Mom, I'm not as menacing as you think I am.* He realized McKenzie was waiting for him to tell her why he'd come. "I, uh… I found this in the rubble." He held up the bear. "Thought the little one might want him. Or her."

Now he was trying to assign a gender to a stuffed bear. What a fool. No wonder he hadn't had a girlfriend in years.

"That's so nice of you." McKenzie showed the bear to baby Jax, who let out a squeal of excitement that touched Duke's heart. She took a closer look at the bear. "Did you clean him?"

"I did. I hope that's okay. He was filthy from the storm."

"That's so kind of you and to bring him to us."

"It was no problem."

"Would you like to sit for a minute?"

"Oh, um, sure. Thanks."

"Tiffany left made coffee on the grill before she went to check on her shop in town. Can I get you a cup?"

"That'd be nice. Thank you."

"How do you take it?"

"Black."

"Ew," she said with a laugh. "You like it with all that crap in it?"

"I sure do. The more crap, the better."

"That ain't coffee. It's coffee milk."

She brought his mug and then one for herself, all while still holding the baby.

"He's a cutie," Duke said.

"I think so, too."

The baby started to fuss, so she produced dry cereal that she put in front of him on the table, immediately satisfying him.

"How do you know what he wants?"

"You don't at first, but over time, you start to recognize the various noises. That was his hungry noise. There's a different one when the diaper is wet or he's sleepy."

"Wow. It's like a secret code or something." He'd love to put the most stunning flowers on her gorgeous skin, not that she needed any enhancements. But he couldn't look at skin like hers and not dream of the art he could create on such a perfect canvas.

"It takes a few weeks to figure out the different needs, but after a while, you find a groove."

"What're you going to do about the cabin?"

"I'm not sure yet. I have a call into the insurance company, but I'm sure they're slammed with claims after the storm. Tiffany said I can stay here as long as I need to, but I hate to put them out."

"Tiffany and Blaine are good people."

"Yes, they are, but no one needs strangers in their house any longer than necessary."

"If you need a place to stay while you figure things out, I have a small apartment over my garage you can use. It'd need a good cleaning, but I can take care of that."

"What's the rent?"

"No rent. No one has lived there in years, so I don't need the money.

I'm happy to offer it to you if it would help you out."

"Why?"

He shook his head, as if he hadn't heard her right. "Why what?"

"Why would you offer it to me? You don't even know me."

Duke tried to think fast, to come up with something that wouldn't seem weird. "I knew Rosemary. She was my friend. You're her grand-daughter. You need help. It's kinda that simple." To his great dismay, she started to cry. "Now don't do that." Nothing freaked him out like girl tears did.

"It's so very kind of you," she said as she dabbed at her eyes with a napkin.

"Well, don't cry about it."

She laughed as she wiped away more tears.

"Seriously. Cut that out."

McKenzie laughed, and then the baby did, too, and he decided the sound of their laughter was one of the best things he'd ever heard.

"So do you want the apartment?" he asked. His tone was testier than he'd intended, but she made him feel like a fool who couldn't get out of his own way.

"I would very much appreciate the apartment while I figure out what's next."

"I'll get it ready."

"Hey, Duke?"

"Yes?" Why did he feel so breathless as she looked up at him with that pretty face and those eyes that seemed to see inside him.

"Thank you for your kindness."

"You're welcome. I'll pick you up at five and drive you home."

"I can call a cab."

He stood and nearly knocked over the chair. "I'll come for you."

She stood to walk him to the door. "Thank you again for this and for bringing the bear to Jax. My grandmother had good taste in friends."

"She was a great lady."

"Yes, she was."

"Well, uh, I'll see you at five."

"We'll be ready."

As Duke went out the door and down the steps to the driveway, he feared he'd made the biggest mistake of his life asking her to stay at his place. She turned him into a bumbling, tongue-tied idiot. But the strangest thing was that he couldn't wait to come back to get them.

CHAPTER 35

*J*oe packed up the kids, thanked his in-laws for caring for them while he was at sea and buckled them into his truck to run by his mother's house before they left.

Big Mac and Linda waved them off, blowing kisses to the kids that made them giggle.

"Wave to Grammy L and Pop."

"I miss Grammy L and Pop," PJ said.

"You just saw them."

"I miss them."

Joe couldn't wait until they were back to stay on Gansett, where they belonged. The time in Ohio had been great, but they were all ready to be home. Janey had this last semester of school before she could come home to take over Doc Potter's island practice. Doc was looking forward to that as much as they were.

At his mother's house, the driveway was full of trucks and other vehicles.

Joe parked the truck, released the kids from their seats and held Viv as PJ ran ahead of him looking for Kyle, Jackson and Burpee. "Stay out of the way, PJ," Joe called after his son as he took in the massive cleanup going on.

"Wow," he said to Seamus.

"You should've seen it before we started. Vic was having a breakdown."

"I can imagine."

"We'll have it ready for the festivities next weekend."

Shannon came over to say hello to them, wiping sweat from his brow. "Are you guys heading home?"

"We are," Joe said. "I wish we could stay for the wedding, but their mom is getting antsy about having her babies home. And I'm antsy to see her."

"I don't blame you at all," Shannon said.

"We hope it's a marvelous day for you both," Joe said.

"Oh, it will be. No doubt."

"Let's go see Grammy Caro," he said, shepherding them inside.

Carolina was in her recliner.

Joe placed the kids carefully on her lap. "Be gentle," he reminded them.

"They always are." Carolina snuggled her grandchildren. "Are you guys heading home?"

"Mommy misses us," PJ said.

"I bet she does. I'll miss you, too, but we'll see you at Thanksgiving."

"That's a long time from now," PJ said.

"It'll go by so fast." Carolina kissed them both until they were laughing. "I love you forever and ever, amen."

"Love you, too, Grammy C," PJ said, hugging her.

To Joe, she said, "Thank you for coming and taking such good care of me after I broke my leg."

"We were glad to be here to help."

"Text me when you get home?"

"Will do."

He kissed his mother, collected the kids, went back outside and signaled to Slim.

"Are you guys ready to fly?" Slim asked.

"We are!" PJ said with a fist bump.

"I'll be back in a bit," Slim said to Seamus.

"Be safe with the precious cargo," Seamus said as he hugged and kissed the kids and shook hands with Joe.

"You and Shannon will pick up my truck at the airport?" Joe asked.

"Yep, we got ya covered."

Joe gave Seamus a bro hug. "Thanks. For everything."

"Thanks for coming when we needed you."

"Always."

Joe hugged Kyle and Jackson, gave Burpee a pat on the head and waved to the others, who were cutting up the fallen trees. "Let's go see Mommy, kiddos."

CHARLIE DROVE AS FAST as he could from New York to Providence, about a four-hour drive without traffic.

Sarah stared out the windshield, unable to focus on anything while she waited for another update from Johnny, who'd sent photos of the latest X-rays that showed several cracks in Jeff's pelvis as well as a fractured hip that would require surgery to stabilize.

The phone rang with a call from Johnny.

Sarah pounced on it, putting it on speaker so the others could hear. "What's up?"

"Jeff wants to say hi. Hang on a second."

She held her breath waiting to hear the voice of her youngest child.

"Hey, Ma."

Her eyes flooded with tears. "Hi, sweetie. What's this I hear about you causing some drama during the storm?"

His chuckle made her smile. "It wasn't intentional, believe me."

"I heard you're a hero with the way you saved Kelsey."

"I don't remember it." His voice sounded much weaker than usual. "She says I jumped on top of her. I'd do it again to save her."

"She's very lucky to have you."

"I'm the lucky one. She's agreed to marry me."

A few days ago, Sarah might've balked at the news that he was engaged at such a young age, but now she was too filled with gratitude that he'd survived to quibble over timing. "That's incredible news. Congratulations, sweetheart. She's a wonderful young woman."

"She's the best. The absolute best."

She'd been dismayed when he gave up his job in Florida and decided to stay on Gansett with Kelsey, working construction while she fulfilled her obligation to the McCarthys. There'd been a time when Sarah would've had no choice but to forcefully object because his father would've blown a gasket over that decision.

But those days were long over, and Charlie had helped her see there was no point in standing in the way of true love. Before him, she'd never known true love. Now that she did, she wouldn't deny anyone that experience, especially one of her precious children.

"I couldn't be happier for you both. How's she doing?"

"She's in a lot of pain after the surgery, but they're working on getting it under control."

"Please give her our love."

"I will."

"We'll be there in about two hours."

"Tell Charlie to drive safely."

"I will. See you soon. We love you."

"Love you, too."

"Well, that's a relief," Adele said from the back seat. "He sounds as well as could be expected."

"I guess so."

Charlie reached for her hand and held on tight, letting her know he was there, come what may. That made all the difference.

WHEN DUKE GOT BACK to his place, he went to work scrubbing the garage apartment from ceiling to floor and everything in between. He threw open the windows to air out the musty scent, put fresh sheets on the bed, plumped the pillows on the sofa and cleaned the bathroom until it shone.

Then he attacked the kitchen, which the previous tenant had left filthy. Hours later, he raised his head from the task to realize it was getting closer to five o'clock, and he badly needed a shower before he went to get McKenzie and Jax. On the way home, he'd stop at the grocery store to get them whatever he thought they'd need for a few days. He had no idea what her situation was, but he was determined to make sure they were taken care of.

And why was that exactly?

He had no freaking clue beyond her being Rosemary's granddaughter.

Before he could further contemplate that perplexing question, his phone rang with a call from Ace, the tattoo artist who'd recently joined his team after his other artist decided to move back to the mainland. "Hey, what's up?"

"Just wondering what the plan is for reopening," Ace said.

"Waiting on power. Until then, enjoy some time off."

"I was afraid you might say that. I'm running a little short on cash after being out of work for days now."

"I can spot you some until payday."

"I hate to ask for that."

"You didn't. I'll Venmo you."

"That's good of you, man. I appreciate it."

"No worries. I'll let you know when we're back up and running."

"I hope it's soon."

"I do, too. Will be in touch."

"Thanks again, Duke."

"No problem."

Duke ended the call, sent some money to Ace to tide him over and ran for the shower so he wouldn't be late for a very important date.

McKenzie was about to leave a note for Tiffany when she came in, toting groceries. She rushed over to help with the bags.

"Thank you. I always try to do it in one trip."

"I do the same, even when it's not practical. I'm surprised the grocery store is open."

"They're running on multiple generators."

Ashleigh came in with Addie and put her sister down to run around.

"I was just about to leave you a note," McKenzie said. "Duke offered me a place to stay in his garage apartment while I sort out the insurance and whatnot for the cabin."

"That's very nice of him."

"It was."

"Everyone likes him. He's a great guy."

"He's been so good to me, and to hear that my grandmother was his friend makes me feel better about taking him up on the offer of a place to stay."

"I hope you know you'd be welcome to stay here for as long as you'd like."

"I appreciate it, but you've done enough for us."

"What're your plans?" Tiffany asked as she unpacked the groceries into a fridge running off a generator. "Will you stay on the island?"

"I guess that'll depend on whether I can find a job and if we can rebuild the cabin."

"I'm hiring at my store. I own Naughty & Nice in town, and my faithful helper, Patty, is moving off the island with her boyfriend, Wyatt, who took a job with the Providence Police Department. They want to live off-island before they settle down to have a family. She and Wyatt just told Blaine and me about their plans earlier today. I've been in denial ever since." Tiffany rested a hand on her protruding belly. "With this little one joining our circus, I'm going to rely more than ever on my backup at the store."

"I'll take it," McKenzie said.

"Really?"

"Yes, of course. I'd just need to find childcare for Jax."

"You could bring him with you to the store. We're a very family-friendly business."

"Seriously?"

"Very seriously. Addie has grown up there. Jax is more than welcome."

"Wow, that'd be amazing. I've been so worried about how I would afford daycare on top of everything else."

Tiffany turned and rested against the counter. "I haven't wanted to pry, but does his father help out?"

McKenzie shook her head. "He left us. We haven't heard from him in months." The sentence still sounded surreal to her, even after all this time.

"You need a lawyer, honey," Tiffany said softly.

"I can't afford one."

"Would you mind if I arranged a meeting with a great lawyer who would probably take your case pro bono?"

"I couldn't do that."

"Trust me when I tell you he'd want you to reach out. He loves to help with cases like yours."

"Are you sure?"

"I'm positive. Shall I call him for you?"

McKenzie couldn't believe it had come to this. "Yes, please."

JANEY GOT to the airport an hour before her family's flight was due to land at John Glenn Columbus International Airport. They'd connected in Detroit and would be arriving in Columbus any minute now. Joe had sent pictures of the kids on the plane and in the Detroit airport.

She couldn't wait to see them.

It had been raining hard all day, making the drive to the airport a further test of her already-frazzled nerves. In the last few days, she'd questioned every life choice she'd made since her kids arrived, asking herself repeatedly who she thought she was to be pursuing this degree when she had children to care for.

That question would've made Joe and her parents and everyone else who loved her angry because they wanted this for her almost more than she wanted it for herself. But it'd been on her mind since they received the call from Seamus about Carolina breaking her leg. She'd wanted to go with Joe and the kids to help care for her mother-in-law, as well as to help with Jackson and Kyle. That's what family did during a crisis. While Joe and the kids went home to care for his mother, she'd had to stay back because she couldn't miss classes.

She had a huge exam tomorrow, for all she cared about that.

Janey didn't care about anything other than seeing her husband and children.

By the time their flight arrived, she was about to come unglued.

Joe texted that they'd arrived and were waiting for the other people on the plane to collect everything they owned so they could deplane.

It took forever, or so it seemed to her, for them to appear on the escalator to the baggage claim area.

PJ let out a shriek of excitement when he saw her waiting, and only Joe's tight hold on his hand kept their son from running down the escalator to get to her. The second they reached the bottom, Joe released him.

Janey lifted him into her arms and squeezed him so tightly, he squawked. "Mommy missed you so much."

"I missed you, too. They let us have extra snacks on the plane, and Daddy let us split a Sprite!"

Oh joy, she thought as she took Viv from Joe. *They're whacked out on sugar.*

Janey hugged and kissed her little girl, who clung to her. "Missed you so much, sweet girl."

Joe put his arm around her and kissed her cheek. "Daddy gets the shaft when there're kids to love on."

"Mommy missed Daddy as much as she missed the babies."

"That's good to know," he said with the grin she loved so much.

Joe collected the bags with PJ's "help," and then they walked to the parking garage.

On the ride home, PJ told her everything that'd happened since they left, most of which she already knew because she'd talked to them every day. But she listened to him with patience and appropriate reactions while holding Joe's hand in both of hers, delighted to be back with them after weeks apart.

"PJ, take a breath," Joe said as he drove them home in driving rain. "We don't have to tell Mommy everything that happened in the first five minutes."

"Jackson ate a bug!" PJ said as if Joe hadn't said anything.

"Ew," Janey said.

"It was so *gross!*"

"Did he really eat a bug?" Janey asked Joe.

"According to all my sources, yes."

"We had the best time with Jackson and Kyle," PJ said, bouncing in his seat. "Did you know that Grammy C is their mom now?"

"I heard that news."

"And there's gonna be a wedding at Grammy C's house, too."

"That's exciting."

They arrived at home, schlepped kids and bags into their townhome, greeted delighted dogs and took the kids upstairs for baths and bedtimes.

"Great job with the Sprite, Daddyo," Janey said as the kids bounced off the walls.

"That might've been a mistake."

"Do you think?"

They laughed as PJ pounced on Joe, wanting to wrestle.

It took another hour for the kids to settle down enough to listen to the two stories Janey read them before they tucked them in. They met in the hallway, and Janey leaned her head on Joe's chest.

He wrapped his arms around her.

"I'm *so* glad you guys are home."

"We missed you so much."

"Not as much as I missed you. The silence was deafening. I found out I need chaos to study."

He laughed. "That's funny."

She looked up at him. "Let's go to bed. I want to be with you."

"There's nowhere on earth I'd rather be than wherever you are."

"Seems to me I've heard that somewhere before."

Smiling, he kissed her and then surprised her when he lifted her and carried her to bed.

CHAPTER 36

*J*eff was dozing when his mother, Charlie and grandparents arrived in a flurry of anxious activity that had his eyes opening to see what was going on.

His mom leaned over the bed to kiss his cheek and stroke his hair. "I'm so glad to see you," she said.

"Same. Sorry to mess up your trip."

"You didn't. That bitch Ethel did."

He laughed and then grimaced. "Don't make me laugh."

"Whoops. How's the pain?"

"Manageable. Hey, Gran," he said when Adele kissed the other side of his face.

"Hi there, my sweet boy. Sorry you're hurting."

"I'm okay."

They moved to the other bed to see Kelsey, who greeted them warmly.

"Mom, Charlie, Gram, Gramps, meet Kelsey's parents, Dave and Liz," Jeff said.

They shook hands and introduced themselves.

"We hear there's a wedding to be planned," Sarah said to Kelsey's mother.

"That's the word on the street."

"We should exchange numbers so we can stay in touch," Sarah said.

As they did that, Jeff said, "Hey, Kels?"

"Yes, dear?"

"Mark this as the moment we lost control of the wedding."

AT THE GANSETT ISLAND TOWN HALL on Monday morning, Finn and Chloe looked for the town clerk's office.

"Over there," Finn said, pointing.

"May I help you?" the woman working at the desk asked.

"We need a marriage license, please," Finn said.

"I can help with that, and congratulations."

"Thank you," Chloe said.

"Is it possible to backdate it by two days?" Finn asked.

"Normally, we couldn't do that, but considering the storm, let me see what I can do."

"That'd be great," Finn said. "Thank you." While they waited, he grinned at his wife. His wife. He still couldn't believe they were married.

"Fancy meeting you guys here," Deacon Taylor said from behind them. They turned to find him and his fiancée, Julia Lawry.

"Need we ask why you're here?" Deacon asked, smiling.

"Probably the same reason you are."

"Congratulations," Julia said, hugging Chloe and then Finn.

"Same to you guys. When's the big day?"

"Later today, but we're not telling anyone," Deacon said, gazing at Julia. "We'll have a party later when Jeff and Kelsey are better and can join us. How about you?"

"We did the deed two days ago," Finn said with a dirty grin for Chloe. "Just making it legal today."

"That's awesome. Congratulations."

"We were so happy to hear you're safe, Deacon," Chloe said.

"Thank you. It was a wild few hours, to say the least."

Julia shuddered. "It was horrible, and I never want to think about that again."

The clerk returned with some forms for Finn and Chloe, who signed where directed and received a marriage license bearing a date of two days earlier.

"Congratulations, Mrs. McCarthy," Finn said, kissing her.

"Congratulations, Mr. McCarthy."

"And now," he said, "for the honeymoon."

"Next year, let's celebrate our first anniversaries together," Julia said.

"Let's do it," Chloe said. "All the best to you guys."

"Same to you," Deacon said as he shook Finn's hand and kissed Chloe's cheek.

Chloe curled her hand around the arm Finn offered her, and they walked out of town hall legally married.

"We need a real honeymoon," Finn said as he held the car door for her. "Where would my wife like to go?"

"I'm perfectly content to be right here with my handsome husband."

"We'll have our whole lives right here," he said when he got in the car. "Let's go somewhere fabulous."

"Like where?"

"Where have you always wanted to go?"

"I've never been anywhere, so you tell me. Where do you want to go?"

"Paris?"

"Seriously?"

"Absolutely. Would you like to go to Paris with me, Mrs. McCarthy?"

"I would love that, Mr. McCarthy."

"Then that's what we'll do."

JULIA AND DEACON arrived back at the garage apartment behind Blaine and Tiffany's house with a marriage license in hand.

"What time did you tell Frank, Katie and Shane?" Deacon asked.

"Six o'clock."

"Whatever shall we do with ourselves until then?" he asked, backing her up to the counter in the kitchen.

"I can't think of a single thing."

"Not *one* thing?" he asked, kissing her neck and making her shiver.

"Nope."

He put his arm around her and lifted her off her feet. "Then I guess I'll have to do the thinking for both of us."

She held on tight to him as he carried her to the bedroom. "I hope you'll understand if I'm a little clingy for a while."

"There's nothing I love more than when you cling to me."

"This is apt to be the suffocating kind of clingy."

"I can handle whatever you're dishing out." He came down on top of her, gazing at her sweet face, committing every fine detail to memory. "All the time I was out there, the only thing I thought about was you." He brushed a soft kiss over lips swollen from a night full of love. "Don't tell my mom that, okay?"

Smiling, she said, "Your secret is safe with me."

Pupwell jumped up on the bed and nosed his way between them.

"Listen, you little cockblocker," Deacon said. "How many times do I have to tell you that you have to share Mommy with me?"

Pupwell whined.

"Don't be mean to my baby," she said, cuddling the dog.

"He needs to share you with me."

"He knows that, don't you, sweet boy?"

Pupwell sighed with pleasure that Deacon certainly understood. Being loved by Julia Lawry was the best thing to ever happen to them.

They spent the afternoon in bed, napping, making love, making plans and snuggling with Pupwell. At five, they got up to shower and change for their wedding.

At five thirty, Deacon knocked on the bedroom door. "Are you ready?"

"Yes, come in."

Julia turned away from the full-length mirror to face him, wearing the dress Tiffany had helped her buy quite some time ago, in anticipation of their wedding.

"*Wow*," he said on a long exhale.

The dress was a creamy off-white silk with spaghetti straps, a fitted bodice and a long, flowing skirt. She'd put her hair up and had put a white bow tie on Pupwell, who would serve as their ring bearer.

A few weeks ago, they'd traveled to the mainland to purchase wedding rings for when they were ready.

"You're... Stunning. How lucky am I?"

His reaction to her in the dress was everything she'd hoped it would be—and then some. "I'm glad you like it." She took in the sight of him in the khaki suit and white dress shirt he'd bought for the occasion.

"Like it?" He put his hands on her hips. "I love it." With a soft, sweet kiss, he added, "I love you, and I can't wait to get married."

"I can't wait either. And by the way, you look beautiful, too."

"Thank you." Deacon took Pupwell's leash from her. "And isn't our little boy looking dapper, too?"

"He's the cutest."

"In case I forget to mention it later, this was the best day of my life," Deacon said before he escorted her from the room.

"The best day of my life was when I heard you'd been rescued."

"Let's go top that, shall we?"

"Yes, please."

"AND JULIA DIDN'T SAY why they were coming by?" Shane asked Katie, who was running around straightening up before her sister and Deacon arrived.

"No, just that they wanted to share something with us."

"Will you stop cleaning up for your sister? This place is immaculate, as always."

Katie stopped suddenly, looked around as if seeing their home for the first time and realized he was right. She'd been doing it again, trying to bring ruthless order to places that didn't need it. The trait was another holdover from a childhood spent trying to please a career Air Force officer who'd been impossible to please. Nothing was ever clean enough, orderly enough, organized enough.

Nothing was ever enough.

"No one is judging you or your home," Shane said gently. "Not me or anyone who will visit you here."

"Thank you for reminding me. Sometimes I still need that."

"I'm here for it, any time."

"I hate how he's still in there, still controlling me."

Shane gathered her in close to him. "He's not controlling you."

"Feels like it sometimes."

"He's out of your life and exactly where he belongs."

"Keep telling me."

"I will. For as long as you need to hear it."

"How about some good news?" Katie asked, looking up at him.

"I'm here for that, too."

"During the storm, I asked Vic to do blood work because I thought I might be pregnant, and I wanted to be sure."

"And?" he asked, breathless.

"I am."

"Oh my God, Katie. How did you keep this from me?"

"I wanted to wait until we could celebrate properly."

He hugged her tightly. "How're you feeling?"

"Anxious but happy." A miscarriage earlier in the summer had devastated them, but they'd agreed to try again right away.

"I have a good feeling that this one will stick."

"I really hope so."

"No matter what happens, we've got this."

"Having you by my side is what got me through before."

They hugged for a long time.

"I'm so excited," he whispered.

"I am, too. I'll try not to be a nervous wreck the whole time."

The moment was interrupted by the doorbell.

"This conversation will be continued later," he said.

"I'll look forward to later."

Shane went to get the door and was surprised to see his dad and Betsy. He pushed open the storm door to admit them. "Hey, guys. What's up?"

"Julia asked me to meet her here," Frank said.

"She did?" Katie glanced at Shane, who shrugged. "Wonder what's going on?"

"I guess we'll find out soon enough."

CHAPTER 37

*A*s Deacon drove them to Shane and Katie's, a million thoughts went through Julia's head, everything from difficult memories of the past to the delightful present she'd found with Deacon and Pupwell. Their little family had brought her more joy than anything in her life ever had, and she couldn't wait to be married to him.

"What're you thinking about over there?" he asked.

"Everything. My whole life and how it's all come down to this—and you."

"I hope you're only thinking about the good stuff."

"Mostly."

"No bad stuff today. It's not allowed."

"Would you mind if I invited Owen, too? I can't do this without him."

"Of course I don't mind."

"Are you sure you don't want to invite Blaine and your parents?"

"Not for this. They'll all be at the party."

Julia sent the text asking her older brother if he could come by Katie's for a minute.

Sure, he replied. *What's up?*

Will tell you when I see you.

Everything is okay tho?

Yes, everything is fine.

Poor Owen was preconditioned to expect disaster.

"Your family won't be angry that we did this without them, will they?" Julia asked.

"They're so thankful I survived my disaster at sea that they'll forgive me. I'll tell them it was a spontaneous thing, which it was, and they'll understand."

"I hope so. I don't want my new family to hate me."

"They could never hate you. They've seen how happy you make me."

"They've seen how I domesticated you."

"That, too," he said with a laugh. "Can I ask for something?"

"Anything you want."

"Oh wow. It's that kind of day, huh?"

She nudged him. "What do you want?"

"Will you sing for me at our wedding?"

"Yes, Deacon, I'll sing for you at our wedding. Any special requests?"

"I'll leave it up to you."

Julia thought about what she might sing to her new husband, something that would summarize how she felt about him and this moment.

Deacon pulled his truck into the driveway at Katie and Shane's and parked behind Frank McCarthy's silver sedan. "Frank is already here."

"Which has them wondering what the heck is going on."

"Let's go tell them. Wait for me."

Deacon got out of the truck and came around to help her out. Then he got Pupwell from the back seat.

Katie met them at the front door, her face going slack with surprise when she saw Julia wearing "the dress," as she'd referred to it when she'd shown it to her twin. "Oh my God, you guys! You're getting married!"

"Yes, and we're keeping it quiet because we didn't invite everyone," Julia said. "We'll do it again with a big party next summer. But for now, we just wanted to be married, and with Jeff in the hospital and after what almost happened to Deacon…"

"You don't have to explain it to me." Katie hugged her and then Deacon. "I get it."

Frank hugged Julia and shook hands with Deacon. "Shall we get this done?"

Owen came in the door a second later. "What's going on?"

"Julia and Deacon are getting married!" Katie said.

"Now?" Owen asked.

"Right now," Deacon said.

Julia went to her brother. "We were going to just have Katie and Shane with us, but I couldn't exclude you. The three of us..." Her throat closed on a lump.

"The three of us are a team," Owen said softly as he hugged his sister.

"I couldn't do it without you."

"I'm honored to be here."

"Will you give me away?"

"Never, but I'll happily escort you."

She took the arm Owen offered her and went with him to the kitchen while Deacon and Shane stayed with Katie, Frank and Betsy in the living room.

"Don't tell anyone about this, okay?" Julia asked. "I don't want Mom and the others to be upset that we did this without them."

"I won't tell anyone but Laura, and we'll keep a lid on it. I promise."

"Thank you. We'll do it all again in the summer with everyone we love there."

"I'll look forward to that."

"Thank you for being here for me."

"Always. You know that."

"I do, and it means everything to me." She felt herself getting emotional and tried to keep it in check so she wouldn't be a mess when she greeted her groom. "Deacon asked me to sing for him, so I'll do that on the way in, okay?"

"You're the boss."

"Are you ready?"

"Just one quick thing," Owen said. "I want you to know how much I love you and how happy I am for you and Deacon. He's perfect for you."

"Yes, he is, and I love you, too. Thank you for everything you did to make it possible for the rest of us to have what we do now."

"I didn't—"

Julia went up on tiptoes to kiss his cheek. "Yes, you did, Owen. You did everything for us, and we'll never forget it."

She took a moment to get her emotions in check, and then she began to sing the song she'd chosen for Deacon. "Can't Help Falling in Love" perfectly summarized what he'd been to her and what he would always be to her. She sang the opening verse before she and Owen appeared in the doorway to the kitchen to find Deacon wiping away tears as Pupwell sat at his feet, seeming to wonder what the heck Mom and Dad were up to now.

She sang the second verse from the doorway, her gaze locked on his, and finished the song as she and Owen walked into the living room.

Owen kissed her and joined her hand to Deacon's. "Take good care of our Julia," he said gruffly to Deacon.

"Always," Deacon said.

"Friends, we're here today to celebrate the love of Julia Lawry and Deacon Taylor," Frank said.

Later, Julia would try to remember what she said, what Deacon said, what Frank said, but it was all a blur of tears and a love so deep, it couldn't be contained. She recalled Katie and Shane's wedding, when he'd convinced her to take a ride on his motorcycle during the reception. They'd started a scandal by disappearing and had been together ever since.

The hours she'd recently spent wondering if she'd ever see him again had been torturous, but as he slid the ring on her finger and promised to love her forever, she felt as if her entire life had come down to this moment and this man. All the hell and heartache, the years of battling eating disorders, the absolute nonsense she'd endured with every other man she'd ever dated… It had all come down to him and them.

"By the power vested in me by the state of Rhode Island, I now declare you husband and wife. Deacon, you may kiss your bride."

As he held her face in his hands, he looked at her with his whole heart in his eyes. Everything he had was hers. Everything she had was his. Just the way it should be.

He kissed her softly and gently, even as his gorgeous eyes flared with desire for much more. There'd be time for that later.

They had all the time in the world for everything.

THE IRISH INVASION occurred as scheduled on Thursday when Slim flew Shannon and Seamus's parents to the island.

Shannon, Victoria and Seamus were on hand at the airport to welcome them to the island, which had been restored mostly to rights after the storm. They were still waiting for the power to come back on, however, but with the ferries operating again, they were able to fuel the generators and keep things running.

It had been a tense week of emotional highs and lows, but now that the folks were arriving, Shannon had tried to let it all go so he could enjoy a moment he'd once thought would never occur for him.

Shannon stood back to watch his aunt Nora hug the life out of Seamus, who indulged his mother as he always did since they'd lost his brothers tragically young. Seamus lifted his tiny mother and spun her around, making her scream with laughter.

"Put me down, ya damned fool," Nora said.

He relished the lyrical sound of her voice, the sound of home, as well as that of his own mother, Breeda, who hugged him with the same enthusiasm that Seamus had received, but with a flood of tears, too.

"Aw, Mam, what's with the waterworks?" Shannon asked.

"I'm just so bloody happy to see you."

"Same. It's been too long." He stepped back and held out a hand to Vic. "This is my incredible fiancée, Victoria Stevens. Vic, meet my mam, Breeda, and my da, John."

His mother enveloped Vic in a fierce hug, which he'd warned her would happen.

"I'm so happy to finally meet you in person," Vic said as she returned his mother's embrace. She'd gotten to know his family through FaceTime calls. Next, she hugged his father and then Seamus's parents. "Thank you all for coming so far for us."

"We wouldn't have missed it for all the world, love," Breeda said, with a tearful glance at Shannon.

He knew exactly what she was thinking. After he'd lost his first love, Fiona, to murder, he'd spiraled so deep that everyone around him had feared he might never resurface. And for years, he hadn't. The best thing he'd ever done was let everyone talk him into accompanying his aunt Nora to Gansett to visit Seamus. He'd known they were worried about him and had manipulated him into going with Nora when it was the last thing he'd wanted to do.

They'd hit him with the trip at a time when he'd begun to tire of his own company and the dire thoughts that plagued him through all his waking hours and in nightmares that surfaced during rare hours of sleep.

He'd met Vic the day they arrived on Gansett, and just that quickly, he'd felt better. She would never fully appreciate the new lease on life she'd given him, even when he'd tried to deny the inevitable with her. He'd been so afraid to fall in love again that he'd nearly screwed up the best thing to happen to him since he lost Fi. But leave it to Vic to make a stand that forced him to confront his demons and choose the happy future he now looked forward to with her.

Just thinking about her, the gift of her love and the commitment they were about to make to each other had put a lump in his throat for days as they counted down to their wedding. Love like this came with risks. He knew that all too well, but Victoria had shown him that their love was worth the risk. She was worth it.

He'd thought about Fi more in the last few weeks than he had in a while, which made him feel guilty amid the happiness he'd found with Vic. Sometimes he wondered what right he had to such happiness when Fi was gone forever. Every time he thought such things, he immediately knew that she would tell him to knock it off.

Life is for the living, she would say. She would remind him that he'd loved her with all his heart during the years they'd spent together, and the only thing he could do after losing her was pick up the pieces and go forward. Shannon knew for certain that Fi would love Vic as much as he did. That helped him to cope with the emotions that had come to the surface as their big day drew closer.

"You're quiet," Vic said when they got to Seamus's house, where their guests would be staying. They'd tried to talk Seamus into putting them in a hotel, since Carolina was injured, but neither of them would hear of it. Carolina's friends Linda McCarthy, Francine Saunders and Betsy Jacobson had been cooking for days to make sure there was plenty of food for their guests. That they'd managed to pull off such a miracle during an island-wide power outage had deeply touched him and Vic.

The island community on Gansett never failed to amaze him. Once they wrapped their collective arms around you and made you part of them, they never let go, showing up as needed for anything and everything that came along.

"I'm just thinking," Shannon said in response to Vic's comment.

"Happy thoughts, I hope."

"For the most part."

She took him by the hand, led him into Seamus and Carolina's bedroom and shut the door. "Anything I can do?"

"You're doing it, love, just by being here and agreeing to marry me and all my demons."

"If you're struggling, I hope you know you can talk to me about it."

Shannon leaned his forehead on hers. "I do know, sweetheart, but thank you for reminding me. I'm okay. Just feeling all the stuff this week."

"Me, too. Mostly, I feel thankful that we found each other, that we have so much to look forward to."

"I'm thankful for all that, but I'm especially grateful for you and the way you fought for us and made it happen."

She went up on tiptoes to kiss him. "We made it happen together, and we're just getting started."

CHAPTER 38

Saturday dawned bright, sunny and cool, a perfect September day for a wedding. The best wedding gift they received was the return of power to the island around noon.

Hallelujah, Seamus had declared in a text, along with photos of him stringing lights through trees in a finishing touch they'd expected to have to forgo without power.

"I don't know how you people can stand to live in such a primitive place," Victoria's mother said for at least the third time since she'd arrived the night before to an island still cleaning up from the storm and functioning without power after nearly a week.

"We love it here," Victoria said, also for the third time. "It's home."

They were in the honeymoon suite at the Beachcomber, where Shannon and Victoria would spend their wedding night.

"What about when you have children? You won't want to raise them on a remote island in the middle of nowhere."

"I can't think of anywhere better to raise them, Mom. This is the best place I've ever lived. The best people I've ever known."

Her mother didn't care for that, but Victoria was about to rescind her mother's invitation to the wedding. "He's still just a deckhand on a ferryboat and could be deported at any time. Are you sure about this, Victoria?"

Vic summoned the patience she needed to keep from punching her mother in the face. It wasn't the first time she'd had to control that urge, and it probably wouldn't be the last. "As I've told you, repeatedly now, Shannon has applied for citizenship and is studying to take the captain's exam."

"And you're certain this wedding isn't about a green card?"

"I'm going to pretend you didn't say that and ask you to leave now so I can finish getting ready."

"It's a valid question, Victoria."

"This is my wedding day, Mom. If you're going to say hateful things about the man I love, you're going to be uninvited to the wedding."

"You wouldn't dare."

"You don't think so? Say one more word about him or our lives, and you'll be officially uninvited."

They engaged in a stare-down that was interrupted when someone knocked at the door.

Victoria walked away from her mother to answer the door.

David and Daisy smiled widely as they greeted her.

"Please come in," Victoria said, relieved to see them. "You guys look gorgeous."

"So do you," Daisy said. "Your hair is incredible."

"Cindy did it this morning." Victoria had gone with an elaborate style that included braids and flowers woven in.

"Wow," David said. "You clean up well."

Victoria scowled playfully at him. "As do you, Doc. Um, this is my mother, Carol. This is David and Daisy Lawrence. David and I work together at the clinic."

"Ah, yes, you're the *doctor*," Carol said. "Very impressive."

"I'll see you at Seamus's house, Mom. You've got the address, right?"

"Yes, I do. Your father and that woman should be on the island by now. I can't believe you had to invite them."

"I'll see you there, Mom," Victoria said, showing her to the door and shutting it behind her. "She's horrible. I'm sorry."

"Don't apologize to us," David said. "Are you okay?"

"I was having a great day until she suggested that Shannon is marrying me for a green card."

David's mouth fell open. "She *said* that?"

"She sure did, while also mentioning that he's only a deckhand on the ferry. She was far more impressed with you."

"I wondered what the doctor thing was about."

"She'd be much happier if I was marrying you."

Daisy curled her hands around his arm. "Sorry, but he's taken."

"You're so lucky to be married to a *doctor*, Daisy," Victoria said, imitating her mother.

"Wow, that's spot-on."

"Sadly, I have years of experience in dealing with her."

"Don't let her ruin this day for you, Vic," David said.

"I won't. Don't worry. I just need to put my dress on. Daisy, can you help me?"

"Isn't that the job of the maid of dishonor?" David asked with a grin.

She and Daisy laughed, and just that quickly, Victoria was back on track, thanks to her closest friends. "Thanks, you guys."

"For what?" Daisy asked.

"Everything. Your friendship means so much to me."

"Same goes for us," David said.

Victoria went with Daisy into the bedroom and closed the door. She closed her eyes and leaned against the door.

"Are you all right?" Daisy asked.

"I'm great. I just needed a second."

"I had a mother like yours, always with a comment to undercut me, to make me question my own judgment, to make me feel small."

"Yes," Victoria said softly. "That's how she's always been."

"You're not under any obligation to keep her in your life. Walking away from my toxic mother was the best thing I ever did, even if it was also the hardest thing."

"That thought has been in my head for a while now. After today, I may need to make a move. I wish I hadn't invited either of my parents to the wedding. All they do is stress me out. They hate each other. They haven't seen each other since my college graduation, another day I'd rather forget because of them."

"We won't let them ruin today for you."

"Thank you for being here with me."

"Of course. Let's get you into this gorgeous dress."

As the beautiful silk dress surrounded her, Victoria felt giddy with excitement and anticipation. Today, she would marry Shannon, the love of her life. As long as she stayed focused on him and their love, this would be the best day ever.

. . .

SHANNON COULDN'T WAIT to see her. He'd dropped her at the Beachcomber earlier with their suitcases and her dress in a garment bag.

David and Daisy would deliver her to Seamus's house in the next few minutes.

He hoped her parents weren't causing any drama for her. They'd debated endlessly about whether to invite them. He hoped they didn't regret asking them to come.

His mother, Breeda, came into Seamus and Carolina's bedroom, where Seamus had told him to wait. Seamus was in charge. Shannon was along for the ride.

"How're you holding up, love?" his mother asked.

"I'm fine. Excited. Ready."

Breeda pinned a flower to his lapel. "There was a time I thought I wouldn't live to see this day. I can't tell you how happy I am for you and your Victoria. She's a lovely young lady, and it's so nice to see you smiling the way you used to."

"It feels good to be happy again, even if I never forget."

She kept her hands flat against his chest. "Of course you don't, love. How could you? Fi would be so proud of how you've carried on. I know I am, and so is your da."

"That means a lot to me. Thank you."

Seamus came to the door. "Are you ready, mate?"

"You know it." He extended his arm to his mother. "Let's get married."

When he stepped outside with his mother and Seamus, he was surprised to see a huge crowd waiting for him. The entire town had turned out for them, or so it seemed. He walked his mother to the front row of the chairs they'd set out earlier and kissed her before he hugged his dad, uncle and aunt Nora, who was already dabbing at tears.

With everything set up for the wedding, it was hard to believe the yard had nearly been destroyed by the storm less than a week ago. Seamus and the rest of their friends had done yeoman's work to get the place ready in time for the wedding. He and Victoria would be forever thankful to everyone who'd pitched in to save their big day.

He, Seamus and Slim had dug a hole for an old-fashioned New England clambake, which had been simmering since the night before. A tent had been raised in the side yard, where Carolina had spent the morning supervising the setting of tables and other preparations.

And now it was time, and just when he might've wondered what was keeping Vic, she appeared with David and Daisy at the far end of the aisle between the two rows of chairs. A white liner covered the aisle. Vic had told him that was intended to protect her dress from the dirt.

Daisy held her own bouquet and Victoria's, which she handed to her.

When they were in position, Shannon signaled to Evan McCarthy and Niall Fitzgerald, who were providing music.

Daisy came first, wearing a champagne-colored dress, and yes, he'd learned from Victoria that champagne was a color.

While Evan and Niall played instrumental music, Victoria took David's arm to begin the walk down the aisle.

"Ought to be me doing that," Shannon heard Victoria's father say.

"Hush," his wife said.

Shannon couldn't have said it better himself. His gaze was fixed on the gorgeous woman who would soon be his wife. She was radiant, her smile bigger than it had ever been as she came toward him on the arm of her best friend. After David delivered her to him, Shannon took her hand, kissed the back of it and stared at the face of his beloved. "Thanks for coming, love."

"Wouldn't have missed it for the world."

Frank gave them what they'd requested—a quick and simple ceremony that made their commitment to each other legal.

In a matter of minutes, he'd declared them husband and wife, and Shannon was kissing his bride, his forever love, his happy ending.

HOURS LATER, the party was still going strong with most of the island's residents—or so it seemed—on the dance floor.

Big Mac and Linda had danced until their feet hurt and were taking a breather with Carolina, Seamus, Ned and Francine, Frank and Betsy, Kevin and Chelsea and baby Summer.

"What a week this has been," Linda said. "A hurricane and three weddings. That must be a record."

"I think it is," Big Mac said.

"How'd you hear about the third wedding?" Frank asked. "That was supposed to have been a secret."

"I have my sources," Linda said with a coy look for her brother-in-law.

"Who else got married?" Chelsea asked.

"We're not telling," Frank said, "because feelings would be hurt if people found out they weren't invited. The couple in question plans to hold a wedding next summer, but they wanted to be legally married now."

"That's very romantic," Francine said.

"Indeed it is," Frank replied.

"And great news from Providence that Jeff's hip surgery was a success, and he's on the road to recovery with Kelsey," Big Mac said.

"Very good news indeed," Ned said. "Can't wait to get them kids back out here where they belong."

"Still no word about Billy?" Kevin asked.

"Nothing," Big Mac said grimly. "The Coast Guard has called off the search, but Blaine and his team are still patrolling the Salt Pond. Deacon was out all day today and said he'll be back out every day until they find him."

"Goodness," Francine said. "What an awful thing."

"It really is," Big Mac said.

"In other news, you all pulled off a miracle here, Seamus," Frank said. "I heard you came home to a real mess after the storm."

"It was bad," Big Mac said. "I was here for a couple of hours the first day, and I couldn't believe the difference when I came back today."

"We had a deadline." Seamus gestured to his cousin and Victoria, who were slow dancing to a fast song. "I couldn't let them down."

"It was a great wedding, Seamus," Linda said. "I love the lights in the trees."

"That was a last-minute addition after the power came back on earlier today," Seamus said.

"He was like a monkey in the trees stringing lights," Carolina said.

The others laughed while her husband feigned outrage at being called a monkey.

"You know I'm only teasing," Carolina told him. "None of this would've happened without you."

"It took a village," Seamus said, "and luckily, ours is the best."

"It sure is," Linda said. "Looks like Piper and Jack are having a good time."

"Laura told me they're smitten," Frank said. "She's thrilled. She loves them both."

"What a week indeed," Linda said.

PIPER BENNETT HAD DECIDED that slow dancing with Jack Downing was the highlight of her life thus far.

"How's it going down there?" Jack asked.

"Divine. Everything is divine."

"No one has ever said that about dancing with me."

"I find that very hard to believe. You've got mad moves, which I already knew."

"I'm glad you like my moves."

They'd spent every night that week together, and she couldn't wait to snuggle up to him later.

Cindy Lawry and Jace Carson danced up beside them.

"How's it going, lovebirds?" Cindy asked.

Piper smiled at the friend she'd made at the Beachcomber. "It's going quite well. You?"

Cindy gazed up at her sexy boyfriend. "It's going very well."

"Hey, you guys," Maddie McCarthy said. "Vic's going to toss her bouquet. Get out there."

"I don't believe in dumb stuff like that," Piper said.

"Oh, come on." Cindy took Piper's hand and gave her a gentle tug. "Don't make me go out there alone. I think we're the last single women on Gansett."

"You're *not* single," Jace said, making Cindy giggle.

"You know what I mean!"

Only because she loved Cindy so much did Piper let her drag her to the middle of the dance floor, where several other women stood, looking as awkward as Piper felt.

"Are we ready, ladies?" the DJ asked. "On a count of one, two—"

Victoria let it go early, and Piper had the choice of either catching the bouquet or letting it hit her in the head.

"Lucky duck," Cindy said.

"Here." Piper tried to foist the bouquet off on Cindy. "You take it."

"Oh no, girl. You won it fair and square."

"Please take it," Piper said. "We're so new, and he's not ready for this and—"

"Here he comes," Cindy said.

"I didn't try to win," Piper said.

"Congratulations," Jace said to Piper. "You're next."

"No pressure or anything," Piper said to Jack.

"You can stop melting down," Jack said with a grin. "All is well."

Relieved by his reaction, she set the bouquet on a table and said, "Let's go back to dancing."

The minute his arms were around her again, she felt better.

"Why're you so worked up about a silly tradition?" Jack asked.

"Do you know what it means to catch the bouquet?"

"Believe it or not, I've been to a wedding before. Including my own."

"We're not ready for that. I don't want you to feel pressured or, well, anything but happy with where we are right now."

"Where we are right now is the best place I've been in years, and I'd like to stay there for a long, long time. If that's all right with you."

"Yes, Jack," she said, breathless and falling deeper in love by the minute with this amazing man. "That's more than fine with me."

"CAN WE GO HOME?" Dan Torrington asked his lovely wife. He could tell that she was exhausted, but she would never admit it to him or anyone else. This kid had better be worth the toll he or she was taking on his or her mother.

"Whenever you're ready."

"I'm ready. Let's say our goodbyes." They made the rounds, which included serious abuse from the McCarthy brothers for leaving early.

"We're right behind them," Abby told Adam, shutting him up.

"I'm not sure why we're friends with these people," Dan said to his wife.

"It's because you've never had more fun with anyone in your life than you do with us," Grant said.

"Something like that," Dan replied. "Call me tomorrow?"

"Will do," Grant said.

Dan and Kara said good night to the bride and groom, to Seamus and Carolina and the others at their table and then spent the next twenty minutes chatting with everyone from Alex and Jenny Martinez to Slim and Erin Jackson to Mallory and Quinn James as they made their way out of the tent.

Knowing Kara was tired, Dan kept moving them toward the driveway, where they finally made their escape. "Wow, nothing like knowing every person at a wedding, huh?"

"That's how we roll on Gansett Island," Kara said. "Everyone knows everyone."

"It was a fun day. Shannon and Vic seem very happy."

"They sure do." Kara had high-heeled sandals dangling from her fingers as she walked on bare feet. "I'm so glad their wedding went off without a hitch despite Mother Nature's efforts to derail things."

They'd parked out on the street and had nearly reached Dan's Porsche when Kara's phone rang. She fished it out of her purse and looked at the screen. "It's my mother. She's called three times. What the hell?" Kara took the call. "Mom?"

"Oh, Kara, thank God you finally answered."

"We were at a wedding. What's wrong?"

"You and Dan need to come home to Maine right away. Your brothers have been charged with murder."

I'm VERY excited to announce that Dan and Kara will be spinning off into the new Downeast Maine Series, beginning in 2024! I've been thinking about this idea for quite some time and took a trip to Bar Harbor and Mount Desert Island last fall to get a feel for the area. I have an exciting story in mind for them as they venture to Kara's home for the first time together to encounter deep divisions within the Ballard family and secrets that could cost them everything.

In the meantime, Gansett will continue with more about Duke and McKenzie in the next book, as well as Jeff and Kelsey and some other new characters who'll be coming to Gansett Island. More info to come on Gansett Island and Downeast Maine!

HURRICANE AFTER DARK is my 100th book! That's so hard to believe! And Gansett Island accounts for more than a quarter of my books. When I was writing Mac and Maddie's story back in 2006, I never could've imagined the journey these characters would take me or how much I would still love Gansett Island SEVENTEEN YEARS later! Thank you for taking this ride with me and the McCarthy family and the entire Gansett Island community. It's still such a thrill to write this series and to know how much it means to so many of you.

It takes a village to write books, and I'm so incredibly thankful to mine. Thank you to the team that supports me every day: Julie Cupp, Lisa Cafferty, Jean Mello, Nikki Haley and Ashley Lopez. To my editors, Linda Ingmanson and Joyce Lamb, I appreciate you both so much. My primary beta readers Anne Woodall and Kara Conrad as well as the Gansett Island betas, Michelle, Jennifer, Amy, Kelly, Jaime, Doreen, Andi, Mona and Katy, are such a huge help to me as is my continuity editor Gwen Neff, and Tik Tok/Instagram guru Rachel Spencer.

Thank you, as always, to my medical consultant, Dr. Sarah Hewitt, family nurse practitioner, who helped me figure out a way to save Jeff Lawry's life.

I'm grateful to Dan, Emily and Jake for always supporting my career as well as the friends and family that surround us and make our lives so much fun. My fur babies Louie and Sam Sullivan (as well as my granddog Tommy Force) are the best companions as I write books, and I love them so much.

To the readers who make it all worthwhile, I am so deeply appreciative for the way you roll with me and support my books. We've changed up a few things with our routine as of this book, and while I'm excited to take advantage of new opportunities, I know that change can be unsettling. Please be assured that my goal is to make as many of you happy as I possibly can, and that will always be my priority.

Thank you for reading!

Xoxo

Marie

ALSO BY MARIE FORCE

Contemporary Romances Available from Marie Force

The Gansett Island Series

Book 1: Maid for Love (*Mac & Maddie*)

Book 2: Fool for Love (*Joe & Janey*)

Book 3: Ready for Love (*Luke & Sydney*)

Book 4: Falling for Love (*Grant & Stephanie*)

Book 5: Hoping for Love (*Evan & Grace*)

Book 6: Season for Love (*Owen & Laura*)

Book 7: Longing for Love (*Blaine & Tiffany*)

Book 8: Waiting for Love (*Adam & Abby*)

Book 9: Time for Love (*David & Daisy*)

Book 10: Meant for Love (*Jenny & Alex*)

Book 10.5: Chance for Love, *A Gansett Island Novella* (*Jared & Lizzie*)

Book 11: Gansett After Dark (*Owen & Laura*)

Book 12: Kisses After Dark (*Shane & Katie*)

Book 13: Love After Dark (*Paul & Hope*)

Book 14: Celebration After Dark (*Big Mac & Linda*)

Book 15: Desire After Dark (*Slim & Erin*)

Book 16: Light After Dark (*Mallory & Quinn*)

Book 17: Victoria & Shannon (Episode 1)

Book 18: Kevin & Chelsea (Episode 2)

A Gansett Island Christmas Novella

Book 19: Mine After Dark (*Riley & Nikki*)

Book 20: Yours After Dark (*Finn & Chloe*)

Book 21: Trouble After Dark (*Deacon & Julia*)

Book 22: Rescue After Dark (*Mason & Jordan*)

Book 23: Blackout After Dark (*Full Cast*)

Book 24: Temptation After Dark (*Gigi & Cooper*)

Book 25: Resilience After Dark (*Jace & Cindy*)

Book 26: Hurricane After Dark (*Full Cast*)

The Wild Widows Series—a Fatal Series Spin-Off

Book 1: Someone Like You

Book 2: Someone to Hold

The Green Mountain Series

Book 1: All You Need Is Love (*Will & Cameron*)

Book 2: I Want to Hold Your Hand (*Nolan & Hannah*)

Book 3: I Saw Her Standing There (*Colton & Lucy*)

Book 4: And I Love Her (*Hunter & Megan*)

Novella: You'll Be Mine (*Will & Cam's Wedding*)

Book 5: It's Only Love (*Gavin & Ella*)

Book 6: Ain't She Sweet (*Tyler & Charlotte*)

The Butler, Vermont Series

(Continuation of Green Mountain)

Book 1: Every Little Thing (*Grayson & Emma*)

Book 2: Can't Buy Me Love (*Mary & Patrick*)

Book 3: Here Comes the Sun (*Wade & Mia*)

Book 4: Till There Was You (*Lucas & Dani*)

Book 5: All My Loving (*Landon & Amanda*)

Book 6: Let It Be (*Lincoln & Molly*)

Book 7: Come Together (*Noah & Brianna*)

Book 8: Here, There & Everywhere (*Izzy & Cabot*)

Book 9: The Long and Winding Road (*Max & Lexi*)

The Quantum Series

Book 1: Virtuous (*Flynn & Natalie*)

Book 2: Valorous (*Flynn & Natalie*)

Book 3: Victorious (*Flynn & Natalie*)

Book 4: Rapturous (*Addie & Hayden*)

Book 5: Ravenous (*Jasper & Ellie*)

Book 6: Delirious (*Kristian & Aileen*)

Book 7: Outrageous (*Emmett & Leah*)

Book 8: Famous (*Marlowe & Sebastian*)

The Miami Nights Series

Book 1: How Much I Feel (*Carmen & Jason*)

Book 2: How Much I Care (*Maria & Austin*)

Book 3: How Much I Love (*Dee's story*)

Nochebuena, A Miami Nights Novella

Book 4: How Much I Want (*Nico & Sofia*)

Book 5: How Much I Need (*Milo and Gianna*)

The Treading Water Series

Book 1: Treading Water

Book 2: Marking Time

Book 3: Starting Over

Book 4: Coming Home

Book 5: Finding Forever

Single Titles

Five Years Gone

One Year Home

Sex Machine

Sex God

Georgia on My Mind

True North

The Fall

The Wreck

Love at First Flight

Everyone Loves a Hero

Line of Scrimmage

Romantic Suspense Novels Available from Marie Force

The Fatal Series

One Night With You, *A Fatal Series Prequel Novella*

Book 1: Fatal Affair

Book 2: Fatal Justice

Book 3: Fatal Consequences

Book 3.5: Fatal Destiny, *the Wedding Novella*

Book 4: Fatal Flaw

Book 5: Fatal Deception

Book 6: Fatal Mistake

Book 7: Fatal Jeopardy

Book 8: Fatal Scandal

Book 9: Fatal Frenzy

Book 10: Fatal Identity

Book 11: Fatal Threat

Book 12: Fatal Chaos

Book 13: Fatal Invasion

Book 14: Fatal Reckoning

Book 15: Fatal Accusation

Book 16: Fatal Fraud

Sam and Nick's Story Continues....

Book 1: State of Affairs

Book 2: State of Grace

Book 3: State of the Union

Book 4: State of Shock

Book 5: State of Denial

Historical Romance Available from Marie Force

The Gilded Series

Book 1: Duchess by Deception

Book 2: Deceived by Desire

ABOUT THE AUTHOR

Marie Force is the *New York Times* bestselling author of contemporary romance, romantic suspense and erotic romance. Her series include Fatal, First Family, Gansett Island, Butler Vermont, Quantum, Treading Water, Miami Nights and Wild Widows.

Her books have sold more than 12 million copies worldwide, have been translated into more than a dozen languages and have appeared on the *New York Times* bestseller list more than 30 times. She is also a *USA Today* and #1 *Wall Street Journal* bestseller, as well as a Spiegel bestseller in Germany.

Her goals in life are simple—to finish raising two happy, healthy, productive young adults, to keep writing books for as long as she possibly can and to never be on a flight that makes the news.

Join Marie's mailing list on her website at *marieforce.com* for news about new books and upcoming appearances in your area. Follow her on Facebook at *www.Facebook.com/MarieForceAuthor*, Instagram at *www.instagram.com/marieforceauthor/* and TikTok at *https://www.tiktok.com/@marieforceauthor?*. Contact Marie at *marie@marieforce.com*.

Made in the USA
Las Vegas, NV
16 June 2023